# VESANYA'S CURSE

Book 1 of The Veseile Conspiracy

* * *

First paperback edition, January 2024

ISBN 978-1-7384190-0-5 (paperback edition)

Published by M. L. L. Publishing

*For my younger self, who always dreamed of this*

\* \* \*

*An Excerpt from 'Origins of the Power: Understanding the Hidden History of the Veseile'*

In the beginning, there was harmony between the Gods. All six worked together to create the humans and forge a perfect world for them to live in.

Meto, God of Harvest and Fertility, created rolling hills for the humans to farm, filling the ground and trees with nourishment for their fragile mortal bodies; Collatus, God of Hunt and Healing, gifted humans the innate desire to protect one another and created animals to sustain and challenge them; Adagna, God of Wisdom and War, gave the humans a thirst for understanding and the insight to document and learn from their history; Dilectya, God of Love and Invention, gave them the complex love that distinguished them from the animals and the unending desire for progress; Vesanya, God of Chaos, breathed life into the first humans, gifting them the unpredictability of free will; and Mortus, God of Death, transformed a portion of the Gods' private realm into the Underworld, where he would guard the humans' souls when they finally came to rest under his protection.

Each God, except Mortus who dwelled in the Underworld, lived alongside their creation for millennia, watching the humans learn, evolve, and flourish. However, with time the Gods desired to improve and strengthen their initial creation. Working individually, they transformed a small portion of the original humans into a race collectively known as the Eile.

Meto created the Meteile, fostering within her creation a

strong affinity for and likeness to the natural world, allowing the Meteile to camouflage themselves amongst nature to better protect the world from any that would harm it.

Collatus created the Colleile, strengthening their bodies and reflexes to aid their ability to hunt and provide, whilst protecting them from injuries that were so common among human hunters.

Adagna created the Adeile. She too, strengthened her creation in mass, giving them hulking bodies and an innate ability to defend themselves, but bestowing them with the increased desire to seek peace, reform, and impartial knowledge before resorting to physical means, in an attempt to avoid the atrocities humans so frequently committed.

Dilectya created the Dileile, choosing to develop the smallest of the humans. Though slight and short compared to other Eile, the Dileile were an equally strong race, with an unending passion for innovation and aptitude for creativity and invention.

Vesanya created the Veseile. Like the other Eile, her creation was distinguished from the humans by their stronger bodies and longer lifespan, but Vesanya also blessed them with a piece of herself. She gifted them pure chaos, in the form of the Power, allowing them to access and wield the elements in their defence and to strengthen their influence over the other Eile and the remaining humans. Her gift marked each Veseile with a streak of unpigmented hair, matching the stark white lock in her own dark tresses.

Finally, Mortus created the Moreile, a race destined to dwell with him in the Underworld and assist his protective duties.

Satisfied with their new creations, the Gods retired to their own Realm, finally reuniting with Mortus and watching Eile and humans coexist from afar.

# I

The king was dying, and it came as a relief to Luelle, for she no longer had to find a way to kill him.

It took a surprising amount of effort for her to conceal the spring in her step as she weaved through the wide, busy halls. Distraught nobles practicing premature mourning interspersed the weary, solemn servants. Luelle kept her head down and expression sombre to match them. Her face wasn't out of place after over five years of working in the castle, wearing a meek, mild mask to avoid detection, but it was important to blend in tonight. Every second of her deception was for this moment.

Of course, she pitied the dying king. She and Alaric had grown as close as a king and a servant could, particularly during the past fortnight as she'd leapt to tend to his every need during the sudden onset of illness. At times over the last year, the elderly man had seemed to prefer her assistance to any other servant, potentially because she wasn't terrified of him or disappointed to be assisting him rather than his younger family, as many others were.

Luelle was grown enough to admit she'd miss King Alaric when his soul departed for the Underworld. She might even grieve his loss. But, not until her job was finished.

Not until she'd taken back every last drop of his Power.

Fortunately, Queen Vonya and the four royal heirs were delayed returning from an overseas tourney in the eastern continent, Stodor. Given his fragile health, Alaric's advisers had insisted he stay behind when his family departed two weeks ago, and his condition deteriorated faster than anyone had expected in their absence.

Luelle was grateful. Her task would've been much harder if the king had gone to the tourney, or if his family had chosen to remain at his side.

Since learning about Alaric's severe decline in health, Luelle had spent every moment plotting her next move. Free time was a rarity, so she schemed as she worked, which wasn't always prudent. Days ago, it led to an embarrassing encounter with a naked nobleman whose room she had entered to clean, thinking it was her usual circuit, only to realise she was on the wrong floor.

Assessing her options to obtain the Power was near-impossible. Choosing a flawed plan could render all of Luelle's work over the past few years useless, and risked her life, but the longer she waited before making the decision, the less time she had to ensure nothing could go wrong.

She'd settled on her final plan two days prior and spent every waking moment since dwelling on ways to perfect it. She would not get a second chance.

Before hearing the rumours of Alaric's imminent demise, Luelle had agonised over how she might kill the king. Finding a moment in which he was outside of his family's supervision had been a significant hurdle to overcome, but the dark scheme had primarily stalled because she did not know if she could retrieve the Power from a corpse.

Fortunately, it was as if the old man wanted her to succeed, taking to his deathbed when his wife and children were no longer around to interfere and fuss.

Prince Malcolm was due to inherit Alaric's Power this evening, on his return, so Luelle had to move fast, but every aspect of her plan was in place. She'd be out of the castle and well on her way before any of the royals knew what they were missing.

Endless artwork lined the hallways, a blur of colourful brush strokes and needlework on either side as Luelle strode past. Stony-faced portraits of previous rulers watched over the crowd, nestled among visual stories of Cerulya's history. Cerulya was the jewel in the crown, the shining capital in the kingdom of Arazia, a land older than time and favoured by all six Gods.

When she'd first arrived in the castle, Luelle had crept out of her room every night for a month to examine the tapestries and paintings, colours more vibrant and thread work more delicate than any she'd ever seen. She stared for so long that the images replayed in her mind when she closed her eyes to sleep. Now, she didn't spare them a second glance. How easily finery became commonplace when one drowned in it for half a decade.

Around her, the castle was alive with panic as flustered

servants prepared for the royal family's return and lesser nobles displayed their exaggerated grief in public. Luelle tightened her arm around the fresh linens she carried, and the parcel hidden within, securing them against her hip as she danced between the floods of people.

Alaric was a good king, as good as any human monarch could be. He'd gone further than previous rulers in his attempts to soothe animosity between humans and the God-made races, the Eile, choosing to marry Vonya several years before inheriting his crown. As a foreign princess and a member of the Veseile race —said to descend from Vesanya, the God of Chaos—Vonya's hand had presented an opportunity to strengthen Arazia's alliance with Stodor as well as calm the turmoil within the nation. From their union, Prince Malcolm would be Arazia's first half-blood ruler, when he inherited the throne.

*If* he inherited the throne.

Who knew how things might change when the royals discovered Luelle had snatched their bloodline's Power from under their noses?

She ducked her head to hide a smile at the thought and continued down the hallways, letting muscle memory guide her to Alaric's chambers.

Things were playing into her hands better than she'd imagined. A little under an hour ago, in a rare lucid moment, the king had requested her aid to prepare for his family's return, dismissing the need for her to use any of her prepared excuses. Since she was the only handmaiden he'd mentioned by name, Luelle wasted no time informing the other servants she must go alone. The argument had not lasted long.

Other servants made no attempt to hide their contempt for Luelle when working together, not that she cared, when working alone made her task easier. Even when loneliness ate at her, she knew she couldn't befriend the other palace workers. Besides, they only wanted to help the king this evening to gain favour with Queen Vonya or Prince Malcolm. All of them were delusional. Luelle was the only one sane enough to realise the royals would never bother to learn one servant's face from another. Any servant could claim they were in the room helping the king tonight and the remaining royals would likely accept the lie as a truth. It might even help Luelle escape if they did.

King Alaric's suite lined the front of the castle, several of his rooms overlooking the outer wall and the city beyond. It had taken Luelle weeks to overcome her shock at the placement of the rooms, but years of reigning unchallenged had lulled the humans into a false sense of security. Guards remained stationed at every set of doors through the suite, monitoring everyone that moved near the king. She kept her eyes on the tiled floor as she passed them, though none of the soldiers stood in her way until she reached Alaric's private chambers within the wider suite.

She offered the pair standing in front of the king's doors a sad smile, dipping into a shallow curtsy to address them. They nodded in return, greeting her as Belle, the false name she'd given when she arrived all those years ago.

During her time in Cerulya, Luelle had avoided the guards wherever she could. Unlike the royal family, they were trained to remember faces and, already, too many of them knew hers, thanks to her favour with the king. She pushed the concern aside. As long as everything continued going to plan, she would be far from the castle by the time the guards pieced her crime together. After leaving the castle, she would journey across the realm to a cavern deep in the Caeleste Peaks, where she would reunite with Zeke, Freya, and Imbryl. Her role in their plot was to retrieve Vesanya's Power, and her chosen family would help with the rest. They trusted her with the task, enough to spend almost six years without attempting to contact her. She couldn't let them down.

"How is he?" Luelle asked in a low voice when the guards didn't immediately step aside to let her in.

"Not good," the woman to the left, Clarisse, said. Her eyes were inflamed, the whites tinged with red. As well as being stationed outside Alaric's private chamber more frequently than any other guards, she and Benjamin were two of the first castle employees Luelle had encountered when planning how to get close to the king in the first year of her stay here.

"He has been asking for you. We must pray that Mortus will let his soul linger here until the Queen and Prince arrive home." Benjamin's heavy brow furrowed with worry, the wiry grey hairs slightly obscuring his vision.

Luelle curtsied again, stifling the urge to roll her eyes. "I'll make him as comfortable as possible until then. Have you removed the other guards from within the chambers?"

Clarisse frowned. She opened her mouth to say something but Luelle continued before the meddling woman could question her.

"His Majesty will not want anyone witnessing as I help him

bathe and dress, to protect his dignity. That's why he only asked for me by name. He specified such when he was preparing me last week, in case the worst was to happen. He said he was going to inform you both, but it doesn't surprise me that it slipped his mind, knowing how his grasp on reality has been fading." She pulled a face.

Clarisse closed her mouth again but continued to block the door. Luelle's annoyance grew.

"Will you be okay by yourself? Are you sure you are strong enough? We can help you lift him if necessary," Benjamin fretted, eyes scouring the hall for a guard he trusted enough to take his place at the door.

"No," Luelle said, her tone a touch too sharp. She shifted her weight and took a breath, composing herself. "He will not want to feel as though he's being fussed over. He has enough to cope with. It will only overwhelm him."

Clarisse made a wordless noise of agreement and finally disappeared into the chambers to retrieve the other guards. Once they'd vacated the room, stationing themselves in regular intervals along the hallway instead, Luelle stepped inside. She turned back to Clarisse and Benjamin before her hand left the door handle.

"Please don't let anyone other than the queen or prince disturb us. I'll come back out once he's ready."

Benjamin nodded. "We shall be right here if you need anything. Do not hesitate to call for us."

Luelle closed the heavy door behind her.

The stench of sickness, urine, and sweat hit her in a wave

when she turned to face the room. It had been growing stronger each time she visited the old man, and was almost overwhelming now. Bile rose in her throat.

Stuffy air filled the chambers, weighing down each of Luelle's steps and sticking her shirt to the curve of her back. Whichever healers had tended the king throughout the day had turned the room into a premature tomb.

Luelle placed her bundle of fabric on a chair beside the door and marched across the wide bedroom to fling the nearest shutters open. It would make no difference if Alaric caught a chill now; he'd be gone within the next few hours. He may as well die in a room fit for a king.

She inhaled the fresh sea air until her nausea settled.

With her stomach under control, Luelle turned to face the king's bed. Larger than any bed she'd ever slept in, it spanned a third of the room, thick solid oak posters stretching well above her head, despite reaching only half the height of the room. Past it, on the wall opposite the windows, two closed doors led to private bathing chambers and dressing rooms, but within the bedroom itself, the furniture was simple and sparse, particularly compared to some of the lower nobles' rooms elsewhere in the castle. Those lords and ladies seemed to believe stuffing their chambers with trinkets and rubbish was the best way to demonstrate their extensive wealth. Alaric kept things more minimal. Besides the bed, the room contained two plain sofas, a small round table with matching chairs, and several unadorned cabinets. Everything else he might need had its own separate room elsewhere in the suite.

Rasping breaths, like stone scraping stone, sounded through the large, bare chamber.

Despite herself, Luelle's heart lurched at the sight of the king.

Grey, sallow skin peeked out from above the blankets tucked tightly around the monarch. His cheeks, which had been fleshy and pink with life when she'd first started working in the castle, now hung from cheekbones that were too sharp. Silver hair, as thin as cobwebs, clung to his brow, limp and damp with a sheen of sweat that hadn't washed away all week.

Luelle turned back to the window. In the distance, past the thousand pinpricks of light in the city, the ship carrying the Queen and royal heirs drifted towards the harbour. She had, at most, an hour before they were docked and escorted to the king's side. Even at a time like this, the city's inhabitants would crowd them, delaying their journey through Cerulya's streets to their home.

Luelle strode into each of the chamber's adjoining rooms, checking in every crevice and behind every thick curtain to be certain no guards remained.

She and King Alaric were well and truly alone.

Rolling up her sleeves, she lifted one of the ornate chairs from the small table where she'd left her parcel and hauled it to the chamber door, grunting under its weight. Slowly, to avoid knocking it against anything that might alert Clarisse and Benjamin outside, Luelle wedged the chair underneath the door handles. It wouldn't stop the guards from getting in altogether but would buy her some precious time if her task took longer than it should.

She scuttled back to the linens and unravelled them to reveal her parcel. Hidden within, she'd brought the longest rope she could find in the stables and a near-exact replica of the royal crystal ball, made of glass. Shops in the city were overflowing with the dupes, pushing them on the countless tourists hoping to witness Prince Malcolm's coronation.

Compared to the troves of jewels and wealth flooding the castle, the royal crystal's value seemed negligible at a glance, but it was worth more than any other gem in the kingdom. Every monarch, spanning back centuries, had used the crystal to transfer their Power to their eldest heir. Without the vessel, Luelle didn't know if the Power would endure, lying dormant in the corpse of its wielder or if it would dissipate on their death. To her knowledge, no monarch had been careless enough to find out.

If anyone looked closely enough, the differences between the crystal and Luelle's cheap replica were stark. Imperfections marred the replica, its surface scratched and cloudy, its size and weight smaller and lighter than the crystal sphere. The real relic was safe with the eldest prince, hence his rush to return before Alaric died, but the king shouldn't notice the flaws in his state. Over the past few days, he'd barely been well enough to hold a conversation lasting more than a few minutes. In fact, he was so impressionable the guards should keep him under constant supervision, but who would expect a quiet, docile handmaiden to cause trouble, let alone commit treason?

When Prince Malcolm realised someone had stolen his Power, the guards would likely be punished, but glancing at the frail, fading king, Luelle found it hard to care about their fates.

Like the king, Clarisse and Benjamin were humans. Their lives would be over before they knew it; spending their remaining years in prison would not be a true hardship. How did humans cope knowing their time in this world was so brief?

Luelle spun the glass sphere in her hands and knelt to open a cupboard behind the table. Stashed within, tucked behind a stack of folded robes, was the small backpack she'd hidden days ago, packed with basic supplies for her journey; a dagger, a cloak, two small parcels of food to see her through her first day of travelling, a water flask, a flint, and a spare set of clothes. In the side pocket, she had a small coin purse, though the contents was worth less than the smallest ornament in the king's chambers. She placed the bag at the foot of Alaric's bed, her rope curled beside it like a nest for the glass sphere, all out of his line of sight.

Luelle strode to the king's bathing room to pour a small bowl of tepid water and grab a clean cloth. He needed to be awake for this.

Whispering a short prayer to Vesanya, Luelle perched on the king's bed, settling the glass sphere and bowl of water at her hip.

She wrung the water from her cloth and dabbed at King Alaric's clammy forehead.

He wrenched his eyes open.

"Belle," he croaked her false name.

"That's right, I'm here," she murmured. She needed him awake and lucid, but not enough to question her.

Sleep and sickness clouded his eyes. Each blink was slow and heavy.

"Do you need a drink?" she asked. There was no point in

torturing the old man. Whoever had been in here earlier had already refilled the chalice on his bedside table, so the kindness cost her nothing.

Alaric gave an almost imperceptible nod.

Luelle folded her cloth over the side of the bowl and put both on the floor. She pushed the glass sphere further onto the bed, propping it against a fold in the thick fabric to stop it from rolling off and smashing on the stone floor.

"I'm going to sit you up."

Alaric started to speak but the words turned into a cough.

She lifted the king's torso with little effort as he cleared his lungs. He'd wasted away over the past two weeks, unable to consume more than a few mouthfuls of soggy food for each meal before nausea overtook him. With another two large down feather cushions behind him, she lay Alaric back into a more upright position.

"Here." She held the chalice from the bedside table to his lips, helping him take several small sips.

He tried speaking again after swallowing the lukewarm water and clearing his throat.

"Is Malcolm here?" He eyed the sphere beside his legs.

"He sent the crystal ahead but he's on his way. He asked us to prepare for the worst, in case he doesn't make it home in time." The lie came easily.

Alaric nodded again, knowing his end was looming as well as anyone else in the castle.

"What do you need me to do?" Luelle asked, digging her nails into her palms to will some patience into her bones.

He gestured for the sphere.

She placed it in his gnarled hands, holding her breath as if the slightest wrong move would shatter the deception. He didn't notice it was lighter than it should be. It must feel as heavy as the real crystal now that his muscles had withered to nothing.

Alaric murmured something incoherent. Luelle watched with wide eyes as the Power glowed in the veins in his forearms, slithering out of his body to become a churning, glowing fog within the glass. She felt its movements like a warm sigh against her skin, raising the fine hairs on her arms.

"Perfect, Your Majesty," she breathed. He was already fading back out of consciousness.

"Malcolm will be here soon. And my family," he croaked, eyelids drooping once again. "I would like to say goodbye."

"Very soon, sire." She took the ball from his grasp and tucked him deeper into the blankets, ignoring the pang of guilt in her heart. "Get some rest before he arrives. You won't need to hold on for much longer."

Luelle squeezed Alaric's hand. His fingers offered a weak twitch in return.

Her heart drummed in her chest as she stood and backed away from the bed.

When she was certain the king was asleep, she darted across the room and wrapped the glass ball back in the linens she'd brought, concealing its glowing light in several hasty layers that she hoped would also secure it from any risk of breaking. She placed it at the top of her backpack, fastened the bag tight over her shoulders and donned her cloak, obscuring the bag altogether.

Summer's waning warmth lingered in the evenings, but the nights were bound to bring lower temperatures as she travelled, with no guarantee of shelter from the weather. Although the heavy cloak was inconvenient, it could save her life during those coldest hours.

She took her rope to the king's balcony, closing the doors to the chamber behind her. The deep, stone balcony stretched the entire length of the bedroom and wrapped far around the corner of the castle. Luelle stayed pressed against the wall as she gazed at the courtyard far beneath her. People swarmed across the bulk of the space far below, preparing for the return of the queen and crown prince, but few ventured down the narrow, shadowy alleys that extended around the edges of the castle. The far end of Alaric's balcony was positioned above one of those dark, quiet passages.

Earlier that week, Luelle had settled on her escape route when scouting those alleys beneath his suite. Nestled far below the furthest corner of the king's balcony were the royal kennels. As she had walked past, the hounds had leapt to life, barking and howling their discontent at being disturbed. At the time, she'd startled, to the amusement of nearby guards, but following that experience, Luelle spent as much time as she could justify in the courtyard, observing the kennels. At times, a breath of wind was enough to set the dogs off. In fact, it was such a regular occurrence that the dog handlers rarely appeared to quiet the animals, although their ferocious noise still deterred most people from straying into the alley unless they had a real need. Even the guards upped their pace as they passed the kennels during their rounds, speeding towards the lighter, more spacious courtyard at the castle's entrance.

It wasn't perfect, but those kennels offered an escape route better than any of the alternatives Luelle had considered, so she'd set to making the plan airtight.

After hours of scoping the surrounding area and memorising the guards' patrols, Luelle had ventured closer to the kennels, ignoring the din the dogs made. The wooden sheds were simple, sufficient to contain the animals securely with no need for comfort. However, a few of the stalls were so dilapidated that they remained empty, used as storage rather than for housing any living creatures.

The furthest edge of the king's balcony was perfectly positioned above one of those empty stalls.

Sunset was long faded, replaced by a dark, cloudless sky. Warm firelight from flickering torches bathed the main courtyard, but the alley beneath the far end of the balcony was pitch black. No one would notice Luelle making her escape even if they did look into the gloom of the passageway, and the next round of guards wasn't due for thirty minutes.

Stars blinked into life, mirroring the city's lights below. Squinting past those distant pin pricks of brightness, Luelle spotted the royals' opulent ship in the harbour, safely docked. Somewhere on the streets below, her enemies stalked closer.

She tied one end of her rope to the thickest column on the balcony's edge, knotting it multiple times and tugging hard to check it would hold before throwing the rest down to the ground. Tightening the straps on her bag, she peeked over the edge to examine the drop, fighting a tide of nausea at the distance.

Why had she thought clambering down the castle's walls would be the best way to make her escape?

Luelle didn't think about how far away the ground was as she swung her legs over the waist-height balcony wall and crouched to grab the rope without looking down. Inhaling deep to steady her shallow, shaky breathing, she ignored the thought of what might happen if her strength gave out before she reached the end of the rope. She weaved it between her feet before starting her descent, in an attempt to try and control her speed and save her palms from rope burn.

Her cloak was as dark as the night around her, flapping against her body in the breeze but further camouflaging her against the shadowy castle walls. The downward climb took all of her concentration, leaving no room to worry about swaying into view of the windows beneath the king's chambers. Days earlier, she'd scouted those lower floors, learning that few of the rooms were occupied and knowing those that were should be empty now, since most of the castle's inhabitants were busy in the common spaces, preparing for the return of the queen and crown prince.

Inch by inch Luelle lowered herself down the rope. The muscles in her arms, shoulders, and core burned with the effort of holding her own weight. She'd had no privacy to maintain her strength as she'd desired while living in the castle, always sharing a room with at least one nosy, gossiping colleague. Servants weren't expected to look after themselves, only those they were tending. Exercising would have given rise to unwanted questions, even if she'd had the energy to do so. Most working days had left her too exhausted to consider it. Fortunately, her daily tasks had required a high level of strength and stamina, so her abilities had not withered to nothing.

Twice, Luelle's grip on the rope slipped and her heart rose to her throat. She choked on screams both times, fighting tears and once biting through the skin of her bottom lip. Her palms would be red raw at the end of her descent. She stayed frozen on the rope for too long each time her grip fumbled, a sudden fear of falling overpowering her fear of being caught.

Glancing down, Luelle located the kennel roof, not far below. She couldn't go back now. Even if there was another way to escape the king's chambers, her trembling arms would never pull her back up the rope. The only way out of this situation was down. Luelle inhaled a shaking breath and whispered a prayer to Vesanya before forcing her limbs to unlock from their frozen state.

She made it a few more metres before her grip slipped again, only this time, she didn't manage to regain her hold.

Pain flared in her palms as the rope slid between them.

The kennel roof collapsed beneath Luelle's weight. Ferocious howls and barks erupted from the next stall along, obscuring most of the noise from her crashing descent.

The landing snatched the air from her lungs. Discomfort sparked through her chest as she drew in a breath. She covered her mouth with her hand to soften the groan that leaked out, tasting blood on the tip of her tongue.

Voices neared as dog handlers rushed to quiet the animals.

Luelle scrambled backwards over the remnants of the roof, shrinking into the darkest corner of the kennel stall she'd fallen into. She shuffled behind a pile of saddles stored within, ignoring the wet, sticky filth she was crawling in and the sting of it against her palms.

Everything hurt.

Curling herself into a small, tight ball, she waited for someone to duck their head into her stall. Her heart pounded in her chest and her ears, but the handlers didn't bother approaching the stalls they already knew were empty. They silenced the dogs with several shouts and kicks to the kennel walls and retreated.

Luelle wiggled her fingers and toes and probed each tooth with her tongue. She stretched her limbs out slowly, checking for any damage beyond scrapes and splinters. She would be bruised and sore for days but nothing was broken, thank the Gods.

Stars glittered above her, visible through the hole where the roof had once been, but her rope was unseen against the castle wall's shadows. Since no one had been waiting for her in the kennels, the people in the courtyard must remain oblivious to her descent.

Pushing herself to sit upright, she shrugged off her bag from under her cloak, each movement stiff with discomfort. With throbbing fingers, she unfastened the top of the bag and fondled the glass ball through its layers of fabric in search of any chips or scratches. She didn't know what would happen to the Power if its vessel was broken before it could be absorbed by someone, but it couldn't be good.

Luck was on her side. The sphere survived the fall. She refastened her bag and slung it over her shoulders once again, adjusting her cloak around it.

Her legs quivered as she got to her feet. Luelle couldn't stifle her groan but it was hidden beneath the general noise of the dogs, who continued to growl at one another, snuffling in their beds.

Peering out of her stall revealed a blessedly empty path to the courtyard.

Luelle sidled from the kennels, limping towards the shadows by the castle wall. She didn't want to imagine how she looked. She tried to pluck the splinters from her hair and clothing as she staggered forward but couldn't do anything to remove the dog piss and stale excrement staining her cloak and leggings.

Rounding the corner of her alley, she stepped into the main courtyard.

Just as the royals were arriving.

Queen Vonya and her four half-human children sat tall on their horses, surrounded by their personal guard. Stablehands swarmed them, helping the royals and their guards descend from their mounts and leading the horses away.

Luelle paused her escape, retreating into the shadows behind her. She ducked her head and fell to a deep curtsy, mirroring everyone else in the courtyard. None of the royals would pick her out from this crowd, even if they had known her face.

Queen Vonya spared no one in the vicinity a second glance. She leapt from her horse in a flap of expensive fabric and strode through the crowd, her dark braid, streaked with a single white lock, streaming behind her. Her face was lined with evidence of fear and worry for her dying husband.

She was not returning to the same man she'd left two weeks ago, but such was the tragedy of their relationship. The queen was only older than Alaric by seven years, but all five Eile races were blessed with considerably longer lives than humans. She looked no older than she had on their wedding day fifty years ago, and likely had centuries of life still ahead of her, but Alaric was a shadow of the man he'd been when they married.

Behind Vonya, the princes and princesses were still dismounting. Princess Vivyenne rushed to her two younger siblings, Zasha and Edwyn, both of whom wore solemn expressions.

Prince Edwyn was the only one of the four half-blood royal heirs who hadn't inherited the typical streak of unpigmented hair that marked all Veseile. He was also the only one of the four who could truly be called a child any more, but fear of their father's looming death made both him and Princess Zasha look younger than their years. Their lower lips trembled as they stared at the doors to their home, eyes wide with fear of what lay beyond.

Princess Vivyenne's own full lips were set into a firm line as she adopted the role of guardian and shield for her younger siblings whilst their mother was preoccupied with grief. She held her sharp chin high and ushered the younger prince and princess inside the castle, away from the prying eyes in the courtyard.

From underneath her lashes, Luelle watched Prince Malcolm dismount. As the eldest heir, his presence before the dying king was the most important but he lingered once off his horse, scanning the crowd. His dark eyebrows pressed together in a deep frown. The evening's shadows accentuated the sharp, straight lines of his face, offset by the curved, crooked nose that all the royal children shared, a trait inherited from Alaric.

Malcolm's frown fell on the spot of darkness where Luelle lurked.

She froze under the weight of his stare.

He took a step forward.

A blond human guard grabbed his arm, breaking the prince from whatever trance he'd been in and murmuring a quiet reminder of the situation's urgency.

Malcolm slowly nodded, throwing a final lingering glance towards Luelle before striding to the castle, flanked by guards.

Once the prince and royal guard were inside the palace walls, the frozen courtyard came back to life. Stablehands and servants rushed to settle the newly arrived horses and complete the tasks they'd been in the middle of before the royals had arrived.

Luelle almost collapsed where she stood.

Had the prince known who she was?

She straightened and shook her head, exhaling a long breath. He couldn't have. She wouldn't still be standing here if he had.

Maybe he was just wondering why one of his servants was covered in dog shit.

Giving a final glance at the castle, her home for over five years, Luelle weaved through the crowd and left the courtyard. The guards stationed at the gate didn't stop her. Servants left the castle every day to enjoy the city's delights at the end of their shifts, and people leaving were of no concern, not now the royal family were safe inside.

With slow, shallow breathing, she forced herself to walk at a steady pace towards Cerulya's busy centre. She'd be out of this damn city before anyone knew what she'd gotten away with.

# 2

Malcolm patted the small leather pouch attached to his belt for the hundredth time, checking that the royal crystal was still there, wrapped in several layers of protective silk. With every step closer to his father's chambers, the crystal's weight grew heavier, a physical reminder of the burden he was about to bear.

Receiving his father's Power, his kingdom's Power, was an honour but the gift was bittersweet, a final sign that his fragile, human father was departing from their world and joining Mortus, the God of Death, in the Underworld.

Before departing for the tourney in Stodor, Malcolm had told his mother it was a mistake to leave. Any other time, he would have thrived at the opportunity to fight, relishing the competitions and the pride that accompanied winning. Grief and frustration had driven him to a level of ferocity he had never before experienced when fighting. He was bringing home more medals than ever before but he felt nothing beyond bitter resentment.

He knew their very distant family ruling Stodor would have understood their absence, given King Alaric's age and the signs of looming illness, but the queen had insisted it was nothing serious. Typically stubborn of her. She'd spent the past year denying the deterioration in the king's health, determined to ignore it as if that might make it go away. She forgot the king was just as important to Malcolm and his siblings.

Did the kingdom always have to come first?

Relations with Stodor weren't in question; the two realms had known peace for several decades, since Malcolm's mother had travelled across the sea separating them to marry Alaric. Any minor damage to relations over one unattended tourney would have been easier to fix than the guilt and shame devouring Malcolm for missing these past two weeks with his father, for their whole family being away when the king had needed them the most.

Malcolm's dark thoughts simmered as he strode through the hallways but he wouldn't voice them aloud to his mother again. She was already blaming herself. On their journey home, she had locked herself away, refusing to eat or speak to anyone. Her melancholy would only worsen when she saw the king and was forced to give up her denial. To be strong for her and his siblings was the least Malcolm could do.

Leena and Theodas fell in behind him without a word, two members of his personal guard and his closest friends since childhood. They knew the problems weighing on his mind well enough. Half the time, they knew him better than he knew himself.

Growing up as a half-blood prince had been lonely, but both Theo and Leena had allied with Malcolm early on, united by their inability to fit in with the rest of the children at court.

Malcolm had encountered Leena first. She was Colleile—a race descended from Collatus, the God of Hunt and Healing. Her parents were nobles, old friends of Queen Vonya's. At her invitation, they emigrated from Nimstall, a warm continent to the southeast, to live in Arazia, making a new home in Cerulya. Malcolm met Leena when hiding from a tutor, retreating to one of his favourite spots deep in the kitchen store rooms, only to find a young girl occupying the space already. At first, they'd both frozen, frightened and suspicious of one another. Leena bared her teeth at Malcolm in a silent snarl, exposing the elongated canines that marked her a Colleile, a much easier trait to notice than the transparent membrane over her eyes eliminating the need to blink lest it interfere with a hunt. Their stalemate persisted until Leena shifted to make room for Malcolm to squeeze in beside her. Together, they hid from the court's crueler children, a silent, tentative friendship forming between them.

Over time, they grew brave enough to talk, eventually agreeing to leave their hiding spot behind, so long as they stuck together. Their duo became a trio months later when they encountered Theo, a pale human child suffering torment from a group of noble Eile children. Leena and Malcolm had defended the small, teary blonde, adopting him as their friend without question.

They became inseparable, spending every minute outside of

private lessons exploring the castle grounds and imagining how they might make the other noble children regret treating them as outcasts once Malcolm ascended to the throne. Their bond had only strengthened over the years.

When Malcolm was crowned king, Leena was to become his spymaster and Theo the captain of his Royal Guard. He wouldn't trust anyone else in the positions, no matter who his father's advisers pushed on him.

Their reunion had been brief when his ship docked at the harbour earlier that evening. Most occasions would have seen them sneaking into the city to drink and play card games as they recounted the highlights of Malcolm's trip and anything interesting he'd missed at home. At the very least, Leena would have coaxed her human sweetheart in the kitchens to slip her a few bottles of wine so they could disappear to the castle roof and play drinking games until they passed out, but this was no ordinary occasion.

Malcolm's footsteps were a muffled, regular beat against the clamour of voices, rustling fabric, and the clinking armour of nearby guards. Overpowering oils and perfumes washed over him as each noble passed, a flimsy attempt to show off their wealth. Their acrid floral scents were little better than his own—musty wood and tangy brine from too long spent above deck on the journey home. It all built to a crescendo, an attack on his senses that threatened to overwhelm him, despite his best efforts to shut it out.

Each step he took was harder than the last. His siblings had rushed ahead, trailing in their mother's wake, but Malcolm's pace slowed. The sooner he arrived, the sooner he had to say goodbye.

Servants stopped to bow and curtsy as he, Leena, and Theodas passed. The sight of their simple clothing nudged his thoughts to the strange feeling he'd experienced in the courtyard.

He fell back to walk alongside his friends. They kept their eyes ahead, tracking the people around them. Servants and nobles stepped out of their path, falling into bows or curtsies until the crown prince moved past.

"Did either of you notice anything strange in the courtyard when we arrived?" Malcolm asked as they ascended a wide, well-lit staircase to the upper floors.

"No."

"Nothing."

They each responded in the same quiet tone.

"Did you see something out of the ordinary?" Leena asked. Her ebony eyes glinted as she raced through her mental list of known deviants that might be reckless enough to attack the royals as they returned home.

"No, but I had a strange feeling." Malcolm frowned, searching for the words to describe what had entranced him. Something about the dirty woman bowing in the stable's shadows had felt familiar, though he hadn't recognised her as one of his regular servants. Something drew his attention to her, but he'd never felt a magnetic pull like that from anyone other than his father. From the king, the feeling was a steady comfort he'd known since childhood but from the stranger it was unnerving. Theo had been right to draw him away, he didn't have time to follow strange impulses today, but it was an oddity that would keep him awake at night for a while. He would have to investigate it the next time he saw her around the castle.

"What sort of feeling?" Theodas shot him a sideways glance.

"It is hard to describe. It was like—" Malcolm paused mid-stride as they neared his father's suite. Distant shouts echoed down the halls.

He exchanged an alarmed glance with his friends before they simultaneously broke into a sprint towards the panicked voices, approaching the king's bedchambers.

Regular thudding began to accompany the shouting.

Malcolm's family were huddled outside his father's chambers, surrounded by a tight ring of guards. More soldiers clustered at the entrance to his father's room. Two of them barged at the closed doors with their shoulders as Malcolm's mother and three younger siblings watched in varying shades of shock and fear.

Servants paused to witness the commotion, wide-eyed, drinking in detail to gossip about later.

"Clear the hallways," Malcolm ordered Theo and Leena, entrusting them to remove the inquisitive onlookers. "What is the meaning of this?" He stormed towards the crowd, demanding of the nearest guard.

"The king appears to have locked himself in his chambers, but he is not answering. We cannot get in," she informed him, her voice trembling.

Malcolm stepped closer to his family, needing the comfort of their presence to stifle the panic rising in his chest. He didn't realise he was clenching and unclenching his fist until Edwyn's wide-eyed gaze dropped to his hand. Malcolm ran the hand through his hair, just to do something with it.

"Why would he have locked the door? Who was guarding the room before we arrived? Did anyone else go inside?" He barked the questions to no one in particular.

His mother's glassy eyes were fixed on the doors, her russet brown skin paler than normal despite their time spent in the sun at the tourney. If she heard his voice, she didn't react.

"Sir, Clarisse and I were on watch." Benjamin, one of his father's favourite and longest-standing guards cleared his throat and spoke up, shifting with discomfort under Malcolm's fierce attention. "The only person that entered was a maid. She has been tending His Majesty for months, Your Highness, and has worked in the palace for several years. She would not do anything to harm him."

"How can you guarantee that?" Vivyenne hissed over Malcolm's shoulder.

Malcolm looked back at his sister. She was next in line for the throne if anything were to happen to him, though he often wondered if she was better suited for the role, faster to make decisions, more ruthless. He pitied Benjamin, cowering under the full force of her wrath, but couldn't bring himself to defend the guard, not whilst his father was trapped in a room with a maid that could be doing Gods-knew what to him.

Malcolm left Viv to torment Benjamin with accusations and strode to the guards at the doors.

"How can I help?"

As he spoke, the doors inched open. One of his father's heavy, ornate chairs was wedged against them.

Fear was a tight fist around Malcolm's heart.

"Out of the way," he snapped at the guards and pushed past them, patience too thin for manners. Blocking these doors had been an intentional act. The king was in danger.

Malcolm reached through the slender gap between the doors and wrestled with the chair for a moment before managing to dislodge it completely.

He shoved the doors open and stumbled inside.

Everything was as he remembered it. Nothing was out of place apart from the chair that had been forced underneath the door handles. The table was upright, its other chair positioned to look out over the room, where his father liked to take an evening drink. To his left, the two familiar lounging sofas remained, cushions fluffed and colourful. The doors to the bathing room and dressing room were both closed, as were the doors to the balcony. Not even the large woven rug that covered most of the cold stone floor was disturbed.

Other than his father's body under the bedsheets, there was no one in the bedchambers. One of the windows on the leftmost wall was open to let a breeze in, or perhaps to let someone out.

"Search the room," Malcolm ordered.

His gaze returned to the large bed, where his father lay, nestled amongst thick pillows. How could someone lose so much weight in only two weeks?

Something was wrong.

Malcolm's mouth dried. The room was too still, the air around him was dead and heavy. The magnetic pull he'd always felt from his father was gone.

Was he too late?

Had the Power that had lived in their lineage for generations disappeared, returned to the Gods, all because Malcolm was too late?

Somewhere behind him, his mother sobbed.

Malcolm staggered to his father's bedside, fighting through a wave of dizziness and fumbling for a pulse in the king's too-thin wrist. Blood roared in his ears, drowning out any noises from behind.

Viv appeared on the other side of the bed, dread and sorrow etched into every sharp contour of her face. Zasha and Edwyn hovered behind her, fat tears rolling down their cheeks.

The queen appeared at Malcolm's side. She clutched her son's arm, fingers digging in so deep that her nails would score his skin.

"Is he..."

"He lives," Malcolm breathed. A delicate heartbeat fluttered beneath his fingertips.

His father stirred at the commotion.

"Father," Malcolm spoke at the same time as his siblings and mother, all of them clamouring for the king's attention to say their final few words.

Malcolm pulled the crystal from the leather pouch at his waist and pressed it into his father's palm.

Alaric opened his eyes at the cool touch of the orb.

"Malcolm?" The king's gaze fell on his son and the rest of his family. His thin, cracked lips curled into a weak smile. "You made it home safe. I missed you all." Wheezing breaths fractured his sentences.

"Father, I am so sorry, but we must act fast. You must transfer the Power into the crystal." Malcolm loathed himself for the words when there was so much else he should be saying.

His father's face scrunched into a frown, deepening the wrinkles on his fair, parchment-thin skin. "It is done, Malcolm. The girl brought me the crystal before you arrived."

The king began recounting some distant memory, an old story he'd repeated over hundreds of lavish dinners about the amazing feats he'd accomplished with the Power and how it was all to come for Malcolm.

Malcolm met Vivyenne's eyes, then his mother's. He swallowed.

As his father said those damning words, Malcolm felt the truth of them. It was why he'd been unable to feel his father's presence when he entered the room, why he'd thought the king was already dead. That buzzing connection, like a magnet drawing Malcolm to him, had always been the Power running through his father's veins, the Power that was part of their bloodline and a symbol of their family's right to rule Arazia.

He tried to swallow again, but his mouth was too dry.

"What do I do?" Malcolm whispered to his mother, feeling much too young to be stepping into the role his father would soon vacate. Inheriting a throne at thirty-four might be normal for a human, but his Eile heritage gave his lifespan the potential to stretch hundreds of years; he felt little more than a child.

Vonya opened her mouth, but a guard interrupted their quiet conversation.

"We found something on the balcony. A rope, Your Highnesses."

Malcolm squeezed his mother's shoulder. Abandoning the crystal on his father's bedsheets, he stepped towards the guard, leading the man away from the bed to give his family some privacy. Malcolm yearned to stay with them but his father was in no state to deal with the problems they faced any more; that was now his responsibility, no matter how little he wanted it.

"It descends into the kennels," the guard continued, leading him outside and gesturing to a rope fastened around one of the thick columns on the king's balcony.

A fresh sense of dread washed over Malcolm.

He peered over the edge of the balcony, gripping the balustrade. A cold wind ruffled his hair, pushing it into his eyes. Far below, the kennels were shrouded in darkness. He moved back towards the courtyard, staring over the edge of the balcony to the ground as he walked. Flickering torches lit the main courtyard, suggesting movement where there was none. It was quieter than it had been on his arrival, with no sign of a thief hiding in the shadows. If his suspicions were correct, she would be long gone into the city by now. He straightened, turning to Theo and Leena who awaited his next orders in the doorway, having ordered the other guard inside.

"Find anyone involved in letting this happen, including guards, and lock them up until we know more about the theft. We will need to interrogate each of them and keep this news contained."

Leena nodded. "Clarisse and Benjamin are already being

escorted to the jail cells. I will find and detain any others."

"There was a woman in the courtyard beside the stables. That was what caught my attention earlier." Malcolm steeled himself with a deep, shaking breath. If only he'd caught a better look at her face. "It was the maid that was in here, I'm certain of it. We must catch her. She must have tricked my father. Retrieve tonight's working schedules from Philip. He will know her identity."

Malcolm's mind raced. He scrambled for a plan to retrieve the stolen Power, for questions to ask Philip, the castle's seneschal, but coherent thoughts escaped his grasp, as slippery as silk. For a brief moment, he feared he might release the contents of his churning stomach over his own feet, splattering across the pale, grey stone of his father's balcony. The world around him spun.

Leena's slender hand fell on his arm. He met her eyes, as dark as the night sky above them and only a few shades deeper than her complexion; he shied away from the concern shining there.

"Stop. We will take care of this."

"I need to—I cannot—"

"Stay and say goodbye." Theo stepped beside Leena. "You cannot waste these moments, Malcolm."

Malcolm swallowed but couldn't eliminate the lump from his throat. He closed his eyes to ward off the tears stinging them. He hadn't even inherited the title of king and already everything was going wrong.

It took a moment to overcome the sense of duty his father had drilled into him for decades but Malcolm nodded. The kingdom could wait.

Theo gathered the remaining guards on the far side of the king's chamber once the three of them walked back inside. Leena stalked into the hallway to investigate any clues left in the courtyard.

"I want two of you stationed on the balcony. The rest, wait outside and give their highnesses some privacy. I will disclose your orders there," Theo commanded, gesturing to where he wanted each of the guards.

Chainmail clinked as they rushed to comply.

Once the doors to the balcony and adjoining rooms clicked shut, Malcolm turned back to the bed. He forced himself to walk the distance, ignoring the weight pressing on his shoulders.

His father looked so weak, so at odds with the figure Malcolm had grown up idolising. Despite his humanity, the king had always been a strong presence. Malcolm had spent most of his early childhood convinced that his father was indestructible. This frail, delicate figure could not be the same man.

The king was talking to Zasha and Edwyn, who were curled on the bed at his right-hand side. Did they remember their father in the same light Malcolm did? Or had he always seemed so fragile to them?

"-And don't cause your mother any trouble when I am gone. Mortus has agreed to give me leave to come back and haunt you if you misbehave."

The two youngest royals sniffed quiet laughs through their tears at the old joke. Like the rest of the world, Alaric had always known his family would outlive him, but the jokes came easier to him than the rest of them.

Malcolm couldn't bring himself to smile at this one.

He perched on the mattress beside his father's legs. His mother had moved to the king's left to caress his fine, white hair in slow, smooth strokes. Viv stayed at the foot of the bed with Malcolm, her arms wrapped tightly around herself. Silent tears streamed down her cheeks, leaving glistening tracks against her skin.

"Everything sorted, my boy?" Focus faded in and out of the king's stare as his eyes fell on Malcolm.

"All under control, Father." Malcolm's voice wasn't as steady as he'd intended. The crystal lay in a nest of bedsheets in front of him, a worthless heirloom now it had nothing to contain. He plucked it from the bed and slipped it back into the pouch at his waist.

He pushed the issue out of his mind and focused on his father.

The king reached out his hands. Malcolm grasped one, Viv the other.

Malcolm no longer fought his tears.

# 3

Luelle darted through Cerulya's crowded streets, adrenaline driving her faster than she should walk if she wanted to blend in. It made no difference, no one paid attention to her. Tonight, she was just another face in the rabble. No other palace workers would be in the city on the eve of the king's death, let alone any that would recognise her, but she tugged her cloak's hood further forward, as a precaution.

So far, no sense of alarm had leaked from the castle into the surrounding city, but Prince Malcolm must now know someone had committed treason against the crown.

She ignored the pit of anxiety in her stomach and shifted her backpack, stifling the urge to check on the glass sphere again.

Around her, Cerulya was alive with activity, despite the apprehension that lingered like a bad smell. Luelle scuttled away from the castle and the threat it contained, walking upstream along the edge of the River Kendra, towards the outskirts of the city. Boats and rafts swarmed the wide, deep channel, creating a liquid road as busy as the solid one she walked.

She scrambled to plan the next stage of her escape as she strode through the city.

Once Prince Malcolm discovered his Power had been stolen, he or his advisers would seal the city gates, attempting to trap her inside Cerulya's walls. Either she needed to be out of the capital by then, or she needed to find an unmonitored exit. The Kendra Gate, named after the city's first human monarch, was the closest; going through it would mean a longer walk around the city's external walls but at least she was less likely to be trapped within.

Outside the capital, she could find somewhere secluded to absorb the Power. Leaving it in the glass sphere for her entire journey was too risky. It could break or her bag could be stolen, putting it in the hands of someone whose motives were inappropriate, or worse, someone with no motives at all that left it to waste and wither.

If Luelle stuck to the river's edge, skirting around the city's main market square, she could reach the main bridge over the Kendra River in twenty minutes and be out of Cerulya's northern gates in thirty. With any luck, that wouldn't be enough time for the prince to get word to the city guards stationed there. If any guards looked too alert, she could double back and find somewhere safer to exit.

Clinging to the edges of the market square proved difficult, even at night. Ever-moving crowds bustled around Luelle, swelling like the tide, their current trying to tug her to their centre.

Voices rang over her head; merchants selling their final wares for the evening, drunkards prematurely celebrating the new king or mourning the one they were losing, and pleasure workers spouting raunchy offers to anyone who made eye contact.

Luelle kept her stare hostile and fixed on her path ahead, constantly searching for space in the sea of people. She gripped the straps of her bag tight enough to turn her knuckles white, warding off any would-be thieves with a fierce glare.

She'd visited the city's streets frequently enough to become well-acquainted with the dangers and the best routes out but rarely for her own pleasure or entertainment during her years working in the castle. No other servants had bothered to invite her when they had time off, but she would've declined even if they had extended an olive branch of friendship. At best, they'd tolerated her quiet company but in many cases that icy indifference stretched to a more vicious form of resentment.

Streets grew calmer as Luelle put distance between herself and the central market. Shops lining the road were long-closed, their darkened windows only broken up by the occasional lively inn or tavern. Patrons streamed inside and gathered in the immediate vicinity, still at a joyous stage of their drinking. They sang and danced to jaunty music. Laughter overflowed the perimeter like the ale sloshing over the rims of their tankards.

In a brief moment of idiocy, Luelle considered staying the night in one, eyeing the large fireplace within. Her mouth watered at the scent of hot, spiced food spilling into the street from the kitchens.

No, it was too risky. Escaping the city would be much harder when they stopped letting people leave in an attempt to catch her. Clarisse and Benjamin would certainly suspect her. By morning, the city would be crawling with guards who knew exactly who to look for, whether the news had spread to the public or not. If she could make it out before then, she had to try.

Luelle continued past the inns, turning from their open doors with reluctance. She'd always known her journey home would be uncomfortable, especially compared to her years of living in the palace. Working as a servant, she'd had her own bed, a regular wage, and clean washing facilities. Her shifts had been long and gruelling but she'd never suffered from sleeping in the cold, nor wondered where her next meal would come from.

She'd forgotten her roots. Before this mission, she'd spent her life sleeping on the street, on hard floors and in caves, hunting and fighting to survive, and scraping together any money she and her companions could for the supplies they couldn't steal, salvage, or forge from scratch.

Her priority now was to find somewhere safe and absorb the Power, not to find a comfortable bed.

Tolhurst, the nearest village at the edge of the Great Forest, was a few days away on foot. She would find somewhere secluded outside the capital, dump the empty glass sphere, and make her way there. When she was in the Great Forest, away from strangers that could be bribed, it would be much harder for the guards to track her.

The bridge over the Kendra River was almost a hundred feet wide, stretching several times that far to cross the water rushing beneath. City guards were stationed at each end of the bridge and regularly across its length. They gathered underneath the moonstone globes positioned every twenty paces, the glowing spheres mined and sent from the underground Dileile communities who lived in the northern Camthryn Peaks. The Dileile descended from Dilectya, God of Love and Invention. True to their God, the Dileile were natural creators, a small, strong race whose eyes were capable of magnifying sights to see details no other beings could manage. Luelle had noticed a couple Dileile nobles in the castle but few lived beyond the Northlands.

Luelle kept her head down as she passed each city guard, cringing into the shadows her hood provided. Walking across the bridge took agonisingly long, as torturous as her descent down the castle wall had been, but after what felt like hours she was on the eastern side of the river and only a few minutes from the Kendra Gate.

She upped her pace, striding through the streets and wrapping her arms around herself when she passed yet more guards, praying they would believe she was rushing to get out of the cold.

No one stopped her.

The roads leading up to and out of the Kendra Gate were quiet. Few people arrived in Cerulya this late, only some late-night stragglers entered the city, likely hoping to attend the burial of King Alaric and Prince Malcolm's coronation in a week.

Fewer still were leaving.

Guards flanked the large gates but none spared her more than a passing glance. Prince Malcolm must not have yet given the order to close the city. Or, he might not intend to send that order at all. He knew more than her about the Power, about what would happen if she died whilst it was in her body. If he knew it would return to him, there was a chance he would isolate news of the theft inside the palace walls and simply send assassins after her.

Luelle continued, trying to leave that uncomfortable thought behind.

A weight lifted from her shoulders as she left Cerulya but the danger wasn't yet eliminated.

Clouds drifted in front of the waning moon, darkening the road from the capital to the rest of the kingdom. Before Luelle had arrived in the city, half a decade ago, she'd poured over maps of the land, committing them to memory. A mile or so south of Cerulya, she'd find a rocky stream. In the daylight, it was visible from the city's taller buildings but no one would see or hear her lurking there at this hour. Absorbing the Power there would be safer than attempting it too close to the capital, even if it meant venturing cross-country with no more than her wits to guide her.

When the guards behind her were no more than shadows in the distance, still lingering at their posts on either side of the Kendra Gate, Luelle pulled off her bag and dug out the short dagger she'd stashed inside. Fleeing would be her best option if she encountered anyone that wished to harm her, she was no skilled fighter, but the slight weight of the blade in her palm was a comfort in the darkness.

She set off again, not giving herself time to overthink the pros and cons of absorbing the Power out in the open.

Previous monarchs had always hidden the transfer behind

closed doors so the exact process was unknown, but unofficial sources suggested anyone with enough Veseile blood would feel the surge. Luelle didn't doubt the truth of it since she'd always felt the Power residing in King Alaric. That innate recognition was a sign the Power belonged to the entire Veseile race, no matter how else humans tried to spin their false history.

Farmsteads and smallholdings littered the land around the capital city. Their lights looked like fallen stars on the flat, shadowy land, but Cerulya outshone them all, a vast, imposing beacon on the horizon.

Luelle stayed far from the isolated homes she passed, eyeing their warmth with envy. She stumbled more than walked for over an hour, tripping over hidden obstacles and falling to her knees several times. Warm, sticky blood seeped through her leggings after her third tumble.

Muttering a curse and wincing through the pain, she pressed on. It was just another ache to add to those still lingering from her fall through the kennel roof.

Her legs throbbed by the time she reached the stream.

In the darkness, the water's edge was hidden. Luelle's heart raced as she almost fell over the steep riverbank. Splaying her arms, she jerked backwards, retaining her balance at the last moment. Visions of falling from the king's chambers flooded her mind.

When her breathing steadied, she clambered down the riverbank, scuttling along the water's edge until she found an outcropping of rock to shelter her from view of the city she'd left behind.

The river was narrower than the one wending through Cerulya and much faster. It bubbled past Luelle, whispering secrets.

Tucked into the darkest shadows her hiding place provided, Luelle knelt on the ground, wincing at the pain that throbbed through her knees. Stones and dirt probed into the scratches and cuts there.

She hunched in silence for a few minutes, thanking her Eile heritage for the gift of elevated hearing. She'd never known her parents but the streak of unpigmented hair above her left temple and her ability to sense the Power was confirmation they'd been Veseile. Both had died before she could form any memories of their faces, but Zeke had been enough of a parental figure to fill the gaping hole in her chest after those early years stuffed into an orphanage.

She crouched by the river until she was certain no one was following her and readied herself for the most important moment of her life.

Pebbles clattered into the water as she pulled her backpack in front of her, plucking out the carefully concealed glass sphere. As she unwrapped each layer of fabric, the glow of the Power within grew brighter, illuminating her small shelter like blue sunlight when it was fully uncovered.

Luelle gazed at it, frozen with awe. It eddied inside the transparent cage like a living thing. Cradled in Luelle's fingers, the glass was warm. The Power pulled at her, whispering like the river, beckoning her to let it in.

Zeke had given her some basic guidance on how she might

be able to will it into herself but he had no true experience with the process. It seemed like an impossible task without him here to support her.

She sat, transfixed by the swirling, shimmering patterns until the call became unbearable.

Luelle closed her eyes and focused on the warmth and weight in her palms.

Human tradition suggested that a new prince or princess's ability to absorb the Power was a sign of their divine right to rule, that if they couldn't, they were unfit for the role and their sovereignty would fail.

Luelle knew how untrue that was.

Anyone with a bloodline blessed by Vesanya, God of Chaos, would be able to absorb it, and once she completed her mission, each member of the Veseile race would once again own and wield the Power without needing to obtain it from a silly relic.

Some Veseile instead believed that eradicating the human race altogether was the only way to retrieve the Power. Zeke had once shared those beliefs but had since found evidence to support a different, less bloodthirsty, theory. He now believed that the Power only needed to be returned to its source; he, Luelle and the rest of their mismatched family had no desire to start a war by assassinating the king or slaughtering an entire race, they only wished the humans would return what they'd stolen.

Luelle pushed away her anger at the deception spread by the monarchy over so many centuries. She took a deep breath, focused on the natural connection between her and the Power, and willed it to enter her body.

For a moment, nothing happened.

Then, the world paused.

It seeped into her hands, sluggish at first, but soon flooding the veins in her arms with heat and settling in her chest.

She couldn't breathe as those final few drops of Power bled into her. Strands of her coppery brown hair floated around her face, tickling her cheeks.

She inhaled a deep breath, and the world started moving again.

Opening her eyes, nothing had changed, yet everything had.

The glass ball in her hands was transparent and empty. She knelt in the same rocky shelter and, though it was once again shrouded in darkness, unlit by the Power, Luelle's vision was sharper, picking out details she hadn't noticed moments earlier, cracks in the dry dirt, insects crawling nearby.

Beyond her shelter, the same endless fields and plains rolled but now she could smell the wildflowers riding the wind in the distance. Looking up, the sky was decorated with thousands more stars than before, despite the distracting glow of Cerulya behind her.

Her aches and twinges from falling through the kennel roof remained but their pain was lessened.

She felt whole.

Luelle shoved the linens that had once concealed the glass ball back into her bag and crept closer to the stream to wash some of the dirt from her bloody knees. When her cuts were cleaner, she snatched the dull glass sphere from the ground and hurled it as far as she could into the rushing water.

It sank straight to the bottom.

She grabbed her dagger, swung her bag back onto her shoulders, and climbed the rock to continue her journey to Tolhurst.

Using the stars to ground herself, she strode in the direction of the Great Forest.

# 4

Malcolm slumped in his armchair, rubbing his hands across his face. Across the room Theo and Graman, his childhood tutor and one of his father's advisers, were seated on a sofa, engaged in a quiet conversation. It was drowned out by the roar of Malcolm's thoughts. Leena had left to retrieve Philip, who could answer some of their questions, but for now, Malcolm had a moment to breathe and recover.

Fatigue weighed down every inch of his body, a physical pain he could feel in his tense muscles and aching eyes.

His father had died less than an hour ago.

Malcolm and his siblings had left their mother alone with the king's body, instructing the guards that no one was to disturb her and delaying the announcement of his death to give her some privacy to mourn. Viv was finding Zasha and Edwyn something to eat, keeping them close since neither she nor Malcolm wanted their younger siblings handed straight to stewards after the night's events. He knew there was a deeper, underlying motivation. Viv didn't want to be alone either, didn't want to face the realities of what happened next. That was Malcolm's job. He was left alone to deal with the biggest problem now facing their realm—catching the thief before his bloodline's Power was lost or used against them.

Tomorrow, the royal council would officially announce the king's death. He would lie in state for six days, one to represent and honour each of the Gods. Historically, the six days were a way to ensure that the coroner's analysis was correct and the monarch's soul was accepted into the Underworld. Modern belief acknowledged that the time was more of an opportunity to mourn the lost monarch and prepare for the upcoming, public coronation, giving the realm's four Thanes time to travel to the capital. At sunrise on the seventh day, Malcolm would officially become king. Later that day, at his coronation, he would perform a demonstration of the Power to validate his claim as the legitimate heir and confirm his divine right to rule.

None of it could go ahead as tradition dictated if he couldn't inherit his father's Power. Without it, what claim did he have other than being raised in the right place?

What would his father think if he could see Malcolm now?

The door opened.

Philip entered, trailed by Leena. The human seneschal dipped into a short, stiff bow, tension clear in the tightness around his eyes.

Leena's brow was furrowed with concern when Malcolm dragged his gaze to meet hers, a mirror to the look Theodas had been shooting regularly in his direction.

He offered his friends a weak smile but the expression felt wrong on his face. Leena looked towards the large table, usually reserved for hosting meetings such as this, but Malcolm shook his head. He gestured at the sofa to the left of his armchair so she and Philip would stop looming over him.

Malcolm's shirt clung to his shoulders, clammy and uncomfortably warm. The room felt too crowded, despite all the space, despite dismissing the guards who had been stationed within and relocating them in the hallway. Any one of them could be traitors to the crown. How was Malcolm supposed to trust anyone after this betrayal?

Philip assessed him with keen eyes before speaking up.

"It is true then, Your Highness?" he asked, face expressionless. As always, his appearance was immaculate; his long, dark locs were swept back and gathered together at the nape of his neck, his clothes neatly pressed to eliminate any creases, his posture erect and unyielding to the late hour.

Leena, after consulting her spies, was certain that Philip was not part of the betrayal, which was as much as Malcolm could bear to think on the subject, for now.

He nodded in answer to Philip's question.

Leena and Theo began questioning the seneschal about the thief but Malcolm zoned out of the conversation, letting their voices blur into the background and slumping further into the cushions behind him.

Why had the gods allowed this to happen? Was it a punishment for something he'd done?

He ransacked his memories, scrutinising every mistake he'd

made in life. His father had always drilled into him the importance of the Gods, ensuring they were a prominent part of his tuition.

Six Gods created their world: Vesanya, God of Chaos; Mortus, God of Death; Meto, God of Harvest and Fertility; Adagna, God of Wisdom and War; Dilectya, God of Love and Invention; and Collatus, God of Hunt and Healing. Working together, the Gods created humans, but individually, they developed their original creation further to produce six races, collectively known as the Eile. Five of those races lived on earth alongside the humans, though myth claimed that the Moreile, a sixth race created by Mortus, lived alongside the God of Death in the Underworld, helping him to care for and protect the souls that resided there.

Belief and mythology surrounding the Gods were the main cause of conflict and tension between humans and Eile in Arazia, particularly between humans and the Veseile race. A fraction of Veseile denied that the monarchy's Power was a gift from the Gods to the humans, despite the evidence of it in front of them. Instead, they believed the Power must belong to them since it originated from Vesanya, the God who created their race. Most Veseile understood the ludicrosity of these ideas, living in harmony with humans, but the minority that didn't were vocal and violent about their beliefs.

Malcolm's father had thought that marrying a Veseile princess would help to unite the two divided factions, to silence that small, aggressive group of Veseile fanatics. If only it could've been that easy.

From a young age, Malcolm had been reminded of his importance to both the Veseile and the humans, but neither camp seemed to fully belong to him. Most human children he'd grown up alongside had rejected his claims that he was like them, laughing in his face when they weren't able to avoid him altogether. Veseile nobles had been just as bad, always responding to him with uncertainty, as if there was a chance he was tainted and might infect them with his human heritage. The two groups had disagreed about a lot but both were certain they didn't accept a half-blood like him as one of them.

Perhaps his inability to understand and embrace either side of his heritage was why the Gods were now choosing to punish him.

He had to catch this thief and retrieve the Power before news spread that his claim to the throne was vulnerable. Despite tensions between the extremist factions of Veseile and humans, general dissent was low after his father's careful, placating reign. Destroying that peace couldn't be Malcolm's legacy.

He tried to push away the dark thoughts, to return to the conversation in the room, but his stomach dropped. He shuddered, tensing as a feather-light touch skittered down his spine. Straightening in his chair, he looked around to try and locate the source of the unsettling feeling in the room.

No one else seemed disturbed, though Leena eyed him as if he'd finally given into madness.

"What's wrong?" Theo asked, interrupting Philip in the middle of a sentence.

Malcolm shook his head, desperate to rid himself of the

urgent feeling that something important was happening. His mouth dried but, as he swallowed, the world settled back into place as if nothing out of the ordinary had just occurred.

"I don't know. I just had another strange feeling," he managed to say.

Graman peered at him over the wire spectacles perched on his short nose. He was one of the few of his father's advisers that Malcolm trusted completely, a large Adeile with a green tint to his skin. Though he was originally from the east of the kingdom, some small town near Sandport, he had lived in the castle for Malcolm's entire life.

"Hm," Graman grumbled, narrowing his muddy brown eyes.

Malcolm met his gaze across the low table separating them. "What?"

"A rushing feeling? In your chest?"

Malcolm nodded, running a hand through his unkempt hair. He didn't feel like a king at the moment. A glimpse in a mirror before retiring to his drawing room had shown dark circles underneath his eyes, bowed shoulders, and crumpled clothes, still unchanged from his journey home. His father had always said maintaining a kingly appearance was a type of power in itself but Malcolm couldn't muster the strength to care tonight.

He'd been preparing to step into this role his entire life, had always known his father would die whilst he was only a few decades old, probably centuries before his own death. How could he still feel so unprepared for it all?

"I've read about this in the journals my predecessors left." Graman's deep tones reverberated through the room. Like all

Adeile, the tusks protruding from his lower jaw brushed past his fuzzy upper lip as he spoke, giving him a slight lisp. "Some inhabitants in the castle have described a rushing feeling when the monarch's Power is transferred from the royal crystal into the next heir, but it wasn't universal."

Malcolm's fists tightened on the arms of his armchair. That couldn't mean—

"The thief." Leena's voice was clipped and controlled.

Graman shrugged, challenging the seams of his tunic. "It could be a coincidence but that is what I suspect."

"How is that possible?" Theo asked.

Malcolm leaned forward to cradle his head in his hands, resting his elbows on his knees. Conversation around him became incoherent again. He scrunched his eyes shut but couldn't escape the image of his father lying too still in bed, couldn't escape the sound of his mothers and siblings sobbing. The sound of his reign commencing was tragedy and loss.

The door to his drawing room opened, revealing two dishevelled nobles, wrestling their arms away from his guards' grip, fury creased into their furrowed brows. Malcolm raised his head, recognising two of his father's advisers—his advisers now, if he chose to keep them. Elena, a human and the Councillor of Internal Relations, and Tym, a Colleile and the Treasurer.

Elena spoke up, her voice a little shrill. "Your Highness, we have been awaiting a council meeting to discuss the night's events. We must know the state of His Majesty's health. The Queen will not admit anyone into the room."

Malcolm gestured for the guards to shut the doors again,

leaving the advisers inside. He had no capacity to deal with this right now. The room felt suffocating with two more people inside.

Decades ago, Malcolm had peeked into his father's meetings through the keyhole in the council room door, given the opportunity by friendly guards who knew the crown prince would soon sit in on those councils. Back then, Malcolm yearned for the day he would sit in his father's seat at the head of the table, when he would make the important decisions to defend his people and strengthen the realm. He'd had a place at the table for two decades and had sat in on more meetings than he could remember but, still, he'd anticipated the day the council would truly belong to him and would respect his word as much as they did his father's.

He had his wish. The council was now his alone, though, given the way two of its members were barging into his private drawing room, the respect he desired wasn't going to be immediate.

"Should we retrieve the other councillors? Meet in the appropriate setting?" Tym eyed Graman.

"I will call the council when I am ready to discuss what has occurred tonight." Malcolm heard the stern words slipping from his mouth. He wasn't ready to deal with their demands and expectations, for their beady, assessing stares as they tried to decide what sort of king he would be and learn how they might best manipulate him. Many had been trying for years already, circling him like vultures. Others had ignored and dismissed him altogether, only deigning to pay him attention when his father requested his opinion on important matters.

"Your Highness, it is vital that we meet." Elena spoke up, smoothing her grey hair. Frown lines gouged the space between her brows like trenches. She was one of those who had rarely acknowledged Malcolm's presence when his father had been alive, leading council meetings. "We must decide on the next steps—"

"That is Your Majesty," Theo corrected her, his normally warm and welcoming brown eyes as cold as Leena's.

Elena sneered in return. "Not until the official announcement of the king's death. Not until he inherits the title and crown on the Seventh Day. He remains the crown prince in the interim."

Malcolm forced himself to straighten in his seat and pay attention.

"Elena, I will call a council meeting soon. What is so important that it cannot wait until the morning?" He didn't bother adjusting his tone to be more pleasant.

She shifted where she stood, shooting another brief glare at Theo. "Rumours are circulating. We hear you do not have the Power, as you should."

Quiet fell over the room, holding for a beat too long.

"So it is true." Tym's face paled.

Elena charged on. "You must send out search parties at once. Interview every worker in the palace and send urgent messages to all four Thanes informing them that the kingdom is on high alert and a dangerous criminal is on the loose," she rambled, achieving a tone that managed to be both smooth and condescending. Tym nodded with approval.

Malcolm shook his head. "I cannot let news of a theft spread to the general public. It risks fuelling further dissent, particularly if this is the work of Veseile extremists." He didn't voice his concern that if any of his Thanes were more ambitious than they appeared, now would be an ideal time for them to stage a coup against him. "Guards and search parties at every corner of the realm would unsettle the people. It would undermine the authority and trust my father established. I need people to feel that same trust in me, to know I can protect them and have control."

"With all due respect, Your Highness, you don't have control if you have allowed King Alaric's Power to be stolen from underneath your nose," Tym sneered.

Malcolm gritted his teeth.

"I understand that but the solution Elena proposes is rash. It would create more problems than it solves, particularly if the thief is working with others. I need time to think it through." He bit out the words.

"You do not have time," Tym retorted. "You have six days after the king's death before you are due to inherit the crown. If you do not retrieve Alaric's Power by then, you shall not be able to continue fooling the people that all is well."

"You will speak to Prince Malcolm with respect," Leena snapped, anger bubbling over at the council members' tones.

The room descended into incoherent bickering.

Malcolm's breathing grew faster. He was drowning in their arguments. All he could see was his father's pale, fragile body.

"Enough," he shouted, standing from his seat. "Nothing will be solved arguing like this." His chest heaved.

"If you cannot solve this matter, perhaps we should take it to Princess Vivyenne or insist that we are allowed into the king's chambers. You have already shown reluctance to punish the guards who let this treason occur. Vivyenne may be better suited to make hard decisions, regardless of the price," Elena remarked in the silence.

Leena and Theo's heads snapped to her but Malcolm held up a hand to prevent them from saying anything that would worsen the situation. They obeyed but Malcolm didn't miss the tension in his friends' postures.

Clarisse and Benjamin, the guards who had let the thief enter his father's chambers, were in the cells beneath the castle. Leena had interrogated them whilst Malcolm said goodbye to his father. She'd reported back to him before leaving to find Philip, describing their apparent remorse. Both guards had readily answered all of her questions, providing any additional, useful details they could think of about the maid that had disappeared from King Alaric's private chambers.

Graman had already warned Malcolm that some advisers might push him to do more in the pursuit of justice, demanding torture or their heads on pikes. Malcolm wanted nothing more than to oblige, and if he stepped foot in the dungeons, if he laid eyes on Clarisse or Benjamin's faces, he was certain he'd lose control and slaughter them. However, giving into that desire would solve nothing. Although it might soothe some of the pain and fury he felt, killing Clarisse and Benjamin was not the right thing for his kingdom or his people. He needed them alive, at least until he caught the thief. They offered a source of information that could benefit his quest to retrieve the Power. He couldn't continue to use them if they were dead.

Once the Power was under his control again and the thief had been dealt with, he could decide their fates. Perhaps he'd simply leave them to rot for eternity, eaten away by their own guilt for failing their king.

"You may not approach my sister or mother. Nor may you ever threaten to force your way into the king's chambers, let alone hours after a breach of security. You are bordering on treason. You forget yourself." He let his wrath leak into his tone, using Elena as an outlet for his rage.

She didn't respond but two spots of colour bloomed on her cheeks.

"If either of you, or any other adviser, dares to disturb my family before they are ready to speak to you, you will have me to answer to. I am still in line to be your king, and I will not forget those who disobeyed me in our kingdom's time of need." He spat the words. "Now, both of you, get out and speak of tonight's events to no one else. If I hear that these rumours are persisting, I will hold each of you personally responsible."

Malcolm didn't watch Elena or Tym leave. He stared at the ceiling, listening to their muttering voices, to the fabric of their clothes rustling, and the soles of their shoes brushing against the floor. He remained silent until the door shut but did not let himself sink back into his seat until they departed. Once this issue was sorted, he would take the time to consider how appropriate each councillor was, replacing the worst with his own trusted choices. His father wasn't a bad judge of character but

Malcolm needed advisers who respected him and his abilities, regardless of his age and mixed heritage. He wasn't their puppet. Growing up alongside them had tainted their opinion of him. They still saw the insecure, uncertain child, not the man he now was.

"Leena, please ensure they do not linger and tell the guards outside not to let them back in under any circumstances. Maybe send a couple after them to ensure they do not disturb my family." Malcolm sighed and slumped in the armchair, rubbing frown lines from his brow. "Graman, have they always been that awful or am I misremembering things?" He looked up at his old tutor, who shrugged.

"They are under immense stress, my lord. They all care a lot for your father. They want the best for the kingdom."

Theo snorted. "That is a yes."

Philip hid his abrupt laugh in a cough.

"They do have a point though, Malcolm. It has happened at an awful time for you but we must plan a way to retrieve your Power." Graman's tone softened.

"He is still mourning his father," Leena snapped, returning from the door. Her sharp expression was at odds with the soft, floral patterns shaved into her close-cropped hair.

"And he will be for many years. That changes nothing."

Theo opened his mouth but Malcolm cut off the retort.

"Graman is right. Do we have any suspects other than the servant?" Grief and exhaustion weighed down his every move and thought but he shoved them aside. His lack of sleep from the journey home was catching up with him, fogging his mind.

"She, Belle, was the last person on rotation to attend the king tonight," Philip confirmed. "He asked for her by name to help him prepare for your return. There were several others, servants and healers that tended to him today. I brought a list of names, but Belle was the most recent before your arrival."

"Is it possible someone could have climbed the rope and eliminated the servant? Perhaps from one of the rooms below, if they had the opportunity to enter the king's chambers earlier in the day and secure the rope," Graman suggested.

Leena shook her head. "That is highly unlikely. Benjamin and Clarisse reported hearing no disturbances and I have eyewitness reports confirming they did not leave their posts. There was no other body in the room, nor any evidence of a conflict."

"Every guard change requires a full sweep of the room. I will check the earlier schedules and make sure none of them saw anything," Theo said.

"Do you think it is likely the servant was working with anyone else in the castle?" Malcolm asked Philip.

"I have checked the records and did a head count before coming here, Your Highness. Belle is the only one who is missing. I would be surprised if anyone working with her chose to remain here, knowing you will now be searching for other traitors."

"I have trusted eyes throughout the castle monitoring for suspicious activity," Leena added. "I don't think it's safe to assume anything at the moment, but the fact that only this servant has disappeared suggests she is working alone."

Malcolm rubbed a hand over his face, weighing up his options. Rumours were already spreading fast. If he ordered a huge chunk of staff arrested, he wouldn't be able to hide the theft for long. It was hard enough hiding his father's death until his family were ready for the announcement to be made public.

"It is more likely the thief met with others after escaping if there are others involved at all. Philip, you said she is Veseile, so I would assume we are dealing with an extremist." Theo ran a hand through his short, blonde curls. "We sealed the city gates and paused all ships leaving the harbour as soon as we could but we cannot ignore the possibility we were too late."

Malcolm leaned his head back against the cushioned seat, staring up at the intricate swirling patterns in his ceiling. As much as he disliked his father's adviser, Elena, she was correct about the urgency of the situation. "We must send ravens to alert the guards in the nearest villages. Even if this thief is working with other people, she cannot have travelled far. Do not tell anyone what has happened or what we are searching for. Simply, say there is a dangerous criminal on the run and that we need her returned here, unharmed, as soon as possible. We can put a reward on her head. If we cannot find her soon, we will have to inform the Thanes of the threat she could pose but I want to avoid that, if possible."

Leena and Theo nodded.

"Have we already sent people to search the city?"

"Yes," Leena said. "I have sent a small group of soldiers I trust, using the information Philip provided about the maid. I have not told them what was stolen, only that she is dangerous. They are due to report back in a few hours but even if they cannot recover anything, the servant could be lying low until we reopen the gates. They are under orders to come straight to me with any news."

"Why did we not see this coming?" Malcolm wondered aloud.

Philip shifted in his seat, frustration clear in the set of his brow. "This servant worked in the castle for just under six years. She was quiet and obedient and underwent the same background checks as every other worker when she first started. I never had any problems with her before."

"The main issue we face is how much of our documentation about her is accurate. We can rely on witness accounts of her appearance but her identity and background could be false," Leena said.

"Who was she close to? We can find out more from them." Theo's brow furrowed.

"I have already tried that but no one claims to know her well. Apparently she was not well-liked."

Philip nodded. "She kept to herself, especially once the king began requesting her assistance more regularly." He glanced at Malcolm.

A pang of anger stabbed Malcolm's chest. How had he not noticed a traitor living amongst them for so long? There were hundreds of servants around the palace but he always made an effort to acknowledge them, to recognise the ones who served him and his family the most often.

"I imagine she stayed away from duties that crossed your path too much," Leena added, seeing the flash of frustration cross his face.

"So, all we have to go on is an unreliable background and a potentially false identity. Plus, we have no way of trusting anyone else in the castle. How are we meant to find her?" Malcolm grimaced at the impossible task he faced. His father would've known what to do.

"We have enough for a starting point," Leena reassured him. "We know she is Veseile. Brunette, with the typical streak of unpigmented hair. She is a few inches shorter than me, has brown eyes and is athletic enough to descend the castle walls. It might be worth getting a portrait drawn up if you wish to put a reward on her capture."

Malcolm nodded, chewing his lip. "Did she ever communicate with the other Veseile working here?" He scanned his memory for the faces of every Veseile servant he knew. The thief had been standing alone when he'd noticed her in the courtyard but that meant nothing.

Philip shook his head. "She typically only spoke to other staff to receive her orders."

"If we can get a portrait drawn up, we can use it when questioning any other guards and servants in the castle. Some might know her by sight, even if not by name," Theo suggested.

Leena made a wordless noise of agreement. "If there was anyone else working with her in the castle, we will find them. Locating people she is working with outside the capital will be harder."

"If she came from the east, she could be going back that way. We should prioritise the roads in our searches," Theo said.

"But we have already agreed she could be lying about her

background." Leena frowned at him.

"We need to start somewhere." He shrugged.

Graman had been watching their conversation but his eyes settled on Malcolm, who was once again slouched in his seat.

"What do you plan to do next, Your Highness?" he asked, murmuring whilst the others continued discussing guards and patrols.

Malcolm met his eyes and took a deep breath. He tried to consider his options but could barely string together a coherent thought.

"Let us meet again in a few hours, before dawn. Just those of us in the room, not the other advisers. I need some sleep and then I will be of more use."

They each nodded and rose to stand as Malcolm stumbled out of the room towards his chambers, though they stayed behind to continue finalising their plans to send ravens and patrols.

He was asleep as soon as he fell into bed.

# 5

Luelle travelled through the night, stumbling through her fatigue until the colours of morning stained the sky. She kept the road in sight but walked as far from it as she could, paranoid that guards, or something more sinister, would be tracking her already. When her exhaustion grew too strong to ignore, she strayed towards a dark, derelict barn standing alone on the horizon. A hesitant step inside revealed it was long abandoned by humans and Eile, only inhabited by spiders and beetles.

Luelle crawled further in, shrinking into the shadows against the rotting wooden walls as dawn broke. Half of the barn's ceiling had fallen to the ground, leaving an open window to the sky. Wind whistled through the gap, swaying the cobwebs and peeling more flecks of paint from the remaining walls, but it was better than no shelter at all.

She curled up to sleep on a pile of mouldy hay, wrapped in the linens that had concealed her glass sphere whilst escaping Cerulya.

She wouldn't rest for long. Even staying here, in such an obvious hiding place, was a risk, but she would be more vulnerable if she continued like a walking corpse, tripping from weariness every second step.

Luelle slept fitfully, flinching awake at every distant sound, yet time still passed too quickly. Before long, she was eating more of her meagre supplies and dragging herself back onto her feet to continue, groaning at the stiffness in her limbs from sleeping on the ground and falling through the castle kennels.

Real rest would have to wait until she reached the Great Forest, where it was safer to tend to her injuries. Until then, she had to push through the discomfort. The faster she returned to the Caeleste Peaks, the better.

As she progressed further from Cerulya, the rolling hills on either side of the road grew wilder. Grass and wildflowers stretched toward the sun, standing tall enough to conceal her entirely when she crouched. Whenever she noticed a figure in the distance behind her, Luelle lay low in the grass, still and quiet until the stranger passed, soon developing a crick in her neck from looking over her shoulder every few steps.

Tolhurst, her destination at the edge of the Great Forest, was a moderate village but still a fraction of Cerulya's size. Under normal circumstances, with better supplies and fewer injuries, she could reach it in a day and a half, even less if she had a horse, but travelling off-road and hiding whenever a stranger appeared slowed her progress. Luelle made good time for most of the early afternoon, breaking to rest her legs every few hours and sneaking to wells to refill her water flask whenever she spotted one in the distance.

Several hours into her trek, a cloud of dust appeared on the horizon behind her, growing larger with each passing second.

She didn't wait to see if the travellers were civilians before darting further from the road and crouching into the grasses, leaving only enough of her head exposed to peer at whoever was thundering down the path in the same direction as her.

A group of guards in glinting, silver, Cerulyan armour passed in a wave of noise and colour. Incoherent shouts permeated the drumming hooves, but Luelle couldn't decipher the snatches of conversation that reached her hiding spot.

She didn't need to hear them to know who they were chasing.

They were the first sign that Prince Malcolm was not going to sit idly by and let her get away with her theft.

A brief note of sadness struck Luelle's heart when she realised it also likely meant King Alaric was dead. He hadn't clung on for long after she'd left him. Had surrendering the Power hurried the process along?

She cringed from the thought, unwilling to dwell on her guilt in case she lost her nerve. More guards would be searching for her. Losing her confidence now would be just as dangerous as abandoning her dagger and continuing her journey unarmed.

When the guards were a speck in the distance, Luelle strayed from her hiding spot, continuing with more caution than before and flinching at every slight noise. More soldiers appeared, though none in groups as large as the first. Their presence became so frequent that Luelle spent most of the next hour hiding in the grass at the roadside. Continuing to travel in the daylight would be pointless. She turned from the road and scoured the horizon for somewhere to rest, settling on a secluded cluster of trees in the distance. She would pause there and gather her strength until darkness fell to offer some protection from her enemies.

Cool speckled shade covered the ground beneath the throng of trees, a blessed relief from early autumn's muggy warmth.

Luelle sat against the trunk of one of the trees and closed her eyes, breathing through the aches pulsing in her legs. She probed her thighs and hips, wincing as she discovered an abundance of new bruises.

Working in the castle had kept her active but her shifts had been laden with breaks. She hadn't travelled this far on foot for years, and it was becoming plain in her heavy breathing and the sheen of sweat sticking her clothes to her skin.

After five minutes of relishing the cool breeze and quiet rest, Luelle shifted onto her knees, wincing as the action tugged the scabs that had grown over her cuts.

If Cerulya's guards and soldiers were now chasing her in bulk, they must know who to look for. Her features weren't uncommon in this part of the kingdom, there were plenty of brunette Veseile women wandering around, but she couldn't predict how observant people in the palace had been whilst she lived among them. Would they know that her eyes were the same shade as burnt caramel? Or that her face was slightly asymmetrical? She'd kept her head down, trying to avoid attention in the capital but she attracted it as soon as Alaric started favouring her.

Seeing her true friends again would be a relief, finally allowing her to drop the facade of unpleasantness. She'd liked several of the people she'd worked with in Cerulya, but pursuing a friendship with them, let alone anything more, would've been impossible given her reasons for being there.

Loneliness had eaten at her during those long nights in the castle. Sometimes, it was intense enough that she'd fled into the city, dancing and laughing with any strangers open to her company. Most of those companions had sought more than friendship, and a few times she'd obliged, when the thought of returning to her own shared chamber, to her hard, narrow bed, was too much. She never stayed the night with her chosen stranger, always returning to that prison of a castle to prepare for her shift in the morning, and she never allowed herself to meet or socialise with the same person more than once. Becoming too familiar with someone would leave them vulnerable to the city's guards once she'd retrieved the Power. Involving other people in her deception had never been an option, particularly not innocent civilians, given the rumours that Cerulya's guards could be over-enthusiastic in their violent treatment of criminals.

The Power might now protect her from those guards but no one else. If she could learn to manipulate it, she wouldn't need physical weapons to ward off their attacks. She'd be untouchable.

Luelle had studied the Power before travelling to Cerulya but feeling it warming her body revealed how ignorant the authors of those sources were. None of them had come as close to it as she was so her learning curve would be steep. There had been precious little source material for her to read, regardless.

Throughout history, most reigning monarchs deemed the study of the Power too close to treason. Not even Alaric had allowed it, despite his liberal attitudes. Since only the current king or queen could wield the Power, there was no need for average, normal people to know how it worked.

If Luelle wanted to use it for her own defence on the journey, she would have to figure it out herself.

She dragged her backpack in front of her, placing it just out of arm's reach.

Witness accounts Zeke collected over the years described kings and queens that could achieve incredible feats with the Power—forming weapons forged of fire, reshaping the earth around them, even controlling people's movements. Writers theorised that skill and willingness of the wielder affected the Power. Luelle was certainly willing, but would her skill level match her enthusiasm?

There was only one way to find out.

Taking several deep, calming breaths, she settled back into a comfortable position, resting on the heels of her feet. Twinges of pain in her legs and back cried out for attention but she ignored them.

She held her hands out straight in front of her, thrusting her palms at her backpack in an attempt to push it away with a gust of wind.

Nothing happened.

Luelle squeezed her eyes shut and searched the deepest corners of her mind and body for the Power, trying to draw up as much of it as she could. Again, she thrust her hands towards her backpack.

But, when she squinted one eye open, the bag hadn't moved an inch.

Her hands dropped to her sides, fingers brushing against the dry dirt and brown fallen leaves.

A move like that must be too advanced for her. After all, the Power hadn't been in her body for a full day. She should have spent more time trying to watch Alaric use it around the castle.

Hours inched by as she tried different tricks—pulling at her backpack, pushing it, lifting it in the air. When nothing worked, she tried with smaller targets, lining up several rocks and then crunchy leaves, but couldn't muster a whisper of wind to shift them. She attempted to manipulate the shadows on the ground, to make them writhe around her fingers, examining her hands for any physical trace of the Power.

The only thing that changed was her growing exasperation.

When the frustration of defeat became too strong, Luelle snatched a handful of dirt from beside her and hauled it at her belongings.

She tried again.

Birds watched from the trees, chirping encouragement. Shadows stretched across the ground, bringing a cool breeze with them. Sweat beaded on Luelle's forehead as she toiled over her impossible challenges, but when the sky began to darken, she had still not discovered how to use the Power lying dormant in her chest.

She got to her feet with a sigh and stretched her aching muscles. Sitting in one position for so long had done nothing good for her injuries. She grabbed her backpack and slung it over her shoulders, adjusting her cloak to fall over it.

Wandering to the edge of the copse, Luelle peered through the gloom towards the road. Everything was still. No more soldiers or travellers materialised on the horizon in either direction.

Travelling unseen would be easier now that the sun had set, but she still wouldn't risk using the road.

She abandoned the shelter of the trees and continued towards Tolhurst, clutching her dagger, gritting her teeth at the thought of how many miles lay ahead, and looking over her shoulder to spot any enemies before they could sneak up on her.

# 6

The skies were still dark when Malcolm returned to his drawing room, only a few hours after fleeing it. He hadn't extended an invitation to his father's old advisers. Instead, he shared the room with Graman, Leena, Theodas, Philip, and the eldest of his younger siblings, Vivyenne. They sat at the table, rather than lounging in the more comfortable chairs across the room.

Malcolm had hoped to enter the meeting fresh-faced, confident in his role and the best course of action to catch the thief, but he'd spent the precious little time he had in bed tossing and turning, somehow waking feeling more exhausted than he'd felt earlier. Every move was sluggish and heavy, as if he'd waded to the room through syrup.

Viv had slept no better if the bruise-like shadows under her eyes were any indication. Even in a simple black gown, she looked every inch a princess, spine straight, shoulders back, expression solemn. Her long, black hair was wound into a knot, twisted around a long hairpin at the back of her head.

They'd spent most of the meeting so far updating her about the information they'd gathered, the thief's identity and their suspicions about how she'd stolen the Power and escaped the castle. Viv's eyes darted back and forth, following the conversation that Malcolm had long zoned out of.

He pulled himself back to attention, straightening in his seat.

A map of the kingdom was spread over the table between them. Markers noted all major trading ports along the western coastline, as well as every known smuggler cove, but their attention was focused on the mass of land to the east of that.

"If she travels east, she may intend to go to Sandport and leave the kingdom altogether." Theo pointed to the large city on the other side of Arazia. "She must have known we would close the ports here as soon as we discovered the treason. Sandport is the easiest place to find a ship to another continent, no questions asked."

"There are plenty of other ports she could use to reach another continent and that's assuming she wants to escape the kingdom at all. We cannot be certain she did not meet with someone else who would go in a different direction," Leena countered. She ran a hand over her shaved head.

"True, but as I said earlier, this is our only lead." Theo frowned, equally unhappy with the situation.

"Have we sent ravens to any other cities?" Viv spoke up, her voice huskier than usual. She cleared her throat.

Theo nodded. "To all of the nearest villages and the major cities in all four other provinces. Cerulya's guards have also been enforcing checks on anyone leaving the city gates and searching boats and carriages for stowaways. They have been told we are cracking down on crime before the coronation and are under instructions to report anything suspicious to us. We have also supplied a description to match the thief."

"We need to think of an explanation for the masses in case we have to delay the coronation," Graman noted.

"Perhaps Malcolm can give a speech once our message is aligned." Viv nodded at their old tutor.

"I will not be here. Viv, you will need to give the speech."

Her head snapped towards Malcolm. A strand of hair escaped her bun, swaying beside her cheek.

"What do you mean you will not be here?" Her eyes narrowed.

"I am going after the thief. I decided before this meeting." Malcolm shrugged.

"Don't be ridiculous." Ire grew in Viv's expression. "You are needed here, you are the king."

"Not yet. And how can I claim that title if I won't risk leaving the castle to track down a single thieving servant? Father would never have sent others to retrieve the Power for him. This is too important to leave in the hands of other people, not to mention too sensitive. We cannot let news of the theft spread. It is my responsibility to get it back." He'd toiled over the dilemma in bed, unable to fall back to sleep once he'd woken. What was the best course of action to protect his people and restore his strength? He couldn't trust any staff in the castle, Clarisse and Benjamin had proven that. If anyone was to catch the thief, it had to be him, but could he justify risking his life in the process?

"It is too dangerous," Viv insisted.

"I shall not be alone. Leena and Theodas will accompany me."

Malcolm's two closest friends looked as if they were more inclined to agree with Vivyenne, but nodded at him.

"Sire, I do not mean to question your judgement, but how would you track her? We have no idea where the thief is going, nor what direction she left the city from. There is a small chance we may still find her in the city itself," Graman spoke up.

"I can... I can sense her." Malcolm pulled a face. "Well, not her. It is hard to explain. I can sense the Power. I could always sense it in Father, feel his presence before he entered a room, things like that. I had not realised it was the Power I was feeling until we came back last night. I couldn't—I thought—"

He swallowed, blinking hard to try and eliminate the tears pricking his eyes. The lump in his throat threatened to choke him.

Graman reached over to place his hand over Malcolm's. Malcolm wasn't a small man. His father had been well-built for a human and his Veseile heritage gave him a considerable amount of extra height and muscle, but Graman's hand dwarfed his own.

He took a deep, trembling breath and carried on.

"I thought Father was dead when we reached his room because I could no longer feel him," his voice was gruff, "but I felt the pull of the Power in the courtyard, towards a servant in the shadows. It must have been her. Belle."

Viv didn't respond, her face paler than it had been moments before.

"That was only hours ago so she cannot be far," Malcolm continued. "I will use my connection to the Power to track her. We will ride east and try to pick up her trail."

"Malcolm, your coronation is in six days. You are needed here. The announcement about Father's death will be made in a few hours."

"With any luck, we might make it back before the coronation is due and the public will not realise anything was wrong." He didn't meet Viv's eyes.

She shook her head, glancing at Graman for support. "We cannot rely on luck in a situation like this."

"Then we will make a contingency plan." Frustration rose as Malcolm listened to his sister. She was only saying everything he'd already considered, already tortured himself with. There was no perfect solution to this problem, why couldn't she just support him? "I need to do this, Viv. Arazia is a small kingdom. The monarch's Power is the only thing that has prevented a successful invasion from the neighbouring realms. Without it, our enemies will think me weak. I would put the entire kingdom at risk of war or a coup from the Veseile extremists within."

"Send someone else to retrieve it instead! I understand your concerns, but a weak king is better than a dead one," she snapped at him.

"Who else can I send? There is nobody else we can trust!" Malcolm's tone rose to meet hers.

"Leena, Philip, have you found proof of any others working with the thief?" Viv turned to the two seated to her left, ignoring her brother's outburst.

Philip shook his head.

Leena shuffled in her seat, eyes flickering from Viv to Malcolm. "I think it is more likely that the thief is working with people outside the city, but there is no way of knowing if she has other allies here until they slip up and reveal themselves. I do not think any of you should consider yourselves safe until the Power is back with Malcolm and we have had a chance to interrogate the thief."

"That is proof that you are needed here." Viv turned back to Malcolm. "Your family needs you, forget about the realm and your strength for a moment."

"I cannot forget about it, Viv. I wish I could but I cannot. The longer I leave this alone, the more time I give the thief to master the Power and use it against us."

"You do not even know that she is able to use it. Father has trained us for decades. She will not manage after a few days, if at all."

"I cannot take that risk. If she is able to, she could harm thousands of our people, could *kill* them."

Graman cleared his throat. "With all due respect, sire, I am inclined to agree with Princess Vivyenne. Due to the rumours and Elena and Tym's visit last night, your advisers are currently aware that the Power is missing. We must work with them to minimise the damage and control the message you want to give before anything leaks to the public, but that will be easier to do with you here."

"And how will I control the message when I am unable to demonstrate the Power at my coronation? Or worse, when the thief shows up and uses it against me at my coronation because I was too weak to go after her?" Malcolm's resolve hardened as he spoke. "I will not put my people at risk like that. The entire city would be vulnerable."

Viv was frowning when Malcolm looked back at her. "Fine, ignoring that, what about the risk to yourself? If this woman is part of a group of rebels, they could easily overwhelm you in sheer numbers alone. You are a good fighter. I know you have experience in small battles and are more than capable of besting your opponents in controlled environments, like the tourneys, but even the most skilled fighter would struggle standing alone against an entire army of enemies."

"I will not be alone. I have already said Theo and Leena are coming with me."

"That is not enough, Malcolm. We have no solid evidence of how many extremists there are spread throughout the realm. A large group of them would not hesitate to kill you if they were able to capture you."

"The Veseile that would go that far are a tiny minority, Viv." He rolled his eyes. "You pay too much attention to fearmongering amongst the human nobles."

Her jaw clenched as she scowled at her brother.

"All rumours have an element of truth. You would be wise to pay attention to them, given that your life would be at risk if you undergo this foolish journey. Is it not enough for us to have lost our father? You want us to lose you, too?"

Shame flooded Malcolm. His gaze dropped to the table. "I am sorry. I will pay attention to the risks, but I will not be travelling alone. I trust Leena and Theo with my life. If we come across any people we suspect of being extremists, we shall not engage with them. We will send word home and track them until reinforcements can reach us, even if we have identified the thief among their numbers."

Viv's frown didn't budge from her expression.

"We will keep him safe," Theo promised her.

Malcolm nodded his thanks to his friend.

"That still leaves the dilemma of the coronation if you do not make it back in time." Graman's troubled expression matched Vivyenne's.

"Can we not simply use a stand-in replacement and keep them far enough from the public that no one realises it isn't me?" Malcolm shrugged.

Viv snorted. "Even you are not stupid enough to truly think that would work. Who would you suggest we use? Shall I hold auditions? Too many people would learn about your absence, and then there is no hiding the vulnerability of the realm or of you, travelling the kingdom with only two guards. A random replacement would also be unable to demonstrate the Power for the public, which is the main point of the ceremony."

"Could you tell people he is sick to delay it?" Leena suggested.

Malcolm shook his head. "No one would believe it. There is no illness serious enough to prevent the coronation. People would think I was dead or dying too, which could cause bigger problems to fix."

Silence returned to the table as they mulled over their

problem. Viv was the first to speak up.

"What if Father was alive again?" She stared at Malcolm.

He rubbed his hand over his face. He was too tired for this. "We would not have this problem at all if he was alive again."

"No, you misunderstand me." She took a deep breath. "The six days between the death of the monarch and the coronation are traditionally a way to ensure the monarch's soul is accepted into the Underworld, correct?" She glanced at Graman who nodded, understanding dawning on his face. "Father has not yet been moved from his room. There are obviously rumours circulating, but the official announcement has not been made. The only person who has actually seen his body other than our family was the coroner. Mother wouldn't even let the guards back in. We can seal the room before his body is moved and say the diagnosis was wrong or that he has awoken again." Her voice trembled.

Malcolm's mouth dried.

"I shall stay in the room with Mother. We can say you are with us, looking after him, so no one suspects that you are vulnerable travelling through the kingdom. Graman can be our point of contact with the outside world, he can bring me updates from you and Philip can provide anything else we need, like food."

"No, Viv, I cannot ask you to do that," Malcolm choked out, fighting nausea at the thought of his mother and sister awaiting his return, locked in a room with their father's decaying corpse.

Her expression hardened. "You did not ask, I am the one suggesting it. That way, we can delay the coronation until you return home by simply stating that the king is still alive. The six days do not officially start until the monarch's time of death has been publicly announced."

"How would you deal with the coroner and the other council members?" Graman asked. "They already know about the Power, and they will certainly suspect Alaric's death by now."

"Arrest the coroner," Leena spoke up, her dark eyes calculating. "I can plant evidence that he was working with the thief if you want a credible excuse, but that will stop him from talking and refuting you no matter whether you claim his diagnosis was wrong or that the king has awoken."

"The council may demand to see the king themselves, for proof," Graman cautioned.

Viv shrugged. "I can deal with them. If we have been betrayed by a servant and one of our coroners, why would I trust the council? Particularly if my father has awoken but is still in poor health. Any one of them could make an attempt on his life. He will need to stay in a room with his family, alone, until we decide he's strong enough to return to the public."

"You must not forget that the council knows about the theft," Graman reminded her.

"We can explain that we were misguided in our assumptions. The servant actually tried to assassinate the king but when the attempt failed, we realised he still possessed the Power, ready to pass to Malcolm. That is why Malcolm must remain in the room with us, in case Father's condition worsens again."

"Viv, it would not work. How would you stop his body from decomposing? People will be able to—they'll smell him from outside the room." Malcolm stared at his sister, trying to relax his horrified expression.

She faltered. Graman spoke up in her silence.

"We may not be able to prevent it altogether, the body will already be breaking down, but there are steps we can take to slow the process or to... contain it, for the comfort of anyone else in the room. We can wrap it or try to sneak up a container of sorts. Sand and ice are both proven to slow decomposition but they would be difficult to explain and source. Salt would be easier, though we cannot stop the body from decomposing indefinitely."

Viv regained her composure, nodding. "That would be adequate. If anyone shows suspicion, I can explain that I am running Father regular salt baths to aid his recovery."

"Okay." Malcolm swallowed. "What about Zasha and Edwyn? This will traumatise them. Besides, Mother will never agree to it."

"I shall deal with them." Viv nodded, regaining her composure. "Mother will agree when I explain it to her. Besides, it will give her more privacy to grieve. Edwyn might be best kept elsewhere, he is still young, but Zasha is stronger than we all give her credit for."

Malcolm stared at his sister over the table. Could this work? Could he really expect his family to do this? It would be for nothing if he got himself killed or if he failed to find the thief.

"Your Highnesses, if we are settling on this plan, we must move quickly. The coroner is due to move the king's body to the morgue at first light and the sun will be rising soon," Graman noted.

Malcolm and Viv locked eyes again, coming to a silent

agreement. This was the best plan they had. It would have to work; there was no viable alternative. His reign would be at risk if he didn't retrieve the Power and chaos could ensue if word spread that someone had stolen it from him. The majority of Arazia's population was concentrated in Cerulya and the other cities, but there were scores of towns and villages that the thief could wreak havoc in, let alone the countless individual homes and farmsteads throughout the rural countryside. While he remained unaware of the thief's destination, Malcolm had to assume all of his people were vulnerable.

"When will you leave?" Viv clenched and unclenched her slender fingers into fists on the table.

"As soon as possible. The longer we remain here, the more time the thief has to meet up with others or reach a coastline." Malcolm looked at Leena and Theo. "We will pack our own things and leave before sunrise. No one else can know what is happening in order for Viv's plan to work. People need to believe I am in the room with her."

"I was going to get a portrait of the thief drawn up today," Leena said. "We will need to wait for that unless you have another way we can identify her."

"I can sense the Power in her."

"What if she transfers it elsewhere?" Theo asked.

"Take Benjamin or Clarisse," Viv said.

Malcolm frowned. "No."

She scowled at him. "They know what happened and they know her face as well as any other guard. I need Philip here so you cannot take him. Enduring their presence on your journey will be more pleasant than spending an undefined amount of time living beside Father's corpse, as Mother and I will be doing."

Malcolm gritted his teeth. It was a bad idea but he did not have time to sit and argue the point to his sister. "Fine."

Leena stood from the table. "I will pack for us now and collect one of them from the cells. Theo can deal with the coroner whilst I am doing that. We will wait for you in the courtyard. Cover your face when you come to meet us. Do not wear anything that would identify you."

He nodded.

"I will say goodbye to Mother, Zasha, and Edwyn, then I will be there."

Theo and Leena left the room to get started. Malcolm waited for the door to shut again before turning back to Viv, Graman, and Philip.

"Make sure the patrols and guards continue their searches in the rest of the city and kingdom, but if they find the thief before us, they must return her alive. I do not know what will happen to the Power if she dies before submitting it to me. I shall keep in touch and send messages back to Cerulya at every village or town we reach to keep you updated on our progress. Monitor Leena and Theo's mail too, since we'll be undercover. Sending a message to the princess might look a bit unusual." He tried to joke.

Viv chewed her lip. She nodded, but frown lines remained nestled between her brow.

"It is only temporary, Viv. I will return with the Power before you know it and we can put Father to rest."

"I wish he was here to advise us."

"Me too." Malcolm lifted the corners of his mouth in an attempt at a smile. "I will go and say goodbye to Mother, Zasha, and Edwyn now, and then I shall head off." He took a deep breath. "Graman, Philip, can you deal with the council? The three of you should come up with an agreement about how often you'll meet and how to get supplies into the room."

They nodded.

"Send Mother, Zash, and Ed to Father's room when you are done," Viv said. "There is no need to tell them our entire plan, just that you are leaving. I will fill them in when you are gone, to save you time."

Malcolm rose and walked around the table to pull his sister into a tight hug before leaving her to a much worse immediate future than his own.

# 7

Luelle walked all night and most of the following morning until Tolhurst peeked over the top of a hill she ascended, laying in wait for her arrival. Beyond the town, the Great Forest loomed, blanketing the horizon with greens and browns.

The shrubbery she'd been using to conceal herself at the sides of the road grew shorter so she abandoned it and ventured onto the manmade path. Each slow footstep dragged through the dirt, sending small puffs of dust trailing in her wake.

This was the most risky part of her journey.

She could skirt around the village to reach the Great Forest— she *should* skirt around the village—but she'd finished the last of her food through the night and had spent the entire morning failing to ignore the dull ache in her stomach. Entering the Great Forest exhausted and underfed would be stupid, given the creatures that lurked in those trees. She would find food in Tolhurst, most likely the last hot meal of her journey, and continue, speaking to as few people as possible.

Guards lounged against the buildings at the outer edges of the village, too engrossed in their conversation to pay Luelle any attention. She kept her head down as she passed, retreating into the shadows of her hood.

Luelle wandered down the widest street, the main road through the village, admiring the mismatched buildings around her.

Treetops stretched over their uneven roofs at the far edges of the settlement.

People of all ages milled the streets, greeting each other by name and eyeing the stranger in their midst. Anyone Luelle strayed close to veered away with a wrinkled nose as her scent wafted over them. After breathing it in all morning, she barely noticed the smell, but the reactions of the townsfolk confirmed her dire need for a wash.

She walked the entire village once, memorising the best routes to the treeline before choosing an inn on the side closest to the forest. Peering through the windows before heading inside, she observed a small dining hall hosting a handful of late risers. Most of the tables remained empty. Stains decorated the wooden floor, the fire was not lit, and there was only one bartender, but it was better than nothing.

A hoppy scent washed over Luelle as she opened the door. She stepped inside the inn and strolled to the bar at the far end, earning passing glances from the other patrons. She pushed her hood back.

The barman didn't look up as she approached. She rolled on the balls of her feet in front of the counter, but he didn't acknowledge her, too absorbed in whatever he was scrawling on a tattered sheet of parchment.

She cleared her throat.

The barman raised his head and levelled her with an unimpressed stare. Grey eyes wandered over Luelle, assessing the interruption.

"You stink." He eyed the remaining muck on her clothes. Most of the dirt and dog excrement had brushed off after drying under the sun but no amount of wiping at the fabric had eliminated the stains or the lingering scent of urine.

Luelle frowned, cheeks heating. "Is that how you speak to all of your customers?"

The barman shrugged. He abandoned his parchment and slid off his stool, stepping closer. An easy smile curved his lips. "Only the ones in need of a bath."

Luelle ignored the remark and took the opportunity to assess the barkeep in return. He was handsome, a Veseile that moved with the full grace of the race. His face, surrounded by a mop of red hair with a single white streak, showed no sign of age, but appearances were deceiving when it came to the age of most Eile races. It was one of the main traits that set them apart from humans.

"Can I get a drink?" she asked after a pause in their conversation.

"No." The barman leaned forward to rest his forearms on the wood between them. He wrinkled his nose, twirling the quill he'd been writing with between his fingers.

Luelle's nostrils flared as she huffed an annoyed sigh. "I have the coin."

"I can't let you sit in here smelling like you spent the night in a dog's arse." He shrugged. "You'll scare off all my customers."

Still frowning, Luelle took a slow, pointed look around the near-empty room. "Looks like you're managing that well enough, yourself."

"Lunchtime rush is gonna be any minute." Dimples danced in the Veseile's cheeks.

"Okay, where can I find the next closest tavern?" Luelle grumbled, shifting her bag on her shoulders. Hunger was making her more irritable than normal.

"I don't wish to be rude, but no bar is going to serve you in that state. You need to book a room and have a wash."

"I can't afford a room. I just need some food before I head off," she snapped. She probably had enough coins for it all but it would leave her without any for an emergency. Her planned route took her to the Caeleste Peaks through the Great Forest and the Godswood, avoiding all traces of civilization on the kingdom's Eastern Road. Paths existed through the forests but the risk of bandits and wild animals meant most people only took them if they were desperate to avoid the tolls on the Eastern Road. Luelle would travel deep in the forests, avoiding even the well known paths, but a few coins could still be a handy distraction if she happened across any bandits lurking among the trees.

The red-haired Veseile looked her up and down, once again.

"Tell you what, I'll give you an hour in our bath house out back, free of charge. When you're done, you can come back in and get your drink," he offered.

Luelle narrowed her eyes. "Why would you do that?" Such kindness from a stranger was rare. Was there already a public bounty on her head that she hadn't noticed?

The barman put his quill down, laying it carefully beside the parchment he'd been writing on. "It's been a slow morning and I'm a sucker for a pretty face. You're still paying for the food."

Luelle didn't lessen her glare or lower her guard, but she wouldn't turn down the chance for a proper wash. None of the guards in the village had seemed suspicious of her; they'd hardly paid her any attention. An hour to rest and replenish her energy might actually improve the speed of her journey, rather than hinder it, and this could be the last time she accessed a real bath house for a while. She nodded at the barman.

He tugged the stained cloth off his shoulder and threw it on the bar, ambling towards a door to his right. He gestured for Luelle to follow.

"Watch the bar, Fee," he called to someone at one of the tables.

Luelle looked back in time to see a human hunched over a bowl of porridge glancing at them. He grunted in reply.

She followed the barman into a narrow hall that emerged back outside, into an enclosed, square courtyard behind the inn. Short, grey buildings lined each edge.

"That way leads to some of our rooms." The barman gestured to the doors on their left, noticing Luelle examining them. "And that door leads to the stables. But no more rolling around with the animals if you want that food," he teased. "Bath house is up ahead." He led her across the cobblestones and opened the door furthest from the bar. Floral-scented steam billowed into the courtyard, floating away into the blue sky.

"Thank you." Luelle nodded her gratitude.

He smiled. "My pleasure. I look forward to speaking to you when you smell nicer." He turned and sauntered back to the bar, whistling a jaunty tune as he went.

Luelle closed the door to the cobbled courtyard behind her.

A large, square pool was the main feature of the room, sunken into the floor. Steam rose from its surface. She had the place to herself, which was probably for the best. Talking too much would put her at risk and the barman was already too chatty for her liking, despite the part of herself yearning to enjoy his conversation and subdue her loneliness for a while. When she got home, she would be surrounded by friends and loved ones, she'd never have to leave them behind again, but here she needed as few people to remember her face as possible. Getting too close to someone in Tolhurst could ruin her chances of making it to the Caeleste Peaks altogether.

She limped to the shelves on the far side of the room, letting the thick, curling steam hide her from the doorway. Soaps and oils covered the shelf. Luelle took her time sniffing each one before selecting her favourite and returning to the edge of the bath with the cleanest washcloth she could find. Hooks lined the right wall, holding dry, fresh towels for when she was finished.

She undressed, grimacing at the wafts of her own body that drifted up to her. She hurled her dirty clothes in a heap far from the bath, wishing she had another spare set so she could abandon the soiled ones altogether.

Before stepping into the water, Luelle examined her injuries. Scabs covered her cuts from stumbling as she walked and falling through the kennels in Cerulya; her body was a patchwork of yellow and blue bruises, hidden under a layer of dirt and dust that had somehow seeped through her leggings and shirt. She prodded at her bruises, hissing at their sensitivity and twisting to try and peer at the ones decorating her back.

Satisfied that none of her injuries were serious, Luelle undid her hair from its braid and descended into the small pool, lowering herself until only her face remained above the hot water.

Tension melted from her sore muscles in the heat. Her hair fanned around her, brushing against her shoulders as the water rippled with her movements. Only when the threat of sleep tugged at her mind did she sit up again.

She dunked her head under the water's cloudy surface, rubbing at her scalp hard with her fingertips to tease some of the knots away. Sitting back up, she grabbed her oils and soaps to scrub the dirt and sweat from her body and hair, hoping that guards were not about to burst in at any moment.

# 8

Malcolm's head throbbed as he left his drawing room. A dark cloud hung over him as he strode through the palace hallways, unable to find the joy in his home that had once felt natural. Colourful paintings looked dull and faded, jests and laughter sounded forced, the faint scent of food wafting from the kitchens turned his stomach. Having the Power stolen from under his nose, from his father's dying body, was an eye-opening warning, a stark reminder he couldn't trust the majority of people in the castle, particularly in the interim period before he became king.

Silence pressed closer around him as Malcolm strode to his family's rooms. He ignored the few people he passed, servants on the earliest shifts and patrolling guards. In a few hours, nobles would join the crowds, seeking him out to offer their condolences. Their sorrow was not genuine, they were looking to climb the social ladder, to use him as they had his entire life. None of them, human and Eile alike, had ever truly accepted him as one of their own. Fortunately, most of them were still asleep this early. Malcolm walked with a grim expression, hoping it would be enough to ward off any approaches.

As always, he was shadowed by a personal guard, but the human and Colleile assigned to him today stayed far enough behind that their company was not an intrusion.

Edwyn and Zasha's rooms were closer than the royal chambers where his mother would be, so he made his way there first.

His younger siblings were in the middle of getting dressed when Malcolm arrived, already preparing to start a long day full of their regular lessons. Arithmetic was first.

Malcolm had questioned Viv earlier that morning when she'd informed him their siblings were to begin their tutoring again so soon but she'd simply shrugged, claiming it would be a good distraction for them whilst she and Malcolm were too busy to help them work through their grief. They would likely beg for a distraction like this when they were locked in a room with their dead father.

Servants were adjusting the laces and buttons on his siblings' outfits—mourning black—as Malcolm entered. Zasha and Edwyn both looked up at him. Their tutor, Shela, who was seated at a nearby table preparing their first lesson, looked up too. Like Graman, she was an Adeile, though she was younger and stouter, with a blue tint to her thick skin.

"Good morning," Malcolm said to the tutor. "I require a moment alone with my siblings."

Her lips tightened around her tusks at the delay to their lesson but she nodded, bending into a short bow before leaving.

The servants followed her. Malcolm instructed the guards in the room to stand outside the chamber doors and ensure they were not disturbed, in part for privacy but also so he could abandon the formality his role required whenever non-family members were present.

As soon as only himself, Zasha, and Edwyn remained in the room, he released a breath and turned to them with a small, tight smile.

"Thank the Gods, I hate arithmetic. Can you banish Shela? Or stay here and chat with us all morning so she cannot force us to complete those stupid sums for hours." Zasha waved a hand towards the door that her tutor was waiting behind.

Malcolm's smile grew. "Sadly not. It is something we must all learn." He walked past them, making a beeline for the sofas ladened with cushions further into the room. What would his father's advisers think if he replaced all of the chairs in the council room with ones as comfortable as this? Zasha and Edwyn didn't wait for an invitation to join him before they were lounging on either side of their eldest brother, undoing the servants' careful work to smooth out their clothing and ignoring any personal space he might claim.

"How are you both?"

They nodded, expressions serious and sombre. There was quite an age gap between Malcolm and his two youngest siblings. Though only six years separated him and Viv, there were just over two decades between him and Zasha and almost three between him and Edwyn. His youngest brother, at eight years old, was still the beloved baby of their family and home, doted on by everyone around him.

"We miss Father," Zasha murmured.

Edwyn stared at the floor, eyes wide and glistening with fresh tears.

Malcolm wrapped an arm around each of their shoulders, pulling them closer. Viv had promised to tell them the details of their plan so he tried to close the topic; he didn't have time to answer the countless questions they would have if he was meeting Theo and Leena in the courtyard before the sun rose. "It is okay to be sad about it. I miss him too. People keep asking me what to do and I just wish he was here to tell me," he confessed. The painful lump returned to his throat.

Zasha breathed a small laugh.

"When you are crowned king, will you still have time to come and see us?" Edwyn asked, his small pink mouth downturned into a frown.

Malcolm squeezed his shoulders. "Of course I will. Father always had time for us, didn't he? Even if my days are busy, I will make time for you whenever you want to see me. You will be sick of me. You will beg the advisors to give me more work," he teased.

Edwyn and Zasha giggled.

"I came here to discuss something serious this morning, though."

"About the thief?" Zasha asked.

Malcolm nodded. "Did Viv already tell you about the situation?"

Zasha shook her head, biting her bottom lip. She was the spitting image of Viv twenty years ago, before her cheeks had lost all of their roundness. "I overheard you all when we got home yesterday. When we were saying goodbye to Father." Her voice quickened. "I know it was a private conversation, but I could tell something was wrong and Mother wouldn't answer me—"

"It is good that you know," Malcolm said quickly, quieting her panic, "but you must not tell anyone else. Someone was working in the castle, one of the servants that tended to Father. We think she must have tricked him the evening we got home, whilst we were still on the boat. She took the Power before we could get back and ran, most likely out of the city. No one else knows, and Viv is going to explain the rest to you so I need you to go and speak to her, rather than finishing your lesson. She will be waiting in Mother and Father's rooms."

Edwyn hugged his knees. Dark curls, unmarred by the white streak that Malcolm and Zasha had, fell over the worry lines creasing his forehead. "Why did Father not stop the servant?"

"His illness got a lot worse when we were away. The guards said he was not himself. He spent a lot of time sleeping and was confused when he awoke. We do not know exactly what happened, but it would have been easy for the servant to trick him, especially if he trusted her."

"Are the other servants going to hurt us?" Edwyn whispered.

"No." Malcolm's voice was firm. "I will not let this happen again. Theo and Leena are keeping a close watch on all the servants and will check all the guards, too. You do not need to be scared around the servants. Most of them have worked with us for a very long time and would never want to hurt us."

Edwyn nodded but the tension didn't leave his narrow

shoulders.

"If you ever see anything that makes you feel uncomfortable or scared, leave the situation and find me. If I am away, find Viv, Leena, Theo, Graman, or Shela. They will always make sure you're kept safe." He ignored the fleeting thoughts of Clarisse and Benjamin, who he had always considered trustworthy.

"Are you going to be able to become king without Father's Power?" Zasha asked.

Malcolm took a deep breath. "This is what I wanted to speak to you both about. I am going to try and catch the thief before she can take the Power overseas. We do not know her plans, which is why I must act fast, before she has a chance to leave the kingdom."

"You must leave Cerulya?"

He nodded. "Only for a little while."

"Who is going to rule?" Edwyn frowned.

"Viv will explain that to you when you go and see her after this."

"When will you be back?"

Malcolm smiled at their unending questions. "As soon as possible. I will try to return before the coronation, but it depends on how far the thief has managed to travel."

A moment of silence passed between the three of them.

"Are we going to have to continue our lessons whilst you're gone?" Edwyn piped up, a glimmer of hope sparkling in his dark eyes.

Malcolm gave him a wry smile. "That is up to Viv."

"Fine," Edwyn sulked, his bottom lip protruding.

"Does Mother know?" Zasha asked.

Malcolm shook his head. "Not yet. I will speak with her once I have finished saying goodbye to you two."

"You really must leave today?"

He nodded again.

"Are you taking guards?" Concern furrowed Zasha's brow.

"A couple, but we will travel in disguise. We will be safer that way."

She nodded but the frown remained.

"Stop worrying, I will be home before you know it. I have to meet Leena soon, though, so you should both pack up your lesson and get ready to go and speak to Viv. I will arrange for Shela to escort you there."

Malcolm hugged each of his siblings and left them to gather their things whilst he informed Shela that their lesson was cancelled, in the hallway. She accepted his orders grudgingly and awaited the youngest prince and princess to escort them to Vivyenne. Malcolm forced himself to continue through the castle. Time was running away from him. As much as he wanted to relish his last moments with his siblings, in case anything happened to him whilst hunting the thief, he had to increase his pace to update his mother before it became too late to meet Theo and Leena in the cover of darkness.

Once a loud, lively presence in the castle, the queen was now little more than a shell. She'd withdrawn from them all on the ship home from the tourney, refusing to eat or speak to anyone. Things hadn't improved since arriving in Cerulya.

Malcolm wasn't sure if his presence helped or worsened her

state. He was just a reminder that her husband was dead. He was stepping into the role of king far too soon. Every time his mother saw him, she would surely wish him gone so she could have his father back.

The guards outside his parents' chambers stood to attention as Malcolm approached. He nodded to put them at ease.

"Is my mother awake?"

They glanced at one another.

"She is not here, Your Highness. We stayed behind to guard her rooms, but I believe she went to the crypt." One spoke up.

Malcolm blinked.

His father's body was still behind those doors, not yet collected by the coroner. Before his body could rest in the crypt, he would lie in wait for six days, and the royal sculptor would complete a life-size likeness of the king, to be his headstone.

"Uh, thank you. My siblings will be along soon. Let no one else into the rooms." Malcolm nodded at the guards and turned to stride in the direction of the crypt. Being in the gloom down there wouldn't help his mother feel any better about the situation, even if she had gone there to seek some peace.

His steps slowed as he neared his destination. More guards waited outside the heavy wooden doors to the crypt, each straightening and saluting as Malcolm approached.

He gave them a tight-lipped smile and pushed through the doors. Lingering outside, too scared to face his own mother, wasn't how a crown prince should act.

Flickering torches lit the stairway and the wide hallway at the bottom of the descent. In their dancing light, the faces of his ancestors, the monarchs before him, came to life, blinking and smiling. Their stone eyes tracked Malcolm's steps deeper into the tombs. Each one was tucked in their own alcove, set back from the path on which he walked.

Thick, dead air filled the crypt. Malcolm gulped it down, pulling at the collar of his tunic, which must have tightened on the staircase.

One day, he'd lie in a grave identical to those around him. His likeness would be carved to watch the rare visitors that strayed below the palace. It should offer him some peace, to know he would remain with his family and home, even in death, but the thought of his rotting body abandoned in this musty tomb made him break into a sweat.

He couldn't remember much of his grandmother, who had reigned before his father, but he could recall attending her private funeral here, as a child. He'd been unable to tear his eyes away as her body was lowered into the dirt, confined in a wooden box that looked too small for anyone to fit in. Back then, he'd clung to his mother's hand, face pressed against her skirts. It had taken all of his willpower to remain at her side, instead of fleeing to the familiar, brighter hallways above, away from the heavy stares of the dead.

After that moment, he'd only been brave enough to explore the dark catacombs with Theo and Leena at his side.

Malcolm could see his mother's slender silhouette deep in the tombs. His footsteps echoed on the stone floor as he closed the distance between them but she didn't look up to see who approached. Still as the statues around her, she stared at the rectangular pit into which his father would soon be lowered.

"Mother, are you alright?" Malcolm's voice bounced off the walls, repeating his question a thousand times.

No reply. She continued staring, her eyelids heavy.

She'd lost weight over the past week, despite his father's death only occurring yesterday. Her cheeks were more hollow, her dark dress looser. Her once glowy skin was dull, exaggerated by the purple shadows under her dark eyes.

Malcolm placed a hand on her shoulder. Jolting at his touch, she turned her head towards him, though her eyes remained glued to the same patch of earth.

He took it as a sign she was listening.

"Mother, I am leaving the city for a while. I need to retrieve Father's Power. Viv will explain everything to you properly, and I will return as soon as I can." He swallowed. "Viv is waiting for you in your chambers."

His mother said nothing.

"I do not know when I'll return, but if you need anything, speak to Viv and she will make sure you are okay. I love you."

His own words responded to him, reflecting from the dark walls. He opened his mouth again to apologise for being here when she only wanted to see his father but the words got stuck in his throat.

Malcolm left his mother alone in the crypt feeling heavier than he had when he'd entered the dark tunnels. He passed by his chambers to swipe a plain, hooded cloak and donned it in a quiet hallway before making his way outside.

Leena and Theodas awaited him in the gloomy castle

courtyard, leaning against an enclosed carriage. The horses at the front of the vehicle snorted as he approached.

"Clarisse is inside," Theo warned Malcolm before he followed Leena into the carriage.

"Does she understand why she is here?" he asked, through gritted teeth. He had no desire to speak to the guard, nor to hear any weak apologies or excuses for her role in the treason.

Theo nodded and swung himself into the driver's seat at the front of the vehicle.

Malcolm braced himself to be in such close proximity to Clarisse, a traitor to his Father and his realm. The carriage lurched into motion as soon as the door clicked shut behind him. Clarisse sat in the far corner, dressed in plain civilian clothes, her wrists tightly bound with rope. Her shoulders were already bowed but she managed to close in on herself further when Malcolm glanced at her. She didn't meet his eyes.

Sharing her bench were three backpacks and an assortment of weapons. More bags were strewn on the floor, lumpy with hidden items.

Malcolm took the seat furthest from Clarisse, eyeing the bulky luggage sharing the carriage with them.

"We cannot bring all of this, Leena. We are meant to be travelling discreetly."

Leena rolled her eyes at him. "Most of this is going back to the palace. We each have a spare change of clothes in those bags." She pointed at the ones at Malcolm's feet. "And supplies for the journey in the others. I did not know which weapons you would favour, so brought you a selection to choose from. This carriage will take us to the edge of the city, outside the walls. We shall change in here and send back anything that could identify you. People will know you are from the palace, but as a soldier, not as the Crown Prince, and no one will see your disguise as you leave."

"Oh, good thinking."

Leena snorted. "Do not thank me yet. You are posing as a prisoner to get out of the city. The guards won't question us, but the palace orders mean they will look inside the carriage. You need to put this on and let me tie your hands." She chucked a coarse sack into his lap.

"Put it on?"

"Over your head. Clarisse will be wearing one too."

Malcolm sighed and held his wrists together for Leena to bind.

# 9

Luelle lost track of time in the bath house. Eventually, she left the warm water behind with reluctance, drying her body and re-braiding her hair. She tugged on her spare set of clothes and wrapped her dirty outfit in the sheet that had once hidden the glass sphere, hoping that would contain the stench. When she reached the Godswood, she could find a stream to wash the clothes, although they might serve her better as fuel for a fire.

Gratitude to the barman flashed through her once again as she caught the scent of the fabric. She'd needed the bath, badly.

After double-checking that no one was about to walk in, she slipped several oils and soaps from the shelves into her bag.

The bar was no busier when she returned to it.

The barman looked up from his writing and flashed her a smile as she approached.

"Feeling better now?" he asked.

Luelle nodded. "Thank you. I needed that."

"Tell me about it." He grinned. "I was worried the smell

would linger in here for weeks after you left."

She rolled her eyes at him. His grin spread wider.

"Can I get a drink now?"

"Absolutely. Take a seat, I'll bring some ale over."

"And something to eat, please."

The Veseile stood and stretched. "Right away, ma'am." He offered her a mock salute.

Luelle turned to find a table. Three other strangers occupied the room. A pair of humans were tucked in the far corner, chatting about Prince Malcolm's upcoming coronation, and the man the barman had spoken to earlier was sitting a few tables down from the one Luelle chose. He leaned back in his seat, boots crossed on the table. Stout fingers danced over the strings of a lute with surprising grace, plucking a quiet, merry tune. Each time a note stumbled, the man cursed and restarted the entire piece.

Luelle took a seat against the wall, giving herself a clear view of the inn's entrance.

"Fee, I'm taking my morning break," the barman called out to the musician as he carried two tankards and a bowl of stew to Luelle's table. A thick wedge of bread balanced precariously on top of the bowl.

The musician shot the barman an icy glare but stood and marched to the bar. He perched on a stool behind it and continued his practice.

Luelle raised her eyebrows at the barman's second tankard, sending them a notch higher when he sat across from her.

"You can keep me company until Fee makes me take over again," he explained. "Consider it payment for the bath house." A smug smile curved his lips.

"I should have known there was a catch." Luelle sighed and pulled the bowl closer to her, dunking her bread in the stew and savouring a large bite with her eyes closed.

He laughed. "What's your name?"

Luelle chewed slowly, considering how foolish it might be to give her real name. She couldn't continue using Belle here if the palace guards were chasing her.

"Anne," she said, after swallowing her mouthful.

The barman raised an eyebrow. "Liar."

Luelle frowned at him. "I am not."

"I can tell. Your eyebrow twitched when you said it."

Her frown deepened to a scowl. "My eyebrow did not twitch."

He shrugged. "It's fine, you don't need to tell me. Are you on the run? You look the sort." His grey eyes twinkled with amusement.

"What's your name?" Luelle ignored the remark.

"Art." He stuck out a hand for her to shake. "Nice to meet you, *Anne*." He wiggled his eyebrows at the fake name she'd given.

Luelle continued eating, ignoring his hand with a pointed look. Art shrugged and lowered it, taking a deep swig of the hoppy ale in his tankard.

"What brings you to Tolhurst, Anne?"

"Just passing through on my way home," Luelle said through a doughy mouthful of bread. The rich stew burned her mouth but she couldn't stop herself from shovelling it in to try and combat the ache in her stomach.

"Where's home?"

"Is this an interrogation?" Luelle eyed Art, who couldn't seem to tear his stare from her face.

He held his hands up, palms forward in defence. His smile returned. "Just trying to make some friendly conversation. And here I thought you'd be better company than Fee."

Luelle ran her tongue along her teeth, poking at a piece of meat caught between two. She really shouldn't encourage a conversation, but Art's easy presence felt like having a friend again. Was there really any harm in talking?

"What were you writing?" She gestured to the bar with her spoon.

His expression lit up at the crack in her demeanour. "A letter to my family. They live further east. I'm planning on attending the coronation next week and they're keen to hear about it. Are you going to it?"

Luelle shook her head. "I'm not a fan of crowds."

He pursed his lips but didn't challenge her. "I can understand that, but the city must be much more interesting than here. The crowds are worth it for that alone. Nothing happens in towns this size."

"Is that why you're so enamoured with my arrival?" she teased him, feeling lighter than she had in months, years, despite knowing it couldn't last.

His dimples resurfaced. "Perhaps. Where are you travelling from?"

She hesitated again.

Art raised his eyebrows. "If you're trying to dampen my

curiosity, it's not working."

She took a deep breath and sighed. "I came from Cerulya." She'd be gone within the hour, admitting this much to a bartender couldn't put her in more danger.

"And you decided to leave just before the most historic event we might ever live through?" His eyes widened.

"We're Eile. A new monarch comes around every hundred years."

Art shook his head. "Not after Prince Malcolm. He's got Veseile heritage too, doesn't he? He's one of us. No one knows how long he's going to last."

"Half-bloods can inherit the lifespan of either parent. There's no guarantee he'll live any longer than Alaric has."

"True, but I prefer to be positive about these things. It would be a tragedy for Queen Vonya if her husband and her children were all destined to die before her."

Luelle took another bite of food to avoid replying. She had no desire to pity the royal family when they were responsible for spreading and maintaining so many lies about the Power. Fortunately, Art had no qualms filling the silence.

"I was going to move to Cerulya, that's why I came to this part of the world in the first place," he rambled, "but my funds ran out pretty early on in my trip. I didn't realise how expensive life was, I suppose. Sheltered growing up, you know? I was passing through Tolhurst last year and saw an advert for a job in this bar. Thought it might be a good idea to build up some funds before I went to the big city, but I've been here ever since."

"Do you have somewhere to stay in Cerulya?"

Art shook his head again, pulling a face. "No. My family are hoping to join me when I'm settled there, but things haven't gone to plan. I think the coronation is my sign to leave." He glanced at Fee, still plucking his lute behind the bar, but the human didn't react.

"Most of the inns have hiked their prices for the tourists. I'd suggest waiting until after the coronation," she advised him.

He pursed his lips. "Maybe I can earn my keep somewhere. There must be a need for extra workers with all the additional people in the city."

"Good luck with that." Luelle swallowed the last few chunks of potato in her bowl and wiped the edges clean with the remaining bread. Once she finished her ale, she'd leave. The risk of getting caught increased the longer she stayed. She'd been lucky so far, but the familiar anxiety and paranoia she'd developed over the last few years were rousing.

"How much do I owe you for this?" she asked.

Art named the amount with a note of disappointment in his voice. Luelle was pulling her coin purse from her bag when the door to the inn opened.

Three guards walked in.

They glanced around the room, dismissing the two humans in the corner and the one behind the bar. Their eyes lingered on Luelle and Art.

Luelle ducked her head, rooting through her bag again as if her coin purse wasn't already in her hand.

Art looked between her and the guards, a slight frown on his face for the first time since Luelle had entered the inn.

The tallest guard strolled to their table, the two others trailing at her sides. She pulled up a chair, letting its legs screech as she dragged them on the floor and spun it around to straddle beside Art. To passers-by, the guard might look like a long-lost friend, lounging at their table, but her smile didn't reach her eyes and her cold stare didn't leave Luelle for a moment.

The two other guards remained standing. Their stances were casual but their hands rested on the weapons sheathed at their waists.

Luelle gritted her teeth and looked up, meeting the guard's taunting smile. Sharp canines gave away her Colleile heritage. Satisfaction glinted in her pale grey eyes, making Luelle's skin crawl with unease.

"Can we help you?" Art spoke up before Luelle had the chance.

"We received an urgent order from the palace in Cerulya to apprehend a thief that escaped the city yesterday. Veseile, brunette, brown eyes..." The guard raised a finger with each descriptor. Her smile widened in Luelle's direction. "You're not from town. When did you get to Tolhurst?"

She stayed quiet.

Art's eyes flickered between Luelle and the guard at their table.

"My friend Anne, here, is visiting me. She's not your thief."

Luelle didn't let any of her surprise show.

"Oh really?" The guard raised her fair eyebrows. "How long have you been friends?"

"Since we were kids." Art took a long pull from his tankard.

"Can Fee get you three a drink?" He raised his voice. The human at the bar eyed them. His practice with the lute had finished the moment the guards walked in.

"No. Your friend is pretty quiet." The guard didn't bother looking at Art when she spoke.

Luelle returned the Colleile's stare with what she hoped was an expression of cold indifference.

"What was stolen?" Art piped up again.

The guard shrugged. "It's none of your concern. But, we need to take this one off for further questioning." She nodded at Luelle. The two guards behind her straightened, readying themselves to step around the table and drag their suspect away.

"I've done nothing wrong. You're not taking me anywhere," Luelle spoke up, indignant.

"You fit the description and you're new in town. We're following royal orders, so you'll find we can do what we want. Can't be too careful." The guard's cold smile returned.

"I'm not coming with you." Luelle shook her head. A wry smile curled on her own lips, a mask of innocent confidence to hide her thumping heart, which was beating so hard they must be able to hear it pounding the wall of her chest.

She could handle herself in a fight if necessary. She wasn't the strongest but she was quick and, with any added strength the Power provided, she stood a chance of beating these guards or at least buying herself some time to escape and hide.

"You can either come along quietly or we'll drag you out of here," the guard said in a slow, condescending tone. "A scene like that wouldn't be great for business." She spared a glance at Art, whose face was paler than it had been moments earlier.

Luelle inhaled a deep breath, huffing it out through her nose.

"Okay, fine, don't get your breeches in a twist." She pushed herself to her feet and swung her bag onto her shoulders. The stew she'd just eaten churned in her stomach.

She stepped over her bench, watching from the corner of her eye as the guard opposite her also rose. The others turned towards the door. Further into the room, the two humans had gone silent to listen to the interaction, but their eyes were locked on their table.

Before the lead guard could step around the table to restrain her, Luelle grabbed her tankard and flung the remaining contents in the woman's face.

The Colleile guard hissed in shock, reeling backwards. As the other two turned toward the noise, Luelle leapt onto the table and soared between them, shoving each one hard in the chest as she passed.

With shouts of surprise, they stumbled away from her, but she didn't turn to see if they pursued her.

One day, after the balance in their world was restored and her task was complete, she would find the time to return and repay Art for his kindness.

Luelle burst out of the inn into Tolhurst's streets and raced in the direction of the forest, scrabbling in her mind for the escape route she'd planned out. She was an idiot for staying here as long as she had.

Citizens cried out as she barged into them, sending several reeling away or falling to the cobblestones. Guards behind shouted frantic commands to one another, instructing anyone to apprehend her and to catch her alive.

Luelle didn't look back. Her feet slapped against the firm dirt beneath her. She flew through the air.

Tolhurst's citizens tripped over their own feet in their haste to escape her path and the flock of guards hot on her tail.

The treeline loomed just outside the village. Luelle was distracted, searching for the house that marked the route she'd memorised earlier, when the first guard tackled her.

She hit the ground with a grunt, teeth clashing together. Air whooshed from her lungs. Pain throbbed through her bruises.

Relying on instinct alone to guide her actions, she twisted beneath the guard, slamming the heel of her hand into his face. Bone cracked beneath her hand, punctuated by a cry of pain. The Power heated in Luelle's veins, burning her from the inside with no outlet. She scrambled away before the guard could cling to her any tighter, taking off in a sprint.

An arrow whizzed past her face. Shouts behind her grew louder. More guards closed in. She raced in zigzags, breath tearing her throat raw. Her cloak flapped behind her.

A second arrow sliced her arm.

Flinching away from it, Luelle hissed through her teeth but pushed through the pain and carried on running.

She was so close now. Two more houses and it was a free sprint down an alley into the Great Forest.

She made the turn, glancing over her shoulder to check the distance between her and the guards. They weren't letting up. She spun back around, ready to sprint with everything she had, but stumbled.

This wasn't the route she'd memorised.

A wall stood at the end of the alley, a head taller than her, blocking the route to the forest between the houses on either side.

Fear washed over her in a cold wave.

She ran towards the wall and leapt up, grabbing at the top layer of bricks. Her fingers scraped the edge but couldn't get enough purchase for her to haul herself over. She dropped to the ground as another two arrows hit the wall at her side, clattering to the cobblestones when they missed their mark.

Luelle fell into a crouch, covering her head and waiting for an arrow to sink into her. The Power swelled in her chest, tingling over her skin.

She was on fire. The pressure became unbearable.

Just as she could take no more of the searing heat within her, it burst from her chest, a wave of pure force in all directions.

The explosion was deafening. Debris pounded her torso as the wall and houses beside her collapsed.

When it stopped, Luelle lowered her arms, blinking through the haze over her eyes. Her ears rang. Dust filled the air, obscuring the entrance to the alley where the guards had been closing in on her. No one stood there now.

Exhaustion washed over Luelle, but she didn't wait for the dust to clear to see if the guards would emerge.

She hauled herself to her feet and clambered over remnants of the fallen wall, stumbling in the direction of the Great Forest. She didn't look back, even as she passed the treeline.

Mossy roots looped up from the ground to trip her. She

scrambled over them, slipping in the dirt as she lurched onwards.

She made it a few hundred metres into the Great Forest before she collapsed on the ground and fell deep into unconsciousness.

# 10

Malcolm swayed in his saddle. His bay stallion followed Theo's horse without any guidance. Leena's mare walked behind, flanked by Clarisse on a smaller mount, riding with her wrists still bound together. Malcolm had done his best to avoid looking at his father's old guard but she hadn't left Leena's keen sight for a moment.

Yesterday afternoon, they had met one of Leena's agents on the outskirts of the city. He'd been waiting with four horses, ready to exchange them for the empty carriage and maintain the secrecy of their departure. Leena hadn't taken the sack off Malcolm's head until the guard had left, reluctant to trust a single soul with the future king's whereabouts.

Malcolm, Theo, and Leena now wore a plain disguise—thick, hardened leather armour with thin, black scarves wrapped around their necks, ready to pull over their faces, concealing everything below their eyes, if another person approached. Clarisse, in contrast, wore plain civilian clothing.

Instead of his usual intricate gold armour to identify him as the crown prince, Malcolm wore a single token of his heritage to serve as identification for any guards that challenged their authority passing through cities and towns, a plain gold amulet that had belonged to his father, engraved with a simplistic arch to depict a rainbow—the symbol of Alaric's reign. Leena and Theo had similar tokens to refer to if any guards or soldiers hesitated to comply with their requests during their journey.

They had no intention of interacting with people unless it was necessary. If the thief was part of an organisation, there was no knowing how deep the threat to the crown was rooted, no telling which strangers conspired against him. For now, Malcolm remained wary of all other Veseile they might encounter.

When Leena had asked them yesterday, the guards at the Kendra Gate described a cloaked woman leaving the city late on the night of his father's death, so they'd spent all of the remaining daylight hours scouring the land surrounding the capital, searching for any trace of a trail Malcolm might be able to follow.

They found nothing.

Conversation had died with the daylight. Theo set up a small camp for them on a flat patch of land, and they'd taken to their beds early, Malcolm sharing a tent with Theo, leaving Leena and Clarisse in the second.

Malcolm lay awake for most of the night, pondering how he could save his legacy and torturing himself by imagining all of the ways he might fail. Morning arrived just as he managed to get some sleep. He was the last to emerge from the tents, bleary-eyed and squinting in the newly risen orange sun. If he didn't get more than a few hours of sleep soon, his body might give up on him altogether.

The four of them shared a quiet, simple breakfast from their supplies and concluded that, since it was their only lead, they would continue their search by travelling east. Malcolm ignored his rising hopelessness and remounted his horse.

What would he do if they couldn't find the trail? How long would he traipse the countryside before admitting his own uselessness and defeat? He couldn't search forever. Viv couldn't fool people that their father was alive again for long, not without proof.

The single benefit of their failing search was that it kept Malcolm away from that awful reality. Returning home would mean facing his father's death; out here, he could hold onto the false belief that the king was still alive and awaiting his return.

They trekked along the Eastern Road, walking their horses at a slow pace so there was no chance Malcolm would miss the tug of his Power. At times, he thought he could feel a weak pull in his chest, an echo of the feeling he'd had in the courtyard, but at other moments, he was convinced he was imagining it all.

A couple of hours into their journey, his despair became too strong to ignore. He fell in and out of alertness, relying on his trusted companions to protect him when melancholy took hold. He was fighting off a depressive cloud when the feeling from the courtyard hit him in a much stronger burst.

He jolted on his horse, almost falling from the saddle. Clutching at the reins, Malcolm stared in the direction of the pull. It shouted to him for a heartbeat before disappearing into the same quiet hum as before.

"What is it?" Theo asked. His hand dropped to his sword hilt.

Leena scanned the immediate vicinity for threats.

"That feeling," Malcolm breathed, "it just hit me again. We are heading in the right direction." He knew it in his gut. He felt more awake than he had in days.

"Let's pick up the pace," Theo said. "Continuing on this road will lead us to the Great Forest. A village lies on the outskirts where we can gather more information before choosing where to go from there."

Malcolm nodded. Kicking his horse into a gallop, he took the lead. His companions followed. Thundering hooves drowned out the opportunity for conversation. Wind tore at Malcolm's face, whipping the soft fabric of his scarf against his cheeks and bringing tears to his eyes. They only slowed twice to water and rest their horses.

The village came into sight in just under two hours.

Their mounts snorted as they passed the first few buildings, breathing hard to cool down after their final sprint. Malcolm tightened his scarf over his face but Leena and Theo kept theirs uncovered so they could speak to the first soldiers they found.

No guards were stationed at the village outskirts. A few citizens milled around the streets but none paid attention to the unusually-dressed visitors.

A hunched human woman with grey hair stumbled past them, carving a crooked path towards a wooden house. Her wide eyes were vacant. Blood dribbled down her temple and cheek from a small cut on her forehead. She clutched the loaf of bread in her arms as if it was a lifeline.

Malcolm exchanged frowns with Leena and Theo.

Nearing the side of the village closest to the Great Forest, the streets grew busier. The amalgamation of voices reached Malcolm's ears before he saw the source of the noise. Crowds gathered in clusters, eyeing a large group of guards who were tending to their injuries and those of several civilians. People stepped aside to let the newcomers through.

The clattering of their horses' hooves slowed. One of the nearest human guards stepped up to stop them from approaching, but Leena pulled out her amulet to signify she was representing the palace.

"What happened here?" She drew her horse to a stop and dismounted in a single, smooth motion.

The guard swallowed. Sweat plastered his hair to his forehead but it didn't hide the dried blood crusting at his temple.

He stepped closer and spoke with a lowered voice, eyeing the groups of civilians gathered close enough to hear. "We tried to apprehend the thief, ma'am. She was here, but escaped into the forest."

Malcolm and Theo dismounted. Clarisse mirrored their movement with some difficulty, having her hands stuck together. Theo handed his and Malcolm's reins to her to hold whilst they gained more information, but kept her in his line of sight.

The pull of the Power was stronger here, calling to Malcolm from the trees behind the houses. His breathing quickened at the thought of its return, of finally claiming his birthright.

Beyond the guards, a short row of buildings lay in ruins. Two had collapsed outwards, showering rubble into piles on the street. None of the crowds ventured close to the devastated homes.

Malcolm's mouth dried at the destruction. The thief must be in control of the Power already. Tolhurst's ruins were evidence of her unsavoury intentions against his people.

"How did she get away?" Leena asked.

The guard inhaled a shaky breath.

"We think she must have had a weapon concealed in her cloak." His voice was so low, Malcolm strained to hear the words. "She was fast so we tried to take her down with an arrow. Not to kill her, we got the orders to keep her alive, but once she was through those buildings, she triggered a—an explosion of some sort." The man stammered, shaking his head in disbelief. "I've never seen anything like it. We were thrown backwards and the buildings, well, you can see what happened. We didn't see where she went, so we've been prioritising helping the injured before pursuing her further. We're preparing to sweep the forest before dark."

"Any dead?"

"Not so far. A few minor civilian casualties, but most of the serious damage was dealt to the guards that were closest to her."

Leena nodded once. "You did the right thing. Did anyone else interact with her?"

"We found her in an inn a few streets over. The Horseshoe. She was talking to the bartender, the Veseile. He claimed to know her."

She dismissed the guard and walked back to where Malcolm and Theo waited.

"It must be her," Theo said.

"The pull is stronger here," Malcolm agreed. "She must still be close."

"We should speak to the Veseile barman before we leave." Leena's eyes were cold. "If he is working with the thief, we should take him to the castle and hold him in the dungeons. My people would be able to loosen his tongue to find out more about her plans and uncover any other threats to the crown."

"No." The objection slipped from Malcolm's lips before he could think it through.

Leena's full brows furrowed.

He itched to keep moving, but it would be stupid to leave a known threat at his back. If one of these criminals had already infiltrated the castle, he needed to find out all he could about potential others, particularly since he was no longer there to protect his family in their vulnerable time of grief.

"I mean, we must make it quick," he amended.

Leena led the way to The Horseshoe, leaving Clarisse under the watch of the guard she'd spoken to.

Inside, a surly-looking human stood behind the bar. Seated at a table nearby, a wide-eyed Veseile nursed a drink. Both were dressed in identical tan aprons. Low, long tables filled most of the room, empty benches and chairs scattered around their edges. Any patrons were long gone to spectate the commotion in the streets.

At the sight of their armour, the red-haired Veseile shrank

back into his seat. His eyes remained on the stained tabletop as the newcomers approached.

Malcolm stayed a step behind the others, praying no one would recognise the upper half of his face, exposed above the scarf. Woodsmoke from the fireplace in the right-most wall and the scent of hoppy, savoury ale infiltrated the fabric. His mouth watered.

Leena sat opposite the trembling Veseile. Theodas perched on the bench next to him, leaving the spot beside Leena for Malcolm.

The man tensed in his seat, his breath quickening.

"I didn't know her, alright? I was lying to the other guard." His eyes darted between them all. He clenched his trembling fingers tighter around his flask.

"What's your name?" Leena asked, resting her forearms on the table. Her dark eyes roamed the man's face, burning into his skin.

His throat bobbed. "Arthyr. Art. Am I in trouble?" A grey sheen tinted his cheeks. For a moment, Malcolm feared the Veseile was going to vomit over the table.

Leena shot Malcolm a glance but he shook his head, keeping the gesture small enough to avoid Art's attention. He had no patience for this interaction knowing the thief was so close. If this man was an extremist, Malcolm doubted he'd be so amenable to the guards or that he'd be trembling and sweating quite this much. They could return to question him properly once the thief was in chains.

"No, Art." Leena softened her voice. "We just want to catch

the criminal. The royal family sent us to reclaim what she stole and return her to the crown prince, unharmed. As someone who spoke to her, you could help us catch her before she hurts anyone else."

Art straightened in his seat. "You're—you're not going to hurt her?" He blinked.

"We only wish to take her back to the capital for questioning and to retrieve what she stole," Leena said.

Art nodded slowly, then once again with confidence. "I'll help however I can."

"Why did you lie to the guards about her?" Theodas asked.

Art pulled a face. "I didn't intend to. It just came out. I could feel this pull towards her, this chemistry. I—" He stumbled over his words, eyes on the table again. "I thought she must be my soul mate. No one's ever made me feel like that."

Malcolm resisted the urge to roll his eyes, tensing at yet more confirmation they were close to their thief. Fleeting confusion arose at the realisation that a stranger could sense the Power as he could, but it was a secondary concern. He tensed in his seat. It took every ounce of willpower not to sprint from the inn alone and pursue her.

"Did she show any other signs of violence before attacking the guards?" Theo asked.

Art shook his head, strands of fiery and pale white hair floating into his face. "No. She was a bit standoffish but she wasn't aggressive. She used the bath house and ate some food, then the guards came in and tried to grab her. She threw her drink at one of them and ran out. The rest of it happened in the streets so I didn't see it."

They concluded their brief interrogation, regrouping outside the inn and leaving Art to process the day's unusual events after they decided he was no threat, just a foolish onlooker that happened to be in the wrong place at the wrong time. Their decision didn't stop Leena from stationing several of the village's guards around the inn to monitor his movements.

Malcolm was done wasting time here.

"We need to continue." He turned to his friends. "We might be able to take her by surprise if we act fast, but we cannot afford to let her get much further. It will be easier for her to hide in the forest, but I can feel the pull stronger from here."

"And if we catch her now, we can be back well before the coronation." Theo squared his shoulders, staring at the treeline.

"Do you want to bring Clarisse with us into the forest?" Leena asked.

Malcolm shook his head. "Leave her here. The guards can lock her away until we have the thief and she is needed."

Leena nodded and stepped away to update Tolhurst's guards.

When she returned, they collected their horses and led them around the buildings, staying clear of the rubble. Malcolm couldn't look at the ruins for too long without his mouth drying. They remounted on the other side of the destruction.

"I will lead the way. Listen out for any noise. She may hide if she hears us approach," he said.

Pine and earth flooded Malcolm's senses as they ventured past the first few trees. Underneath the cover of the forest, the air was cooler, even through his armour. Dirt and moss muted their horses' hooves, a blanket of quiet permeated by the occasional snapping stick. Birdsong and scurrying animal footsteps drifted from the branches above.

And the pull drawing Malcolm to his Power grew stronger.

# II

Luelle's head throbbed with an agony unlike any she'd experienced.

Her thoughts swam as the world spun and twisted beneath her.

Something was pressed against her cheek, squishing the softer flesh up against her eye and cheekbone, distorting her mouth into a sneer. Saliva had dried and crusted on her chin. The smell of dirt and pollen overpowered each breath.

Groaning, she opened her eyes, wincing against the blinding beams of buttery sunlight filtering through the leaves far above her. She was laying in a small, circular glade.

Taking a deep breath, she gathered enough strength to sit up, picking off the twigs and bark indenting her face.

Memories from earlier in the day slithered back to her, each worse than the last.

The guards in the inn.

The chase through the village.

The wave of defensive force erupting from her moments before she should have been captured or killed.

Luelle turned her hands in front of her face, examining them for any trace of the Power. No markings marred her skin, besides her familiar callouses. Her skin no longer burned, her chest no longer ached with pressure. Could she do it again?

How many people had she hurt? None of the guards had pursued her here.

...Where was here?

Slowly, so slowly, Luelle looked around, desperate to avoid worsening the ache pounding in her temples.

She'd made it to the Great Forest.

Memories of entering the treeline danced beyond her reach, but she couldn't be far from Tolhurst, not when using the Power had drained her to the point of exhaustion.

Luelle allowed herself a few moments of recovery before untangling her limbs and pushing herself into a tentative standing position. She straightened her backpack over her cloak, wincing at the twinge in her shoulder. Everything ached. Draining herself of the Power must have reminded her body of its injuries.

She swayed where she stood, eyes closed to chase away her fleeting nausea and the urge to lie straight back on the ground.

Once her body decided to cooperate, she analysed the clearing.

Indents of squashed flowers and clover contrasted the surrounding tall greenery. Anyone that walked through the glade would see evidence of her passing through.

On the bright side, her trail of destruction pointed in the direction of Tolhurst, assuming she'd stumbled from the village in a straight line.

Miles of woodland made up the Great Forest, brought to an abrupt stop by the Ophidian Channel. Across that wide, winding river was Luelle's next destination, the Godswood. She'd passed through it years prior, on her initial journey to Cerulya, though this time she didn't have Freya and Imbryl to keep her company. They'd travelled on the forest paths, distracting each other with jokes and laughter and defending one another against the threat of bandits. Since Luelle was travelling alone now, she'd be safer sticking to the unmarked routes. The journey might take slightly longer but she was more likely to survive it.

Avoiding the thieves in the Godswood and the creatures inhabiting the Great Forest hadn't seemed such a chilling task in her friends' company. They'd passed through without any issues, but now, Luelle was an easier target, lacking the luxury of a companion to watch her back.

Arachnids, malevolent sprites, and wolves, were just some of the most problematic beasts she could encounter here. Light glinted on thick cobwebs stretching between the branches far above, a subtle reminder that the giant, malicious spiders were ever close. They were more cunning than the other threats she might come across. Sprites only attacked in defence and wild animals on instinct, if an easy meal appeared. Arachnids were calculated hunters, relishing the chase and the fear they inflicted.

They could already be watching her from the distant shadows, assessing her threat level and deciding whether there was enough of her to provide some rewarding entertainment.

She sighed and shrugged off her bag, rooting through it to find her flask. Taking a sip was almost enough to empty the container. Muttering a curse, Luelle shoved it back into her backpack. Toldhurst's guards had apprehended her before she'd thought to refill it and she was too disoriented to know where the nearest water source might be. She could ration what she had left until the end of the day, but finding water was a priority, second only to finding a clearing large enough that she could use the sun's position to align herself and locate the Ophidian Channel.

Before closing her bag, she slid out her dagger. It would do nothing against an entire swarm of arachnids but even a sword would be useless in that situation. Her best hope was to avoid them altogether and hope there was more interesting prey nearby. Worrying about them before they'd even shown themselves was a waste of energy.

Luelle strode away from her old footprints, leaving her tracks plain in the foliage. Covering them would take too long, especially if Tolhurst's guards were already tracking her through the forest.

Each step was stiff, though the movement eased the tension in her muscles. At the very least, the discomfort in her limbs offered a distraction from the ache in her head, which had settled into a dull throb behind her eyes.

Around her, the forest passed in a blur of green and brown. Without the threat of an enemy to hold her concentration, her ambling thoughts returned to the Power. It had acted out of her control in Tolhurst, on her behalf, as if it had a mind to defend its vessel from danger. But, it hadn't lashed out at her when she'd taken it from King Alaric or when she'd absorbed it from her fake glass sphere. Was that confirmation that the Power belonged to her people? Did it recognise her Veseile heritage?

She needed to improve her control over it. Though the Power had saved her by acting on her behalf, it had drained her in the process, leaving her more vulnerable than before. If the guards caught up to her soon, she wasn't sure she'd have the strength or ability to use it again, nor to fight them off.

Luelle ducked under a branch and trekked around a large oak, relying on instinct more than anything else to guide her in the direction she needed. After a few hours of walking, she found a clearing large enough to show the sun's position, dipping lower between the trees. She adjusted her path to travel east and set back off with more confidence.

As long as she continued east, the Ophidian Channel would cross her path at some point. It was named, in part, for the way it wound through the land like a serpent, but also for the water snakes inhabiting its rushing depths. Over those waters, she'd find the Godswood, and from there she could walk downstream until the Channel met the Caeleste River. Following that upstream would lead to the valleys between the mountains where her friends awaited her.

It would be a long trek, but if she stayed ahead of her pursuers, it should be uneventful.

Luelle dragged her thoughts back to the present, glancing at the branches above to make sure she was still walking alone. The Power thrumming in her chest connected her to the world in a way she'd never imagined it could, as if a vital part of her had been missing but was finally returned. How had she survived so long without it?

She would never let just one person hoard it again.

Veseile beliefs about the history of the Power varied, but Zeke had shown Luelle evidence to support his theories, smuggling in ancient documents from overseas and gathering personal writings from private collections. It was a God-given gift, bestowed to all Veseile by Vesanya, the God of Chaos, when she'd created the race.

After Zeke shared the truth with her as a child, Luelle spent every free moment inhaling stories about the Gods, dwelling on the little they knew and drawing her own tenuous conclusions from the available information. Myths described Gods that walked the world alongside their creations. Some portrayed the Gods as omnibenevolent beings who would bestow their people with blessings and favours but other, darker tales suggested tensions among the Gods, detailing epic battles for dominance that threatened to destroy the universe in the process.

Luelle chose to believe the former.

Many Eile and humans alike dismissed the stories as nothing more than myth, but Luelle believed the Gods had shared their realm in a literal sense. The Power was proof of their direct influence. She might never know why the Gods no longer had a physical presence in their world, but she knew deep in her heart that Vesanya would not want the Power to remain in the lineage of the human who had originally stolen it from the Veseile people.

Prince Malcolm, with his Veseile heritage, was more deserving of the Power than any of his ancestors. Ironic that he was who Luelle was taking it from. He would get it back before long, and perhaps when that imbalance was set to rights, the Gods would return.

A decade ago, Zeke, Luelle, and their other companions had been losing faith that they could restore the Power to the Veseile, coming to yet another dead end in their research and living in the wilderness near the Godswood, low on funds, scavenging for food every day, fighting among each other. Several of their companions abandoned the mission altogether.

However, Luelle knew the Gods still influenced events in the world when she stumbled across a long-abandoned pilgrimage site in their search for a new home. Together, she and Zeke explored the cave system in the Caeleste Peaks, finding a cavern deep and low in one of the mountains.

Within the cavern stood a tall statue of Vesanya, humming with energy that made the fine hairs on Luelle's arms stand on end. Beside the God was a stone archway, similar to the many sketches in their documents depicting a doorway between their world and the realm of the Gods. On the other side of the cavern stood a pedestal, hosting a sphere of cloudy crystal, similar to the royal crystal but much larger, just bigger than Luelle's head. Something about that cavern filled her with renewed hope.

She and her companions weren't extremists in their beliefs, like some Veseile. Before discovering the cave, Zeke had believed they must only kill the reigning monarch to set Vesanya's Power free, rather than all of the humans in the realm. However, their theories evolved when they stumbled across the cavern. One night, whilst they'd been sitting around the crystal, drunk on mead that Imbryl had brewed, Luelle wondered aloud if the orb in the cave had inspired the relic monarchs used to pass the Power to one another.

Zeke ran with her theory, suggesting the two orbs could be made from the same crystal, that the royal crystal's origin explained how the humans had been able to steal the Power in the first place. If the Power originated in this cavern, where Vesanya's presence was so strong, perhaps returning it would naturally restore it to the Veseile people. Killing the reigning monarch could remain as a last resort if this plan didn't work, but restoring the Power to its source was something they could test first, without such a high risk of losing their own lives in the process of an assassination scheme. So, they hatched their plan to steal King Alaric's Power when his human lifespan came to an end and bring it back to their home, its potential true source.

As Luelle travelled, musing over her mission and its potential consequences, birds trilled and chirped conversations in the trees. Their songs rode on the gentle wind that caressed her hair. Walking through each passing beam of sunlight, the temperature flicked from warm to cool. Glittering particles danced in Luelle's wake as she trudged on, glancing regularly at the sun through the trees to ensure she was still walking in the right direction.

Her thirst grew, drying up her mouth and throat. The Ophidian Channel was deep in the woods but it was only one of a thousand water sources in the Great Forest. If she kept walking straight, she should stumble across a stream or pond eventually. If her thirst became too unbearable, she would dig for groundwater and find a means of straining enough to fill her flask.

If she didn't find the Channel before sunset, she would need to continue travelling through the night. Sleeping this far in the Great Forest without at least one other person to watch for arachnids was a death sentence.

She walked all afternoon with no breaks and no real clue as to how far she'd travelled. Her pace grew ever-slower as thirst, hunger, and exhaustion mounted.

Sunlight mellowed from bright yellow to moody orange. As dusk approached, the feeling of eyes on her back made Luelle's skin crawl.

She continued walking, her stare fixed on the path ahead, but the feeling lingered. Her fingers tightened around the handle of her dagger.

The lack of crashing undergrowth suggested it wasn't the guards from Tolhurst but something more sinister. Arachnids or sprites would be curious enough to pursue her. Most other things in the Great Forest would flee or hide at her scent and the noise she made traipsing through the undergrowth. Unless they were starving, of course.

Luelle emerged in another glade, a perfect circle of tall oak trees. Evergreen vines hung in loops from their branches, decorated with delicate, violet flowers. Light bounced off the silver cobwebs swaying between them.

She paused, feigning interest in the blossoms but listening for movement.

Someone was following her.

# 12

As they ventured further into the Great Forest, the trees huddled closer together, like Cerulya's guards gathering under the courtyard's torches in the winter. Malcolm and his friends ducked and weaved in their saddles to avoid colliding with the lowest branches. After several miles of dodging, they dismounted and led their horses. No one voiced the added bonus of continuing on foot—to put some much-desired distance between them and the shimmering cobwebs looming overhead. Malcolm clutched his reins and followed the pull in his chest, Leena and Theo walking their own horses close behind.

The further they travelled, the stronger the tug of his stolen Power became.

The thief wasn't far from him now. It was all he could concentrate on.

When the buzzing pressure in his chest began to feel as strong as it had when he'd been a room or two away from his father in the castle, Malcolm drew his sword, gripping it in an aching fist.

After what felt like years of travelling, he froze.

Far ahead, a lone figure stood in a clearing, visible through the slender gaps between the trees. Malcolm edged his horse sideways and looped his lead rope on a low branch, motioning for his friends to do likewise. They left their mounts to graze the surrounding plants and approached a closer space that offered a clear view of the cloaked stranger.

It was her—the woman from the courtyard.

Leena and Theodas crept to Malcolm's sides.

In the clearing, the thief was examining a flower growing from a low-hanging vine.

Her back was to Malcolm but their vantage point was close enough that he could see stray hairs escaping from her braid and loose threads ferreting from the seams of her backpack. Her cloak was cleaner than it had looked in the shadows of the courtyard at home, but the pull of his father's stolen Power was just as magnetic as it had been then.

This close, it was like a fork of lightning between them.

"Definitely her?" Leena's voice was no more than a breath.

Malcolm nodded once. "I will try talking to her before we do anything else."

Theo eyed his king-to-be but nodded. "We will circle to the sides, in case she tries to run."

They crept away from him, leaving Malcolm alone to assess the criminal. He pulled his scarf over his face, binding it tighter so it wouldn't slip down.

The stranger didn't look like a thief, sniffing at the purple blossom resting on her fingertips, but from the little information Philip had been able to provide, this woman had been planning her treason for a while, plotting against her king even as she tended him through his illness.

Imagining the ways she must have taken advantage of his father in his weakened, vulnerable state set a fire of hatred blazing in Malcolm's gut. He ground his teeth and stepped forward, fighting to control the emotions screaming at him to take back what was his.

A twig snapped under his foot.

The stranger whipped towards him as he emerged into the clearing.

With his scarf covering all but his eyes, the thief must not realise who she was glaring at, but he got a good look at her.

She was short for a Veseile, though still taller than most human women. Cold, calculating eyes roamed over his armour, lips set into a harsh line. Some people, like the gullible barman in Tolhurst, might consider her pretty, if that stoney face ever melted into a smile, but all Malcolm could see was a monster.

"Who are you? What do you want?" Her stare darted around Malcolm. She glanced above and beyond him but found no companions.

He was close enough to see her pulse thrumming in her neck.

Rage burned inside him. It stained his vision with a red hue and choked the words in his throat. His fingers tightened on the hilt of his sword as he considered slashing it across her neck right there. No matter how strong that desire was, he couldn't let things go that far. He didn't know how to retrieve the Power if it wasn't willingly given, as it had been every time it was passed from monarch to child by his ancestors.

And the destruction in Tolhurst lingered in his recent memory. If the thief turned the Power on him and his friends, they'd be dead in an instant. He'd promised Viv he would return, that he wouldn't do anything stupid.

The thief's eyes dropped to his weapon, reading the thoughts plain in his stance. The dagger she clutched would be useless against his sword. Her hand shifted on its handle nonetheless, knuckles whitening at the strength of her grip.

"I have no money," she said, eyes dancing between Malcolm's murderous gaze and his sword. "I'm just passing through. I'm not looking for any trouble."

A laugh burst from his throat, startling the thief where she stood.

"That's rich," he sneered. "Scared of someone stealing from you, is that it? How ironic." Malcolm's voice was alien to himself; he'd never sounded so cold.

Her eyes roved his outfit once more but the rest of her stayed frozen, as if moving risked breaking whatever restraint was holding Malcolm back. "The prince sent you?" she asked.

Without his regular decorative armour, embellished with gold and black onyx, there was nothing to identify Malcolm's status. His father's amulet was tucked away, cool against his chest.

He didn't bother answering the question.

"You can either surrender and come with me peacefully or I will force you to return to the capital."

The thief's lips curled into a mocking smile.

"How about a third option? I'll continue on my way and let you crawl back to the capital unharmed. You can tell whoever sent you that I beat you in combat and you won't actually have to suffer the embarrassment of the defeat."

Malcolm's blood boiled.

Leaves at the edges of the clearing rustled. Leena and Theodas emerged from their hiding places on either side of the thief, their scarves concealing the lower halves of their faces, like Malcolm's.

A muscle jumped in the thief's jaw as her gaze moved between the three of them, assessing her dwindling odds of fighting her way free. She swallowed.

"I think I shall stick with the first two options." Malcolm didn't take his eyes off her.

"Stay back. I don't want to hurt anyone." Her voice trembled.

"If only we could say the same." Theo stepped closer to the thief.

Malcolm held a hand up, halting him.

"We will not hurt you if you come quietly. Willingly."

The thief chewed on her bottom lip, glancing around to find an escape route that didn't exist.

"What happens if I return with you?" she asked. "Is the prince going to execute me?"

Malcolm shrugged. Right now, his fury was enough that he might.

"You must return what is rightfully his. Your fate will be decided at the castle."

The thief sneered. "You're blind to the true history of the realm—of the monarchy," she spat. "The Power was God-given to all Veseile. It belongs to me just as much as it does the prince."

Malcolm gritted his teeth, biting down on the retorts that came to mind. There was no point continuing to argue with a crazy person. She was a fanatic, an extremist who believed violence would solve all of the realm's issues. She knew nothing of the work his ancestors had done to maintain peace and prosperity for their people, too focused on a false history based on no evidence.

"I will only ask you one more time. Are you going to return with us peacefully?"

The woman's eyes wandered above Malcolm's head. The corners of her lips twitched.

"No, I don't think I will."

Leena ripped her glare from the thief long enough to follow her line of sight. Her own dark eyes widened. Before Malcolm could blink, Leena's sword moved to her left hand and her right yanked a dagger from her belt. She threw it in his direction, a blur of steel.

Malcolm ducked his head as a screech exploded above him.

He leapt sideways and looked back in time to see the hairy, writhing legs of an arachnid. Blood seeped from the enormous body that hit the ground where he was standing only moments ago. Thick silver cobwebs pooled on the beast, tangling in its kicking limbs. Its many beady eyes rolled and its fangs clicked together, snapping at Malcolm as he stumbled away.

Terror washed over him. He'd been seconds away from

becoming a meal for that creature. Forcing down his fear, he whipped his head back to where the thief had been standing.

She'd disappeared.

He'd looked away for only a moment, but she'd fled into the undergrowth, leaving rustling leaves in her wake.

Theodas and Leena rushed to Malcolm's side.

"There are more of them," Theo barked, head tilted up and grip tight on his sword's hilt. He fell into a fighting stance, rotating to analyse his enemies.

Above them, the branches were alive with wriggling bodies. Arachnids descended on glistening webs into the clearing, blocking the path that the thief took and spreading out to force their prey into narrower spaces.

"I must go after her. Keep the horses safe and follow me when you can," Malcolm ordered.

Leena and Theo grunted their acceptance.

Leena flung a second throwing dagger into the heart of one of the giant spiders and wrenched her other small blade from the first writhing arachnid she'd hit, ending its life with a flash of her sword.

Malcolm lurched forward, his own sword in hand. He sliced and jabbed at the screeching arachnid blocking his path. It danced around him as he swung, but his second attempt drew blood. His third severed a leg.

The beast retreated enough that he could dart past.

Away from the chaos of the clearing, he sheathed his sword, unwilling to fall on it as he chased the thief. The sound of battle remained behind him, screeching arachnids, shouts from his friends, the whistling, thudding, and squelching sounds of weapons racing through the air and hitting their targets.

Instinct screamed at him to turn back, to help his friends through the fight, but if he stayed with them, he would lose this opportunity to catch the thief. Leena and Theo were two of the best fighters he knew. They could handle themselves.

With a stab of guilt, Malcolm raced deeper into the darkening woods, doing his best to dodge oncoming trees as the pull in his chest dictated the movements of his feet. His breath tore in and out of his throat as he sprinted through the forest.

He didn't once glance up, unwilling to let his fear of the monsters slow him. Adrenaline fuelled his pace. He leapt over boulders in his path and flung himself under a felled tree, skidding through the dirt.

In the distance, the shadowy form of the thief appeared. She was running hard but limping, faltering.

Fresh rage flooded Malcolm.

He poured every ounce of energy he had into the chase, shrinking the gap between them.

When he was close enough, he leapt at the thief, tackling her. His arms became a vice around her waist.

The thief lost her footing under Malcolm's sudden weight, sending them both tumbling to the ground and down a hidden hill, bereft of trees. They rolled over one another's bodies, tumbling over rocks, fruit bushes, and fallen branches.

A stray, thorny stick snagged Malcolm's scarf as he fell, tugging it free from his face, but he didn't loosen his grip on the thief.

They slowed at the bottom of the hill. He regained his wits before she did.

He straddled the thief, shoving her face into the ground and gripping her arms together behind her back, holding her wrists awkwardly below her backpack. Glancing desperately around, Malcolm searched for something to bind her hands with but could only see wood, stones, and dirt. Not even his scarf was in sight any longer. Her dagger had fallen from her grip during their descent, landing several feet from them, too far for her to use against him.

"Stop, you're hurting me," the thief gasped out.

Malcolm eased up his grip, an automatic response, his fury dissipating at the pain in her voice.

He realised her deceit too late.

The woman shifted her weight, snatching a hand away and jerking her hips back to twist beneath him. She flung dirt in his face. He lost his balance in his attempt to shield his eyes. She shoved him away, evading his scrambling hands. Stumbling to her feet, she continued through the forest, abandoning her weapon in her haste to escape him.

Malcolm cursed and sped after her.

They both ran slower after their fall down the hill. Pain shot up one of Malcolm's ankles each time his foot touched the ground but he ignored it. His body would be a tapestry of bruises tomorrow.

He reached out as he ran, managing to snag his fingers in the thief's hood. She jerked away, out of his grasp.

The second time, he got a better grip, wrapping his fingers

around her braid and yanking it hard, pulling her back.

She cried out, nails clawing vicious red lines on his fist, teeth exposed in a silent snarl.

"Get off me," she spat at him, twisting in his grip as he tried to capture her hands once again.

The thief outmanoeuvred him and slammed the heel of her hand into Malcolm's nose.

Pain erupted across his face, jolting his head backwards.

He stumbled away, losing his grip on her once again.

Tears welled in Malcolm's eyes, obscuring his vision. He blinked hard, sending them streaming down his cheeks as he gave chase again. Foul curses cascaded from his lips. Blood dripped from his nose into his mouth. He smeared it away with his forearm, sending another wave of blinding white pain across his vision.

Over his panting breath, the sound of rushing water whispered.

Malcolm upped his speed.

If they'd already reached the Ophidian Channel, they were much further east than he'd anticipated. He prayed to the Gods he could catch the thief before she made it to the water. If he pursued her across it, it would be near impossible for Theodas and Leena to track him. There were no permanent bridges across the water to prevent the arachnid from spreading into Meteile territories, so his friends would lose his trail almost instantly.

Over the next hill, the wide river came into view, a churning mass of white between the trees. It was only a few hundred metres away.

Malcolm's limbs screamed as he pushed himself to his limit.

The thief had pulled away from him again but she couldn't run forever. With the pull in his chest to link them, he'd never stop chasing her.

He closed the gap, gritting his teeth against the pain in his body and face.

They neared the river.

The thief leapt forwards, diving into the roaring current.

Malcolm followed, arms outstretched.

His hand found her ankle and didn't let go.

The current flung them like ragdolls. Malcolm fought to keep his head above the water as hard as he fought to retain his grip on the thief.

His leather armour, soaked with the freezing water, threatened to pull him to an icy death. The pain in his nose and limbs was forgotten in this new battle.

Malcolm lost track of direction and time in the depths, able only to concentrate on keeping his grip and on taking a gasping breath when the rare opportunity arose. At times, he plunged below the surface for long enough that his lungs burned.

The thief kicked her legs to evade him but his hand was a shackle on her ankle.

Just as his fingers began to numb, the river calmed from rapids to a gentler current. It curved, sweeping the two of them to a muddy bank on the opposite shore.

Malcolm released the thief's ankle as they washed ashore. He waded out of the shallows and collapsed onto the dirt near her, retching and spluttering dirty water between his hands. Shivers wracked his body.

"You idiot," the thief snapped at him between hacking coughs, as she cleared her own lungs of the freezing water. "Why did you hold me like that? We could've both drowned."

She glared at him, but as Malcolm raised his head to meet her gaze, she faltered.

Without his scarf, his identity was bare. If she'd worked in the castle for as long as Philip suggested, there was no way she didn't know who he was, even if his nose was still dripping blood, his teeth were chattering, and his wet hair was plastered to his face. He shook his hair out of his eyes, flicking an arc of water to one side. The movement sent a fresh wave of agony through his face. Tears pricked his eyes. He hissed at the pain.

The thief confirmed his suspicions as she knelt, frozen, a few paces away. Her eyes were wide, the white around her muddy irises stark in the gloomy evening.

"What are you doing here?" she whispered. Her eyes flicked to his nose; she winced at the damage she'd caused.

"You stole my Power," Malcolm retorted. He shifted his weight to sit cross-legged and fingered his nose with a feather-light touch.

"It doesn't look broken," she offered, once she'd recovered from her state of shock. Shivers wracked her body. "You won't need to reset it."

He hoped his glare was as withering as he intended. "No thanks to you."

She set her jaw in response, scowling at the ground. Their clothes dripped icy water onto the dirt, a regular beat against the backdrop of the river.

"We need to make a fire, or we're going to freeze." The thief pushed herself to standing and limped around the clearing, gathering the driest wood she could find and clutching it in her trembling hands.

"Oh, you no longer wish to fight me?" Malcolm's tone was acid. The overwhelming anger he felt towards this woman increased each time he looked at her.

She ignored him and continued collecting branches. Once she'd gathered an armful, she chose a spot a few feet away from him, dug a shallow pit, and stacked some of the smaller sticks inside. She moved to the nearest tree and dug her short fingernails into its trunk, peeling off several thin strips of bark for kindling.

"Give me your knife." She unhooked her bag, which had somehow stayed closed in the river, and dug through its contents. She pulled out a wet pile of fabric and slapped it on the ground beside her firepit. Unhooking her cloak, she peeled off the layer and added to the pile before she started laying the bundle of fabric out more neatly, separating an entire outfit from a large sheet.

"No." Malcolm stared at her. Did she really expect him to hand her a weapon after she'd stolen his Power and punched him in the face?

"Okay." She crouched back to her bag and threw something at him.

Malcolm caught the flint.

"You start the fire."

He held his glare for a heartbeat longer, but couldn't suppress his shivers for long. Cold seeped into his bones, threatening to make a permanent home of his body.

He knelt by the small fire pit and struck his knife with the flint. Why didn't she just use the Power for this? Did she believe it was only a weapon? Perhaps she was eager to embarrass him. Heat flared in his cheeks long before it appeared in the wood. He repeated the motion until his arm ached. He was on the verge of giving up when a spark caught.

The thief cupped her hands and leaned close, breathing life into the flames. She made no comment about how long it had taken him to complete such a simple task.

Huddled on opposite sides of the pitiful fire, they remained as far from each other as they could get without leaving the shred of warmth before them. The thief's fingers drummed on the next branch as she waited for the flame to grow strong enough for more fuel.

Malcolm's shivers eventually slowed as the fire grew larger.

"Is Belle your real name?" He broke the silence when his teeth were no longer clattering together.

She ignored him, setting his temper rearing again.

"I am not going anywhere, so you may as well tell me. I can feel the Power you stole from my father on his deathbed," Malcolm spat the words. "That is how I found you. We are connected, you and I. You cannot escape me. So, you can either confirm your real name and make our time together slightly easier or continue being stubborn until I have recovered enough to take you back to my home. I am sure the torturers will relish getting the information from you." His heart pounded in his chest. Knowing she could strike him down with his own Power at any point made his voice tremble, but he couldn't stop the threats from pouring out. Hopefully, the thief would think his shaking was a reaction to the cold, rather than from fear.

Her nostrils flared at his words but she spoke up.

"My name is Luelle."

Malcolm huffed a breath through his mouth, since his nose was too swollen, and nodded. "Right. Good." Perhaps she was still lying but he had no way of truly knowing and had no desire to argue with her whilst his nose was still throbbing.

The sky had darkened during their chase but clouds covered the rising moon, disguising the time.

Malcolm's tremors came to a stop, replaced with a kernel of warmth.

He didn't initiate conversation again, concentrating instead on planning how to get Luelle back to the castle and reclaim his Power.

# 13

Thirst was no longer a problem for Luelle since she'd swallowed half of the Ophidian Channel trying to escape from the prince.

She stole glances at him through the flames, but didn't need to worry about subtlety, he didn't once look at her. He stared into the fire as if she wasn't even there.

Luelle had known he'd be angry but hadn't expected such pure, violent hatred.

She hadn't expected to see him again at all. In the castle, she'd only ever glimpsed the prince from a distance. Like most of the nobles, he was oblivious to the hundreds of servants bustling around, and wouldn't have spoken to her even if he had seen her. Their stations were miles apart, any communication on a personal level would have been inappropriate and would've risked her job, destroying everything she'd worked for. Besides, Alaric had always been her sole focus. In her attempts to stay near him, most of her duties kept her away from the other royals.

Details she'd never noticed before caught her eye now the

prince was so close. Faint lines crinkled the outer corners of his hazel eyes. Sparse freckles dusted his brown skin. A small, pale scar marred the skin above his left eyebrow. His curved, crooked nose was swelling from her hit, but his cheekbones and jawline were just as defined up close as they had been from a distance.

Other castle servants in Cerulya had wasted hours mooning over the crown prince, working their fingers to the bone for the honour of attending him. One woman had been the talk of their quarters after claiming she'd been lucky enough to turn down his bedsheets, bringing back a stolen silk pillowcase to sleep beside.

Despite paying Prince Malcolm little attention during her years in the castle, Luelle could see why people were so infatuated.

He met her gaze through the flames. She looked away too late.

"What?" he asked, the word short and curt. He didn't sound very regal, with his blocked nose and foul attitude.

Luelle shook her head, unsure what she could say that wouldn't make the situation worse. She certainly wasn't going to admit taking the opportunity to admire his regal features.

Her earlier headache had retreated but her body ached from their fighting. Shallow cuts and scrapes decorated the space between her old bruises, which were throbbing from the fresh beating they'd taken.

This wasn't how her plan was meant to go. No one was meant to have caught up with her. Prince Malcolm should be nestled with his family in the castle, grieving his father, not tackling her down hills in the Great Forest.

She hadn't anticipated such a strong connection to the prince but it made sense. Alaric's presence had been magnetic in a way no one else's had, thanks to the Power. It hadn't occurred to her that others would know how to isolate and follow that feeling.

Shedding the prince without killing him would be tough but Luelle would have to find a way. His two companions would track him if they escaped the arachnids, and there were bound to be others following close behind them.

Lighting the fire was a risk, as much as they'd needed the warmth. Any smoke that rose over the trees would be a beacon to their location, but she hoped that the darkening skies would obscure it. Letting more soldiers catch up with her would ruin her plans and potentially lead to an early grave, so Luelle would keep moving. Outrunning her pursuers wouldn't be hard; none of them knew where she was going, and the prince had no way to get word back to them from here, even if she couldn't shed him. He could threaten to follow her all the way to the Caeleste Peaks, but the Power in her chest gave her an advantage over him. Whilst it remained within her, their fight was uneven. He couldn't drag her back to the capital by himself, and he couldn't stop her from returning the Power to its source. The fact he was here at all suggested he couldn't simply kill her to get it back.

But, would she be able to use her Power against the prince if the need arose? She hadn't controlled it in Tolhurst. A defensive blast like that might kill him, which was the last thing she needed. Her entire mission was designed to avoid his death, to restore her people's rightful Power without causing more loss and chaos.

She pushed the dilemma to the back of her mind for now. She could worry about her inability to control the Power if that time came. She was resourceful, she didn't need it to escape her enemies.

Her stomach growled.

When she could feel her fingers again, she removed her empty flask from her bag.

"Do you have one?" She raised it in the direction of the prince, who, since catching her staring, watched her every move like a hawk.

He shook his head. "My supplies are with my horse." Worry flashed across his face. He looked out over the river to the Great Forest, looming on the far bank. He must have fought through the spiders to continue chasing her as quickly as he had.

"The arachnids won't follow us here. They don't cross the Channel." Luelle tried to reassure him when that worry didn't fade from his expression.

"I am not concerned about myself," the prince snapped, sneering at her with disgust.

Luelle swallowed her growing annoyance and shuffled to the water, wincing at the pain in her leg. "Your guards," she guessed. "They'll be fine if they fled. Your horse is probably dead though." She knelt at the river's edge to refill her flask.

"That makes me feel much better, thank you."

She ignored his sardonic tone and swigged several mouthfuls of the cold water. She held the flask out, offering it to the prince.

After a second of stubborn hesitation, he shuffled forwards

and took it, finishing off the water inside.

"We'll have to stick to the rivers since you don't have a flask or any other supplies. It'll take a bit longer than going cross-country, but it will still lead us to the valleys within the Caeleste Peaks. I can find the way from there, anyway."

The prince lowered the flask, staring at her in disbelief.

"We are not going to the Caeleste Peaks," he said. "We are returning to Cerulya. My coronation is in five days."

She snatched her flask from him to refill it again before returning to the fire's warmth and tucking it into her backpack.

"I'm going to the Caeleste Peaks." She met the prince's eyes. "You can come with me, like you claimed you would, or you can retreat to your city alone."

His lips tightened into a scowl.

They relapsed into tense silence until Luelle's stomach growled with more urgency. She'd give anything for another bowl of stew from the inn she'd fled that morning. Had the guards gone back to interrogate Art after she'd escaped them?

"We need to find some food." She broke the silence again, knowing the prince was already watching her.

"I am not letting you out of my sight."

"I'm not trying to get away from you!" she snapped, exasperated. He might be heir to the throne, but he was also a blockhead. "We need to eat. I'll see what I can gather from here. I don't want to go far, anyway, and it's too dark to make anything to fish with. We can look for craybugs in the shallows tomorrow."

Prince Malcolm's scowl deepened, but he didn't attempt to stop Luelle as she moved around their small patch of the

Godswood, plucking berries and nuts where she could find them, digging for soft roots, and gathering seed pods. She avoided anything she didn't recognise. This journey would be unpleasant enough without giving herself food poisoning.

She routinely deposited handfuls of the food beside the fire until they had a small mound of snacks. Luelle tossed a blackberry into her mouth and gestured to the pile.

"Help yourself, Prince."

He glared at her.

"I know it isn't the level of catering you're accustomed to but it's going to have to be enough for tonight." Luelle rooted through the pile until she found a sweet nut and crunched it loudly.

The prince picked at the food initially but was soon shovelling berries into his mouth faster than Luelle, ignoring her smirks. Even sitting cross-legged on the ground, lips stained red with juice from berries, his posture revealed his upbringing. Luelle slouched over her knees, whilst his spine was straight and tall, wide shoulders pushed back, a stance that must have been drilled into him from a very young age.

By the time both had eaten their fill, only a few small nuts and roots remained, attracting ants and beetles. Making no attempt to hide his disapproval as Luelle wiped her fingers clean on her trousers, the prince stood and rinsed his own in the river.

Luelle added another stout branch to the fire, ignoring the prince as they walked around one another, moving back to their positions on either side of the fire. Wood cracked and snapped, devoured by the flames, shooting up the occasional sparks.

"Why did you steal it?"

She looked up to find the prince's gaze still on her, heavy and intense. Shifting where she sat, Luelle returned her own stare to the fire.

"The history you've been told is false. The Power belongs to all Veseile, not just one monarch. Especially not a human monarch."

"It has been in my family for generations. Pick up a book. Any historical text shows it being passed down from ruling monarch to eldest child. The tradition goes back millennia," Prince Malcolm retorted. "Whatever claim you think you have, it is false."

Luelle hugged her knees closer to her chest. Knowing she was right didn't make the confrontation any easier.

"The Power is a gift bestowed on the original Veseile bloodlines by Vesanya. There were even schools dedicated to teaching people how to wield it, once, not that the human monarchs allowed any of that instruction to survive for common folk."

He scoffed. "Nonsense. You are ignoring the evidence in front of your own face. Documentation would exist if that was true. If it belonged to the Veseile, if it was so ingrained in society, how did humans get it? Why did the Veseile not simply revolt and take it back?"

"One of your ancestors, Queen Arabella, a human, decided she no longer wanted to be at a disadvantage to the Eile races. She used your crystal to steal the Power from its source in the Caeleste Peaks, ripping it from the world so that only she could wield it. Of course the Veseile wouldn't be in a state to fight back immediately after such a core part of them was torn away. Zeke, the person who revealed the Veseile's true history to me, has theorised that the Gods might even be able to return to our realm, to live among us as they once did, when we return the Power to its true source and restore balance to the world."

The Prince stared at Luelle as if flowers were sprouting from her ears.

Laughter burst from his lips but there was no amusement in the sound. Heat rose in her cheeks at his disdainful expression.

"None of that is true." He shook his head. "Even if it were true, that does not actually explain how Arabella supposedly stole the Power. There would be written evidence of such a feat. Besides, it is a myth that the Gods physically walked among us. I have studied the history of our realm extensively with the best tutors available, and the Power has always belonged to the human monarchs. They are the ones who Vesanya blessed. They are the true source. You have been lied to. Whoever Zeke is, he has fed you a false narrative."

"Arabella censored the truth. She burnt thousands of documents, destroyed the evidence and details of her crime, and closed off the kingdom to outsiders so no one suspected the lies she spread," Luelle insisted. "I'll show you proof when we reach the Caeleste Peaks if that's what you want. We have sources that have been smuggled over generations, some from beyond the kingdom's borders, too."

"Your proof is false. Do you think I know nothing about people like you? Pureblood Veseile who wish to incite a war between yourselves and the humans." He glared at her. "I was warned about terrorists like you from the time I was a child. None of your stories align because there is no truth to them, you all believe different things. The only thing you share is a desire for violence and genocide."

Luelle's cheeks burned hotter. "I have no interest in hurting anyone, let alone an entire race of people. I only want to return the Power to the people it belongs to."

Prince Malcolm set his jaw. "The Power belongs to my family. You committed treason by stealing it."

"If that's true, why does it respond to me?" she challenged him. He flinched at her words, prompting her to continue. "Only those who descend from the original Veseile bloodlines can harness the Power."

"Then how do you explain the thousands of humans who have used it throughout history?"

"They stole it!" she repeated, frustration growing in her tone. "If it was never stolen from its source, they never would have been able to use it."

"It is a sign of my family's divine right to rule," the prince said, through gritted teeth. "My ability to wield it is proof that the throne belongs to me."

"Oh!" Luelle exclaimed, smiling at how her sudden reaction made his face darken. "I guess I *should* return to Cerulya then. Since I can wield the Power, I need to claim my crown."

Malcolm changed the subject rather than responding to her taunt.

"Who else was working with you at the castle? I do not know

a Zeke."

"No one."

"Do not lie to me."

"I'm not lying," Luelle insisted. "I came to the capital alone. My companions are waiting for me in the Caeleste Peaks, at an ancient pilgrimage site. It's where the source of Vesanya's Power is located."

The prince eyed her, unconvinced.

"I swear it to you." She met his gaze. "I was alone in the castle. I had no accomplices. It was just me, so if you're hurting anyone there for information, you're doing so in vain."

"You are the only one here who has hurt anyone," he snapped.

A tense silence fell between them. Luelle shuffled away from the firepit, overheating all of a sudden.

"You should get some sleep," she said, after another few minutes of uncomfortable quiet. "I can keep the first watch. If you're serious about following me, you've got a couple of weeks of hard travelling ahead and you already look exhausted." She wasn't lying. The shadows underneath the prince's eyes weren't just bruising from his injured nose.

"I am not an idiot." He sneered at her. "As soon as I fall asleep, you will flee again and I will have to chase after you."

"I give you my word that I won't. You can accompany me to the Peaks. It'll be safer travelling as a pair."

"Oh, brilliant. A criminal gives me her word." His cruel, jeering smile resurfaced. "You have stolen my Power, most likely broken my nose, and now I am to trust your word?"

Luelle shrugged. "Suit yourself. Wake me if you hear anything."

She lay down and turned on her side, facing away from the prince. Stones and twigs poked into her torso but she was reluctant to shuffle around whilst she could still feel his eyes on her. His cold glare on her back offset the warmth of the fire and the embarrassment still burning in her face.

She stared into the shadows flickering and pulsating between the trees in front of her.

How had this journey become such a mess? Allowing the prince to follow her to the Peaks could be detrimental to her mission, not to mention to the peace of the small home Zeke had built there.

She might need to deter the prince from following before she arrived at the cavern, to find a way to send him back to the capital alone, but would he even survive that journey? He couldn't have much experience travelling without servants and guards to provide him with food and protect him from harm.

Anxiety churned in Luelle's chest as she lay staring into the distant forest.

Sleep took its time claiming her.

# 14

Though he tried to fight it, Malcolm drifted into a fitful sleep at some point through the night.

Birdsong floated into his dreams, tempting him back to consciousness after a few hours. A delicious smell captured his attention. Saliva pooled in his mouth. His stomach voiced its interest, gurgling audibly.

He shifted where he dozed. How was the scent of the kitchens reaching his chambers when they were separated by so many floors? And why was his bed so uncomfortable this morning?

Memories of yesterday flooded back to him, reminding Malcolm why his mattress was so firm and why his face ached with dull pain.

He jerked awake, hauling himself upright. His heart raced.

Luelle shot him an alarmed look from beside a small, fresh fire.

"You are still here," Malcolm breathed. She wore the same

clothes as yesterday, hair messy from sleeping on the ground but clinging to the same braided pattern.

"Your eyesight is very good, Your Highness."

Malcolm glared at Luelle but bit his tongue. He wouldn't continue to stoop to her level. He was better than that. Back home, people engaged in proper debate if they disagreed with him, respecting his points and his voice, supporting their own beliefs with facts. Last night's childlike bickering was not something he wanted to repeat any time soon.

Reaching over his shoulder, he began kneading some of the knots and pains in his upper back. If sleeping on the ground was to be a common feature of their journey, he already wished it was over. The sooner Leena and Theo caught up with them, the better.

Perhaps he could convince Luelle to travel outside of the Godswood and stay in a nice inn on the Eastern Road. She'd already risked going to one in Tolhurst, so couldn't be that averse to them. Despite losing the majority of his things, he had a few coins in an inner pocket, and could always reimburse the innkeeper. His amulet was proof of his identity.

He would insist on it for their journey back to the capital. Even if he was forced to follow Luelle to this supposed source of the Power before his friends caught up with him, the thief would realise she'd been lied to and would have no choice but to return his Power and face the punishment for her crimes. He couldn't risk restraining her by himself, not while she could use his Power against him, but perhaps he could convince her to trust him and return it willingly.

The thought of trying to befriend her turned his stomach.

Theo and Leena would have escaped the arachnids and be following them by now. They would know to bring reinforcements from Tolhurst, there had easily been enough guards there to form a party. Even if he failed to recover his Power alone, Luelle would have to comply once reinforcements reached him. He knew not to underestimate her manipulations now.

He stole glances at her as he rubbed small circles into his neck and shoulders.

Somehow, she'd caught four craybugs from the river while he slept and speared them on a thin stick. Humming a tune he'd heard from other servants at home, she rotated the craybugs over a small, fresh fire, working as if he didn't exist.

She seemed happy to let the morning pass without conversation, but he was so used to the constant company of his friends, family, and advisers, even servants, at the palace that the lapse of chatter soon became unbearable.

A conversation would also distract him from the ache in his cheekbones. How could a nose injury cause pain in his entire face?

"How long have you been awake?" Malcolm tried to initiate an amicable discussion.

The thief glanced at him. "An hour or so." She shrugged. "Next time, wake me up when you're too tired to stay on watch. If we were still in the Great Forest, your snoozing would've gotten us killed. The Godswood is only slightly safer."

"It was not intentional." Malcolm scowled at the berating. He wasn't a child.

Luelle shot him a sweet smile. "Well, don't let it happen again."

"You cannot speak to me like that. I am still your king." His temper flared. He snatched Luelle's flask from the ground and took a long, painful drink.

Was everyone outside the palace this irksome?

"My king? Did I miss the coronation?" She let out a mock gasp.

Malcolm ground his teeth. "You know very well you are preventing that." He bit the words out. "But I will be crowned as soon as you return my Power, and I am still your prince, so show some respect."

As he ranted, her smile grew, infuriating him further.

"You have a leaf on your head, *Your Majesty*." She gave an exaggerated bow where she knelt, flourishing the craybugs.

Malcolm swiped at his hair, heat rising in his face. Luelle laughed at his flushed cheeks.

"Has anyone ever told you how easy it is to wind you up?"

"You have a lot of audacity," Malcolm hissed at her. There was nothing funny about their situation. "You stole my father's Power, taking advantage of a sick man, and now you sit here mocking me, taunting me when you're putting my entire kingdom at risk."

Luelle's laughter died. Her expression faded into one of equal incredulity.

"I'm the one working to save the realm, Prince." She shook away the wisps of hair drifting into her face. "You'll get your Power back. As will your siblings, your mother, and every member of a bloodline it truly belongs to. If you take the right steps afterwards, you could strengthen Arazia like no monarch has before."

"Excuse me if I choose not to take advice on ruling my kingdom from a criminal."

Luelle looked away from him, rotating the craybugs again. For a brief moment, he thought he saw her roll her eyes. "I don't expect you to understand yet."

Malcolm took several deep breaths and changed the subject before saying anything he would regret, or something that would provoke her to burn him to a crisp using his Power. He was still to be king, he should act like it.

"How far is the nearest road through the forest?" Regular complaints from local lords and ladies provided a constant reminder of the untolled routes through the forests. It was perfectly legal for his citizens to take whatever paths they desired, but Malcolm's father taught him to anticipate lengthy, whining letters whenever landowners raised their tolls and didn't receive the money they expected.

"We're not taking the roads unless you want to run into a group of bandits. We'll continue along the Channel until it meets with the Caeleste River. We can follow that upstream to the lower Peaks and then it's just a case of getting to the cavern. It's not a difficult climb."

Malcolm glanced around, cold concern spiking within him, but no bandits revealed themselves. "How long will that take?" The longer they spent travelling, the better the chance that his friends would catch up to aid him in apprehending the thief, but the longer he would be away from home and the duties that awaited him there.

Luelle shrugged, refusing to look at him again. "Under two weeks if we make good progress."

Malcolm resisted the urge to groan. His coronation should have been in four days. Every moment he delayed getting his Power back was more time Viv had to live a lie to postpone the original timeline of events. Thousands of people travelled to Cerulya for the event, from surrounding towns and distant cities; the capital would be bursting at the seams with citizens expecting something he couldn't give them, and to pass that extra time they'd resort to drinking and brawling, not to mention that his advisers would start harassing his family before long, demanding to see the king in person.

"We should leave the forest and travel on the Eastern Road. There are plenty of villages along it, so we could at least bathe and eat some real food." Malcolm spoke, trying to distract himself from those dark concerns. If they passed through another village, he could send Viv a message or get one to Tolhurst where either Theo or Leena might still be waiting.

Luelle raised an eyebrow. "You're welcome to do that, but I'll be continuing through the forest. It's faster and I'm not risking another run-in with some of your arrogant soldiers."

"I am not leaving you alone." He frowned. "I only hoped to talk some sense into you so we could avoid sleeping in the mud every night. And those guards were under orders from the capital. They were doing their job. You were the one putting innocent people at risk."

She had the grace to look ashamed, as fleeting as the emotion was.

"If you're adamant you must come with me, get used to slumming it, Prince. Don't worry, I'll look after you well enough. And, I'll turn my back so you can bathe in the river without prying eyes." A smile played at the corners of her mouth. "Though I won't offer a helping hand if you aren't sure how to clean yourself without servants. Those days are over for me."

Malcolm's frown evolved into a glare, heat creeping into his face again.

"I know how to bathe myself," he snapped.

Luelle grinned, eyeing his armour as if she could see the bare skin beneath. He resisted the urge to cross his arms over his body. Not even the noblewomen at court were so forward, despite the affection and innuendos they weaved into their small talk. Luelle had the subtlety of a battering ram.

"Here." A grin lingered at the edges of her mouth as she held out the craybug stick to him. "Take two. Do you know how to peel them?"

Malcolm took the stick between his finger and thumb, eyeing the creatures' claws with apprehension. A lie lingered on the top of his tongue to avoid admitting his lack of practical skills, but the thief would realise he had no idea what to do with the crustaceans as soon as he started attacking their shells to access the meat beneath. He shook his head once, jaw clenched.

Luelle took the stick back and slid the first two craybugs off, placing them on a large leaf beside her. She handed the stick back to Malcolm.

"Copy me." Short, deft fingers ran along the creature's small body, cracking its claws and peeling off the upper shell to reveal its pale flesh.

Malcolm blinked. "Can you do that slower?"

She smiled but nodded. To his relief, she didn't take the blatant opportunity to mock him further.

He copied each of her moves as she did it. The thief stopped him in between steps when he pressed the wrong spot, to explain how his movements would shatter the shell rather than crack it open if he didn't adjust his thumb.

Stumbling through, Malcolm soon had his meal, though some parts were crunchy with rogue pieces of shell. The second bug was easier. The meat tasted nothing like his meals at home, lacking the butter and herbs that usually accompanied similar crustaceans, but it was hot and filling, more satisfying than the nuts and berries they'd snacked on last night.

Once he'd all but licked the shells clean, Malcolm discarded the remainder of his meal and washed his hands in the Channel. He splashed a few drops of water on his face, hoping its chill would soothe his burning nose or at least relieve some of the swelling, which was bad enough that he'd been forced to breathe through his mouth all morning. When he turned back toward the embers in the fire pit that Luelle had been crouched beside, the thief was standing and untying the laces that held her shirt together.

Malcolm spun back to the river, eyes glued to the distant sky.

"What are you doing?" he snapped.

"I need to wash." Luelle's voice was torn between amusement

and annoyance, but Malcolm refused to glance back at her expression. "Sorry, Prince, I didn't realise a woman's body would come as such a shock."

Footsteps crunched to his left so Malcolm whirled to the right, moving his gaze to the trees and away from the thief. He tried not to look at the clothes she'd abandoned on the forest floor, undergarments and all.

She gasped. Malcolm couldn't stop himself from glancing over, checking for whatever threat she must be responding to. His heartbeat picked up and his hand dropped to the sword at his waist, thoughts snapping back to the thick, hairy legs of the arachnids and their glossy, beady eyes.

He twisted back to face the forest when he realised Luelle was only responding to the temperature of the water. His face blazed at the image of curves and creamy skin now seared into his mind.

It wasn't as if he hadn't seen naked bodies before. He'd had passing romances, though none had ever meant much. Whoever he married would potentially end up leading the kingdom at his side, and no one he'd encountered so far had proven themselves worthy of the honour.

At a young age, his father had explained that his feelings might not matter when he had to choose a partner. Love wasn't something the royal advisers considered important when selecting a match for the reigning monarch. Although their union was political, his parents had been lucky that such strong affection blossomed between them; most pairings only found dispirited acceptance.

He wanted to find love as strong and passionate as his parents' but couldn't shake the paranoia that any romantic interests approached him with a bigger aspiration in mind. Sustaining a relationship with someone inappropriate would be selfish and his life was too hectic for that at the moment, anyway. Thanks to his Veseile blood, he had decades to find a partner. The loneliness wasn't so bad. It was just a natural downside to being the crown prince.

Luelle resumed her earlier humming as she washed, interrupted by occasional vigorous splashing.

Malcolm struggled to find things in the surrounding forest to keep his attention on.

He concentrated on the sounds the thief made, ensuring she wasn't taking the opportunity to flee.

She must know how improper she was being. Though, Malcolm couldn't deny he needed a wash, too. The Channel's icy depths were much less appealing than the heated baths at home.

Had the thief been this improper around his father? Philip had said Luelle was one of the king's favourite servants. He'd requested her assistance before Malcolm's arrival home, she hadn't needed to sneak into his room.

Thoughts of his father made Malcolm's throat burn. Tears pricked at his eyes. Grief snatched his breath, sudden and overwhelming. Swallowing the lump that rose in his throat, he blinked hard. He could mourn soon, when Leena and Theo caught up and helped him escort the thief home. Until then, there was no room for any feeling except determination and caution. The thief could try anything to get rid of him. He'd seen the destructive potential of his stolen Power at Tolhurst. If she chose to use it against him, there'd be nothing left of his body to take back to the capital.

"Everything okay, Prince?"

"Yes." His voice was a little too brusque for someone who was truly fine. Though, if Luelle was content with being improper, he certainly didn't need to watch his manners or tone around her.

"Must be weird being out of the palace."

"I leave the palace all the time. I was out whilst you stole my Power," Malcolm retorted.

Luelle sighed. "I meant out of the palace on your own. Can't we have a single conversation where you don't bring that up?"

Malcolm almost turned to scowl at her but stopped himself at the last moment, remembering she was still bathing in the shallows. "I am only here to retrieve it. You forget who you're speaking to. We are not friends on a casual outing."

Water splashed behind him, followed by dull thuds of droplets hitting the earth.

"If you're going to be this brutish the whole way, you should just go home now. I'd rather face the journey alone."

"I will not let you out of my sight," Malcolm repeated his words from last night, wishing more than anything to be home with his family. "Not until I get my Power back." It was a symbol of his reign, a sign he was fit to rule; his father had repeated the declaration a million times before sickness stole his mind.

"You will get it back. I promise." Luelle's voice was softer than usual.

Malcolm turned his head a fraction.

"I'm decent, you can turn around." A smile was back in her voice.

He turned. She was standing in her loose shirt and undergarments, stepping into her trousers. Malcolm looked pointedly at the leaves above but kept the thief in his peripheral so she couldn't dash away. Not that she'd get far from him with the connection between them.

"So, you will return my Power?" Hope flared in his chest.

Luelle nodded, lacing up her trousers. "As I said, it will return to everyone with Veseile blood once it's back at its source."

Malcolm's heart sank. Closing his eyes, he took a deep breath that sent a twinge of pain through his face. "I need it back before then."

"Look, you'll get it back then, whether you accompany me or not, so just go and wait in your castle. You're not cut out for this." She waved a hand around their small camp.

Annoyance reared its head. Perhaps he should try tying the thief to a tree until Theo and Leena arrived to help him. If he knocked her unconscious, she wouldn't get the chance to use his Power against him. Though, he had nothing to bind her with.

"I keep telling you, I am not leaving."

"Then try and loosen up a little." Luelle rolled her eyes. "This is going to be an awful journey otherwise."

"I find nothing about the situation amusing." Malcolm spat the words across the embers of their firepit that divided them.

Luelle shook her head in exasperation but refrained from another witty remark. "Do you want to wash before we head out?"

"You will only flee if I do." *Or do something else inappropriate,*

Malcolm added, in his head.

Luelle straightened, placing a hand over her heart. "I give my word that I will not run off whilst you're washing," she vowed.

"I have no reason to trust you."

"I didn't keep your dagger after using it to light the fire this morning."

He said nothing, tensing at the realisation she'd taken it from him as he slept. How could he have been so careless? What else had she done to him while he slept?

She shrugged, eyeing him up and down. "Suit yourself." She began packing her few things and tied her hair in a loose braid over her shoulder. "You'll have to wash at some point, though, otherwise you're going to stink."

Malcolm scowled but helped kick dirt over their fire pit, imagining he was kicking it over her smirking face. Other than his weapons, which he vowed to keep a closer watch over, he had nothing to pack. Everything was with his horse.

His thoughts returned to his friends once he started following the thief through the Godswood, staying a few steps behind her, but close enough to grab her if she dashed off. Should he try to leave more evidence of their presence for Theo and Leena to follow? He had nothing to leave behind as a trail but he might be able to wreak some obvious damage or score some tree trunks with his dagger.

If they hadn't survived the arachnids, there would be no point.

The thought made his mouth dry out.

They survived. He wouldn't believe anything else. Both were

excellent fighters, the best he knew.

They'd stumble across his scarf, wherever it had fallen, and track him from there. He and Luelle had left a trail of destruction as they'd fought, rolling over bushes and squashing flowers. Blood had poured from his nose for the last half of their chase, painting the way to the Channel.

His friends would find him again. They had to.

# 15

After all of the sharp words and blunt insults she'd suffered through that morning, Luelle didn't bother initiating another conversation with the prince. She walked ahead of him, not once looking over her shoulder to check if he was keeping up. From his threats, it didn't seem like she'd lose him any time soon.

She needed his dagger. She'd considered keeping it after lighting their fire that morning but knew it would only lead to a fight when he assumed she was attempting to kill him in his sleep. For all she cared, he could keep the sword, but they'd be safer if they were both armed. Beasts in the Godswood weren't as intelligent or sinister as those in the Great Forest but that didn't mean they were any less deadly. Bandits prevailed in the absence of the arachnids and though most of them stuck to the roads, staying away from both the heavily populated Meteile camps and the less travelled paths, Luelle preferred to prepare for any outcome.

The prince was a good fighter. Stories and gossip regularly

circulated the castle following his successes at tourneys and any small quests he undertook in the company of Cerulyan soldiers to hunt down criminals. If she hadn't resorted to manipulation, Luelle wouldn't have escaped his grip in the Great Forest, especially not when she had been so sluggish from using the Power. But, he might not hold up in a fight against an entire group of bandits, particularly any that recognised him and got thoughts of a ransom stuck in their heads. Desperation made fierce fighters of those who otherwise might not care to put in the effort.

They travelled hard and fast in moody silence for two days, scavenging food and picking a precarious route along the winding curves of the river. Breaks were short, few and far between. They stopped to rest and refresh when the latest hours at night descended, darkness making it too difficult to pick a safe path, or when one of them needed to relieve themselves. At first, Malcolm had been reluctant to let Luelle out of his sight to take care of those needs but agreed it was necessary when she threatened to empty her bladder in front of him.

They made good progress, always keeping the Ophidian Channel in sight but walking among the trees, far enough from the riverbank to avoid stumbling back into that strong, icy current. Several times, Luelle contemplated leaping into the water to escape the prince but didn't doubt he'd jump straight after her.

Their two days of silent travel gave her plenty of time to scheme a way to get the dagger from him but she couldn't settle on a plan that would work. The prince needed to trust her. Alaric had trusted her completely by the end, for whatever reason.

Though, the dead king's warm, charming nature didn't appear to run in the family.

On their third full day together, Luelle's restless anxiety evolved into a sombre, murky depression. Loneliness returned with a vengeance, consuming her despite the prince's quiet presence never more than a few steps away. Five years without the company of someone to call a friend weighed on her, eroding who she'd been before this mission.

Alaric had been the closest thing to a friend she'd had in that time, but thinking of him did nothing to improve her mood.

Luelle didn't regret what she'd done but she did regret that there hadn't been another way. Zeke had prepared her well for most of the hardships she'd experienced in the capital but he'd said nothing to ready her for the emotional turmoil of her task.

Would Alaric have considered helping her if she'd made the leap of faith and explained her beliefs when they'd been alone together? Would any human be capable of understanding her reasons for needing to do this? She'd never found the courage to broach the topic in the king's company, but even now couldn't imagine he would have willingly given up something that gave him such an advantage over any Eile in his midst.

Had her friends heard, by now, that she'd succeeded in retrieving Vesanya's Power? They must know about King Alaric's death. Zeke always seemed to learn information faster than it could travel, not that he'd ever revealed the secret behind that talent to Luelle.

How different would things be when she reached her home, her chosen family? Zeke and the others were no true relation to her but she couldn't imagine caring for blood relatives any more than she cared for them. Luelle didn't know her parents, nor any other family she may have once had. They'd been long gone by the time Zeke found her, claiming her as one of the many lost things he collected, amongst other people, histories, objects, and secrets.

Luelle never gave much thought to her real family. Freya and Imbryl were siblings to her. They'd always been an inseparable trio in Zeke's cohort. Memories of growing up with them had helped her through the loneliest nights at the castle; she cherished them. As adolescents, they'd annoyed each other beyond belief, but their bond was unbreakable. She'd give her life for either of them in an instant and knew they would do the same for her.

Zeke had found the three of them at a similar time, two and a half decades ago, when they were still children. He was the reason they were alive today. Helping him with the task of returning the Power to its source, which had been his strongest ambition since Luelle could remember, was the least she could do to repay him for everything, even if guilt nibbled at her each time she glimpsed the Prince's mournful, green-flecked eyes.

She tried to stop meeting his gaze by their third day travelling together.

The morning started as any other they'd shared. They rose in silence, falling into their routine of eating something caught in the river, packing up camp, and walking, never speaking beyond necessary communication. Even working in the palace, Luelle had not experienced such pressing quiet. There, noise had been constant. Conversations in the servant quarters buzzed at all hours, though few had involved her. The kitchens were always alive with sounds and smells. Distant noises from the surrounding city leaked in from every open window, accented with piercing cries from seabirds that drifted by and nested in the tallest towers.

The prince didn't appear to care about the lack of noise. He grew more glum as each day passed, but seemed resigned to his fate of travelling with Luelle. Understanding his hatred for her did nothing to quell her irritation at his sullen nature.

Morning turned to afternoon, marked by the gurgling vocalisations of her stomach, but Luelle kept walking, ignoring her hunger pangs for as long as she could bear. A couple of hours later, through the trees, Luelle saw the point where the Ophidian Channel and the Caeleste River met, melding together and flowing south. They'd made good progress. For the rest of their journey, they'd follow the water upstream. She stopped in her tracks and turned to face the prince, who was trudging further behind than usual.

"We need to find some food." She broke the silence. Food was as safe a topic as any. The prince would bicker with her about any subject.

He nodded.

Luelle's annoyance flared.

"Are you really planning to refuse to speak to me the entire way?" She placed her hands on her hips. Of course he was angry but was there any need for him to be so unpleasant? She'd told him time and time again that he'd get his Power back soon enough.

The few times she'd spotted the prince from afar around the castle, he'd looked friendly enough, all charming smiles and witty jests. He must still view her as a servant, as someone well beneath him. It would explain why he was content to leave the responsibility of keeping them both alive to her. He hadn't once tried to catch fish or craybugs in the river or suggest a suitable place to spend the night; he just watched her do everything in silence, with dull eyes and a sour expression.

Malcolm dragged a hand over his eyes and up through his hair, mixing the dark and light strands together. The swelling around his nose and eyes had gone down but his face was still puffier than normal.

"I have very little to say to you," he muttered, examining the leaves around them—anything to avoid looking at her.

"You're much ruder than your father, do you know that?" She was under enough stress without a pompous prince making her life harder. At this point, she'd rather face off all the guards in Tolhurst again than continue putting up with him, dragging his feet and staring daggers into her back.

The prince's eyes snapped to hers, his mouth curling with disgust. He stepped closer, looming a head taller than her, but Luelle lifted her chin at the loathing in his expression, unwilling to cringe under its intensity. She'd never been one to back down from a challenge.

"Do not speak about my father." His voice was icy with rage.

His tone sparked her own fury, warming her from within, as it always did when they argued. It was a pleasant contrast to the numb, emotionless trance she'd fallen into. She reacted without thinking about the words tumbling from her lips, desperate to hold onto that feeling of life within her.

"Why not? I helped him through those last few weeks, through the pain and humiliation of it. Where were you when he needed you? Was a tournament really more important than his final days?"

Alaric's requests for his family had grown more frequent towards the end of their trip away. His memory failed faster after each of Luelle's reminders that they were at a tournament in Stodor, an event he would have once attended with them. Although his family's absence made her theft easier, it had been hard to watch Alaric's sorrow and fear of dying without them at his side worsen over the course of the two weeks.

The prince recoiled from her as if he'd been struck. A flash of hurt replaced the anger on his face before he could school his expression into its usual calm, unfeeling mask. Unlike Luelle, who was grasping at any feelings she could find, the prince shoved his deeper after every interaction.

"Where can we find food?" His voice was monotonous, though his fists were curled tight at his sides.

Had she gone too far? She only wanted to get a reaction from him. Walking in silence was sending her mind to the darkest places. Arguing with him would offer a distraction from her thoughts, and if he wouldn't have a regular conversation with her, she had no alternative but to start a fight. The irritation on his face every time she called him Prince was like a reward for her goading.

Besides, there was some truth to her accusations. Alaric had been helpless in his family's absence thanks to the clueless, careless guards. She would have never left Zeke or another member of her chosen family alone, particularly not a fragile human nearing the end of their lifespan.

"We can look at the bases of the trees for mushrooms. There should be nuts around, too." Luelle rolled her shoulders. Last night, she'd dreamed of the hot meals she'd eaten in the castle, of fresh bread with cheese and fruit, of baked oats with honey, of joints of meat with crunchy, herb-rolled skins and roasted, buttery vegetables. She woke with dried saliva on her chin. Gods, she missed that food.

Prince Malcolm paid her no attention. His eyes were back on the trees, frown in its usual place.

"You can forage your own, just check with me before eating anything, otherwise—"

"Shush," he interrupted her, frown deepening.

"Excuse me?" Luelle's anger blossomed anew. "How dare you —"

The prince abandoned whatever manners he'd been keeping in check.

He closed the gap between them in three strides, spinning Luelle around and placing a large hand over her mouth to shut her up before she could finish her sentence.

The moment she recovered from her shock, she fought against the arm wrapped around her, heart pounding. He'd finally decided to act, but he couldn't drag her back to the castle, she wouldn't let him. Why wait this long, anyway? Her muffled protests struggled to breach his fingers. She clawed at his leather-clad forearm.

"Be *quiet*," he hissed, breath hot against her ear. His dark hair tickled her cheek.

Luelle's fury was an inferno, but just as the Power began to tingle in her palms, she heard what had caught his attention.

Voices.

Quiet, and deep in the forest, but getting closer.

She wriggled once more and Prince Malcolm released her, a cold breath of air swooping down her back where his chest had been moments ago.

She shot him a glare and leapt into a crouch behind the nearest shrubbery, trying to pinpoint the voices. He lowered himself beside her, leaving the usual gap between them.

"Bandits?" he whispered. His hand hovered over the hilt of his sword, every inch of him tensed to leap into a fight.

Luelle squinted into the trees. "I don't know. Sounds like a lot of people. I've never known bandits to travel in large groups this far from the roads, but I've been away from this part of the world for a long time. Things might've changed since I was last here."

"Should we run?"

She shook her head. "Too noisy. If they're hostile, they'll chase us. We'll do better hiding until they're past. Though, if they're friendly, we might be able to get some help from them."

"Are you insane?" he asked, turning to look at her.

"Bandits aren't the only folk that live here. Is one commoner bad enough for you to spend your time with, Prince? Don't want to risk meeting a second?" Luelle couldn't disguise the bitterness in her voice. The sooner she was back with friends, the better.

The prince scowled. "I cannot risk being recognised. My position is vulnerable enough after the havoc you've caused. You clearly know nothing of the dangers I am in by pursuing you—this is not a game. I have to think about the future of the realm, and of my family, not just my own safety."

Luelle glanced sideways at him. "I know the dangers, Prince, but I doubt anyone will recognise you. You don't look very regal at the moment. You didn't even wash this morning."

His cheeks flushed pink. He opened his mouth to retort but closed it as figures emerged in the distance. Both of them leaned forward to watch through the leaves.

Strangers streamed through the forest, a column of people that seemed never ending.

"You should give me your dagger," she breathed.

"Absolutely not."

She turned to him. His glare was as fierce as her own.

"You would use it against me the second my back is turned. It is hardly my fault you were careless enough to lose yours in the Great Forest."

"I wouldn't have dropped it if you hadn't attacked me like a wild animal. Besides, Prince, if I wanted you dead, you would be. When will you believe I don't want to hurt you?"

"You punched me in the face!"

Luelle paused. He had her there. The swelling was still quite bad.

"I was scared for my life?"

He scoffed and turned back towards the strangers in the

forest. They continued towards the water. If she and the prince hadn't stopped and bickered, they would have collided with the group where the two rivers met.

"If anything, I helped you. No one's going to recognise you whilst your face looks like that. And you did attack me first." Luelle defended herself in a whisper.

He ignored her. A muscle twitched in his jaw.

Lilting, melodic accents drifted to them from the strangers, who chatted and called to one another with little regard for being overheard. A few lithe forms ran across the thickest branches far above their companions, who walked in a long, weaving line. Their skin ranged in colour from mossy green and rosy pink, to greys and browns as rich and varied as the stones and soil around them.

"They're Meteile!" Luelle exclaimed in a hushed tone. She relaxed where she crouched. The Meteile race descended from the God of Harvest and Fertility, Meto. They were amicable people for the most part, but protectors of the natural world above all else. In the few encounters she'd had with them, the Meteile had been generous and altruistic.

"Are you certain?" Malcolm asked, leaning further forward to peer at the distant figures.

"Pretty sure," Luelle replied. "Haven't you seen any before?"

"We have representatives of every race in the castle. The Thane of the Midlands is Meteile, but I have never visited any of the forest communities." He smiled at a memory. "My father once —" He stopped himself, his smile dying as quickly as it came.

He glanced at Luelle as if preparing himself for another jibe, but she didn't push him.

"Are you happy for us to approach them?" she asked. "We can act as travellers on our way east."

He frowned. "Will they not question why we are travelling so far from the paths?"

"Only one way to find out."

Part of her wondered why she bothered to offer him the choice. She didn't need to make peace with the prince, just because she'd said something hurtful earlier in an attempt to make herself feel better. It made sense to approach the Meteile; they might offer some better supplies for her journey, and it might be useful if they recognised the prince, just to take him off her hands.

Yet, another part of her pitied Malcolm. It wasn't his fault he'd been misled about his history. And, despite his brutish, ill-tempered nature, he could still be useful to her. Luelle couldn't control the Power. In Tolhurst, it had flared as an automatic response but it drained her in the process. If she didn't learn to control it, she might not make it to the Caeleste Peaks. Since he hadn't killed her on sight, he either must not be able to retrieve the Power through her death or he wasn't willing to take the risk. She didn't care which was true; for now, it was a guarantee of protection. Whilst the Power remained inside her, the prince would keep her from harm.

Prince Malcolm searched her face for any sign of deceit.

"Are you going to tell them who I am?"

"No." Luelle's brows pulled together. "I've said we can travel together a hundred times, I won't break that promise."

He nodded, though he didn't look convinced. "They may have some food they could share with us."

Her mouth watered at the thought.

"Okay, if any of them ask, we're childhood friends travelling to the Iron City. Incorporate the truth into your lies and it'll be easier to keep track. You're from a large family, from Cerulya, but left seeking a fortune elsewhere."

The prince hesitated but nodded again.

"Don't worry, just follow my lead. I've had to do this before. Feign exhaustion and leave the talking to me if you're worried you can't manage."

"I can manage." His expression hardened at the challenge.

Luelle gave him a tight smile. "Great, let's go."

She stood, straightening her clothes.

"Try to act as if you can tolerate me. We're supposed to be friends, after all." She winked over her shoulder and turned to continue their trek.

She didn't quite hear what the prince muttered under his breath, but her smile widened as she walked. She felt more alive than she had in years.

Luelle made plenty of noise as she walked, snapping twigs, stomping through bushes, and humming to herself as they approached the shallow river bank where the Meteile were gathered.

Their chatter quieted. Cautious curiosity lit the faces that observed their arrival.

Luelle paused when she stepped into their view, letting the prince collide into her back with a grunt.

She widened her eyes, startling as she looked up. She took a step backwards, pushing against the prince. He stepped away from her.

"Oh! Good afternoon."

She didn't feign her awe as she took the strangers in. Up close, the Meteile were even more beautiful, the natural world come to life. Their skin ranged in texture and colour from tree bark and stripped wood to autumn leaves and pale petals. Flowers wound amongst their hair, and fungi sprouted like moles on a few.

"Good afternoon." A muscular female close to them spoke, watching the newcomers with a hint of amusement. Her skin was the shade of walnut wood and her hair a bundle of lush vines, tied atop her head.

"Sorry, you alarmed me. We didn't expect to see anyone this far from the roads. We're a little disoriented. This way is east, isn't it?"

The Meteile nodded. "Following that river upstream will take you east." She gestured to the Caeleste River that merged with the Ophidian Channel they'd been trailing up to this point.

Luelle breathed a sigh and rested her palm on her chest.

"We were travelling in the Great Forest but we were ambushed by arachnids." She swallowed. "We fled to the river to escape them but the current was so fast. We've been wandering lost for the past few hours." She glanced around the crowd before her with wide eyes.

"Better to wander lost in the Godswood than the Great Forest. The arachnids won't stray here." The tall female examined them with vibrant, green eyes. "You have surprisingly few supplies for your journey."

"We lost most of our things in the Great Forest."

The Meteile continued her silent evaluation for another few heartbeats. Her eyes ambled to Malcolm's weapons. Behind her, the other Meteile watched the conversation with interest but none spoke up.

Luelle probed further to break the silence.

"Are you Meteile?"

The stranger nodded. "My name is Anwyn. We live in the forest and protect it from any who intend it harm. I'm surprised to come across any travellers heading east, especially this far from the marked paths. Most we've met are rushing to the capital for the coronation."

Luelle felt the prince tense behind her, but she simply smiled.

"We're going to the Iron City. We were going to wait until after the coronation, but I never cared much for crowds and the capital is stuffed to bursting. We thought cutting through the forests would be faster, but heard the roads through the woods are rife with bandits. Turns out we didn't account for my poor sense of direction when we decided to find our own way. I'm Anne, this is Mac." She gestured to the prince. He glanced at her but showed no other surprise at the false name she'd chosen for him. It was close enough to his actual name that he shouldn't give them away by forgetting it or not answering to it.

"You have a long journey ahead of you," Anwyn observed. "We're taking water back to our camp. If you can provide some help, we will share our home. We cannot offer much, but we can gift you warm food and a bed for the night. You both look as though you need it." Her eyes lingered on Malcolm's bruised face.

The Eile behind Anwyn whispered to one another, eyes lingering on the unfamiliar pair.

"If you're sure it's no trouble." Luelle's relieved smile was genuine.

"Of course. We may even be able to help replenish a few of your lost supplies." Anwyn returned the smile and tilted her head, gesturing towards the rows of large pails by the river bank where her people returned to work.

A pair of Meteile stood knee-deep in the Channel, skin slate grey and hair as straight and fine as cobwebs. They dunked each pail in the water, filling it halfway before handing each one to another pair on land for the return journey to their camp.

Luelle and Malcolm joined the queue for a bucket.

Conversation resumed amongst the Meteile as Luelle and Malcolm faded into their numbers. Luelle kept her eyes ahead but listened for any information that could be useful.

No one spoke about the theft from the castle, nor Alaric's death. Either someone in Cerulya was working hard to keep the truth from spreading or it hadn't made its way to the forest communities yet.

At the front of the queue, the two Meteile standing in the river held out a full bucket, large enough that Luelle could curl up inside it. She took one of the handles and Malcolm grabbed the other.

"Where do we take it?" Malcolm asked.

"Follow the others," one of the males in the water instructed, pointing to the figures retreating into the forest.

Anwyn stepped to Malcolm's side.

"I will accompany you back, to ensure you do not get lost. Though, I doubt you could miss our noise." She flashed a warm smile and stepped in front of them to lead the way.

Luelle staggered under the weight of the pail. She tried to relax as they walked but her shoulders ached with tension. If Malcolm said the wrong thing, they'd have to leave, fast—or she would have to flee alone, particularly if he sought misguided help from these strangers. She should have spent longer preparing him, instead of throwing him in the deep end like this. Meteile communities, as far as she knew, were at peace with the crown, but it was impossible to predict the political views of individuals. Violence was more common among the Veseile, but she couldn't assume these Meteile were safe just because they were kind. As infuriating as Prince Malcolm was, losing the king and the crown prince in the space of a few days would devastate the realm, especially when she returned the Power to those it belonged to.

"Is it your first time away from home?" Anwyn asked over her shoulder, loud enough for them to hear her from behind. In the distance, another pair of Eile hobbled with a bucket between them.

Luelle opened her mouth to speak but the prince beat her to it.

"No, but it is our first time travelling together." His tone was more agreeable than it had been during any conversation with Luelle.

She shot an offended glare in his direction.

"What are your plans when you reach the Iron City?" Anwyn glanced over her shoulder. "If you've lost most of your supplies, you'll need a home to go to if you want to avoid living on the streets."

"I have family there. We shall stay with them until we can support ourselves," Malcolm said.

Luelle raised an eyebrow at him. He was doing well enough, but could he keep track of the deception he was weaving?

She shifted her grip on the bucket, grabbing the handle with both hands to relieve some of the pressure digging into her fingers. The prince must be letting her bear most of its weight since he didn't appear to be suffering at all.

Fortunately, the Meteile's home was not far.

Anwyn led them to a tree larger than any Luelle had ever seen, its trunk as wide as some of the smaller homes in Cerulya. To the right of the trunk, winding around the tree, was a staircase constructed from planks and branches, bound with vines and woven grass ropes.

Anwyn walked to the left. A section of the trunk was carved hollow to reveal a platform and a system of ropes.

"Place the pail here and tie the ropes to the handles," she instructed.

Awe flooded Luelle as they shuffled inside the trunk. Though its hollow interior was a fraction of the tree's width, it was large enough to fit all three of them inside, with space to walk around the pail of water. Looking up, a distant hole of light shone above them like a pale sun.

She and Malcolm did as instructed. Once the handles were secured, Anwyn gave two sharp tugs on another rope and the bucket began to ascend. Water sloshed inside it.

Anwyn led them out of the hollowed interior, guiding them up the staircase that wound around the outside of the tree. Though the steps were wide enough for all three to walk side by side, Luelle and Malcolm continued to hang back.

Luelle's legs burned by the time they reached the top of the staircase and their destination revealed itself. The Meteile camp was as large as a town, nestled among the branches of the Godswood. Circular rooms were carved into the tree trunks and built on extended platforms, connected by swaying bridges. Small spheres of moonstone hung on twine from the branches, bathing the walkways and bridges with an ethereal glow.

It took Luelle's breath away.

They paused at the top of the stairs to recover from the climb and admire their surroundings, stepping to one side to leave space for the Meteile who were desensitised to the ascent and the view. Anwyn nodded for her guests to follow her once more when their breathing slowed.

"This is incredible." Luelle looked around as she walked to soak in as many of the new sights as possible. A similar expression of awe decorated the prince's face.

"I have heard of Meteile living in the trees, but this..." he murmured.

Anwyn chuckled, a deep, throaty sound.

"You are too kind. We are very proud of our home. I'll give you a brief tour and show you to the room you will sleep in."

Anwyn strode to the nearest rope bridge. It swayed as she stepped onto it.

Luelle froze.

Malcolm gestured for her to step on first.

"Go on," he hissed when she made no move.

She swallowed and placed a foot on the bridge.

The wooden plank beneath her foot creaked. Thin ropes held the planks together, weaving into hand rails that came up to her waist on either side; they were all that stood between her and a long, long drop to the forest floor. As she put her second foot on the bridge, it shifted beneath her. The world tilted.

Memories of descending the rope from the king's bedroom flooded her. Falling through the kennel roof had hurt. This fall would be fatal.

Luelle grabbed at the rope on each side of her with clammy hands but the flimsy handrails weren't solid enough to hold her weight up. She jerked back as they dipped, careening into the prince, who was still waiting to get on the bridge behind her.

Her face heated.

"You cannot tell me you are afraid of heights after you scaled my castle on a rope," he muttered.

"I just don't love dangling over them on tiny, swinging bridges," Luelle snapped over her shoulder.

"Do you need me to hold your hand?" the prince crooned.

She gritted her teeth and clenched her fists, nails digging crescents into her palms.

Anwyn had reached the other side. She turned back to see what the holdup was.

"The slower you go, the more it swings," she called, cupping her hands around her mouth.

"Just avoid looking down," the prince suggested, his voice still tainted with irritation.

Luelle forced herself forward. Her breathing was shallow and her progress was slow, but she made it across. By the time she reached the far platform, her violent shaking had settled into a tremble.

"Do you want the good news or the bad news?" Anwyn asked when their feet were back on a still surface.

Luelle and Malcolm froze. Luelle's heart was still racing from the bridge and didn't slow at their host's words. Did Anwyn know who they were? Had she waited until they were trapped in the treetops before revealing her plans for them?

Anwyn continued when her guests didn't respond.

"The good news is that I've sent someone ahead to heat a bath for you. The bad news..." She stepped aside to reveal several more bridges spanning a network around the trees like cobwebs. Several Meteile didn't bother using the rope bridges, instead running along the branches above and leaping over the gaps between them.

Luelle groaned.

To her surprise, Malcolm laughed.

She shot him a glare, which he shrugged off.

"After you." He held out an arm, gesturing for her to follow Anwyn, who had taken off over the next bridge.

"You'll make quicker progress if you go ahead."

"True. But then I would not get to witness your discomfort."

He held her glare as if dropping it first would be a defeat, but Luelle, at least, remembered their cover story. She let her scowl dissolve into a sickly sweet smile and leaned close to him, trying not to take offence at the way he recoiled from her.

"Careful, *Mac*. You have to pretend you can tolerate me in front of others, remember?" she murmured. "We don't want anyone asking any difficult questions."

He scoffed, though his reply was equally quiet. "As if you would care whether anything happened to me after what you did to my father." It took him longer than Luelle to relax his own glare.

"When will you get it through your thick skull that I'm not working against you?" Luelle asked. "If I was that desperate for harm to come to you, it would have by now. If you insist on travelling with me, the least you can do is be a bit nicer."

"Do you realise you just insulted me and requested that I am nicer to you in the same sentence? That makes you a thief *and* a hypocrite."

"I beg your forgiveness, my dear Prince. From this moment on, I will shower you with compliments and praise. I will be blind to your flaws and preach of your beauty and honour to every creature with ears, inform them your head is not thick but simply filled with excess brains and wit." She flourished a bow at him, attracting curious glances from the nearest Meteile, many of whom were now straying close enough to hear their whispered argument.

"You are intolerable." Malcolm's lips curled into a smile as he looked around at the strangers observing them but his eyes remained cold with annoyance. "Anwyn is waiting for us. Lead on."

# 16

Fury simmered in Malcolm's core, distracting him from the wonders around him as he followed Luelle and Anwyn through the Meteile camp. This was an experience he might never have again and he was missing it, all because of the thief and her desire to infuriate him.

He stared daggers into Luelle's back as she edged across yet another rope bridge.

Anwyn slowed her pace to match so she wouldn't lose her guests, informing them about her people and home as they walked.

Theirs was one of many Meteile tribes inhabiting the Godswood. Around them, the camp bustled with life, noise, and light. Though it felt large to Malcolm, walking through the midst of it, Anwyn explained their settlement was small by Meteile standards. Some had bases as large as cities hidden in the treetops. He'd read plenty about them, but the descriptions paled in comparison to the real thing.

The first stop on their tour was the heart of the camp.

Their path opened onto an enormous platform. Bare tree trunks pierced the decking in random intervals, their branches sawn away to create a large, open area. Rope ladders ascended each trunk, leading to another level. Small moonstone globes lit the space, hanging on strings that stretched the entire distance of the platform. Wooden seats and tables of all shapes and sizes filled with space between the tree trunks; many were already occupied by Meteile who looked as unique as their furniture.

"This is the Core. It is our communal area for mealtimes, but in the morning and early afternoon, the space is used for education. It's the centre of our settlement." Anwyn spoke as they walked, weaving between tables and bright cushions. "After you have had the opportunity to wash, come back here. I will get some hot food for you both. I'm sure there are plenty of others who will be eager to meet you if you would like some company your own age."

The second stop on their tour was the room Anwyn was providing for them. She stopped outside the door to part ways.

"There's a bathing room attached. I shall leave you to settle in. If you need anything else, you will find me at the Core."

They smiled goodbye and watched her walk away before ending their facade of friendliness.

Luelle turned away from Malcolm and stalked into the room. Her face was still peaky from the rope bridges, which Malcolm had coaxed into swaying with more vigour as he followed close behind her—not that he would ever admit being so childish if she accused him of it.

He entered the room after her, closing the door behind them.

To his relief, there were two beds, each a narrow mattress on the floor, laden with woven blankets, furs, and cushions. The other furnishings were simple: a small bookshelf, a wooden table, and two chairs. Along the right wall, another room was sectioned off with an opaque screen.

Malcolm frowned as Luelle placed her backpack on the bed nearest the door. Was she going to try escaping through the night?

She wouldn't get far. There were too many bridges between her and the stairs to the ground.

Malcolm had nothing of his own to place on the second bed. He wouldn't leave his weapons there, where Luelle could swipe them again. Yes, she'd helped to keep him alive so far but he couldn't let his guard down. He kept his dagger and sword strapped to his waist and wandered to the screened-off room.

Tall shelves lined the furthest wall, piled with rough towels, soaps, and unlabelled bottles. Malcolm opened one to peer inside and was hit with an overpowering waft of floral fragrance. He replaced it quickly.

In front of those shelves, taking up the majority of the room, was a large round pail, not unlike the one they'd carried to the camp. Inside was a shallow layer of water.

Malcolm leaned over and dipped his finger in. It was still warm.

"Do you wish to bathe first?" He walked back through to the main bedroom to see Luelle lying on her mattress, staring at the ceiling with her hands clasped behind her head.

Her gaze fell on him.

"No, you can. You're the Prince."

"You shouldn't mention that, even in here. Anybody could be listening."

She rolled her eyes.

He turned away from her, wishing—not for the first time today—to be back at home with his friends and family.

Leena and Theo must have made progress tracking him by now. Would they be able to find him here? Perhaps he could find a way to send them a message or at least one to Viv. The Meteile must have ways to communicate with people outside of the Godswood. But, how could he do so without revealing his identity? Or at least revealing some of the lies about their disguise.

Malcolm undressed in the bathing room as he pondered his dilemma. Even if he could find a way to send them a message, he'd have to encode it, in case anyone intercepted and read it. Anwyn had been friendly enough so far but her hospitality might not stretch as far as he needed it to if she learned his secret.

He grabbed several oils and soaps from the shelves, uncaring how they smelled, and lowered himself into the tub. Sighing at the water's warmth, he leaned back against the waxed side. He took his life in the castle for granted, he knew that now. Even when travelling on ships, he had private bathing facilities and a luxurious bed. Washing in a river could never compare to a warm bath like this, and this cramped tub could never compare to the hot baths at home that stretched large enough to lie in and filled with steaming water at the pull of a lever.

He washed as fast as he could, fearful of Luelle continuing her shows of impropriety and walking in on him. When he was done, he towelled himself off and was about to step back into his armour when he heard the door shut.

The thief was making her move.

Heart racing, Malcolm hastily wrapped a towel around his waist and rushed from the bathing room, expecting to enter an empty room.

He stopped short when he found Luelle a step away from the door with a stack of folded fabric in her arms.

She raised an eyebrow, eyes descending to the water dripping from Malcolm's hair and body onto their bedroom floor, pooling into a small puddle at his feet.

Heat rose in his cheeks. He gripped the towel tighter.

"I—uh, I thought you left."

"I went to get us some fresh clothes."

To Malcolm's relief, Luelle ignored his exposed skin as she moved around the room. She separated the fabric into two piles, throwing one on her chosen bed and stepping closer to hand the other to Malcolm.

"Anwyn said whatever we needed, right?" She gave him a tight smile. Her eyes drifted to his father's amulet, still hanging around his neck. Was she going to try and steal that too?

Malcolm didn't return her smile. He snatched the clothes she offered and retreated to the bathing room to get dressed before she could say anything else.

The clothes were more casual than his leather armour, similar to the outfits worn by the many Meteile he'd observed on the treetop pathways during Anwyn's tour. Clean undergarments, plain brown trousers, and a white, long-sleeved shirt. Malcolm rolled the sleeves to his elbows and attached his sword belt so he didn't have to leave his weapons with his armour behind.

He hung his towel to dry, grabbed his armour, and returned to the bedroom. He didn't look at Luelle again. They'd interacted more than usual today. Every word he said to her felt like a betrayal to his father, his family. Pretending to be her friend in front of the Meteile made his skin crawl.

He lay with his back to her, ignoring the dampness seeping from his hair into the pillow. The leaf-stuffed mattress was a blessed break from the floors he'd been forced to sleep on. It cradled the parts of his body that were still tender and stiff from fighting in the Great Forest and walking non-stop for days.

Luelle took her turn in the bathing room. Malcolm waited for the sounds of her clothes dropping to the floor before rolling onto his back and having a better look around the bedroom.

The ceilings were the same carved wood as the rest of the room, curved at the corners, but high enough that he could stand straight in all parts of the space. The furniture was simple and fashioned from similar wood, with delicate, repetitive markings on the joints hinting that it was all hand-carved with care.

Malcolm rose from his bed and approached the short bookshelf. Some of the titles were familiar but many more were new to him, and some of the spines had no titles at all. He pulled out one of the blank books and took it to his bed. Before settling down to read it, he detached his scabbard from his belt and slid it underneath his mattress, hiding his sword from Luelle in case she tried to steal another of his things. He kept his dagger attached to his waist, in clear sight so she would think twice about attacking him.

Scrawling words lined every page inside the book, sketched out in dark ink to fill the gaps between intricate, faded drawings. The text detailed some of the history of this Meteile tribe, how they'd set up their camp, their daily routines, and their connection to the Gods—particularly to Meto. Scientific sketches of flowers filled one chapter, complete with labels and the occasional dried example loose amongst the sheets. Malcolm poured over the annotations, reading about how the plants were manipulated for their healing or numbing properties, cosmetic uses, and even as poisons that could kill in seconds or send someone to sleep for a predetermined amount of time depending on the dosage. Some he recognised from visits to the doctors in the castle.

He became so absorbed in the book that he didn't notice Luelle until she was standing at the foot of his mattress, clearing her throat. Her new clothes were as simple as his, loose, navy trousers and a white top that wrapped around her torso. She'd left her damp hair loose. It hung around her shoulders in waves, tucked behind both ears.

"I'm going to get some food."

At the mention of food, Malcolm realised how hungry he was. He put the book down on his bed with reluctance, but he'd learn more about these Meteile by interacting with them. This was an opportunity he might never get again, to speak with regular people that weren't altering their behaviour to suit his royal status. Excitement fluttered in his stomach.

They retraced their steps to the Core in silence, travelling in the same direction as most other Meteile they saw. Luelle's speed across the bridges improved a fraction with each new one they crossed.

Noise from the Core reached Malcolm long before he could see it, a buzz of voices and laughter, entwined with upbeat music. Earlier, the social area had been spacious and open. Now it teemed with Meteile of all shapes, sizes, and ages.

Malcolm almost lost himself in the crowds as he trailed Luelle, distracted by the flashes of colour from each new person he passed. Their bodies shielded him from the gentle breeze that whispered through the branches and leaves, warming him to a slightly uncomfortable temperature. A sheen of sweat coated the back of his neck. Several of the Meteile glanced at the newcomers with trepidation and wariness, though more greeted them with a shy smile or gazed from afar with warm curiosity.

Crowds were not a new phenomenon to Malcolm. He'd attended many overstuffed ballrooms, and his kingdom's people always crowded Cerulya's streets to call out to him and his family when they travelled to and from the castle, but the fleeting intimacy of being pressed against so many strangers was new. Even in his own home, Malcolm rarely travelled without guards defending his personal space.

It was a relief to see Anwyn had saved them seats at one of the many wooden tables. She beamed and waved when she spotted Luelle carving a space through the crowds towards her.

"You both look refreshed. Please, come and sit with us."

Anwyn raised her voice over the buzz of the crowd.

Malcolm and Luelle took the two remaining seats at the table. He ended up between Luelle and Anwyn, sitting close enough that their shoulders brushed against each other with the slightest movement. He gritted his teeth at the contact, unable to keep his usual distance from the thief.

"Thank you for the clothes," Malcolm said to Anwyn, ignoring his proximity to Luelle and raising his own voice.

"It's my pleasure. I am glad to see I predicted your sizes correctly. You suit our fashions." Anwyn's mossy eyes were bright in the moonstone light. "Let me introduce you to Pansy, my daughter, and Trent, one of our most valued scholars and tutors." She gestured to the two strangers sitting on the other side of the table.

Malcolm and Luelle murmured a greeting. Luelle spoke first, introducing herself with her false name—a subtle reminder for Malcolm to do the same.

Anwyn rose from the table to get them some food, leaving them alone with Pansy and Trent.

Despite his excitement to be in this new place, Malcolm's stomach churned with nerves at the inevitable, impending conversation. He'd never tried to deceive anyone like this before, let alone an entire group of people. What would happen if he slipped up and misremembered one of their lies? What if he contradicted something Luelle said when he wasn't paying attention?

Pansy was the first to break the awkward silence that fell over the table in Anwyn's absence.

"What happened to your face?" she asked. Her eyes bored into Malcolm's.

He was taken aback by her blunt question.

"I—uh, I injured it escaping from arachnids in the Great Forest," he stammered, shifting underneath her intense stare, willing the heat in his cheeks to disperse. Surely these people would see through any lies he told them. He was a fool to think he could do this. How would they react when they realised he was the crown prince?

"I've never seen an arachnid."

"Count yourself lucky," Luelle spoke up. She leaned forward to rest her forearms on the tabletop, brushing against Malcolm's shoulder in the process.

"I've never been to the capital before, either. Ma says that's where you're travelling from," Pansy announced. She shared many of her mother's physical traits, though her round eyes were set wider apart and she'd plaited her thick hair over one shoulder, intertwining pink flowers down the length of the braid.

Malcolm could admire the beauty of the Meteile for days on end.

Luelle raised an eyebrow at Pansy's statement. Malcolm swallowed. The younger Meteile continued to make eye contact with each of them, seemingly unaware of their discomfort. A small smile rose on Trent's lips, though he kept his own gaze on the steaming mug in front of him, reluctant to join the conversation.

"Well?" Pansy demanded, eyebrows knitting with annoyance. "What's it like?"

"Beautiful," Malcolm said at the same time as Luelle muttered–

"Overrated."

He shot her a sideways glare.

Pansy leaned back on the bench to cross her arms, her frown deepening.

"It is beautiful," Malcolm repeated. "The sunsets over the sea are incomparable. The city is full of life and joy."

Pansy's expression turned contemplative.

"But, Mac liked to spend his time in the nicer parts of the city," Luelle said. "He rarely ventured out of his home to the busier central markets and the backstreets. Those parts are dirty, smelly, and full of leery drunks. If you don't stay alert, pickpockets will walk away with everything but the shirt on your back, and a pleasure worker will be waiting in the shadows to take that from you, too."

Malcolm frowned and opened his mouth to defend his home, but Pansy spoke before he could.

"Is that why you left?" she asked.

"We left for adventure. It was the right time." Luelle shrugged. "Would you ever leave the Godswood?"

"I have left." Pansy straightened in her seat, offended by the implication of Luelle's question. Malcolm watched them both, trying to fade into the background as Trent was managing. Luelle, as the more experienced liar between them, was faring much better under Pansy's frank interrogation.

"Oh really?" Luelle challenged.

"I've been Above."

Luelle's expression was baffled.

"She means she's ventured to the platforms at the tops of the trees," Trent broke his silence, a smile still playing at the corners of his lips. "I keep trying to tell her that doesn't count but she won't hear it."

"It's outside the forest." Pansy set her jaw.

Luelle grinned at Trent. "Definitely doesn't count."

As Pansy opened her mouth to reply, Anwyn returned with a tray filled with bowls and mugs. She placed it on the table between them all.

Pillars of steam rose from the bowls. Malcolm's mouth watered at the spicy scent wafting from the food. Anwyn dispersed the food around their table, settling the last bowl in the empty space where she'd been sitting. Malcolm helped her hand out the additional mugs and cutlery before tucking into his meal, as Pansy and Trent were already doing. Anwyn shot him a grateful smile.

He savoured his first bite before hunger became a sudden, desperate urge. Still, he managed to remember some of his manners, unlike Luelle, who was hunched over her bowl and shovelling in mouthful after mouthful. Even his brother Edwyn had better table manners.

On their brief tour around the Meteile camp, Malcolm hadn't seen any kitchens like those at the palace, but he wouldn't question where the food came from. After days of eating whatever scraps Luelle could forage, this could be a meal sent directly from the Gods, for all he knew.

As they ate, more people managed to cram themselves into

the Core. Malcolm zoned out from the conversation at the table, hardly able to distinguish it above the general roar of noise, but he couldn't tear his eyes from the crowds, seated at tables around them and weaving between them. Few Meteile sat without smiles on their faces and fewer still sat alone. These were his people—he was witnessing the lives of the people he was sworn to rule and protect.

He hadn't lied to Pansy about his love for Cerulya, but now, in the middle of this Meteile camp as a welcomed stranger, Malcolm could see how restricted his experiences were, locked away in the capital to reign from afar. He knew nothing about the lives of the individuals he was ruling over, their habits, their problems, their dreams. He'd thought his father was a perfect king, but even he couldn't have known the true intricacies of his people, not when everything was passed to the monarch from lords, ladies, and advisors who were just as alienated from the majority.

Perhaps something positive would come out of this strange start to his reign.

For the first time in days, Malcolm let his thoughts drift away from his father and his family waiting for him. He lost himself in the noise and buzz of the crowd, smiling along with the laughter, without really consuming the content of the conversations around him.

He was jolted from his stupor when Luelle rose from her seat on the bench.

"Where are you going?" He straightened in his seat.

She looked down at him, her shy excitement dissolving into

the usual irritation she directed his way.

"Trent asked me to dance with him, weren't you listening?" she snapped.

Malcolm frowned.

Anwyn chuckled at the pair. "We can go too, Mac. I'm eager to watch tonight's festivities." She stood, stacking their bowls and sliding them across the table to Pansy, who disappeared with them into the crowd.

"Oh, of course." Malcolm nodded, trying to hide his initial confusion at his false name.

Luelle and Trent rushed ahead, hands clasped to avoid losing one another in the throng. Tension built in Malcolm's shoulders as Luelle retreated far ahead of him and Anwyn, who was still shuffling around the table. He could feel the pull of his Power, harboured in the thief, despite no longer being able to see her, but he had no desire to chase her through the forest again.

Didn't she realise how foolish it was to separate from one another among so many strangers?

Re-entering the crowd made Malcolm's chest tighten. Each new breath was harder to find. Luelle had already proven he wasn't the best judge of danger. She'd lurked in his home for years without him noticing the threat to his family and kingdom. Any of the people here could intend him similar harm if they recognised his face.

Anwyn threaded her arm through Malcolm's, jolting him from his spiral of panic.

"The crowds are always thickest at the tables." She looked at him with knowing eyes. Meteile were already filling the seats they'd vacated.

The Meteile parted for Anwyn as she pulled Malcolm across the Core to an area where the tables had been cleared away. They walked in silence, conversation made impossible in the noise. Music grew louder with each step they took. Fast drum beats vibrated through Malcolm's chest, matching his heart rate.

At the edge of the crowd, two young Meteile offered their seats to Anwyn and her guest.

Malcolm settled into the round, cushioned chair as well as his tense muscles would allow, concentrating on his breathing in an attempt to stifle the dark sense of unease gripping his heart. He shoved his trembling fingers under his thighs so Anwyn wouldn't see his weakness.

The chairs were angled to watch the Meteile in the cleared space. Pairs twirled and danced to the music, weaving around one another. Their loose clothing spun out from them as they moved. Pounding footsteps joined the drums and stringed instruments to create a crescendo of noise. This raucous, wild joy was nothing like the atmosphere of the parties Malcolm attended at home, where each dance was choreographed and the partners were only connected by carefully placed hands.

He searched the whirling dancers until his eyes landed on Luelle. His racing heart calmed a little, knowing his Power was still within reach.

She and Trent were both laughing as they danced, spinning and stepping around the others on the floor. Her face was flushed and her smile broad, matching Trent's. As they twirled closer to one another again, he grasped one of her hands, his other resting on her waist, tugging her close to his chest.

Her joy grated on Malcolm.

"Does she know?"

Malcolm glanced at Anwyn.

"Pardon?" His eyes flickered between Luelle and the woman beside him. Anwyn knew who he was—this was the end for him.

"How you feel about her."

Malcolm frowned at Anwyn.

"What do you mean?"

"Well, you haven't been able to take your eyes off Anne since Trent asked her to dance. You were searching for them as soon as they disappeared into the crowd. I know she said you're only friends at dinner but it's clear your feelings are stronger." A small smile played on her lips.

Malcolm sat in shocked silence for a moment. He should've paid more attention to the conversations whilst they ate. A laugh bubbled out of him; the thought of having feelings for the person who stole his Power was ridiculous enough to distract him from his anxieties. Once he started, it became harder to stop, loosening the tight feeling in his chest. Anwyn's smile faltered at his peals of laughter.

"I apologise," Malcolm choked, wrestling some control over himself. It felt so good to laugh. "Sorry, no, you misunderstand." His expression settled into a tired smile. "Lu-, uh, Anne just has a tendency to run away with her stupid ideas." He stumbled over her false name. "She is better at all this, the travelling, than me. I cannot make my way where we're going without her. If I lose her along the way, I would only end up returning home, and I doubt

I could forgive myself for not seeing this through."

Anwyn nodded but didn't seem fully convinced.

They returned to observing the dancing in silence. The first song came to an end. The musicians paused to sip from their drinks and lap up the applause and whooping cheers from their onlooking audience.

"Don't feel like you must sit with me," Anwyn spoke up. "If you would rather dance, that is. There are plenty of young folk here who are very curious to meet you if their stares and glances are any indication."

Malcolm took a deep breath and shook his head. "I am not feeling up for dancing at the moment. I..." he hesitated, but they were only here for one night. He would never see Anwyn again; she didn't know who he really was. Opening up wouldn't put him in any danger as long as he didn't mix up his lies. He swallowed. "I lost someone before we left. It is why we left when we did. I haven't had a chance to let it sink in. It does not feel real. I have not been myself since."

Fresh understanding dawned on Anwyn's face.

"I'm sorry to hear that, Mac."

The music started afresh. Malcolm didn't trust himself to speak again, not without letting the emotion constricting his throat spill out.

"Would you like to go somewhere a little quieter? If you feel comfortable leaving Anne here for a while."

When Malcolm hesitated, she continued.

"I promise she's in good hands with Trent, but I can ask someone to bring them to us once they're done dancing."

He thought it over for another long moment but found himself nodding. The tightness in his chest was returning and he was curious to see more of this place, to learn about his people and what might make their lives better when he was home and able to make a real difference. If Luelle ran again, he'd find her.

Anwyn led Malcolm from the dance floor, beckoning her daughter over on their retreat from the thickest part of the crowd.

"Please bring Anne and Trent Above when they're finished. I'm taking Mac there for some peace and quiet."

"Oh, you don't want to dance?" Pansy asked him.

Malcolm shook his head. "I apologise. I need a moment away from the crowd."

Disappointment shone on her face, but Pansy nodded and continued on her way to the dance floor, striding faster to catch up with the friends she'd left seconds earlier.

Malcolm followed close behind Anwyn, concentrating on her form to avoid thinking about the other people brushing against him. Instead of moving along the rope bridges they'd travelled over earlier, she stopped at one of the ladders hanging down the tree trunks in the Core and scurried up with surprising speed.

Malcolm peered after her once she'd ascended but shadows concealed his destination. He followed with shaky limbs, gripping the ladder rungs tight. Curiosity and a desire to be out of the crowd urged him forward.

At the top of the ladder were more walkways and spiralling stairs, somehow leading even higher into the trees. Anwyn led Malcolm up until they emerged onto a circular platform, ringed with a waist-height bannister to prevent people from falling.

Malcolm cleared the last few steps, emerging into the cool night air. His mouth dropped open at the view.

The Godswood stretched for miles in all directions, an ocean of green leaves rustling in the evening breeze, peppered with brown and orange to signal autumn's imminent approach. Above it, the sun dipped in the sky. Orange and pink stained the blue background. A handful of clouds dusted the horizon, pierced by sun rays.

Malcolm stumbled to the edge of the platform, gripping the railing hard as he stared over the forest. He turned in a slow circle. In the distance, behind Anwyn, the Caeleste Peaks rose over the trees, larger than he'd expected them to be. He looked away quickly, turning back to the setting sun.

"We have a few platforms like this, supported by several trees at once." Anwyn's voice drifted from behind him. "Be careful near the edges, it's a long drop. I'll go and get us some drinks and perhaps a blanket or two. It can get quite cold as night descends."

Malcolm whipped around as Anwyn's footsteps retreated, the knot in his chest a little tighter after seeing the Peaks.

"Wait, before you go."

She paused on the stairs to look back at him.

"Do you have the facilities for me to send a letter to Cerulya? My sister works at the palace. I wish to give her an update about our journey."

"Of course. I'll bring up some parchment and we can send a woodpigeon with it in the morning."

Malcolm nodded. "Please do not say anything to the—I mean, to Anne. I would hate for her to worry."

Anwyn smiled. "Your secret is safe with me."

"Thank you," he blurted. "For all of your kindness."

She smiled a moment longer and continued on her way.

Malcolm turned back around and lost himself in the view. The pressure in his chest eased as long as he didn't glance at the mountains.

At some point, Anwyn returned with hot drinks, paper, and a quill.

Malcolm scribbled a note on the parchment she'd brought, addressing it to Leena. He chose his words carefully, in case any curious eyes peeked at his letter before it reached his sister's hands. He described the hospitality of the Meteile they were staying with and informed her about a detour they were planning to make through the Caeleste Peaks, hoping she would understand. As long as Graman and Viv were monitoring Leena's communications, as they'd agreed, they would be able to send backup ahead to meet Malcolm in case Leena and Theo didn't make it to him in time. Silently, he thanked the thief for being so open about her destination.

When he finished, Anwyn disappeared with the letter down the stairs. On her return, they sat beside each other in content quiet, watching the stars slowly blink to life above them. Malcolm lay back on the wooden deck to gaze at the familiar constellations, the ones he'd spent so much time observing whilst growing up.

Homesickness smothered him. Graman had taught Malcolm

about star maps and constellations for hours outside of their designated time together when he and the king had learnt about Malcolm's love of the night sky. What was Graman doing now? Was he helping Viv? Were Viv and his family coping, shut in the suite with his father's body?

He let his anxieties ebb away, floating up to the stars. Those twinkling lights above were a reminder that things were much bigger than him and his problems. His gaze naturally sought out his favourite constellation, the Time Turner, shaped like two triangles atop one another, connected by one of their points. It represented Mortus and the Underworld, a reminder that all life ended.

Malcolm didn't notice Luelle arrive until she was nudging him from the space Anwyn had vacated earlier. She was lying beside him, wrapped in a blanket.

"We should get some rest," the thief murmured. "I want to get moving as early as we can tomorrow."

He stared at her. Her skin shone silver, illuminated by the light of the stars and the waning moon. She didn't look like someone that could commit treason and hurt a helpless old man in this light, but the night hid a lot of flaws.

He nodded and pushed himself up.

# 17

Luelle woke before the prince, her body still in its familiar routine of waking just after sunrise to start chores, as she'd had to in the castle. Pale, early morning sunlight filtered through the thin fabric over the window to her right.

Soft snores drifted from the prince's open mouth. Luelle watched him for several breaths. His peaceful expression, framed by a tangled mess of hair, was at odds with his usual bearing towards her.

She hadn't said much to him last night. Guilt nibbled at her for abandoning him so she could have fun with Trent, but he'd been content to sit in sullen silence all through dinner, leaving her to do all of their talking and she'd needed the break. It wasn't her style to shy away from new experiences like this, anyway. She'd spent so long cooped up in the castle with no friends, no real life, she'd grab any opportunity for fun and friendship now, any opportunity to feel alive again.

Anwyn had looked after the prince in her absence, taking

him to the viewing platforms above the Meteile camp. Luelle wasn't sure he'd even noticed when she'd given up dancing and come to lay beside him.

She got up from her mattress and crept to the bathing room to refresh and slip some clean clothes on. Another new set each had been waiting on their beds when they'd returned to the room last night, along with a pot of cream and a note instructing Malcolm to use it on his nose to soothe the remaining inflammation.

Luelle let the prince continue sleeping once she was dressed. She left her backpack on the bed so he would know she hadn't run off without him, since he still didn't trust she wouldn't. After losing her dagger, there was nothing in the bag she cared about him stealing if he rifled through it in her absence.

She glanced over at him a final time, but his weapons were hidden from sight. It wasn't worth the risk of waking him to try and find his dagger.

Anwyn was waiting at the Core when Luelle reached it, seated at a square table by herself. A smattering of Meteile lounged at the tables around her. Their quiet, murmured conversations were a shadow of last night's noise.

"How did you sleep?" Anwyn asked as Luelle slid into the seat opposite her.

"Well, thank you. Mac is still sleeping. I thought I'd let him rest a bit longer before we leave if that's alright."

"Of course. I imagine he needs it, after everything."

Luelle eyed her. What had Anwyn and Malcolm discussed when Luelle had been busy dancing? She'd been a fool to leave him alone, no matter how much she'd needed the release of stress and energy. The prince was nowhere near as practised when it came to lying and maintaining a false identity. If he'd let something slip to their host, it could be much harder for Luelle to make it through the Godswood. Evading Cerulyan soldiers would be easy enough since they were as unfamiliar with the territory as she, but the Meteile knew these woods better than anyone.

And there was a chance the prince hadn't slipped up at all but had given the truth freely. It was no secret that he wanted to take Luelle back to the capital. Did he hope to find allies among these people? She wouldn't hesitate to use the Power against them if she needed to, he must know that. Or had he guessed that her control was tenuous at best?

She struggled to gain hold of her panic but fought to keep a blank expression until she knew more.

"Did you get much out of him last night? He's usually pretty quiet."

Anwyn took a sip from her drink. "A little. He told me he'd recently lost someone."

Luelle nodded once. "He's been finding it hard, but I'm hoping the journey will keep his mind off it." She changed the subject before Anwyn could press for further details. If she knew the truth, she wouldn't hide it in vague statements like that. "Where can I get some breakfast?"

"Let me show you." Anwyn stood, brushing off her skirts.

Luelle followed her across the Core in silence, hoping to avoid any more probing into their backstory. Trent hadn't been so invasive last night. He'd been happy to dance together, filling the quiet between them with raucous laughter, wandering hands, and heated stares rather than conversation. If Anwyn kept asking questions, Luelle would forsake breakfast and wake Malcolm early. Despite the Meteile's kindness, she still had a job to do. Getting held up here wasn't an option.

Several tables had been moved into a line along one edge of the Core. Behind them, a row of unfamiliar Meteile prepared fresh fruit, slicing it into bite-sized pieces and layering colourful handfuls into bowls, atop a mixture of nuts and oats.

Luelle joined the short queue, stepping back to let Anwyn go first. When she reached the front, an elderly Meteile woman with sand-coloured skin and eyes as grey as a storm handed her a bowl of food and a cup of hot tea.

Back at their original table, Luelle ate in silence, watching the Core grow busier. When Malcolm turned up, his hair was only slightly smoother than it had been whilst he was sleeping but his face looked dangerously close to normal, thanks to the cream Anwyn had left on his bed. He'd chosen to wear his leather armour again, though he must have left his sword in their room, as he had last night. Against the surrounding Meteile's casual attire, the prince's clothing made him look particularly fierce.

Luelle stayed at the table alone while Anwyn showed him where to get his own breakfast. Her knee bounced beneath the wood. Time was dragging this morning. A night of proper rest had rejuvenated her; she itched to continue her journey.

"Are you sure you must leave us so soon?" Anwyn asked when she and Malcolm were re-seated across from Luelle.

Luelle nodded. "We have a long trek ahead."

"Well, at least let us offer a few extra supplies to take with you. You'll need them if you're set on travelling all the way to the Iron City."

"Thank you, that's very kind." Luelle smiled.

Anwyn left, promising to drop the supplies at their room.

"Did you sleep well?" Luelle was the first to break the silence.

"We have no need to make small talk."

Luelle raised her eyebrows at the near-empty bowl in front of her.

"Alright."

They ate in silence, smothering Luelle's hope that the rest of their journey would be as fun as last night. Instead, they'd return to their usual routine of ignoring one another until it was necessary to bicker about food or a location to camp.

After they'd cleared their places, they returned to their room, almost colliding with Pansy and Anwyn on one of the walkways. Pansy was carrying a bundle of stacked, folded fabric, whilst Anwyn held a bag similar to the one Luelle had stashed in their room. The two Meteile women accompanied them, chatting aimlessly, oblivious to Luelle's rising impatience to be gone.

At their bedroom, Luelle opened the door to let the others in first.

Malcolm moved straight to his bed, where he started strapping on his sword. Luelle eyed his dagger in its sheath at the prince's waist but felt no closer to gaining his trust in order to obtain the weapon for herself. If they encountered any bandits, she'd have to rely completely on the Prince for defence, unless she could wrangle some control over her Power.

He caught her staring at the small, sheathed blade and tensed, hand falling to rest possessively on the handle. She averted her eyes.

Pansy and Anwyn helped them repack Luelle's bag and pack the second they were providing for Malcolm. Luelle didn't miss the shy glances Pansy took at Malcolm when his attention was elsewhere. She bit down on a smile, wondering if the young Meteile would be any bolder if she knew who she was really interacting with.

In the palace, a few nobles and servants had been brazen in their interactions with the prince but most were like Pansy, content to admire from afar at all hours of the day. How did he cope with it all? Was he really so oblivious to the constant attention? Luelle would go insane if she suffered from the same lack of privacy.

Anwyn and Luelle wrinkled their noses in unison at the spare set of clothes Luelle pulled from her backpack to repack her supplies.

"Uh, can I leave these here?" Luelle held them up, still wrapped in the white sheet.

Anwyn nodded but threw the bundle onto the walkway outside the room so they didn't have to continue breathing in the stench as they prepared to leave.

As well as two fresh sets of clothing each, Anwyn gifted them two blankets for the cold nights, a spare water flask, and filled every spare inch of space in their bags with food—jerky, flatbread, fruits, nuts and vegetables, all wrapped in large leaves and tied with rough, slender twine.

She bade them farewell with a warm hug.

"Tell Trent I said goodbye." Luelle smiled at the woman as they broke apart. She nodded a small goodbye to Pansy.

"Of course. You must call in on us again if you ever return to the Godswood."

Malcolm nodded, his smile tired but genuine.

She and the prince descended to the forest floor down the same staircase Anwyn had first led them up and traipsed off east. Luelle glanced up whenever there was a break in the trees to ensure their path wasn't straying too far from the direction they needed to travel in. She hoped to cut off a chunk of distance by walking diagonally to the Caeleste River, rather than heading back to where it and the Ophidian Channel met, further downstream.

Her bag straps wore familiar grooves into her shoulders, though the weight of their replenished supplies was less than that of the silence between them. One night of relaxing would never have eradicated the tension, but it had been nice to be free of the burden for a while.

After several hours of walking, Luelle realised she couldn't hear the prince's heavy footfall behind her own.

As she turned, the ring of a sword sliding from its scabbard sliced through the air.

Any warmth that had been on Malcolm's face when parting from the Meteile had disappeared. He glared at Luelle, feet spread in a fighting stance, sword unsheathed and pointed at her chest.

"What are you doing?" Luelle asked, more aware than ever that she was unarmed. Her only defence was the stupid Power in her chest that she couldn't control. Even a child's wooden training sword would be better.

"I will not continue this game any longer. You have wasted enough of my time." The prince's quiet voice trembled. "We are returning to the capital."

Luelle didn't move, eyes flickering from Malcolm's face to the blade clutched in his large hand. His other hand was balled into a tight fist.

"You know I'm not going to agree to that."

"I am not asking!" Malcolm half-shouted the words. The blade shook. He gripped it tighter. "Today was supposed to be my coronation. My family cannot even lay my father to rest because I am pandering to the whims of a stubborn thief rather than taking back what is rightfully mine."

Now didn't feel like the best time to correct that statement once more.

Luelle had forgotten that King Alaric's public funeral would have happened yesterday, the day before Malcolm's coronation. Outside the capital, where news took so much longer to circulate, life seemed to pass at a slower pace.

She swallowed. "I'm sorry about Alaric—"

"I told you not to say his name," Malcolm interrupted her, his voice low. He stepped closer but Luelle retreated in line with him, keeping the same distance between them. "Do not ever say his name again."

She took a deep breath. "I'm not stopping you from going

home." Her palms were clammy with sweat.

"You are coming with me."

Luelle didn't drop eye contact with the prince across the clearing, but she said nothing. She made no move closer.

"Damn it!" Malcolm exclaimed, mouth curling into a snarl. "Stop messing me around. I am finished with this delay. You have already killed my father, stolen my family's Power and my time to mourn—" His words broke off in a choke. He blinked hard and swallowed, face paling. When he'd regained his composure, the prince raised his sword and closed the distance between them in several quick strides, the point of his blade inches from Luelle's throat.

She raised her hands, slowly, her mouth suddenly dry.

"Don't make me force you," he murmured.

She met his hateful glare with a grim stare of her own. They stood, frozen, in a tense impasse.

But she couldn't return with him. She'd worked too long and hard for this. She had sacrificed the only life she'd known to put the balance of the world to rights and to do so without hurting the prince, as some other Veseile hoped to do. Could he not see that?

Luelle lowered her hands to her sides and edged forwards, close enough that swallowing would prick her skin against the point of the blade. Malcolm's eyes widened at her movement. Did he know what would happen to the Power if that blade slashed across her throat? The weapon trembled in his hand.

"Well, Prince, we're going to run into a problem pretty quickly because I'm not returning to Cerulya. You can try to force me and we can fight again, but I'd give up my life to see this through. How far are you willing to go? Would you kill me for this? *Could* you?"

Malcolm flinched at her last few words. His stare roamed her face, mouth twisted downwards in a sorrowful frown.

Their stalemate continued for several more racing heartbeats, Malcolm pointing his sword at Luelle's throat and her welcoming the blade.

She meant every word she said to him. She'd rather die than fail in her mission, though she'd fight to her death to evade the prince, even if she had no desire to kill him.

Malcolm twisted away from her, letting the tip of his blade drop to the ground.

"Just go." His voice was a whisper.

Luelle stared at the intricate scales of armour covering his back, shocked into stillness.

"What?"

"Go! Leave me!" he shouted at her but turned away once more and flung his sword across the clearing. Light glinted on the short blade as it spun before hitting the ground with a thud. The prince crouched and fisted his hands in his dark hair.

Luelle backed away, before turning and running from the clearing.

She sprinted through the forest, weaving between the hundred tree trunks until her breath was tearing from her chest and she could hear the Caeleste River rushing in the distance.

She stumbled to a stop, looking over her shoulder to make sure the prince hadn't pursued her, intent to follow through with his threat. His angry words and vicious accusations echoed in her mind.

She leaned against a tree trunk, breathing hard. She rubbed at the tension between her brows, willing her heartbeat to calm its rapid pace.

Continuing without the prince was what she needed, what she'd been yearning for, for days. He'd been a drain on her progress and her mood, not to mention that he was bound to get himself hurt or killed on their journey. In all honesty, it would be a miracle if he made it back to the capital in one piece, but without him slowing her down, Luelle would reach her destination sooner. She could leave behind the royals for good. She could return to her friends and liberate the Power that should belong to her entire race, not just to one person.

She should be celebrating.

So why did she feel so bad?

# 18

Malcolm remained in the quiet clearing, hunched over his knees until his body grew stiff. Birds sang cheerful melodies around him, taunting his depressive state with their innocent joy. Sweet wildflowers rode to him on a gentle, cool breeze that pushed at the curls in his hair, sweeping them against his face. The fine hairs at the back of his neck rose in response to the chill.

Under regular circumstances, he would be named king today, but so far he'd done nothing to prove himself worthy of the title. Throughout his childhood, Malcolm had idolised his father, shadowing the king and throwing himself into his studies so he could live up to the example Alaric set. As his father aged, Malcolm had known losing him would feel like receiving a wound that would never heal. However, he hadn't known how hard it would be to realise he would never be half the ruler nor half the man his father had been.

If Alaric could see him now, he would only feel disappointment.

On this journey, Malcolm had succeeded in wasting his own time, abandoning his family when they needed him the most, and letting the thief that stole his Power leave, rather than dragging her back to the capital for a just punishment. As far as his people knew, his father wasn't even dead yet—if Viv had succeeded in deceiving everyone, as they'd planned.

He could still track Luelle. Unless he died, he would never escape the pull of his Power in her body—even now he could feel it retreating from him—but what was the point in following it? She'd been right to call his bluff. He didn't want to kill her, even if he had a guarantee that his Power would remain unscathed and would return to him.

He was a coward.

He'd killed before; his father had insisted it happen early in life so he became accustomed with the practice, able to do it to protect his realm if necessary. Memories of the first time it had happened were blurry, untouched in some distant part of Malcolm's mind. Only glimpses of the day remained, haunting him at night when he was unable to sleep; passing recollections of his father's tight-lipped expression, acid burning in his throat as he vomited until nothing came up, Leena and Theo sitting with him in his chambers long into the night while he sobbed. He'd had better control after that first time, knowing more what to expect. In his teenage years, Malcolm had accompanied knights and soldiers on frequent missions to eliminate bandits, and death was a common sight at tourneys, whether accidental or not. But, ending someone's life, human or Eile, never became natural or comfortable for him, no matter how much his father had insisted it would with time.

Malcolm lost track of the time he spent beating himself up in the small, circular clearing. He lost himself in grief for his father, for his family, his kingdom, and himself. When his tears dried up, they were replaced by a sharp, throbbing headache.

His sword lay, abandoned, on the ground not far from him.

Since Luelle left, the forest felt quieter, though the same birds sang and the same small mammals scurried in the branches above. It made no sense since he and the thief hadn't spoken much to one another during their time together. She had tried to initiate more conversation than him, but it always descended into an argument and sullen silence, since he still could not look at her without seeing his father on his deathbed.

His own words echoed in his mind. Of course, he knew they were false; Luelle hadn't killed his father. Malcolm had been by the king's side when death claimed him, but blaming someone, someone who had already wronged him, eased the darkness that had settled over him since that night, even if only a little.

He rubbed at his face with a calloused hand. No matter how strong his despair, Malcolm could not cower in this clearing forever. The world hadn't stopped turning in time with his grief. He pushed himself to his feet, stooping for his sword and re-sheathing it.

Two options remained for him—return home and admit to Viv and his mother that he'd failed or retrieve his Power.

The former was out of the question. He had to follow the thief to the end of this journey. His family were sacrificing so much to give him the opportunity to retrieve it, he couldn't let that be in vain. Besides, no monarch in written history had been crowned without the Power dwelling in their chest. His people may very well reject him if he was too weak to recover it. As long as Viv's plan was working, the ceremony would be delayed whether he turned back now or in a few days. He needed to track Luelle down and hope that Viv sent soldiers to intercept them at the Caeleste Peaks when she received his letter.

However, the thief could be anywhere by now. Malcolm was capable of blindly following the pull of his Power, his earlier tracking had proven that, but if Luelle wanted to evade him out here, she was more than capable. Compared to her, he knew nothing of surviving in the wild. He hadn't even known how to de-shell a craybug.

There was only one thing for it. He had to find her, fast.

He brushed the dirt from his armour and looked around. Every part of the Godswood looked the same, but the pull in his chest was a fraction stronger from one direction, so he trusted his gut and started walking.

Should he apologise to Luelle when he found her again? He hadn't lashed out because of what she'd done, though he still hated her for that and had every right to. She was a criminal. She'd committed treason and she was putting the balance of his kingdom and rule at risk. But, something made him believe her when she promised to return his Power once they reached this supposed pilgrimage site. He'd get it back when she realised she was wrong about it all. It was hardly her fault she'd been brainwashed to believe a false history. Deep down, he pitied her for that.

No, he'd lashed out primarily because of his anger towards himself, in part fuelled by his failure to retrieve his Power, but mostly for yesterday.

Whilst his family were back home, living in a room with his father's decaying corpse and pretending that the king was still alive, Malcolm was conversing with strangers, learning about his people, and watching the sunset over the Godswood. He was... having fun. He enjoyed being away from the castle, being around people that didn't recognise him or adjust their interactions with him based on his role as prince.

Failing to get Luelle back to the capital, being unable to kill her—he could excuse himself for those things. Leena and Theo always joked he was too soft-hearted, and he had no desire to get himself slaughtered if the thief turned his Power against him. But, enjoying himself while he gallivanted through the country days after his father had died? Allowing himself to believe the false truth he'd created, that the king was still alive, to ease his own conscience? That was unforgivable.

Malcolm listened for Luelle as he walked, straining to hear her soft, crunching footsteps or her melodic humming. If she had any respect for his dignity, she wouldn't taunt him for crawling back to her. She must know he couldn't find his way home without her, anyway.

He strolled through endless trees, hearing nothing more than his own heavy footsteps. Somehow, in Luelle's absence, he'd even managed to lose the Caeleste River, one of the largest, longest rivers in his kingdom. He'd tried walking in the direction Luelle had fled from the clearing, but it felt as though he was traipsing in circles.

Despair grew in Malcolm's chest with each step he took. Several times he stopped to reassess, but every inch of the Godswood was identical. Soon his legs began to ache. His shoes rubbed and pinched at his toes and heels but he persevered.

Fat raindrops started pattering through the canopy of leaves above. Malcolm sighed. This was just his luck. He shoved his hair away from his face and upped his speed.

A glimpse of grey stone broke up the monotony of greens and browns in front of him.

Malcolm peered at the anomaly through the gaps between the trees and stumbled forward to find out more, uncaring of any potential strangers. Perhaps he would find some shelter from the rain. Or perhaps Luelle would be here. The pull in his chest felt stronger than it had earlier.

How would she react to his return? He had threatened her, there was no misinterpreting that situation. Would she want to retaliate?

He wiped the rain from his face and approached the stone with renewed caution.

No noise drifted from up ahead. He edged forward, emerging in front of a small, overgrown temple. Several neat rows of headstones stood before it, lining either side of a mossy, cracked path. Crawling plants sought to obscure the path to the temple as much as they attempted to take over the building itself.

Malcolm paused. Though the forest was claiming back the space here, there was still a clear line of sight to the sky, leaving him vulnerable to the full brunt of the rain. He pushed his hair back once again, fighting the urge to shiver at the chill water on his face. His throat constricted at the sight of the small cemetery.

Without thinking, he moved to the first gravestone and knelt in the wet dirt before it. His thoughts strayed to his father. If not for their status, would he lie below a stone like this, forgotten and uncared for? Would Malcolm, in turn, be forgotten when his body was cold in the crypts underneath the castle?

Using his short fingernails, he scraped away the damp moss and plants that were infiltrating the stone. Beneath them, the gravestone was bare. Signs of age marred its surface but no tools had scored a name into its pocked face.

Frowning, Malcolm moved along each row, cleaning off the headstones as he went. All were blank.

When all of the stones were cleared of debris, he stood to gaze at them. A tremor rocked through his body at the chill of the rain.

Who was buried here? Was it a local practice to bury people in the forest with no indication of their identity? He'd read of no such tradition in the journal he'd briefly examined, back in the Meteile camp.

Though he had no way of knowing their names or when they'd lived, Malcolm hoped the people buried here would appreciate the time he'd taken to clean the small portion of forest devouring their resting place.

He brushed the dirt from his knees and strayed closer to the temple's entrance. Like the headstones, the temple walls were made from crumbling grey stone. Cobwebs obscured part of the entrance, stretching from wall to column. Malcolm ducked underneath them, into the shadows of the shelter, taking a break from the fat raindrops.

The pull of his Power remained a consistent pressure. Like him, Luelle must be sheltering from the rain, which, if the blanket of grey clouds were any indication, wouldn't be stopping any time soon, so Malcolm retreated into the building. He may as well dry off a bit before finding her again or getting further lost in an attempt to find her.

Inside, the temple was larger than he'd expected, stretching long and thin. At the far end of the room, a small statue of Meto, the God of Agriculture and Harvest, stood on a stone plinth. Behind it, the roof and part of the wall had collapsed inward. Beams of muted light shone through onto the depiction of the God, highlighting their outstretched arms and mane of feathers, each individual one carved with extraordinary detail.

A slim, cracked path led to the statue, framed on either side with rows of low stone benches.

Malcolm strolled further inside, peering into the shadows at the walls.

Each wall, unlike the bare gravestones outside, was etched with lines and lines of text, columns of words spanning the entire room. He squinted at the script, just about able to read them in the lack of moonstone light. Starting at the entrance, the text described how all six Gods worked together to create the world and humans, but their ambitions didn't stop there.

Individually each God built on the template humans provided to make a distinct race of new human-like creatures—the Eile. They bestowed gifts like a longer lifespan and greater strength, speed, and stamina; any traits they desired to create the ideal people to represent them on earth. Five of the Eile races lived on earth alongside the humans. The Moreile were the only ones chosen to live elsewhere, instead assisting Mortus in caring for the dead souls in the Underworld. Though humans and Eile alike worshipped all six Gods, each Eile race fostered a particular devotion to the God that had created them. The etchings on these walls paid specific attention to the Meteile people, hailing them as the protectors of the natural world.

It was the same tale that had been drummed into Malcolm, like every other child in the kingdom, from a young age.

He wandered the length of the temple and back to the door as he read, relishing the nostalgia of the tale. The final section described the Gods departing their realm, leaving behind humans and Eile to live in harmony and worship their creators from afar.

This was the part of the creation story that most sane people knew to be a myth, though a few stubborn zealots, like Luelle, believed it in a literal sense. The Gods had never truly walked the earth alongside their creation. Malcolm ran his fingers over the grooves in the stone, tracing the lines and curves of the letters.

What would the world be like if it was true—if the Gods could walk among them? Would people still suffer? Would his role as a leader and protector be redundant?

His stomach grumbled, interrupting his philosophies. He was about to turn back to the benches to eat some of his food when a noise outside the temple made him freeze.

Footsteps.

He glanced around the building, searching for somewhere to

hide from whoever was approaching but the benches were too low to conceal him and the plinth and statue too slender. The hole in the roof at the back of the temple was too high to climb through. Besides, whoever was outside would see the clean gravestones and know a stranger was in the area. The temple would be the first place they checked and the front door he'd walked through was the only viable exit.

He was trapped in here. Getting outside was vital but he wouldn't make it away without being seen by whoever was out there. The Meteile they'd encountered had been safe, friendly, even. Could these strangers be the same?

Malcolm slid off his bag and placed it just inside the doorway so whoever was out there had less to grab at if it came down to a fight. He drew his sword and stepped into the doorway, his entire body strung tight. His eyes took a moment to adjust to the daylight.

Outside, two slender men walked towards the temple, eyeing the newly cleaned graves. Malcolm's heart pounded. From here, they looked human, no visible traits suggesting Eile heritage.

They slowed to a stop several feet away from Malcolm as he stepped into the temple's entrance.

"Who are you?" one asked—a man with short, thinning, brown hair. His voice croaked, emerging from between chapped, cracked lips.

"I want no trouble," Malcolm said, keeping his weapon lowered. Perhaps he should've kept his bag on so he didn't leave behind any of his things if he had to flee. Blood roared in his ears. He'd trained in multiple forms of combat for two decades.

Two human civilians posed no real threat to him, particularly two as malnourished as this, but he had no desire to hurt his people and knowing he was approaching a potentially hostile situation without any allies was an unfamiliar, discomforting feeling. It set him on edge.

The men exchanged glances and turned back to look him up and down, swaying where they stood. Their pupils were blown out, obscuring almost all of the colour in their irises.

"We don't get many strangers in these parts." The second man slurred as he spoke, taking a lurching step forward. His breath whistled through the gap where one of his front teeth was absent.

Malcolm held his ground, tensing and spreading his weight in anticipation of conflict.

"I will take my leave now."

"Don't leave on our account. We can all share this space, and anything else we might have." The brown-haired man smiled at him. Hungry eyes wandered over Malcolm's body and flickered to the temple entrance, scouring the shadows. Raindrops slid down the man's face, running into unblinking eyes.

"Or do you think you're too good to share your things with us, little Godling?" The gap-toothed man's tone soured.

Malcolm was familiar with the derogatory moniker some humans gave to Eile, though this was the first time it had been directed his way. Most Eile shrugged off the term, but humans rarely intended 'Godling' as a compliment. Rather, it was an insult mocking their supposed heritage from the Gods and the superiority that some Eile believed came with it.

Malcolm looked between the men. It probably wasn't worth telling them he was only half-Eile. In his experience, it had the opposite of the desired effect, making him seem all the more alien. What would Leena or Theo say to diffuse this situation?

What would Luelle say?

"That's a nice sword," the gap-toothed man continued when Malcolm stayed quiet. "Did you steal it?" His fingers twitched at his sides.

"No."

The gap-toothed man turned to the other stranger, raising his eyebrows. "Must be pretty wealthy if he didn't steal something like that."

"Yeah, talks like a nobleman and all. Wonder if he's got any other valuables here." The brunette man's eyes roamed Malcolm's outfit. The amulet against his chest burned under that gaze but there was no way the stranger could see it through the leather.

Malcolm's heart raced.

"I have nothing but some clothes and food. I want no trouble, I just wish to continue on my way."

"We're not stopping you." The gap-toothed man's smile was sinister.

Malcolm took a step back into the temple where his bag awaited. The brown-haired man followed him, closing the distance between them.

Malcolm raised the tip of his blade, halting the human in his tracks. He was pinned against the temple. If he went any further inside, it would be harder to fight them off. The gap-toothed human watched their standoff with bulging eyes, from the other side of the gravestones.

Malcolm continued holding his weapon up as he leant sideways to pick up his bag, but the brunette man darted forward. Malcolm reacted on instinct, slashing at the outstretched arm.

The man retreated in a spray of crimson, shouting out as the blade cut through his hand. He raised his palm in front of his face and stared, uncomprehending at the gushing stumps where fingers used to be. Four pink digits lay on the grass, leaking blood.

"Stay back," Malcolm warned. The man had to be intoxicated by something to display such an aloof reaction to losing his fingers like that. He should be in agony.

The man clutched his injured hand but didn't retreat further than a few steps. His gap-toothed friend froze by the gravestones, eyes glued to the nubs of flesh on the ground.

On his second attempt, Malcolm grabbed the strap of his bag from inside the temple and swung it over one shoulder. He switched his sword to his left hand to place the other strap on, glaring at the brunette man, who watched, waiting for another opening, injured hand dangling at his side. Blood dripped steadily onto the grass. His irises were almost entirely black.

As Malcolm passed his sword back to his lead hand, the brunette man moved again. Malcolm leapt out of the doorway and swung at him, slicing into his bicep, but the uneven, rain-damp ground outside the temple left him off balance and unable to press the advantage. He stumbled backwards, away from the temple, gripping his sword tighter to keep from dropping it. He backed away from the doorway and edged along the first row of gravestones, keeping the tip of his blade pointed in the general direction of the two strangers. Retreating towards the treeline, he kept the temple to his left so his sword arm was free to swing. The humans followed his slow steps, refusing to let any distance grow between them. Any pretence of friendliness had vanished. The brunette man was unfazed by the blood he was losing.

As Malcolm reached the edge of the temple, a sharp blow connected behind his ear.

He staggered sideways, grunting at the pain cracking through his already aching head. He spun. The back of his fist connected with a short figure. A new, feminine voice cried out in pain but Malcolm had no time to stop and examine his third enemy—the first two men took advantage of his distraction and were sprinting towards him. He had to escape but knew he'd have no room to use his sword in the forest. If he had any hopes of escaping quickly, he needed to stay in the clearing and eliminate the threat altogether.

He stumbled away from the temple and the unseen enemy behind it. With some distance to protect him from any more surprises, Malcolm turned and lashed out at the brunette man he'd already injured, attempting to take out the closer, weaker target first.

It didn't take long.

The man was no fighter. He tried to evade Malcolm's strikes, but either the drugs he was on or his injuries made his movements sluggish and awkward. His bleeding hand swung at his side, a dead, pendulous weight. The man's eyes widened as Malcolm's blade cut deep into his stomach, spraying the nearest gravestone with blood. He dropped to his knees, clutching at the gaping wound. The man's intestines spilled out into his hands. Blood oozed between the gaps in his fingers, saturating his clothes. He sank sideways, the light in his eyes fading.

Malcolm spun towards his next victim, blinking blood and rain from his vision.

He stepped past the dying brown-haired human, closing in on the gap-toothed man, but as he drew back his sword, Malcolm was pulled off balance by someone yanking his bag. He lost his footing in the slippery gore coating the ground and fell on his back. His sword flew from his grip, clanging against a headstone a few feet away.

The woman who had been hiding behind the temple had snuck around and pulled him off-balance, but she didn't stick around to fight him. She fled towards the temple again as he fell, a blur of dirty clothing and bare feet.

Malcolm scrambled to his feet as soon as he hit the ground. He shook his hair from his eyes, smearing blood out of his vision with his forearm. The gap-toothed man was running towards his sword.

Malcolm leapt through the air, clearing a headstone to tackle the man before he reached the weapon. The human grunted as he took the impact of their fall. They scrambled in the dirt together, wrestling for control of the hold. The man's bones jutted out further than any healthy human's should, but whatever drugs were flowing through his bloodstream fuelled his strength, providing more of a challenge than Malcolm expected.

After a few seconds of grappling, Malcolm freed his left arm and yanked his dagger from his belt. He thrust it into the man's chest. The stranger's eyes bulged. Malcolm drew back and stabbed him again and again, gritting his teeth together in a silent snarl. Grief, rage, and frustration poured from him with each thrust of his blade. He lost himself in the emotion as he made a pincushion of the man's chest, forgetting the third enemy lurking in the temple's shadows.

# 19

Luelle trudged through the forest, retracing her steps in the direction she'd left the prince. Rain filtered through the leaves above, plastering loose strands of hair to the sides of her face and dripping from her lashes onto her cheeks like tears. She'd left her cloak at the bottom of her bag, not unpacking it after the first few drops fell in the hopes that it would be a fleeting shower.

It hadn't been. But, getting the cloak out now would be a silent admission that she was wrong about something else, not just about leaving Malcolm behind.

She didn't dwell on her reasons for seeking out the prince again but once she'd made the decision, it had been easy to find his tracks. After returning to the area in which they'd parted ways, she simply followed the path with the most destruction.

The prince was very heavy-footed.

It was a bad idea to follow him. He'd instructed her to leave. He'd made his feelings quite clear—he didn't like her, didn't trust her, and didn't want to continue with her to the Caeleste Peaks.

But, there was no way he would find his way back home alone. The least she could do was escort him back to the Meteile camp they'd left this morning. One day of travelling in the wrong direction wouldn't harm her overall mission that much, and he'd be much safer in Anwyn's company. It was the right thing to do.

So why did the thought of confronting him again fill her with such unease?

Why was it so hard to face such blatant dislike from a person she barely knew? It should be a familiar feeling after her lonely years working in the castle. Outside the palace, Cerulya's people had been warm and affectionate but no one within the castle walls had bothered trying to connect with her. She couldn't have entertained it if they had but it would've been nice if some had tried.

Luelle clenched her fists and took a deep, shaking breath, picking up her pace.

She was stronger than this. She could face another uncomfortable conversation, another argument—whatever this reunion would be.

Leaves and sticks crunched under her feet as she walked. She lost herself in her brooding thoughts until a distant shout jerked her from her daydreams. Luelle froze, holding her breath to hear better. Someone cried out in pain.

Alarm washed over her in a cold wave. The voices were coming from the direction that the prince's path led.

She broke into a sprint, weaving between trees and following the noise until a small temple came into view. In the cemetery before it, Malcolm was straddling an unfamiliar man.

The prince was panting heavily, covered in blood and staring at the blank face of the body beneath him. His arms hung loose at his sides, shoulders slumped, dagger almost falling from his fingers.

A scrawny woman approached him from behind, taking slow, careful steps to remain unseen. Both of her bony hands were wrapped around the hilt of Malcolm's sword. She adjusted her grip, attempting to find the best hold to raise the weapon above her head.

Luelle didn't stop to think.

She ran towards the woman and leapt, tackling the stranger around the waist before the woman could get a proper grip on the sword. The prince's blade scattered to the floor, leaving him unharmed.

Momentum carried Luelle and the stranger into a nearby headstone. Both of them grunted in pain. Hitting and pulling at whatever parts of the woman she could, Luelle fought, suffering as many scratches and whacks as she doled out. The gaunt woman managed to wriggle higher and wedge a foot against the headstone, pushing herself away from it and shoving Luelle off her. She didn't pursue the fight. Instead, she scrambled to her feet and fled into the treeline behind the temple, stumbling as she ran.

The prince appeared at Luelle's side, his sword back in hand. For a second, Luelle's heart stuttered, expecting the weapon to slice down at her. Malcolm was pale beneath a layer of gore and dirt, hair messy and eyes wild. The man he'd been straddling remained on the ground, glazed eyes staring, unseeing, at the sky.

Luelle fought the urge to retch, looking at the mess that was the dead man's chest.

Malcolm held out a hand to help her stand, drawing her eyes away from the corpse. He gripped her hard to stop her hand from sliding through his, slick with the dead man's blood. It transferred to her skin. Breathing heavily, both of them scoured the surrounding forest for any more enemies. None appeared, but Luelle noticed another body lying closer to the temple, guts oozing from a long slash across his stomach. Like the first, the second human's eyes were open and glazed, his skin pallid.

She didn't need to ask what happened to them.

Luelle looked back at the prince. They stared at one another. Irregular, heavy raindrops fell as the rain slowed to a spit.

They tried breaking the silence at the same time.

"I—"

"How—"

Luelle fought an inappropriate smile, nerves squeezing her stomach tight. Would she have shared the same fate as these humans if she hadn't run from the prince?

"Uh, you go first."

"How did you find me?" The prince's eyes darted beyond her, still scanning the treeline around the clearing.

Luelle shifted where she stood, gripping the straps of her bag to stop her hands from twitching. "I tracked you."

Malcolm frowned. "How?"

"I followed the squashed plants. And then I heard the fighting."

"Oh."

He remained where he was standing, a few feet away from her, but he lowered his weapon. "Thank you for your aid."

"What happened?"

"I found this temple and went inside to get out of the rain for a bit. When I was inside, I heard footsteps and saw those two men approaching." He gestured to the bodies. "I attempted to leave but they attacked me. The woman was hiding. She must have been waiting to support them with a surprise attack."

"Did they hurt you?"

"The woman hit my head with a rock, I think, but it is a shallow cut." His hand drifted to the back of his head. Luelle couldn't tell if it came away with any fresh blood because of how much already coated his fingers.

"Do you feel okay? Any dizziness or pressure?"

He shook his head. "I am not concussed."

"We shouldn't linger here. The woman probably won't return but others might," Luelle said. "Noise inspires curiosity in these parts."

The prince stared at her for a moment but nodded. He dipped to rip some fresh moss from the ground and used it to clean his sword and dagger before sliding them back into their scabbard and sheath.

They walked away from the temple in silence, their pace fast enough to keep their heart rates high. Luelle led him until they reached the river, trying to forget the scene she'd just witnessed. Despite Zeke's talk of violence as she'd grown up, she'd never seen death as violent as that before. It was easy to forget that the prince was a trained soldier when he simply trudged behind her in silence.

She turned back to him when they stumbled into a gap between the trees large enough for them both to sit.

"Shall we eat?"

He nodded. "I cannot believe I was walking parallel to the water this entire time." He scowled at the river.

She snorted a laugh, some of the tightness in her shoulders drifting away. Unpacking one of Anwyn's food parcels revealed a selection of dried meats, bruised fruit, and baked oat bars, all misshapen from rolling around on the ground with the human woman at the temple.

Luelle didn't look at the prince as he unpacked his own meal but the tension in the air between them was a heavy weight pushing against her. She ignored it as she ate.

By the time she finished her last mouthful, Luelle had plucked up enough courage to speak again.

"I never hurt your father," she blurted, replying to the angry words he'd spat much earlier that day. The accusation that she'd killed the king had repeated in her mind on a loop since leaving the prince. She stared at her hands as she spoke, tearing the leaf that had held her food together into tiny pieces.

"I... I cared for him, by the end. I didn't think I would. I certainly didn't want to, but he was kind and funny. He always talked to me when I was working, even just to ask about the other tasks lined up in my day. He saw a lot more than people realised, before... before those last few weeks. I didn't expect his decline to be so abrupt. Sometimes, I wonder if he knew my reasons for working in the castle were a lie, if he could see how troubled I felt at times."

The prince's eyes burned into her head but Luelle couldn't look up to meet his gaze. She pushed on, forcing the words out.

"I know he won't get the chance to understand why I had to do what I did, and I wish there had been another way, a way that didn't bring so much pain to you and your family, but I never hurt him, not that night and not before it. I deceived him. I gave him a glass sphere and told him it was the crystal. He thought I was taking it to give to you, in case you didn't arrive in time. But, I swear, I never hurt him as I took it." She glanced up, but couldn't read Malcolm's expression past the tension in his jaw.

The unease between them didn't fade as Luelle's stare returned to her hands.

For several minutes, only the rushing river filled the silence.

"Did he speak about me?" Malcolm's voice was quiet when he responded. "In those last two weeks, I mean."

Luelle looked at him. She swallowed at the vulnerability laid bare in his expression and nodded.

"You were all he talked about. He said less as time went on but every time he spoke it was to ask after you and your family or to tell me some tale about what a great king you would be." She wasn't sure if the answer would make him feel better or worse.

Malcolm looked away. His normally immaculate posture was hunched, making him appear smaller than usual.

She turned her attention back to tearing up the leaf in an attempt to give him a semblance of privacy in his grief. The last few pieces fluttered to the floor by the time the prince spoke again.

"Why did you come back for me?"

Luelle glanced up to find him looking at her again. His earlier vulnerability had disappeared but the sadness in his eyes remained. Walking in the sun for a few days had browned his skin further, likening his appearance more to the Queen's and disguising the shadows under his eyes.

"I didn't want to leave you alone in the forest. I know you're not as familiar with it as I am, so I'll at least escort you to the Meteile camp before I continue. I'm sure Pansy would accompany you to the capital from there. Trent said a few of them want to go when they get the chance." She turned away from the prince's heavy stare. He held so many of his emotions inside, she struggled to know what he was thinking at any point, even after days of travelling together and observing his mannerisms.

"I cannot go back to Cerulya yet. I cannot return without the Power. I will come with you to the end or until I can convince you to return the Power to me."

Luelle raised her eyebrows at him.

"I am... I apologise for threatening you." He cleared his throat and shifted on the ground, straightening to his usual height. "I do not wish to be that sort of ruler and I do not want to start my reign that way. I will not gain anyone's trust by simply killing those that defy me. As irksome as you may be, you are still one of my people, still in my duty of care."

She ignored the insult.

"Not to mention you'd lose such good company if you killed me."

He shot her a flat look. "I didn't say that."

"Don't worry, Prince. I know you were thinking it." The corners of her lips tilted up.

He rolled his eyes.

"You don't need to apologise." Her smile died. "I understand. And I hope you'll be able to understand my actions too, soon."

Malcolm exhaled a heavy breath, his eyes wandering to the water. Luelle followed his line of sight. If they stood at the water's edge and looked upstream, the mountain tops would be in clear sight over the treetops. They'd start their ascent soon, though the entrance to the cavern they were seeking wasn't too high.

"Are you sure you want to come with me? The journey won't get easier once we reach the Caeleste Peaks. And, as I've already told you, your Power will return to you as soon as it's back in its source, whether you're there in person or back in your home."

The prince nodded. "I am sure. If you are mistaken, I must be there to retrieve my Power, whatever it takes."

Luelle chewed at the inside of her cheek. She believed that. A day ago, she'd thought the prince didn't want to hurt or kill her but, for a moment during their argument, she'd believed he would follow through with his threat, whether he thought it would bring his Power back to him or not. The mutilated bodies at the temple proved he was capable of violence, willing to dole it out if he deemed it necessary.

What could trigger that reaction a second time? Would he have the same restraint if they argued again?

"What makes you so sure that you have located the source of the Power?" Malcolm asked.

Luelle toyed with the end of her braid, looking at the trees on the other side of the river as she recalled her earliest memories of the cavern. "We stumbled across a cavern when we were searching for a new place to live for a while. Zeke believes we found an ancient pilgrimage site to Vesanya. We have no idea who created it, or when, but within there's a statue of Vesanya and a larger version of your crystal relic, the one your ancestors have used to transfer the Power to one another. We believe this source is what Arabella modelled her smaller replica on."

"Do you truly believe such a thing would exist in Arazia, of all places?"

Luelle shrugged. "I don't know. It's as likely to be here as anywhere else in the world."

The prince didn't respond. Tension lined his jaw as Luelle glanced over at him.

"Are you going to try and stop me once we get there?"

He met her stare, considering her question.

"I don't know," he murmured.

Luelle swallowed. She would deal with that problem if and when it arose. If all went as planned half a decade ago, Zeke and the others would meet her at the cavern anyway. They'd keep her safe from the prince. And, once his Power was returned, he could admit she'd been right all along and return home to rule his new and improved kingdom.

"We have a few hours of daylight left today and you're still covered in blood. Go have a wash. I'll gather some firewood. Once your armour is dry enough, we can walk a bit further before we make camp for the night."

Malcolm nodded, looking down at his blood-soaked armour. He made no immediate move to stand so she remained seated beside him until he was ready to be sure that he didn't actually have a concussion. Shock jolted through her as she noticed their proximity, sitting close enough to touch one another with an outstretched arm rather than as far away as possible, as they had during their first few days travelling together. The prince didn't notice her reaction.

"Who do you think those graves belonged to? At the temple, I mean," he asked.

"Probably the priests that once served there. Or maybe a smaller Meteile community that once lived nearby."

"Do you find it sad?"

Luelle glanced at the prince. "Find what sad?"

"The fact that whoever is buried there will not have their names remembered. The headstones were covered in moss but when I cleaned them there was nothing underneath."

"You cleaned them?"

"Of course."

Luelle frowned at him but he was busy staring out over the water. She followed his gaze, watching the ever-moving flow. "Well, Prince, that's not something you'll ever have to worry about. I doubt anyone will forget your name."

She smiled hearing Malcolm huff a sigh. This was the nicest he'd been to her on their entire journey. Their argument must have gotten something out of his system. Or, perhaps he trusted her a fraction more after she'd saved him from a gruesome injury at his own sword. With any luck, the rest of their journey might not be quite so dull. He might even give her his dagger.

She got to her feet and made them a fire whilst the Prince was washing. She even managed to catch another pair of craybugs to supplement the berries and seeds they ate for their dinner. They were both warming themselves beside the flames when Malcolm started another conversation.

"Why did you choose not to use the Power earlier today?" He prodded absentmindedly at the ground with a stick that had been laying beside him.

Tension returned to her body. She met his intense stare but said nothing.

"You cannot control it, can you?"

"I used it in Tolhurst." She eyed him, uncertain whether the conversation would lead to another fight.

"Intentionally?"

Their eyes locked. She said nothing.

"What happened there?"

She took a deep breath and averted her stare, gambling on honesty. "The guards were chasing me. I took a wrong turn and was trapped between them and a wall. When I started to panic, the Power burst from me in a wave." She scrunched her nose trying to describe the force that had blasted from her.

Malcolm nodded. "I saw the buildings. The guards said you knocked them from their feet. You hurt several of them quite badly. However, that doesn't explain why you failed to use it back there."

"I didn't mean to use it in Tolhurst," Luelle confessed, clenching her fists as if the Power would spill out again at any point. Would he attack her again if she admitted that she couldn't control it?

"What do you mean?" The prince cocked his head at her. He added his stick to the fire, which consumed it with a greedy crackle.

"It just came out. Like the Power acted of its own accord, in my defence."

"Have you tried using it since then?"

"Not since then, but I had tried one time before I reached Tolhurst." Luelle frowned. "I couldn't do anything with it." Her earlier frustration returned.

"What was it like to use it?"

She shifted on the ground and turned to face the prince. "What's going on? I don't mean to complain about the conversation, because it's much nicer than passing the time in silence, but what's with this sudden change in attitude? You've ignored me for days, almost chopped my head off this morning, and now you're bursting with questions." She narrowed her eyes at him. He must be planning something.

Malcolm's fingers twitched. He avoided eye contact with her.

"I don't know. I suppose I am curious about it. The Power was a part of my father and I have spent my entire life waiting to inherit it. I have spent as much time dreading it as I have dreaming about how it would feel to wield it. If you will not return it immediately, you can at least tell me about it."

"Oh." She hadn't considered that. Of course he was curious. "Didn't you ever ask the king what it was like?"

Malcolm lifted a shoulder. "Yes, of course, but he was too

familiar with it. My grandmother died when I was a child so he inherited it from her when I was still too young to understand the implication of it. He was an expert at controlling it by the time I knew what questions I wanted to ask. Your time with it has been brief compared to his, so you are a better source for me. You must remember how it felt to absorb it."

Luelle nodded. "It would be hard to forget."

"What was it like?" he pressed.

"When it was in the glass sphere, it looked like a living thing. I put my hands on it and opened my mind, willed it into myself. It's hard to describe." She frowned. "It was warm, though. I could feel it slithering through my arms. It settled in my chest." Her hand drifted to her sternum, where the Power still lay, dormant.

"Did you feel changed?"

"A bit. Everything felt more vibrant. My senses felt heightened."

"Yet, you remain unable to use it?"

"Yeah." A bitter laugh escaped Luelle's lips. Zeke would disapprove of her failure. She must've studied the Power for nearly as long as the prince, albeit with fewer resources. Being unable to wrest the most basic level of control over it was a crushing blow to her self-esteem and not a fault she enjoyed admitting.

The fire crackled.

"I could teach you."

Luelle's head snapped towards the prince.

"If—if you swear not to use it on me, that is." Malcolm's

expression was stern.

"Why would you offer that knowing I could use it to hurt you?" She searched every inch of the prince's face for the answer to her question.

"You protected me at the temple. You had no reason to since our last interaction involved me threatening you, so I believe that you do not want me dead. And, since you refuse to return the Power to me, it is actually more dangerous for me to travel with you whilst you remain untrained. You are more likely to hurt me if I don't teach you, particularly given your current haphazard control. If we are attacked again, I would rather you were able to defend us without blowing me half the way back to the capital."

Luelle raised her brows at the prince's haughty speech.

"Do we have an agreement?"

"Fine. Yes. That would be useful."

Malcolm nodded, looking infuriatingly pleased with himself.

"Are you aware of the range of things you can do with it?" he asked.

"I know as much as any member of the public could, but since no monarch has shared their personal experience, I've only had access to witness accounts. Mainly people who have seen it used in battles." Luelle wracked her brain.

"It isn't solely a weapon." Malcolm rolled his eyes. "There are many things you can do with it. It is tied to the elements, to everything the Gods created, in a way. You can use it to move things without touching them, to manipulate the natural world around you. My father was able to create thunder and rain on the sunniest days and bring heat and flame into our chamber hearths with only a thought."

Luelle didn't miss the slight hitch in his voice at the mention of his father.

"And you can teach me all of that?"

"All of that and more. Though, likely not on this journey, I hardly imagine you would pick it up that quickly." He stared out over the river again, ignoring the daggers Luelle scowled into the side of his head. "We can start on it when we take a break tomorrow."

The prince didn't turn back to see the small smile on Luelle's face.

# 20

They walked for a few more hours before resting for the night. At dawn, the following morning, a small part of Malcolm was surprised to see Luelle was still there. A much larger part of him was filled with glee to discover she'd fallen asleep during her shift watching over their camp—something she'd scolded him for too frequently on their brief journey together.

A smile crept over his features. He would enjoy rubbing this in her face today.

He'd slept in one of the spare sets of clothes Anwyn had given him, giving his armour another opportunity to dry out. Carefully unwrapping himself from his blanket, he got to his feet, avoiding stray sticks and crunchy leaves that might wake Luelle if he trod on them. Once standing, he stretched his arms above his head, tilting his neck to ease the cramps he developed every night sleeping on the floor.

He could wake her immediately, feigning an attack to show her the error of her ways.

No, that was irresponsible. She'd admitted her poor control over the Power—she could lash out at him in fear. Besides, he could take the opportunity to prove he wasn't as useless as she thought.

Moving away from their camp to freshen up, Malcolm washed his face in the river and tended to his needs away from where they slept.

He resolved to make breakfast for them whilst Luelle was sleeping. After her help at the temple yesterday, it was the least he could do. Last night, they'd agreed to save Anwyn's food parcels for the mountains, where foraging would be harder but they could top up their supplies as they walked today. Luelle would need a rested mind and a full stomach if she wanted success when she practised using the Power.

And in a few days, the Power would be back with him, where it belonged.

A pang of disappointment flashed in his mind at the thought of their travels ending so soon. Malcolm frowned. Since their brief stay with the Meteile, he had realised how much he enjoyed being away from the capital and the responsibilities awaiting him. It wasn't the company he travelled with—this trip would be much more enjoyable if his reign wasn't on the line and if he was with actual friends, instead of a temperamental, thieving servant—but he could ignore his father's death out here, away from the constant stream of memories home evoked. He could forget that his mother and siblings were still trapped in a room with his father's corpse, all because of his failure to get home quickly.

He pushed away thoughts of his family, latching onto Theo and Leena to keep his grief at bay, replacing it with anxiety. His friends must be in the Godswood by now. If Luelle had found it so easy to track him yesterday, Leena would have no trouble, as long as she'd escaped the arachnids in the Great Forest after he'd abandoned them.

Malcolm spread a large leaf on the ground and found some berries and nuts to arrange atop it. If he couldn't find much more in the trees, he'd surrender one of his meals from Anwyn. Luelle had foraged enough in the earliest days of their journey that he knew several safe options.

Returning to the nearest shrubbery, he plucked a few handfuls of berries from the bramble bushes, only pricking his fingers twice, and some mushrooms from the base of the trees, avoiding anything he didn't recognise. He couldn't catch fish or craybugs like Luelle could but if she wanted those things when she woke she could get them herself.

She was still asleep when he reached their clearing again, though she'd rolled onto her back. Her hair framed her face like a mane. Heavy, deep breaths huffed from her open mouth.

Malcolm arranged his foraged pieces on the leaf he'd laid out, adding two baked bars from his own supply. He'd gathered a veritable feast. His mouth curved into a proud smile at his work. Days earlier, this would have been an impossible task.

He was finishing off one of the baked bars, topped with a few mushrooms when Luelle woke with a start. Washing the food down with a swig from his flask, he cleared his throat and raised his eyebrows.

"Sleep well?" His voice was sickly sweet.

"Shit, sorry." She rubbed a hand over her face. "I must've been more tired than I realised."

"You have drilled the importance of staying awake on your guard shift into me. We both know that is no excuse."

Malcolm fought a grin as Luelle glared at him.

"Okay, I get your point."

"What point? I'm not making a point. I am only reminding you how important it is that we stay awake when it is our shift to guard the camp. Who knows what horrors could occur if we were irresponsible enough not to wake the other one when we are too tired to do so? The bandits from yesterday could have tracked us, seeking revenge and attacking whilst we were vulnerable, for instance. Or perhaps someone even worse. I know you would never risk letting that happen."

Luelle rolled her eyes. "You're enjoying this, aren't you?"

"Very much."

Her gaze dropped to the last bite of the baked bar in his fingers and the food in front of him.

"You foraged some stuff?" Her voice lilted with surprise.

"Turns out I am not entirely useless." He shoved the last bite of food into his mouth, a warm flush of pride spreading over his chest and neck. Surviving in the wilderness was easy.

Luelle crawled towards him. She stilled as she examined the food up close.

"How many of these mushrooms did you eat?"

Malcolm swallowed his food. "Uh, I don't know. They are the same ones you have been picking."

A sinister smile twisted her lips as she raised her head. A seed of anxiety took root in his stomach, prickling on the back of his neck.

"The ones I've been picking are brown."

"Those are brown." Malcolm peered at the mushrooms. The heat on his neck and face deepened as his pride soured into concern and embarrassment. "They are the same as the ones you have been picking," he repeated.

"These are tan."

"That means brown."

"There's a big difference."

A nervous giggle slipped through Malcolm's lips. Luelle's smile widened into a grin that brought a dimple to her cheek. He frowned at the urge to touch it, stifling that feeling.

"How many did you eat, Prince?"

The copper sheen in her hair was more vibrant than usual this morning, catching the early morning light that reached the forest floor.

"Three or four?" His voice felt detached. He looked around, but the sound must have come from him since there was no one else here with them.

"And you're certain they were all like this? You didn't eat any with different colouring? With stripes?" Her grin was replaced by a serious frown.

Malcolm felt himself mirroring her expression. The heat in his chest increased. His skin was burning. Would she look away if he took off his shirt?

Luelle waved a hand in front of his face. Her fingers blurred, prompting a wave of nausea that made him avert his gaze.

"Hey, Prince, this is important. If you ate anything poisonous, you will need to make yourself vomit."

"Stop calling me that. My name is Malcolm." He clenched his fingers in the dirt at his side. His skin tingled with sensation.

Luelle sighed. "Malcolm. Were all the mushrooms you ate like this?"

He looked back to see her holding one of the mushrooms in front of his face. He reached for it but she moved it backwards. His fingers closed around air, instead. He managed a nod, though his head was heavy on his neck.

"This is going to be a fun morning," she muttered.

The edges of her face blurred and distorted. Malcolm focused on her eyes instead, examining the darker ring of colour at the edges of her irises. He had never looked close enough to see quite how many shades of brown her eyes contained.

"You've eaten hallucinogenic mushrooms."

Malcolm giggled again, though the sound was cut off by a sharp pang of panic in his chest. Grabbing at the point of pain was like dragging his arm through syrup.

"Am I going to die?" His voice was a whisper. He could almost see the words floating up on a stray breeze to the treetops. The edges of the trees grew less clear with each breath he took.

"Haven't you ever taken them before? Loads of nobles in the castle do." Luelle sounded like she was frowning but Malcolm couldn't drop his head to look at her again.

His breathing came faster but he couldn't get any air.

"Malcolm."

Panic overwhelmed him.

Two small circles of pressure pushed against his cheeks, tugging his head down. Luelle pulled his chin until he was looking into her eyes again. He could feel every line of her fingerprints against his face.

"You're not going to die. I'm going to stay here with you until this passes. You're safe."

He struggled to make sense of her words, but the fist gripping his heart loosened.

"Breathe," she instructed.

He obeyed.

His eyes dropped to her lips, a delicate curve of pink. She took an exaggerated breath. He matched her slow breathing until she let go of his face.

When she got to her feet, he moved to try and follow but could only make it to his hands and knees before the vibrant, pulsating forest made him want to fall back down.

"Luelle."

"I'm getting you some water, I'll be back in a moment." Her voice drifted to him as he stared at the ground.

Blades of grass poked through Malcolm's fingers, tickling skin that he never realised was so sensitive.

Another laugh bubbled out of his lips but this time it didn't stop. He laughed at the sensation of the grass until tears rolled down his face, falling onto the backs of his hands like rain. He marvelled at the splashing drops.

Pressure on his shoulder pulled him back into a sitting position.

Luelle's face bobbed into view. She pressed something into his palm.

"Have a drink."

His face still ached with the remnants of his smile. The air was especially cold against the traces of tears lining pathways to his chin. He gazed at the thief's dark lashes, brushing against the freckles on her cheeks with each swoop. A heavy blanket of peace settled over him when he removed his attention from the overstimulating life in the forest. He focused on one of the small specks of colour on Luelle's cheekbone.

"What are you looking at?"

Her voice reached his ears on a delay, pink lips moving without sound for a moment.

Malcolm lifted his hand to point to the freckle that had caught his attention but his arm didn't want to do as he instructed.

Luelle's lips curved into another smile, as bright as a full moon on a cloudless night.

Malcolm closed his eyes against a fresh wave of dizziness. He kept them closed, watching the show of colours and shapes dancing behind his eyelids. Throbbing heartbeats vibrated through his entire body like the drumbeats from the Meteile camp's festivities.

He didn't hear Luelle ask any more questions, but opened his eyes when he felt her touch guiding him to lie on the ground. Shifting to his side, he buried his fingers into the blades of grass and the soft, springy moss around him.

A beetle gazed back at him from a nearby stone.

Compared to the tiny insect, Malcolm was an immense creature. He could squish the beetle with just one of his fingers. He wouldn't, but he could.

Did it see him as a God? Maybe his own Gods saw humans and Eile as tiny insects. To them he was a beetle, preoccupied with pointless tasks like ruling his kingdom. It all meant nothing in the grand scheme of the universe.

Malcolm found the beetle's minuscule eyes and locked his stare with them. Those black specks held an infinite knowledge. It stared back at him as if it knew every thought roaming in Malcolm's head. Could they communicate without words? He narrowed his eyes and attempted it.

Maybe he had it the wrong way around. Perhaps this tiny creature was one of the Gods.

He whispered his questions to it, losing track of the time that passed and straining to hear the precious answers over the sounds of his own breathing.

# 21

Luelle watched the prince lying on the forest floor, whispering nonsense to himself. She'd long given up trying to figure out what he was saying.

Pulling the food he'd prepared earlier towards herself, she started to eat, avoiding the four remaining mushrooms. She had to stifle a laugh every time she looked at them or the prince. At least he was trying to be helpful now, even if that help had disastrous results.

She nibbled on the nuts and berries. This would delay their progress. The prince might recover by this afternoon but he wouldn't be up for travelling at their usual pace.

His state also made it very unlikely he'd be able to teach her any control over her Power, as he'd promised yesterday.

Her gaze wandered back to where he was lying. Curls spilled over his forehead, falling into eyes with pupils so large they exterminated almost all of the surrounding colour. His hand clenched in and out of a fist in the dirt beside him.

As amusing as it was, she was getting bored. Malcolm wasn't able to hold a conversation and seemed much more eager to talk to the ground anyway, but she wouldn't leave him alone like this, particularly not after the attack he'd suffered yesterday. The Godswood might be safe compared to the Great Forest, but he was still soon to be king. She couldn't let anything happen to him.

With nothing else to do, and Malcolm likely unable to remember if she embarrassed herself, she decided to try using the Power again. She didn't have to wait for him. Wresting some control over it before might even make things easier when they did start working together, if he truly was willing to go through with his promise.

She lined up a row of circular berries on the leaf plate Malcolm had fashioned and straightened where she sat. Inhaling three deep breaths with her eyes closed, she reached inside herself to feel the Power. It was there, dormant but alive.

She raised her hand, holding it straight towards the berries. Visions of them flying backwards towards the prince and last night's fire pit filled her mind.

When nothing happened, Luelle clenched her teeth, straining harder for any movement from the berries. She'd accept a roll backwards. A tremble.

Nothing.

Hours passed. She worked until beads of sweat rolled down her temples, but no matter how she twisted her imagination, the berries stayed still.

Would she ever be capable of using it?

Rage grew in her chest as afternoon approached. She plucked a berry and put it in her mouth, chewing fiercely and turning away from her makeshift target practice in disgust.

Her eyes fell on Malcolm's sword. Unlike usual, it wasn't by his side.

Scouring the clearing, she also found his dagger, lying discarded by the firepit.

She inhaled a gasp and held her breath.

The dagger was much closer to the prince, but he wouldn't be able to prevent Luelle from grabbing it in his current state, even if he noticed what her intention was before she reached it. The sword was only a few feet from her. It was the safer option.

She shuffled towards it. Malcolm didn't glance up as she moved, his eyes fixed on the same patch of dirt as before. He hadn't moved all morning, silently riding out his high, but her eyes had continually strayed back to his chest to make sure he was at least still breathing.

Luelle didn't remove her stare from the prince until her fingers were closed around the hilt of the sword, the weapon that had been pointed at her throat and his back only yesterday.

Her heart thundered. Frozen to the spot, she gripped the sword so hard that her knuckles ached.

Malcolm still refused to part with either of his weapons, no matter that he was leaving her defenceless since she couldn't control the Power. It made sense that she should get one of the blades, particularly after the attack he'd experienced.

But, he didn't trust her enough for that.

She looked down at the blade.

It was a nice weapon. Much nicer than anything she'd wielded before, not that she was an expert at fighting. Zeke had trained her plenty, with all of the others that followed him, but it didn't come naturally to her. Imbryl and Freya were better. Luelle excelled at lurking in the shadows, at retaining snippets of information to use against someone in a battle of words or manipulation. It was why Zeke had chosen her for this job. Imbryl and Freya had the brute strength but lacked the patience and planning the past five years had required.

Freya and Imbryl would salivate over a sword like this.

Luelle kept her hand on the weapon and looked back at the prince. A soft smile was in the place of his regular stern frown. Her heartbeat didn't slow at the sight of it.

He'd surprised her at the temple, asking to continue travelling with her to the Caeleste Peaks. His reasons made sense; he still didn't believe her plans to return the Power to the masses would work, but she couldn't prove it to him until they arrived at the cavern.

Stealing his sword now could jeopardise the tentative peace that settled between them yesterday. It could trigger an attack from him and Luelle had no confidence in her ability to beat the prince, even with the weapon in her hand. There was no guarantee he would let her live if it came to that. She might end up as mutilated as the human men at the temple. Worse, he might rescind his promise to teach her how to use the Power, and he was the most knowledgeable person about it in the kingdom at this point. After they separated at the end of this trip, she might never get another opportunity to learn the information passed to

Malcolm from Alaric and every other monarch before him.

As much as she wanted a physical weapon to defend herself, she couldn't lose that opportunity to learn more about the Power passed down from the Gods.

She took a shaking breath and clenched her fist around the sword hilt once more before laying it back on the ground.

Luelle rose from where she was sitting and wandered to the prince, who was still lying on his side.

"Hey, Prin—Malcolm, how are you doing down there?"

He mumbled something.

"Have you had something to drink—wait, are you talking to a beetle?" Luelle squinted at the insect cradled in the prince's hand.

"He's talking to me," Malcolm murmured.

Luelle didn't bother trying to hide her grin. Twigs and stones pressed into her legs as she knelt beside him. "What's he saying?"

"He is a God."

Luelle laughed so hard her head tipped backwards and she almost lost her balance.

Malcolm looked up at her, a deep chuckle bubbling from his own lips. His pupils were closer to their usual size, leaving space for the tiny flecks of green and gold in his irises.

"That has to be the funniest thing I've heard in years."

"It does sound a bit silly, now that I think about it." His brow furrowed as the insect flew off his hand.

"Have a drink. I'll prepare some food that won't have you speaking to bugs." Luelle swiped her bag and unpacked some of the food from Anwyn, leaving two more parcels for the next few days. She would forage for more tomorrow, once they got moving again. If she could save Anwyn's food for their climb to the cavern, she would. Facing her friends after five years, miserable from hunger, wouldn't be ideal.

Malcolm pushed himself on shaky arms into a sitting position to sip from his flask and watch Luelle prepare their lunch.

"How are you feeling?" She glanced at him.

"I am alright." His voice was slower than usual, as if he was struggling to understand his words until he heard them. "Things look more normal again now. Everything was so bright. Colours do not usually move like that."

Luelle snorted. "Maybe leave the foraging to me in the future."

"I was only trying to help." His expression was wounded.

She smiled and handed him some dried meat. He nibbled at its edge.

"I appreciate the thought. And, it was funny."

The prince's glare wasn't quite as vicious as normal.

"So, what were you and the divine beetle talking about?"

Colour rose in Malcolm's cheeks. "The universe."

"Makes sense." Luelle's face ached from grinning.

"I hope you forget about this soon," he groaned. "Perhaps you should try some of the mushrooms so you might know what I am talking about."

"I've already experienced the wonder of those things." Luelle pulled a face. "My friends and I took them together when we were younger and had nothing better to do, but I don't particularly enjoy giving up control like that. And I can't recall ever speaking to insects whilst on them."

"I doubt my friends would ever believe I had eaten those." The smile lingering on the prince's face was a sign he must still be under the influence of the mushrooms.

"You're lucky you didn't pick poisonous ones." She raised her brows at him. "You can wake me up if you want help with it in the future. I'm more than happy to teach you what's safe."

The prince met her gaze. "I presumed you must need the rest if you were careless enough to fall asleep when you were meant to be watching over our camp."

Luelle scowled at him.

"Let's call it even. I fell asleep during my shift, but you tried to drug me."

Malcolm's cheeks flushed. "I did not intentionally try to drug you."

She grinned.

He took another sip from his flask. "When will we reach the valley?"

She pursed her lips. "A couple of days. We can set out earlier tomorrow to make up for the time we lost today."

He nodded.

"What did you do before you came to Cerulya? Before, you know, everything."

Luelle met the prince's gaze. His pupils were definitely still engorged.

She took a deep breath. Talking about herself did not feel

natural after half a decade of hiding her true identity, but there was a slim chance he wouldn't remember their full conversation if he was still under the influence of the drugs. It wouldn't do that much harm to open up.

"Not much. We did odd jobs to bring in money when we needed it. Preparing for ways to return Vesanya's Power to the masses, mostly."

"We?"

"I lived with a small group of people."

"With your family? Zeke?"

"You're full of questions today, Prince."

"It cannot hurt to know a little more about the person I am travelling with. Nor what awaits me at the end of this journey." He didn't drop her gaze. Luelle was the first to look away.

"Not my family by blood," she admitted. "Zeke collected us all. He already knew some of the others before I met him, I don't really remember the early years. He found me and my friends when we were young. We've lived together since then, moving around quite a bit."

"Who is Zeke to you? You mentioned him before. You keep saying he found you."

Luelle frowned. How could she describe Zeke? "He's the closest thing I've got to family."

"Where is your real family?"

She chewed her lip. "I don't know. Probably dead, or maybe they just didn't want me. Zeke found me begging for food on the streets in Vidamere." It didn't make her heart ache as much as it used to. Blurry memories of those cold, lonely days didn't haunt her dreams as often.

"How old were you then?"

"I'm not sure. Less than ten, I think."

"You think?"

"I don't know if the orphanage kept any records on me. I followed Zeke from the streets and never went back to find out more."

"Do you even know your birthday?" Malcolm frowned at her, leaning back to rest on his elbows.

"I tend to count the day Zeke found me. We never really had time to celebrate our birthdays, anyway."

"That's sad."

Luelle stiffened at the judgement in his tone.

"Sorry, I meant no offence," he said, seeing too many of Luelle's emotions for her liking. "I only mean, do you not feel as if you are missing out?"

She shifted where she was sitting, tugging blades of grass out of the dirt. "Not really. I don't know. I've never thought about it. I hadn't seen people celebrate their birthdays until I came to the palace." The royal family members' birthday parties had taken extravagance to an extreme Luelle had never known. Even the servants had celebrated between chores and drank themselves into oblivion at the ends of their shifts.

He changed the subject. "Do you truly believe the Gods once walked the earth?"

Luelle met Malcolm's heavy-lidded gaze and nodded.

"What happened to them?"

She shifted her position, toying with another piece of her

food. "I don't know. Zeke says they were banished and trapped in their own realm when Queen Arabella stole Vesanya's Power from the Veseile."

"What do you believe?" His eyes explored her face, bright and curious.

Luelle looked away, towards the water still gushing past them in the river. What did she believe? She'd always accepted Zeke's beliefs as her own, though occasionally she wondered if that was only because she'd never known anything different.

"I believe the Gods walked the earth. I don't know why they stopped," she admitted.

"Do you believe in the Underworld?" he asked.

Most Eile and humans believed Mortus, the God of Death, welcomed the souls of the dead in another realm, caring for them for eternity.

"I've never given it much thought." Luelle plucked another blade of grass from the ground. "Do you?"

Malcolm's eyes dropped from hers.

"I hope it exists. I would like to think my father has found some peace. Or that I may reunite with him, one day." His voice was quiet.

She watched him stare out at the forest. Though he hid his feelings well, grief shadowed the prince's face and hovered over him like a cloud. Were her own parents in the Underworld, if it truly existed? Would she be able to find them there, eventually?

"I think your father is at peace."

His gaze flicked back to hers. He nodded and turned away once more.

Luelle finished the food she'd been nibbling on, lost in thoughts of home and what she might return to. Should she expect some of her friends to be gone, their souls passed on to the Underworld, as King Alaric's had? She hadn't been able to communicate with Zeke, with any of her friends, in over five years. It hadn't occurred to her until now that anything could have happened to them. They could have suffered illness, misfortune, injuries... death.

The sooner she got back to them, the better; the sooner she could stop tormenting herself wondering.

# 22

Malcolm felt normal again the following day, if a little fragile. He had taken over from Luelle, watching over their camp, in the early hours of the morning, staring at the surrounding forest, glimpsing nothing more than a flash of orange—a passing fox sniffing for food—and listening to smaller, hidden creatures shuffle and snort in the undergrowth. Birds woke as the sky lightened, chirping greetings to him from above.

He wasn't sure what to make of Luelle caring for him yesterday, nor of the strange conversation they'd had in the afternoon. The rest of the day had passed without either saying much as they'd made further slow progress through the forest, allowing Malcolm to get lost in thoughts about home and guilt that he still wasn't back to relieve his family from their subterfuge. Sleep had been a blessed reprieve but the thoughts had returned with equally vicious intensity this morning.

He glared at Luelle as she snored, wondering how one person could cause him so much trouble, when an idea occurred to him. She'd taken his Power by willing it into herself from a vessel, as he would've done if everything had happened as it was meant to. Could he take it back from her using that same process? As far as he knew, no one had tried that before—or, if they had, it wasn't documented anywhere.

Shuffling closer to her, careful not to make too much noise, Malcolm analysed the thief. Would he need to make contact with her skin or would it be enough to touch her shoulder over her clothes?

He decided not to risk it and rested his fingertips against her forehead. Closing his eyes, he took several deep breaths to ground himself.

The intoxicating pull of the Power remained the same as it always felt when he was this close to Luelle. Birds continued to sing to each other in the trees above and the river nearby was a steady babble. Malcolm tried willing the Power into his own body, as Luelle said she'd absorbed it from the glass sphere. When nothing happened, he scrunched up his face and tried harder.

"What are you doing, Prince?"

Malcolm gasped. His eyes flew open. Leaping back from Luelle, he jerked his hand from her forehead as if he'd burnt himself. She was looking up at him with an expression somewhere between suspicion and amusement. Humiliation burned in his cheeks.

"Did you eat more mushrooms?" Luelle raised an eyebrow and pushed herself up, brushing dirt from her side.

"N-no," he stammered, wondering how he could explain why she'd woken up with his hand resting on her head.

"Was that a strange royal custom that I'm too poor to understand? Do you make your servants wake you with their cold fingers each morning?"

The temperature in his face rose.

She gasped. His eyes flicked to hers but he was too uncomfortable to hold her stare.

"Were you trying to steal the Power back? After I told you how I did it?"

He shifted where he sat. "I only wanted to see if it would work."

Her head tilted back as she laughed. "That's brilliant." She grinned at him. "You know, I actually considered trying the same, a few years back."

He looked over at her, his embarrassment easing slightly. "You did?"

She nodded. "It was pretty obvious that it was too risky, but I'm glad someone tried it so I have proof I didn't waste the last few years working my fingers to the bone."

He scowled at her.

They didn't spend long in their clearing. They ate, washed, and started walking, pushing hard to make up for lost time. The following day saw another early morning, but before long, the land on either side of the river grew steeper and the trees grew sparser, signalling the looming edge of the Godswood.

Luelle dragged Malcolm as close to the edge of the steep banks as either of them dared, to gaze out over the view before they started the worst of their climb. The Caeleste River continued rushing, but the trees on either side of the water were set against the backdrop of several enormous mountains that had crept up from nowhere. Greenery grew most of the way up those mountains, dying out towards the highest points and leaving nothing but grey stone dusted with infrequent patches of snow. Though the Caeleste Peaks were small compared to the other mountain ranges in the realm, they were no less magnificent.

Malcolm and Luelle hadn't said much to one another since he had tried stealing the Power whilst she slept. The day before that was a blur of nauseating memories. His blatant embarrassment had done nothing to stop her from mocking his foraging skills or asking if he wanted to stop for a chat every time she saw an insect, but the quiet atmosphere was more civil than the frosty silence during their first few days travelling together.

They stopped to eat lunch gazing at the mountains, resting before starting their ascent to the cave. Luelle knew the path, so Malcolm followed as blindly as always.

Their climb led them away from the river, obscuring most of the view behind tall tree trunks and leafy branches. Leaving it behind sparked a pang of regret in Malcolm, like saying goodbye to an old friend. When he caught a glimpse of it in a rare gap between the foliage, it was always more beautiful than the previous time. Water fell from hundreds of spots on the mountains framing the valley, feeding into the river's depths. From this far, they looked like tiny trickles, but he was certain he'd find enormous, roaring waterfalls if he got close enough.

They walked for hours after lunch before taking a break on a flat, wide piece of path. To one side was a steep, rocky wall, stretching around ten feet tall. The other side of the path opened out to offer a view of the valley, obstructed by only two trees. Malcolm breathed hard as he stared at the river growing smaller beneath them. Choosing to wear his lighter clothing from Anwyn, rather than his leather armour, had been a wise decision. His shirt clung to the sheen of sweat on his back.

Luelle, too, gazed at the view, though much further from the edge than Malcolm, sitting with her back against the rock.

This seemed as good a place as any to bring up the topic.

"Do you want me to start teaching you to use the Power?" Yesterday, they'd been too busy trying to make up for lost time and the day before he'd been too affected by the mushrooms to teach her anything worthwhile.

Luelle's eyes were wider than normal when she raised her head to meet his gaze. Pink stained her cheeks from the effort of their climb. Several hairs escaped her braid to caress the sides of her face.

"Yes!" she blurted. "If you're sure."

Malcolm nodded, looking around at the track they were on. "This will be better than anywhere else we have seen so far. We need somewhere with some space, in case anything goes wrong." He walked the width of the path. They had around thirty paces to play with.

"What are you going to teach me?" Luelle breathed.

"We will start small. Maybe moving something."

Malcolm looked around the clearing and settled on a rock smaller than his clenched fist. He picked it up and bounced it in his palm. It might be too light but he didn't want to discourage her too fast if she struggled.

Resting it in the centre of the path, he turned back to Luelle, who was now standing and staring with apprehension at the rock, jaw tight, brow furrowed.

"Stand a few paces away." He ushered her several steps forward. "How have you tried using it before? What was your process?"

Luelle's throat bobbed. "I slowed my breathing and tried to envision what I wanted to happen, I suppose."

"Okay. What do you know about the Power? We should start with the basics."

"Do you want the real truth or the lie that you believe?"

Malcolm fought the urge to sigh. She was only trying to bait him into an argument to procrastinate, probably out of fear of failing to use his Power once again. "Tell me what you think is right and I shall correct your inaccuracies."

Luelle crossed her arms over her chest, straightening where she stood to rise to the challenge in his words.

"It was originally a gift from Vesanya, when the Gods could walk the Earth, to all members of the Veseile race that she created. Then your ancestor, Arabella, sealed the Gods in their realms, cutting off the connection and the gifts they bestowed, keeping the last trace of Vesanya's Power for herself by trapping it in the crystal relic and absorbing it. That's how the whole tradition started, passing the Power down on a monarch's deathbed and giving full-blooded human rulers an advantage over the other races."

Malcolm tilted his head back to face the sky, taking a slow, deep breath to calm his annoyance. He was certain she hadn't been this rude when they'd discussed the Gods a couple of nights ago, though his memories of that day were still slightly fuzzy.

"How do you even think Arabella stole the Power? There are so many inconsistencies in your story. She was a human. It is highly unlikely she would have been able to steal from an entire race of stronger beings, let alone banish six Gods from the world."

Luelle scoffed. "Oh, you're an expert now?"

"No, I simply cannot understand how you believe the nonsense you are spouting! I thought you had some measure of intelligence but it turns out I was mistaken." Malcolm's fury grew hot inside his chest.

Colour stained Luelle's cheeks. "I don't know exactly how she did it but that's only because she took precautions. Arabella spent the rest of her reign punishing those who spoke out against her leadership, she replaced the Eile in the palace with humans and destroyed any documents detailing the use of the Power in the general population."

"You said the other night that you weren't sure you even believed that myth," he pointed out. "You said that Arabella stealing the Power and banishing the Gods was Zeke's belief."

"I'm surprised you can remember that given how you spent most of that day."

Malcolm rolled his eyes. Broaching this topic was always going to shatter their tentative truce and return them to their bickering.

"I don't see what this has to do with learning how to use the

Power anyway."

"You need to understand its history before you can wield it. It provides a connection to the natural world, to the elements and to everything else the Gods created. In order to use the Power, you must enhance your own connection to nature."

"Oh great, that's easy. Let me do that now." Luelle's tone dripped with sarcasm.

Malcolm glared at her. "Do you want my help or not? Because I can rescind the offer."

She pressed her lips together into a thin line.

"Apologise first, then we may continue." Malcolm crossed his arms.

He suppressed a smug smile when Luelle's nostrils flared.

"I'm sorry."

"I forgive you. You were on the right track with the breathing exercises but I doubt you were going far enough to ground yourself to your surroundings." He gestured to the stony path. "It might be easier if you sit, at first. Take several deep breaths and focus on the world around you. Try to isolate each sense. Focus on individual things, everything you can hear, everything you can feel and smell. My father always said he could feel the Power come alive inside him when he took a moment to ground himself like this."

"How long is that going to take? I'm not always going to have time to sit and meditate before using the Power. I wouldn't have had time to save you from that human in the forest if I'd had to sit and meditate first. What if I need to defend us again?"

Malcolm suppressed his retort. She didn't need to worry

about long-term control of the Power if she was truly to fulfill her promise of returning it once her silly mission failed. Though, his hope that Leena and Theodas would find them before it got to that point grew slimmer by the day.

"It becomes easier and faster with practice. Father was almost always connected with the natural world. Harmony with nature was everything he taught me since I was unable to practise with the Power itself."

Luelle sighed and lowered herself to sit cross-legged on the ground.

"At first, this process will also increase your awareness of the Power and your control over rationing it. Apparently, it is common to exhaust yourself the first few times you use it since you will be unfamiliar with the habit of conserving the majority of the Power or only using what you need for a certain task."

She grunted. For once, she straightened her slouched posture. Her eyes fluttered shut, hands resting on her knees.

"So what do I do? Just listen for stuff?"

"Place your hands flat on the ground at your sides and focus on isolating your senses. Identify everything you can feel, hear, and smell."

Malcolm watched her fidget in silence. His patience ran thin when she scratched her arm for the fifth time.

"Do you have fleas?"

Her eyes flew open. "I can't concentrate! This is ridiculous, I don't see how this will help."

"I have already explained to you how it will help, you simply aren't trying hard enough. To succeed, you must let go of any other thoughts. Ignore your distractions and focus."

"When will I get to try using the Power?"

"When you learn some patience."

Luelle's brow furrowed but she squeezed her eyes shut and slowed her breathing once more.

Watching her poor attempt to meditate elicited painful memories of Malcolm's own training with his father. On occasion, he'd trained with Viv but their age difference had only made that possible in the past decade. His father had trained him all over the castle, starting in the quiet privacy of his chambers and moving into increasingly busy areas so Malcolm could master his ability to ignore any distractions. He still wasn't sure it had been necessary to do so in the middle of the courtyard, before a crowd of nosy nobles and servants, nor in the depth of the crypts with the eyes of his ancestors crawling over his skin. Yet, the process was now as natural as breathing, something he did without realising, particularly when his emotions surged.

He recognised Luelle's frustration. In his early years of training, he'd felt the same, but it had all been worth it, knowing one day he would wield the Power his father could. The king had shown Malcolm it was more than a weapon; he'd achieved such delicate tasks with it, fashioning birds and butterflies from the water in the castle garden fountains and making them flutter around Malcolm and his siblings. He'd even lit everlasting fires in every hearth in the castle to leave physical fuel for others in the city that needed it more. Each one of those fires stopped burning the night the king died. How was Viv explaining that to the council?

Malcolm rubbed a hand over his face. Would he be able to face returning home when this trek was over? He wouldn't be able to walk down a single hallway without thinking of his father or what he forced his family to do so he could be here. Travelling like this made it possible to forget but he wouldn't be able to escape his sorrow at home. The thought of reliving the memories that caused his heart to ache every day was almost too much to bear.

He dragged his attention back to the present, ignoring the inky shadows of grief a while longer. Luelle's breathing had slowed, her fidgeting stilled. When he was certain she hadn't fallen asleep, as he had a few times during his early years of training, he spoke again.

"Can you feel any difference?"

Luelle answered after another few steady breaths. "Yes. It's like a living thing in my chest, but it's part of me. I can feel it."

"Good. Now open your eyes and hold onto that feeling, that awareness. Don't imagine the rock moving, will it to move. Use the Power to shape your will into reality."

Luelle opened her eyes as instructed and held out her hand.

"Stop that." He frowned, instructing her instinctively before realising how foolish it was to teach her so thoroughly. "Movements like that are a crutch. You do not need to direct the Power with your body, it comes from within. People can predict your intentions if you rely on movements like that."

"Oh." Dropping her palm back to the ground, she lowered her chin, levelling a stare at the rock.

Malcolm watched with equal intensity, heart pounding. His

grandmother and father were the only other people he'd seen use the Power. Witnessing someone else wield it was as terrifying as the thought of using it himself.

Luelle scowled at the rock, her hands curling into fists at her sides.

Time froze around them, locking in that state. Pressure flared in Malcolm's chest.

The rock flew backwards, disappearing over the edge of the path and bouncing between the trees beyond, toward the valley floor far below them.

Luelle gasped, her breath catching in her throat.

Malcolm met her wide eyes and let himself smile at her without guilt for the first time.

"Good job. With more practice, your control will improve, but that is an excellent start."

She turned back to the empty spot where the rock had rested. A laugh bubbled from her throat.

"I can't believe it." She turned to grin at him. "Thank you."

Malcolm nodded, heart still thundering, thoughts still tangled in his father's memory and the shame that he wasn't the one learning to manipulate the Power. Concern flooded him at the thought he might never do so, but Luelle had promised to return it. He wouldn't think about what he needed to do if she refused to give it back to him when they reached their final destination. If that happened, he wouldn't hesitate again, as he had during their confrontation in the Godswood. He couldn't.

"Can I try again?" Her voice broke through his dark thoughts. "I feel more energised than the last time I used it. I feel like I can control it more."

"Do you want to try something a little harder?"

When she nodded, he reached underneath his shirt and unfastened his father's medallion. Her eyes were wide as he placed it gently on the ground where the stone had been. He took a deep breath.

"This was my father's. Lift it into the air."

Luelle frowned. "Are you sure this is a good idea?"

No, he wasn't.

"It means a lot to me so I would rather you didn't fling it into the valley like the rock, but sometimes high stakes are necessary to learn control. You need to manipulate a smaller amount of the Power. Enough to lift it but not so much that the medallion flies too high, out of your control."

Determination settled over her expression and posture. She frowned at the medallion whilst Malcolm returned to his own earlier position, sitting a few feet away from her. He took care to steady his breathing, to let go of the tension in his shoulders and the concern that this was an awful suggestion.

The sun dipped in the sky as Luelle wrestled a fraction of control over the Power inside her. Beads of sweat rolled down her temple before the pressure in Malcolm's chest changed again, familiar yet different from the feeling he'd experienced every time his father had used the Power.

The medallion was shaking and slow when it rose from the ground. It ascended several inches, the chain trailing underneath the pendant, before falling back to the earth as Luelle released her breath.

"Well done," Malcolm said, releasing a breath of his own.

She grinned at him. "I can't believe it." She scrambled forward and grabbed the medallion, turning it in her palms as if she would find invisible strings that had lifted it into the air.

"How do you feel?"

"Tired." She passed the medallion back to him with a small smile.

He refastened it around his neck, tucking it inside his shirt once more. His father had explained how the Power drained a person's energy, more so in the earlier days when someone was still learning about it. All of Malcolm's preparation was designed to prevent that loss of control. How would he fare when he first attempted it?

"That's enough for today. You can try again tomorrow."

Luelle's eyes shone. She smiled and nodded.

"Thank you," she repeated her earlier words, staring at Malcolm with an earnestness that made his stomach twist.

He got to his feet, brushing off the backs of his legs and ignoring whatever that look meant. He extended a hand to help her stand. She took it, splaying her arms to steady herself as if overcome by dizziness. Before Malcolm could ask if she was okay, she was speaking.

"I used the Power twice!" she exclaimed, beaming over the valley as if she could still see the small rock flying down it. "It was nothing like in Tolhurst. It felt like a connection to the world, just as you said it would. If I've managed this now, how good do you think I'll be in a year? Or five?"

Malcolm frowned. Of course, she still believed she would

keep the Power for life but he knew her hold on it was only temporary.

He opened his mouth to remind her of the fact, but was interrupted by an ear-splitting shriek.

# 23

Luelle and the prince stumbled back, shielding their heads on instinct. They turned to look up the mountain, in the direction of the noise.

"Shit," Luelle whispered.

Leaning over the edge of the ledge to one side of their path, a troll stared down at them. Tusks protruded from its gaping mouth, glistening with saliva that dripped onto the path Luelle and Malcolm stood on. Ragged fur clung to its lanky, muscular body, matted and stained with old gore and dirt.

"What is that?" The prince's voice was notched at a higher pitch than normal.

"A troll."

Luelle looked around, but their options were limited. The path they were on was wide and open, giving the beast more room to swing its long arms and catch them with its knife-like claws, each one as long as Malcolm's dagger. They were exposed, and since the troll already had the high ground, running would only leave their backs vulnerable. Now it had seen them, it would track their scent until it killed them. Fleeing risked sending it into a frenzy.

Plus, she was so close to the cavern, to returning Vesanya's Power to its source. She couldn't die now. It was kill or be killed.

The troll straightened and shrieked again. Birds burst from the trees behind the beast, flapping an escape route through the bright afternoon sky.

Standing at full height, it neared seven feet tall, towering several inches over the prince. It was smaller than the last troll Luelle had seen. That had been years ago, living in the cavern, when Imbryl thought it would be a fun idea to lead her and Freya from their beds to hunt the enormous creatures. She'd accompanied her friends the first time, but seeing a fully grown, ten-foot troll from afar had been terrifying enough that she'd never accepted Imbryl's offer again. This beast couldn't be fully grown but, despite the years of development it had ahead, it was packed with muscle, twitching for a fight.

"Split up. Slowly." Luelle pushed at Malcolm's bicep, taking a long, deliberate step away from him. She didn't drop her eyes from the troll.

"Wait." The prince unsheathed his dagger from his belt and handed it to Luelle, his own eyes also locked on the beast.

Her racing heart lurched as her fingers closed around the handle of the weapon. All it had taken was the threat of death and it was finally hers. The dagger wasn't much against a troll but it was better than nothing. She had the Power dwelling inside her but did she have enough energy left to defend them with it? Her tenuous grip on it had slipped from her grasp when she saw the troll, the heat in her chest smothered by icy fear. If she was going to use it, she'd need to rely on a defensive blast like the one she'd caused in Tolhurst, but her timing would have to be perfect to kill the troll and avoid harming Malcolm.

"Thanks," she breathed.

They edged away from each other. The troll's head darted back and forth between them, thin lips peeling back to expose several rows of sharp teeth. A deep, guttural growl leaked from its throat.

The three of them stayed frozen in that moment, tension thick enough for Luelle to slice with her dagger.

When the troll moved, it was faster than she anticipated.

It leapt from the ledge, landing between them with a thump and a snarl. Beneath her feet, the ground shook with the impact. The troll scurried towards Luelle in a blur of snapping fangs and slashing claws.

She dodged to her right, out of its path. Pain scorched her arm as the beast's claws sliced her skin on its way past. If trolls were more agile creatures, she would already be dead. She scampered back along their path, frantically searching for something to give her an advantage. Finding nothing, she took the opportunity to put some distance between herself and the creature. The troll turned to track her.

Beady orange eyes locked with hers. Saliva dribbled down the beast's chin, hanging in swaying strings as it bared its teeth again.

Luelle's breath came hard and fast. She gripped the dagger's handle tight enough that her fingers ached, widening her stance to stay balanced. The troll roared at her, spraying spittle.

She braced as it took a lumbering step forward but it didn't move far. It let out another thunderous screech and spun towards the prince, who had made the most of the distraction to sneak up behind the beast.

Malcolm retreated as quickly as he'd approached. Crimson dripped from his blade, staining the rocky ground. Through the hair and muscle, Luelle spotted a deep, fresh cut running the width of the troll's lower back.

Adrenaline rushed over her. She dashed forward to help the prince as he darted around the troll. He flicked at the beast with the tip of his sword, leaping away from claws and teeth that slashed and bit at him. Luelle joined the dance, ducking under a long, swinging arm and lashing out with her much smaller blade.

The troll's roars grew louder as its frustration mounted.

Circling the beast, they managed to keep it in one spot. They landed a collection of shallow cuts but nothing deep enough to end the fight.

Though she'd only used a small amount of Power, exhaustion soon slowed Luelle's movements but she didn't stop fighting when the troll was distracted by Malcolm. When the beast next turned away from her, she leapt forwards, impaling her dagger deep into its upper back. The troll spun with a roar.

Her blood-soaked fingers slipped from the handle before she could wrench it free, leaving the weapon embedded in the creature's left shoulder.

Luelle stumbled backwards in an attempt to avoid the troll's claws but lost her balance and tripped over the uneven ground. Air wheezed from her lungs as she landed hard on her back.

The troll seized its opportunity. Gripping her leg with one massive hand, it swung Luelle in a circle towards the prince. She couldn't draw in enough breath to scream.

Malcolm twisted, thrusting his sword out of the way to avoid slicing her in half. Her weight colliding into him knocked him clear off his feet. His sword soared away from them, clattering to a stop inches away from the edge of the mountain path.

They landed in a tangle of limbs. Luelle briefly locked eyes with the prince's wide stare. He scrambled out from underneath her and darted to retrieve his sword.

Pain jolted through Luelle's body. She lurched to her feet and ran, limping, in the other direction. The troll followed her. One of its arms hung slack by its side; stabbing it hadn't been useless after all.

"Its left arm is injured," she shouted out to Malcolm, but the prince didn't reappear from behind the troll. Luelle backed away until she felt the sheer wall of rock behind her.

The troll closed in, opening its jaws wide to roar at her. Spittle splattered on her face like rain. Rancid breath washed over her as the troll revealed its two rows of teeth up close, flecked with old meat.

Luelle suppressed a gag and tried to wrest some more control over her body and mind. Deep gashes oozed blood all over the beast's body, matting its fur. The handle of the dagger she'd embedded in its back poked over the beast's shoulder but she couldn't reach for it without running straight into the troll's arms.

Her breaths were shallow. She reached inside herself, grasping for the Power she'd used earlier, but she was exhausted. Clutching at the depleted connection in her chest, she willed the dagger to come towards her, burrowing further into the beast through its body. Almost collapsing from the effort, she clenched her fists, but the Power kept slipping from her mental grasp.

Strands of hair brushed against her face, loose from her braid after she'd been thrown through the air. Trembling legs held her up, but if this was how she left this world, so be it. She would fight until the end. Sweat rolled down her face, clammy and uncomfortable on her temples.

The dagger didn't budge.

The troll loomed over her, shading Luelle from the last sunlight she'd ever get to see. It opened those awful jaws one last time to screech in her face.

Luelle met the roar head-on. Baring her teeth in a silent snarl, she tensed for the final blow. Agony throbbed through her aching body. She ignored it, staring her death in the face.

But, it didn't come.

Malcolm's fingers wrapped around the dagger handle. He hoisted himself up onto the troll's back. Silver flashed as he shoved his sword clean through the side of the creature's neck, halting its cry with a wet crunch.

The prince wrapped his legs around the troll's waist to steady himself. Clenching his teeth, he gripped the top of the creature's head to brace it and yanked his sword out in a sweeping motion, splitting the beast's neck half open with a horizontal slice. Warm blood freckled Luelle's face anew as the blade emerged, sweeping an arc above her head.

The troll's beady eyes dimmed, staring at Luelle for another heartbeat until its entire head rolled backwards to hang against Malcolm, held on by only a small piece of tough flesh.

Malcolm leapt to the ground, breathing hard as the troll's large body collapsed sideways. Sticky gore coated him, the same type that Luelle could feel on herself. He stared at the troll's body as if convinced it would stand again to continue fighting, fist tight on his sword's hilt. Several minutes passed before he lowered his weapon.

The prince dragged his eyes from the corpse. Grime clumped in his hair, obscuring Vesanya's pigmentless mark entirely. He wiped it away from his face with the back of his hand, smearing crimson over his forehead.

"Are you alright?" His voice was rough.

Luelle's legs finally gave up on her. She slid to the ground, wincing at the pulsing in her temples. Each injury screamed for attention now the immediate danger was gone.

"I think so," she whispered. She moved her limbs and wiggled her fingers, holding her breath until she was sure nothing was broken. Bruised and battered but not irreparable.

The fight had drained what little energy she had left. Black spots speckled her vision. Her fingers trembled, energy still surging through her veins.

The prince wiped his blade on the troll's fur and resheathed it. He yanked his dagger from the beast's shoulder, wedging a foot against its torso for better leverage. With his weapons safely returned to his belt, he crouched in front of Luelle.

"You're bleeding." He inspected her, moving her head from side to side with a gentle grip on her chin. "I thought you were dead." His voice trembled. His eyes met hers for a second but jerked away. His hand dropped.

Luelle couldn't muster the strength to check her injuries in any detail. Her eyelids drooped, too heavy to hold fully open. She would worry about fixing up her cuts and scrapes after she'd had a chance to rest. Zeke and the others weren't far now. They would have supplies for her to raid if her injuries were still an issue when she reached them.

"You saved me." Leaning her head back against the rock, she examined the prince for any injuries of his own. His clothes were bloodied and torn but, other than several shallow scratches, he seemed unharmed. He certainly had more energy than her.

Both of them would need to wash and change before travelling much further if they wanted to avoid attracting other predators. The stench of blood would call to any hungry, opportunistic creatures around.

"Is that a surprise?" Malcolm frowned.

"It was only a few days ago you were holding that sword to my throat." Memories of the men Malcolm had slaughtered flashed in Luelle's mind, a glimpse at the fate she'd avoided.

The prince stiffened. His eyes returned to hers, colder than they'd been a moment earlier. "It will be harder for me to retrieve my Power from a corpse."

Her mouth dried. A sinking feeling rushed through her.

Luelle averted her eyes from his fierce stare. Malcolm stood and stepped back. In the timid peace that had settled between them since their last explosive argument, she'd forgotten they were only travelling together out of necessity. Of course, the prince didn't truly care about her. She was so desperate for affection, she was seeing amity where there was none. Their relationship was not one of care or friendship, just stubbornness and mistrust.

Malcolm would stay with her until he could find a way to get the Power and then he would leave. It was the only reason he hadn't followed through with his threat to kill her. She'd been misguided in thinking anything different, in thinking he'd stopped wanting to harm her or had started to enjoy her company. How could he care for someone who had betrayed his father, the very man whose loss was still such a raw wound? She didn't miss the way the prince would get lost in his thoughts, eyes glazing over and welling up, breath hitching from painful memories he chose not to voice aloud, particularly at night when he thought she was sleeping and unable to hear his quiet sorrow. Bitter grief trailed him every step of their journey.

"We must move away from here and find somewhere to wash our injuries if we want to avoid infection." His voice was still curt.

Luelle nodded. She pushed herself into a standing position, ignoring the hand Malcolm offered, forcing her weak limbs to hold her weight.

A fresh wave of dizziness washed over her.

She held herself against the rocky wall until those pressing black dots passed from her vision. When she could see clearly again, she stepped around the troll, grabbing her bag from the ground. She led the way onwards without turning to look at the prince again.

# 24

Malcolm watched the back of Luelle's head as she limped a few feet in front of him. She walked in silence. She hadn't even accepted his hand to help her stand after they'd decided to leave the troll's body behind, despite needing to steady herself on the wall.

Shame settled in Malcolm's chest, all the more uncomfortable because he wasn't sure where the feeling stemmed from.

She'd flinched when he spat those nasty words at her. Regret flooded him as soon as the words had left his mouth, even if they were true—he didn't know if he could retrieve his Power from her if she died. Admitting he was fighting to save her for any other reason was a betrayal of his father's memory and of his family, trapped with the king's body at home.

But, being so blunt about it had been cruel of him. She brought out the parts of himself he didn't want people to see; the bitterness, the resentment, the anger. He yearned to be a good ruler, kind and just, as his father had been. Why was it so hard? Had it always come naturally to his predecessors or had they needed to work as hard as Malcolm?

Three times now, he'd opened his mouth in an attempt to break the stiff, awkward silence that had fallen and three times he'd snapped his mouth shut, unsure what he could say that would fix things—unsure if he should even care about fixing them.

He took a deep breath and tried again.

"What are you looking for?"

Luelle jerked and glanced back, as if she'd forgotten he was walking behind her.

"A cave. I need to rest before we continue. The troll's den will be nearby. They don't have large hunting ranges at this time of year."

Icy fear gripped Malcolm. He stumbled over a pebble in his path, remembering the troll's guttural growls, teeth that could tear the flesh from his bones, and claws as sharp as his dagger. The stench of its blood still clung to him, tainting every breath he took.

"What if there are more of the beasts?"

"Trolls are solitary." She didn't turn back to speak to him this time.

His nerves grew.

Walking at a slower pace due to Luelle's injuries, they eventually reached the ledge that the troll had first leapt from. Malcolm took the opportunity to gaze at how far they'd travelled. Back in the direction of home, the Godswood blanketed the horizon, thick and crowded compared to the sparse trees around them now. Moody orange sunlight kissed the distant treetops. Far below, the Caeleste River carved a route through the valley. The walk still ahead of them was as daunting as the drop, leading him to an unknown destination full of people that hated him, all because they believed in a false history.

He lay his hand against the trunk of a thin tree near the edge of the ledge and looked down at the troll's corpse.

Its once grey fur was brown with blood. Gore spilled from the creature's neck where Malcolm had almost sliced off its entire head. Flies hovered around the mess in uneven, staggering flight paths.

Malcolm looked away before his nausea evolved into anything physical. Somehow, the troll looked more fearsome laying limp, slain so brutally.

When he turned around again, Luelle was almost out of sight, clambering over boulders half hidden by thorny green shrubs.

His heart jolted. He rushed after her, glancing around for anything else that might attack them. His muscles ached but he wouldn't let his guard down until they were somewhere safe and quiet.

Landing on the other side of the boulders, he almost collided with Luelle, who was standing still, staring at a narrow, jagged cave entrance extending into a steep wall of rock.

"How did you know this was here?" he asked, stepping to her side.

"I knew it would be nearby. There were tracks." Her lids were heavy over her eyes. She swayed where she stood. He resisted the urge to reach out and steady her, as he might if she were a friend.

She'd faced the brunt of the troll's ferocity. Panic had broken through his adrenaline when the beast had flung her like a child's toy. He'd believed they were both doomed when he heard the air leave her lungs after that impact. If the troll had followed him, rather than continuing its tirade against Luelle, perhaps they would've been.

And perhaps the panic he'd felt at her demise was part of the reason he'd lashed out after checking she was okay.

"How can we be sure this cave belonged to the troll and not some other beast?"

"Only one way to find out."

Malcolm stayed at her side as she lurched on, smothering the impulse to offer any assistance—he couldn't help the manners that had been drilled into him from a young age. The cave entrance was wide enough for them to fit walking side by side. Immediately inside, it widened to form a large, deep shelter.

Bones littered the floor, some still half-dressed in flesh, others licked so clean they gleamed in the dying daylight filtering through the cave's entrance.

Luelle pressed on, wading through the stench of decay. Malcolm followed with his arm covering his nose and mouth.

Further into the cave, the smell was less overpowering.

"Is it wise to continue walking blind?" he whispered. He'd paused at the edge of the evening light on the floor, letting Luelle venture into the darkness alone.

"It doesn't go much further." Her voice echoed to him. "The

cave twists. We might be able to light a small fire back here without being seen from outside. Most things will stay away if they know the troll lived here anyway, at least for a night or two."

"Okay. I'll fetch some firewood."

Luelle emerged from the shadows, startling him.

Her face was paler than usual. She took an unstable step forwards, but Malcolm grabbed her arm, stopping her from walking past him.

"Wait here. You are clearly exhausted. Clear a space for the fire instead, I shall return in a moment."

She opened her mouth to argue with him, as she always did, but closed it again and nodded.

Before leaving, Malcolm placed his bag on the ground and unstrapped his dagger from his waist, holding it out to her.

She didn't raise her hand to take it straight away. He couldn't read her expression when she eventually accepted it.

He left the cave without asking what she was thinking, walking with his head held tall and his gaze straight to avoid looking at the bones carpeting the floor.

Their cave was set back from the main path up the mountain. Shadows stretched towards Malcolm from the surrounding trees as he ventured back out into the world. A light breeze brushed his exposed skin, raising goosebumps on his arms.

He got to work collecting dry branches and sticks, balancing them in his arms until he could no longer bend down to pick up more without dropping any from the top of his pile.

On his return to the cave, Malcolm's eyes adjusted faster, the contrast between the light outside and in their shelter no longer as stark. Luelle sat in the darkness beside a cleared patch of floor. The dagger glinted beside her hip.

He dumped the wood on the floor.

"Can you make that while I look for somewhere to wash?" he asked. The dry gore on his skin cracked with every movement.

"There's probably a waterfall nearby. Don't go far now it's getting dark."

Malcolm nodded.

With a change of clothes and a bar of soap in hand, Malcolm left the cave again. He followed the edge of the mountain that their shelter burrowed into, looking over his shoulder every second step, in case another fearsome monster emerged from the shadows. None did.

After a few minutes, he stumbled across a trickle of water, cascading down a steep wall of stone, collecting in a small pool before overflowing again. Cupping his hands under the water and splashing it onto his body, Malcolm washed quickly, scrubbing at himself with his old shirt until the pool was stained red.

Pink and orange hues stained the sky when Malcolm returned to the cave, mostly free of troll guts and carrying another armful of firewood. Despite scouring his skin until it felt raw, he still felt sticky with phantom dirt. He had never missed the washrooms at home more.

Luelle had lit the fire in his absence and was half asleep beside the flames, sitting with her knees cradled to her chest, eyelids drooping.

"Don't sleep until you've washed." His voice startled her.

"You need to clean your wounds. Infection is more likely if you do not."

Fatigue diluted the withering glare she shot his way. Perhaps he'd pushed her too far too soon with the Power. This exhaustion wasn't from their battle alone, though that couldn't be helping things.

Wincing, Luelle pushed herself to her feet as he explained where she could find the small pool. She grabbed her bag, not bothering to separate her things, and wandered into the darkening night. Malcolm watched her leave with a frown. If she wasn't back before long, he'd assume she tumbled down the cliff and would go searching for her.

Whilst she was gone, he sorted through the remaining supplies in his bag.

He had another two small meals from Anwyn and some nuts and fruits they'd found in the forest before reaching the mountains. At his request, they'd avoided any more mushrooms. He wanted his Power back as soon as possible, but Luelle needed to rest and re-energise, even if that meant delaying their progress.

Unpacking some of the food from his bag, he spread a small meal in front of him. Selecting a slender stick from their pile of firewood, Malcolm pierced some pieces of bread and meat, rotating them over the flames.

Time dragged as Malcolm waited alone in the cave, thawing his limbs and drying his hair in the fire's warmth. Had Luelle found the same trickle of water? Had she stayed conscious long enough to wash?

He was preparing to go after her when he heard her shuffling steps returning.

Hunched over, with dirty clothes bundled in one arm and her bag dragging along the ground beside her, she didn't appear refreshed from the cold waterfall, but at least she was no longer covered in blood.

"How are your injuries?" he asked.

She sat a few feet away from him. He didn't miss her wince as she lowered herself to the ground.

"Fine." She pulled one of the leafy plates of food towards her, accepting the heated meat and bread with a mutter of appreciation. Malcolm found another stick to heat some more food for himself.

"Have you bound them?"

She shot him an annoyed look.

"I know how to look after my wounds, Prince. Besides, we have no supplies to bind them with."

"We can tear up the blanket Anwyn gave me. It may not be as sanitary as a bandage, but it will stem further bleeding from your cuts." He dragged his backpack towards himself and pulled out the material. Before Luelle could further object, he sliced into it with his dagger. "How many do you need?"

She inhaled a deep breath through her nose. "Maybe three or four."

Malcolm rolled his eyes. He passed the first strip to her. The blanket was long enough that a single length of the fabric would easily wrap twice and tie around her waist, not that he'd seen the troll cut her there. He tried not to remember the terror in her eyes after the troll had thrown her on top of him.

"I need to take my trousers off," she said, pointedly.

He turned away and continued slicing the blanket into strips as she undressed.

When he turned back to hand her the rest of the strips, his gaze automatically fell to the cuts on her thigh, shallow, red slashes, vibrant against her pale skin. She was dabbing sticky blood from them with the first strip.

Malcolm stilled, staring at the gory cuts. An expectant look from her made him avert his eyes once again. She snatched the rest of the strips from his hand and began wrapping one around her leg.

"That looks painful."

"It could've been worse."

"Did it get you anywhere else?" Images of the troll's claws flashed up in Malcolm's mind. She must be in agony.

"Don't worry, the Power isn't going to ooze out of my injuries," she snapped at him.

He gritted his teeth, but couldn't begrudge her attitude after what he'd said to her.

"I apologise for what I said back there." His father would've been ashamed to hear him speak such hateful words, even to an enemy. He was a grown man, not a child prone to lashing out whenever he was angry.

"Don't apologise, Prince. You were right, after all. I haven't fooled myself into thinking we care for one another." She tightened another knot around her waist. Blood darkened the material before she wrapped the next one around. "I know you're only here to get your Power back. I know that's why you didn't kill me before."

Malcolm set his dagger down, laying the final few strips in between them. Any she didn't use, he would pack in his bag, in case they suffered another assault. He toyed with his food. Was it worth being honest? It wasn't as if Luelle could repeat anything he said to anyone of importance. She'd have to return to Cerulya to face her punishment for stealing his Power once he got it back but he could easily monitor whoever tried to visit her in the palace dungeons. Nobody would believe anything she said about him, anyway.

"I apologise for that, too." He watched the flames dancing in front of them as he spoke. His voice felt too loud, echoing back to him in the cave. "I was angry at myself that day. Don't get me wrong, you committed an act of treason, and I should be taking you back to the capital. I should have already taken you back. But, that is what I was truly angry about—my own failure to do what is right, not your actions."

Sounds of movement from Luelle paused, but Malcolm couldn't look up at her. He continued, unable to stop bleeding this internal wound now he'd started.

"I keep telling myself that no matter what my duty is, there must be a peaceful method to achieve it and I know in my heart that is the truth, but it isn't the whole truth. Part of me simply has no desire to return to Cerulya." The words emerged as a whisper. "Everything will change when I return. My father will not be there, I will have new responsibilities and less time to spend with my friends and family. Nothing will be private, even more so than usual. I likely won't even get a say in who I marry.

And, this week has shown me I barely know any of the kingdom I am to rule over, not really. This is the first time I have spoken to ordinary people without them knowing my identity and adjusting their actions accordingly. The Meteile were so different than I imagined, despite learning of their communities from my father's advisers. I know my father would be disappointed in me and that my family is suffering at home right now, likely sick with worry about whether I am even alive. I know my friends might never have made it out of the Great Forest when I left them alone there to fight off the arachnids, but I can pretend none of that is true whilst I am out here, not facing it. I have no desire to return because for the first time in my life, I can pretend to be a normal person."

Malcolm slammed his lips shut at the end of his speech, preventing any more of his secrets from spilling into the night.

He met Luelle's gaze but couldn't read her expression in the flickering shadows.

"King Alaric wouldn't be disappointed in you," she murmured.

He averted his eyes back to the fire, but she continued.

"He was proud of you, Malcolm. It was clear every time he spoke about you and your family. He loved you more than anything. You forget I saw the chaos of his life whilst I was working in the castle. I understand how hard his role could be, how much it affected him behind closed doors. You shouldn't blame yourself for wanting to put that off for a while. I think anyone would feel the same."

Malcolm swallowed. He stayed quiet until he was certain he

wouldn't choke on the emotions overwhelming him.

"You can use the Power to heal," he said after a long while. Flames devoured the sticks he added to their small fire.

Luelle raised her brows at him.

"Father used it to heal our cuts and scrapes when we were children. Though, you need a good understanding of anatomy, and I wouldn't recommend trying it tonight. You should rest before using it again."

She nodded.

"Maybe we can try it tomorrow."

"Let's not get ahead of ourselves."

"Can you wrap the cuts on my arm?" Luelle asked, after shuffling back into her trousers.

Malcolm nodded. Pushing his food to one side, he shuffled closer to her. She lifted her sleeve to reveal a pattern of fierce puncture marks over her outer bicep. He cut the blanket strips shorter and wrapped them around.

"Do you need me to help with any of yours?" she asked him after he'd tied off the last strip needed on her arm.

"No, my injuries are not that bad. I may have a few bruises but nothing serious."

After binding the last of her cuts, she settled down to sleep, leaving Malcolm to stew in his thoughts and feelings about everything he'd admitted tonight. Speaking the venomous thoughts aloud eased his guilt a little, though they still ate at him from within.

# 25

Luelle slept through the entire night. When she woke, Malcolm was no longer sitting next to the burnt-out fire pit. She pushed herself upright, ignoring the aches and shooting pains in her thigh as the movement pulled at her injuries. She grabbed the two flasks from beside their bags and got to her feet.

For a brief moment, she wondered if the prince had fled or if he'd been killed by another creature living on the mountain, but she found him sitting against the wall toward the mouth of the cave, watching the sunrise. At some point in the night, he'd pushed all of the troll's old bones and meals to one side of the cave, away from his chosen seat.

He looked back as he heard Luelle approach.

"Sorry for sleeping so long," she said. "You should've woken me."

The prince shrugged. His shoulders were hunched compared to normal, eyelids drooping over his hazel eyes. "How do you feel?"

"Better. You should get some sleep before we head out."

"I will be fine."

Luelle resisted the urge to roll her eyes. "You were hurt in the fight, too, even if only a little. And, it's still a couple of days before we reach our destination. Swallow your pride and rest while I get us breakfast." The words came out sharper than she'd intended.

A muscle jumped in Malcolm's jaw, but he nodded and stood, sweeping past Luelle towards the darker parts of the troll's den.

She didn't wait around to see if he tried to get any proper rest.

Her movements were slow and stiff as she walked to the cave mouth but her muscles loosened with each step. Pain throbbed through her thighs and waist, worse than she cared to admit to herself or the prince. Sleeping on the floor had done nothing to ease the discomfort of her injuries, adding twinges and aches where there had been none yesterday. It didn't seem real that in a few days, she might be sleeping in a bed again.

How different would her home look now? A lot could change in five years. Perhaps Zeke and the others were no longer living in the mountain's cave systems. They couldn't stay there if the site became a pilgrimage location once again, as they'd suspected it once was, or if it became a doorway to the realm of the Gods, as Zeke predicted it would.

Excitement blended with the nervous anticipation in Luelle's stomach as it hit her anew how close she was to seeing her family.

She walked towards the trickle of a waterfall she'd washed in the previous evening and pictured herself reuniting with her friends. Were Freya and Imbryl as excited to see her as she was to see them? They must know about her return by now. News of the king's death would've travelled further and faster than her at this point, even if news of his lost Power was still being hidden.

When she reached the waterfall, Luelle refilled the two flasks and tied their leather straps to either side of her waistband. Splashing water onto her face, she scrubbed at her eyes and neck. She considered washing her wounds again, but glancing down her waistband at the dirty, makeshift bandages, discoloured with whatever had oozed out of her overnight, it seemed like too much work. She'd be better off waiting for Zeke to look over them with proper medical supplies.

After scrubbing her face, she lingered away from the cave. Malcolm would need more time to sleep and she hadn't been gone long. Instead, she explored the foliage, foraging for their breakfast. As eager as she was to complete their journey and be rid of the prince, part of her clung to the secrets he'd admitted last night, the knowledge that he'd enjoyed parts of their time together or at least enjoyed being away from the castle, even if not Luelle's company. It was getting harder not to form a sense of attachment to him, to his solid, steady presence, even when he made it clear he didn't feel the same, as he had yesterday after their fight with the troll.

Thinking about him now wasn't helping anything, either.

She forced her thoughts elsewhere until she'd gathered enough food to see them through the morning. The mountains were less bountiful than the Godswood but the shrubbery here still offered some sustenance. Their path wouldn't ascend to the highest parts of the Peaks, where only the hardiest plants grew. It would take another week of hard, fast-paced travelling if they wanted to reach the tips of these mountains, taking them well beyond the destination they were currently seeking.

The prince was dozing when Luelle returned to the cave. He lay curled on his side, mouth parted and hair mussed. His large hand was closed around the hilt of his sword as if he'd fallen asleep waiting to defend himself against something.

Luelle chewed on her lip and took the food she'd gathered back towards the cave's sunlit entrance, leaving him in peace. Placing the food on the ground, she sat looking out of the cave's opening, suppressing a groan as the movement tested her sore body. She ate her share of breakfast and contemplated the many things she and her friends would do together when they were finally reunited.

When she was down to one final fruit core, she perched it on the stone floor in front of her and practised the grounding techniques Malcolm had started to teach her yesterday. Her body cried out for a physical break but sleeping through the entire night had recharged her mentally. It might be a better idea to save all of that energy, in case anything else attacked them on their trek, but ever since she'd succeeded in using her Power, Luelle had been itching to try again.

Closing her eyes, she sought out every sensation, every sound, every scent, no matter how unpleasant or distant.

Despite growing used to it overnight, she smelled the bones

and gore not far from her. It overpowered almost everything but she took deep breaths until she could distinguish summer's final few wildflowers outside and the prince's faint musk behind her.

A stray breeze wandered into the den to caress her cheek, a cold kiss against her skin. Its breathy whisper melded with her own breathing and that of the prince. Birds trilled far beyond the entrance to the cave.

As she isolated each sense, the Power inside Luelle's chest glowed hotter, brighter.

She opened her eyes and stared at the fruit core in front of her. Keeping a tight grip on her awareness, she turned her concentration to the core and willed it to rise, teasing away the smallest amount of the Power within her to do so.

Three breaths passed with no movement. On the fourth, the core rose, trembling, until it was in line with Luelle's eyes. It hung in the air in front of her.

A breath burst from Luelle, but she held the core where it floated. She willed it to rotate.

As if in slow motion, the core spun to show off each of her bite marks.

Her smile spread wide.

"Well done."

She started, twisting towards the prince's voice. The core fell to the floor with a wet thud. Malcolm was leaning against the cave wall behind her, expression blank.

"Thanks," she said, willing her heartbeat to slow. Heat spread across her face at the realisation he'd been watching her attempt to practise grounding herself. At least she'd succeeded in using the Power, this time. She might not have lived it down if he'd watched her fail without his help.

The prince wandered closer and sat beside her, reaching for the food Luelle had foraged. "Did it feel easier today?"

Luelle shrugged. "Easier to manage the amount I used but not necessarily any easier to control. You were right about the meditation, the mindfulness stuff, though."

"Good to know. Will we reach the cavern today?" He bit into a plum. Red juice ran down his long, slender fingers, too reminiscent of the troll's blood.

Luelle averted her eyes as he licked it away, forgoing his usual etiquette. "Not quite. We should by tomorrow as long as nothing else delays us."

She couldn't decide if the prince was pleased about that or not as they sat in silence, waiting for him to finish eating. Perhaps he wished to stay away from Cerulya longer, given the secrets he'd spilled last night.

"Do you want to try and get more sleep? You must still be tired."

He shook his head. "I will be fine once we start moving."

She wasn't convinced but didn't push it.

They gathered their things once Malcolm was done, leaving the remnants of their meal in the cave with the bones. The prince insisted on changing into his leather armour before they departed, in case of any other unwanted interactions with the mountain's inhabitants. His sword and dagger remained strapped to his waist.

Morning passed with little conversation. Luelle was fine

with it, as long as it meant no more arguments. As much as she enjoyed bickering with the prince, his comment yesterday stung too much to throw herself straight back into their usual routine.

She blamed homesickness for her mood. Somehow, her loneliness grew stronger with each step she took closer to her home and friends.

Rain began falling from the gloomy skies above them an hour or so after they'd left their shelter. They agreed to push through it, rather than delay their progress further. If it got heavier they could stop.

Anxiety and paranoia ate at Luelle as they walked, souring her mood further. Dark thoughts clouded her mind like the skies above, most notably that her friends wouldn't feel the same when she returned. She'd been gone for a long time, it wouldn't be unusual for them to have grown closer to others in her absence. She'd missed out on countless experiences with them over the past five years, and she'd changed during her time at the castle, so the same would be true of them. What if those changes were too large to ignore—too large for their shared history to hold them together any more?

Once, Luelle thought she stayed with Zeke out of necessity because she was unable to make a way in life alone. Her time working in the castle had disproven that, even if it had been to serve his goals. Now she knew she could live alone, did she have an excuse to keep putting his desires before her own? Did she even *have* any desires of her own? Could she find another reason to stay with Zeke once they achieved their goal of returning the Power to the Veseile race?

Would she have anywhere to go if she couldn't?

"May we stop for some food?"

Luelle spun around. She'd forgotten the prince was behind her, his footsteps drowned out by her roaring thoughts. They'd eaten a late breakfast, and in her foul temper, she'd pushed through any hunger pangs for lunch.

The sky was already darkening behind the grey clouds.

Her clothing was soaked from the rain still pattering around them. A shiver wracked through her.

"I'm sorry. We should've stopped sooner." She wrapped her arms around herself, hugging any warmth that remained inside.

The prince shrugged. His dark hair was plastered to his face. He pushed it out of his eyes. "It is fine. We both have reasons to want this journey over sooner rather than later."

Luelle looked away from his intense stare. "We'll find somewhere to stop for the night and eat the rest of our supplies from Anwyn. We've covered more ground than I expected today."

He nodded.

She led the prince on, both looking out for anywhere that might provide them with some shelter. Luelle picked food from any bushes and trees she saw as they walked, gathering a few nuts and fruits to bulk out their meal. They found no more caves like the one they'd slept in last night but stumbled across a ledge overlooking the valley, tucked away from the mountain path and offering protection from the rain.

# 26

Malcolm sat with his back against the rocks curving up and over their campsite for the night, cringing back against the occasional raindrops that blew in. Their shelter was just large enough for him to sit upright in, though if his spine was straight, his hair brushed against the ceiling of rock above them. Back to back, he and Luelle changed into dry clothes and laid out their wet clothes in the only other space untouched by the rain beneath the overhanging rock, in the hopes that they would dry overnight.

Luelle was trying to light a small fire but no sparks would catch on the wet wood. He didn't bother pointing out that she might be able to achieve it with the Power, regardless of the rain. She was getting a better grip on the Power, but she must still be tired from their travels and her injuries. Failing to use it to light a fire would dishearten her and he shouldn't keep encouraging her to use it when he needed her to return it as soon as her plan failed. If she grew accustomed to using it, she might refuse to give it back or even use it against him.

A voice deep down questioned why he'd taught her in the first place, but he couldn't deny it was safer travelling with her now she knew the basics. His father had taught him how the Power was linked to its wielder's emotion and there was bound to be a lot of that when he commanded her to return to the capital with him at the end of their journey. She couldn't continue believing the fantasy that she'd escape this unpunished.

He shivered against the wind that whipped into their shelter. Set back into the rock, they avoided the worst of the gusts but didn't escape it all. Gloom from the oncoming night shrouded their view out over the valley. Above, the sky was equally bleak, a patchwork of grey clouds, hiding the sunset and its remaining light.

"Should we try to find another cave?" Malcolm asked when Luelle's attempts to light their fire grew more aggressive.

She kept her back to him. "You really want to get in another fight just for a slightly warmer place to sleep?" she snapped.

Malcolm scowled at her back, hunched over the pitiful excuse of a firepit. "There must be some caves around without trolls or anything else living in them."

"It won't be worth the energy we spend trying to find one. This will be fine for one night. We're lucky the weather held out until now, anyway. It's not cold enough that we'll be in any real danger sleeping without a fire now we're in dry clothes."

Malcolm looked around at their scant shelter. He had no clue how they'd manage to sleep in such a small space. Surely she only intended to stay here until the weather cleared up. "There is barely enough cover to keep us out of the rain," he pointed out.

If he rolled over in his sleep, he might fall halfway back down the mountain.

"It's not even raining any more."

He frowned. Yes, the raindrops had slowed but they still slapped against the stone and leaves around them. Besides, the clouds above left no promise that the night would stay dry.

Luelle flung the dagger and flint to the ground after another five minutes of failing to produce a flame. Her expression was as dark as the sky above. Malcolm had hoped her mood would improve as they got closer to the end of their journey, where she said her friends awaited her, but perhaps her motives were more complex than he'd anticipated. Or, perhaps she'd been lying to him about their destination all along.

Could she have lured him here only to kill him? Plenty of the extremist Veseile groups would be willing to go that far to destroy the human monarchy they claimed wronged them, despite their lack of evidence. Her time working in the castle proved that she was capable of such deceit.

A knot of anxiety tightened in his stomach. He spoke up, putting the thought out of his mind.

"Let me try. Eat some of your food." He'd been travelling with her long enough to know that her most waspish moods were usually a sign too much time had passed since their last meal.

She said nothing but did as he requested. They switched places, awkwardly brushing against one another to squeeze past. He banished the unwanted memories that flashed in his mind at such close proximity to her—of the brief moment he'd accidentally looked at her washing in the Ophidian Channel and of her pale thighs last night, slashed with angry red cuts from the troll they'd fought. Embarrassment flooded through him, setting his face on fire. He was grateful to turn his back to her so she had no opportunity to wonder what thoughts were causing such a reaction. Isolation from his regular life must be driving him insane.

Malcolm copied Luelle's movements as well as he could, striking his dagger with the flint repeatedly, gritting his teeth in concentration. His bicep ached by the time Luelle had eaten most of her food, but there was no further sign of a flame.

Rain returned, falling heavier again, though thankfully outside of their shelter.

He leaned back to sit on his heels. "I do not think we will manage a fire tonight." He crawled back beside her.

She huffed a sigh. Food hadn't done much to improve her mood.

Malcolm shuffled where he was sitting, leaving several inches of space between them and trying to find a comfortable position on the rocky floor. He moved his bag to block some of the wind.

They stared out at the dark valley in silence, side by side.

"Is everything alright?" he ventured, considering it a safe enough question after a brief internal battle.

"Yes." Luelle wrapped her arms around her knees, hugging them close to her chest.

"Are you sure?" Malcolm eyed her. Scanning the past few days in his mind, he tried to locate anything he could've said or done to prompt such a frosty attitude. Of course, he'd been cruel after their fight with the troll, when he claimed he'd only saved her to protect his Power, but he'd apologised for that last night; she couldn't still be holding it against him.

"I'm sure."

It was going to be a long evening.

Malcolm stared at the mountains looming opposite them, on the far side of the valley. Night approached earlier with each passing day. Stars blinked to life in the occasional distant gap between the dark, rolling clouds.

His thoughts turned to home, to everyone awaiting his return. Before long, this journey would be a distant memory. He'd be back in the safety of the castle walls, surrounded by his friends and family, working to protect and strengthen his kingdom. What were they all doing in his absence?

Had Viv received his letter and sent soldiers to help him from the confines of their father's rooms? Had Theo and Leena found a way to figure out where he and Luelle were travelling? He leaned his head back against the rock. Last night's confession lingered like a sour taste, his fears that his friends never made it out of the Great Forest alive. As much as he didn't want to believe it, there was a chance they hadn't escaped the arachnids after he abandoned them to chase Luelle. He had to accept that sooner or later. He had to face the potential that he'd led his friends to a premature death.

Luelle spoke up, startling him out of his morbid thoughts.

"I'm scared," she blurted. "Of seeing my friends again."

Malcolm turned to look at her but she kept her own stare straight ahead, eyes locked on the dark horizon. Tension lined her jaw.

"Why?" His voice was quiet against the dying rain.

She shrugged but didn't loosen her arms, clasped around her legs as if they were the only thing holding her together. "I've been away a long time. People change."

"Are they not the ones that sent you away?" He frowned, trying to piece together the scant information she'd offered him about her past. It hardly mattered if her friends had changed—she couldn't stay with them.

"No. Not really. Kind of." Luelle shook her head in exasperation. "Zeke was the one who brought us all together. We've all worked to help him. I was best suited for this task so it made sense that I was the one who went."

"It must have been daunting to leave everything you knew." He couldn't imagine being in a situation like that, starting afresh in a place where no one knew his name. At home, everyone knew his name. He couldn't escape strangers claiming to know him, even if he'd never seen them before in his life.

"It was. I was terrified."

"Yet, your friends still made you go?"

She shook her head again. "You don't understand. I went gladly, despite my fear."

"Why did you have to make the return journey alone?"

"What?" She turned to him, a frown on her face.

"Why did Zeke not send companions to escort you back? Our trip together has been dangerous. If getting my Power to this cave was so important, I would presume you should travel with a company of guards at the very least."

"They know I can handle myself. The others have done far

more dangerous things than this trip." Her tone grew defensive.

"But you said Zeke's entire life goal was to steal my family's Power. Surely bringing that to him should earn you some protection. Aren't they supposed to be your friends?"

"You're not helping me feel any better," she snapped.

Malcolm shut his mouth. Staying quiet felt better than saying the wrong thing but the quiet would cause a spiral of dark thoughts; images of Theo and Leena being torn apart by arachnids, echoes of his family's cries when his father died, imagining the brutal death Luelle was most likely leading him to.

"I apologise. It must have been hard for you, being away from your loved ones for so long," he said, hoping she wouldn't recognise it for the lame attempt to keep their conversation going that it was. "I would not like to do it."

Luelle chewed at her lip. She nodded. "It was really hard. Living in the palace was lonely." The rain had stopped, but the wind continued whistling through the valley.

Malcolm frowned. "Do...do the servants not get along with one another? They always seem happy enough when I see them." He hated how oblivious it made him sound, but their welfare was the responsibility of others in the castle. Philip, the castle's seneschal, dealt with the servant's needs so the monarch never had to. Malcolm tried to treat all of his servants with the respect they deserved—they certainly worked a lot harder than him—but there were so many of them, he had difficulty keeping track beyond the ones who served him and his family day to day.

Luelle snorted. "Some do. But, they form cliques. I didn't fit in with any of those."

His frown deepened. "Were they cruel to you?"

She shrugged, eyeing him in a way she hadn't before. He wasn't sure what the expression meant. "More cold than cruel. They would never jeopardise their chances of working their way through the royal household to serve you or your family. A lot of people were jealous that Alaric took to me so fast, I guess, even though they would've preferred to tend to you. It happens to more of them than you'd think, but a lot of the outcasts gravitate towards each other so they aren't truly alone."

Malcolm's food soured in his stomach. People were being ostracised just so that others could work closer to him? Were his current servants acting like this towards others? Maybe this was something he could fix, something he *should* fix, when he returned.

"Who acted like that towards you? Tell me their names," he demanded.

Luelle gave him a tight-lipped smile. "Absolutely not."

"Luelle, tell me." He poured every ounce of authority he could into his tone, though he didn't feel like royalty when he was travelling with her. What was his title if not something to use to improve people's lives?

"No. Your interference would only make it worse." She shook her head, stubborn.

Malcolm gritted his teeth. He'd set Leena or Philip on the task of finding out when he returned home.

"Regardless, I am sorry you experienced that. I do not want anyone in my home to feel like an outsider, particularly not because of me. I know some of how you feel." He hesitated but pressed on. "My position made things lonely, growing up. I never knew if people were only befriending me because of my title or because they actually wanted to be around me. The latter was rare."

She stared at him. "Did you have many true friends?"

"Only two that I still trust to this day." He offered a wry smile to the valley, though it was short-lived as his thoughts strayed back to his friends fighting the arachnids.

Luelle watched him in silence until Malcolm shifted with discomfort under her gaze.

"What?"

"You remind me of the king."

Malcolm swallowed. He couldn't run from the pain of his father's memory forever but instinct still made him rear back from it.

"Sorry, I don't know why I keep bringing him up. I promise I'm not trying to be cruel."

"I know. I thought you were at first, but I believe you when you say he meant something to you, too. He had that effect on people. He could turn anyone into a friend." Malcolm felt a smile pulling at his lips from the memories.

Above them, the clouds had thinned, revealing the night sky beyond. Malcolm automatically scanned the stars for his favourite constellations and the brighter faraway planets, peeking out from behind the patchy remains of clouds.

"What's with you and the stars?" Luelle interrupted his search. "You're always looking at them. Whenever it's your turn to watch our camp, I wake to find you staring at the sky."

Malcolm glanced at her, but his eyes drifted back up. It was easier not to look at her when they were being so open with one another, easier to forget who he was really talking to.

"I have always loved them. They make me feel small. It is a nice break from being told how important I am all day." He breathed a laugh. "At home, we have an observatory. Father showed it to me after he found me sneaking from my room to stare at the skies from the roof every night as a child. He even moved my chambers so they were in the same wing as the observatory when he realised how much I loved it. We spent a lot of time there, tracking the stars and other planets. I feel like he's still with me when I look at them. And, I rarely get to see the stars as clearly as I have the last few days. The city lights stain the view."

From the corner of his eye, Malcolm saw Luelle tilt her head to stare up at the skies with him.

"I was jealous of you, you know."

He furrowed his brow, turning to look at her. "Because I'm a prince?"

She breathed a laugh, smiling, but kept her eyes on the skies. The details of her face were harder to discern since night had fallen.

"No, because you have a family that loves you. That's all I wanted growing up. It was clear how much King Alaric loved you and the others, even from the brief time I spent with him. I resented you for it. It made it easier to do what I needed to."

"I thought you said the people you live with are like family to you."

"They are but it's not the same. I still wonder how different my life would be if I knew my parents or if I had a proper home. I want to know how different my life would be if I was normal."

"I think everyone feels like that sometimes."

"Maybe."

Malcolm uncrossed his legs and stretched them long in front of him now the rain had stopped. Gazing out, the stars appeared in ever-moving holes in the clouds, creating an illusion that made the night sky look like it was racing over him.

"Do you think we would've been friends if we'd met under different circumstances?"

The question came from nowhere. Malcolm turned to meet Luelle's stare as he considered every conversation they'd had, every annoyance, every biting insult, and the few shared smiles. He swallowed, remembering the panic he'd felt when the troll had almost killed her and the guilt and shame when he'd hurt her feelings following that confrontation.

"I do not know," he murmured.

Her guarded expression melted into an amused smile.

"A lesser person would have lied to save my feelings."

A small, matching smile curved on Malcolm's lips. Maybe, if circumstances were different, she was right and they could've been friends. But, if the circumstances were different, would they be the same people? This trip had opened his eyes to a lot of things he hadn't considered before. He didn't feel like the same person he'd been before he left the capital.

"We should get some sleep."

"Will we have enough shelter here?" Malcolm looked again at

the space around them. The ledge above offered shelter from the weather but not the temperature. A chill had settled deep into his bones, made all the worse by his rain-damp hair. Night would only bring a colder climate, and his blanket was in strips wrapped around Luelle's injuries.

"I hope so. We can try making another fire but the wood won't have dried out by now, and it would just be a beacon to anything looking for food." Moonlight glinted off her eyes, unveiled by a passing cloud. Her grim expression mirrored the one he'd seen her wear when facing down the troll yesterday. "Sharing body heat is going to be the safest way to stay warm through the night."

"Sharing..." Malcolm slammed his lips shut when he realised what she was suggesting. At least the darkness hid the heat flushing his cheeks this time.

"If you're not comfortable with it, we don't have to. We will probably be fine, and if it gets too cold, we can look for somewhere else to sleep or risk trying to build another fire," she blurted.

She must be able to see his horrified expression. He tried to smooth the lines of his face. Was all of this a ploy to get close enough to stab him in his sleep? No, that was ridiculous. She could've killed him several nights over if that was her plan. He'd slept in her presence multiple times with no consequence.

"No, you are right. It will be safer this way. I did not survive a battle with a troll just to be taken out by a cold night." His laugh was frantic, but he couldn't pin down why the thought of sleeping so close to her made him feel sick.

It was inappropriate to sleep beside his enemy, a traitor to his crown, but nothing about their travels had been appropriate, from their first interaction when Luelle had nearly broken his nose.

She moved their bags to the edge of the ledge, fashioning a small windbreak. She lay down first, beside the bags. Malcolm twisted, bending his legs so she had room.

"You should let me sleep on that side," he said, discomfort a heavy weight in his chest. "It will be colder there."

She wriggled as if the rock beneath her body might mould itself to fit her better. "You've slept in warm, fluffy beds your entire life, I hardly think you'll be comfortable exposed to the wind."

Malcolm scowled at her, relieved their verbal sparring could take his mind off having to lie down next to the person who'd stolen his bloodline's Power. "I will not be comfortable sleeping on either side, and I have not slept in warm, fluffy beds my entire life, I'll have you know."

"Our time travelling together doesn't count." She grinned up at him.

"I don't mean these weeks. I have slept on ships, in tents—I do not need to list the places I have slept to you," he snapped. It wasn't worth mentioning that he'd been given stuffed mattresses and goose down pillows in all of those locations.

Luelle laughed. "You're stalling, Prince. You slayed a troll just yesterday with no fear, but you're shaking in your boots at the thought of laying beside a woman. Do they really keep you so sheltered in the castle?" she taunted him.

"I have no qualms with lying beside a woman." His cheeks heated again.

"Oh, so it's because I'm a commoner?" She propped herself up onto her elbows.

"No! This is simply for warmth and you are twisting how it sounds like more to make me feel uncomfortable," he accused.

Her lips curved into a mocking smile. "I would never, my Prince."

Malcolm gritted his teeth and shuffled to lie beside her on the ground, banishing any inappropriate thoughts from his mind. How long had it been since he'd experienced this sort of proximity to another? He lay on his back, limbs stiff enough that they might snap at any moment. His entire arm was flush against Luelle's. If he lay on his side, he'd have more room but would be forced to turn his back to her, which didn't seem a sensible choice, or turn to face her, which was even more daunting.

He stared at the rock above him. He couldn't even twist to look at the stars without appearing to lean into her.

Despite feeling her body shift as she adjusted her position, Malcolm didn't glance over.

Luelle pressed closer, rolling onto her side and pushing her chest into his arm. Warmth rolled from her. His heart raced. Her breath tickled his ear as she spoke.

"You know, Prince, we'd warm up faster if we took our clothes off."

Malcolm jerked away from her, eyes wide. Peals of laughter escaped her as he almost smashed his head into the wall behind him, trapped between that and her, like a frightened animal with no escape route.

"Forgive me, I couldn't help myself." Luelle reined in her laughter. She unclasped her bag, pulling out her blanket from Anwyn. "It's too easy to rile you."

Taking a deep, calming breath, he forced himself back onto the ground. He could survive one night sleeping beside her. At least he knew the Power was safe whilst she was so close to him.

Luelle lay the blanket over both of their legs, though their feet poked out of the bottom when she pulled it up to cover more of her torso.

Malcolm lay stiff and uncomfortable, listening to her even breathing until sleep claimed him.

# 27

Luelle was warm when she awoke. The cool breeze against her face was a pleasant contrast to the heat of her body. She shifted where she lay, but the weight around her waist didn't move.

Her eyes snapped open when she remembered she'd fallen asleep beside the prince, that those were his legs entwined with hers, the weight around her waist was his arm, and the firm pressure pushing against her rear was—

They scrambled away from one another at the same time, sharing the same silent realisations. She grabbed at their bags after almost knocking them over the ledge of their shelter.

Malcolm's head collided with the rocky wall that had protected them from yesterday's rain. He hissed, raising both hands to cradle the point of impact.

"Are you hurt?" Luelle blurted but made no effort to move closer to him. Her face was aflame thinking of how entangled they'd been in one another's limbs, of how pleasant his arm felt draped over her. She was happy enough to tease Malcolm, to push his buttons and entertain herself with his reactions, but he was still the prince. He was still the descendant of a long line of traitors to her entire race and still someone she'd only truly known for a couple of weeks.

"I am fine," Malcolm said from between gritted teeth, still clutching his head. He didn't look up at her.

Luelle shuffled backwards, moving their bags aside to create more space away from him.

"Are you bleeding?"

He drew one of his hands in front of his face. "No." He scooted away from the wall and rubbed at his head with the other hand.

"I'm sorry, I didn't mean to startle you."

"You did not, I apologise, too. I did not—I mean, it was not —" He didn't meet her eyes, cheeks crimson.

"You don't have to apologise, it's perfectly normal. Let's drop it." She averted her own stare, knowing her cheeks must be as red as his. She tried to change the subject. "If I remember correctly, there's another waterfall just a short way off our path. We can wash there and try to find some food on the way." She toyed with the straps on her bag, staring out at the view over the valley. Low fog drifted between the mountains, hugging the banks of the Caeleste River and hiding the spaces between the trees.

"Will we reach it today?"

She looked at him.

The prince looked far from the man he'd been at the start of their journey. When he'd first confronted and attacked Luelle in the Great Forest, he'd still been the figure she'd known from a distance over the last five years, poised and polished in both personality and appearance. Their days together without real washing facilities and only each other for conversation had shattered that perception.

In plain clothes, he was a less intimidating presence. Any swelling around his nose was long gone, returning the sharpness to his features. His skin had browned further in the sun and his facial hair had grown to a length Luelle had never seen on him, like a shadow hugging his jaw. Dark smudges had settled beneath his eyes but they emphasised the green in his irises. His hair was wild, curling around his ears, instead of being pushed back and carefully styled as it always had been in the palace.

And with those superficial changes came others Luelle hadn't expected. Layers of his personality had peeled back over their most recent days together. In Cerulya, he was a distant, regal figure, someone who had been easy to steal from. On their travels, she'd felt herself warming to him, looking out for his regular habits, like the way his neck flushed with colour when she teased him or how he'd rub his eyes, stretch and yawn loudly every morning before donning a more princely demeanour. She was discovering who Malcolm was—not the prince but the person behind the title.

She preferred this version of him.

Meeting his eyes again, she found him staring at her, his question unanswered whilst she'd been musing about him. He raised his brows at her.

"Oh, uh, what did you say?"

He rolled his eyes. "Will we reach the cavern today?"

"Yes." She nodded. "It's not far from here."

Part of her was eager to push on and complete her mission, to reunite with her friends and her home, but a smaller part, a part she was trying hard to ignore, was desperate to delay their progress. Since Malcolm had admitted his secrets to her after their battle with the troll, that he was enjoying their journey together, she realised she felt the same. Not quite in the same way as Malcolm, none of these experiences were new or as freeing to her, but she'd been enjoying herself more than she probably should have.

He'd relished the opportunity to be nobody, to be normal and escape his royal duties. She'd relished the simple comfort of a regular companion and some independence to make her own choices rather than working under someone else's command. What if working for Zeke again felt as stifling as working in the palace had?

Malcolm had made it very clear he did not care for her and was only there to retrieve his Power, but his barbed company was the most consistent she'd had in years. Luelle hadn't realised what a shadow of herself she'd become until she'd stepped away from her false persona in Cerulya and been free to do and say whatever she pleased once more.

As soon as they reached the cavern, everything would change once again. It had been hard enough adapting to life with Zeke and then to life on her own in the castle. Her future was murky with possibility and the unknown had always terrified her.

"Are you going to try and stop me when we arrive?" she asked.

Malcolm met her eyes again. His throat bobbed.

"I don't know." The words were a whisper. "Are you going to return the Power if your plan does not work?"

Luelle couldn't find the answer. Even if she wished to do so, would Zeke allow it? The concern in her chest grew from a seed to a fist. If only last night could have lasted forever. She had fun talking to the prince and, for a while, he seemed to enjoy her company too. Speaking to one another in the darkness was easier, allowing them to admit things they weren't brave enough to voice in daylight.

She couldn't blame him for not trusting her completely. He'd been raised in ignorance. The whole kingdom had. But, he was smart enough to make the most of the changes that would happen today, to turn them to his advantage and use them to strengthen his realm. He could be the king who re-gifted the Power to the nation.

"Are your people going to hurt me?" Malcolm asked when she didn't reply to his first question.

Luelle frowned. "No, of course not. Zeke only wants the Power returned to its source, to the Veseile people. That has always been his goal. He doesn't agree with the groups calling for revenge against the monarchy." She didn't admit that he'd once supported that position.

The prince stared at her, unconvinced.

"I won't let them hurt you."

He snorted at that.

"What?" Luelle asked, indignant. "Do you think they wouldn't listen to me? I might remind you that we're here together because I beat you in a fight."

"I would hardly say you beat me, and that wasn't a fair fight." Malcolm cocked one eyebrow but the corners of his lips tilted upwards ever so slightly. "However, I am aware that you have no loyalty to me. I need to know if there is a risk things will escalate. I have my family and kingdom to think of."

She nodded. "I haven't seen or communicated with Zeke and the others in over five years, but before I left, they only wanted to retrieve Vesanya's Power."

Malcolm said nothing.

"If you'd rather, you can wait here and I'll come back for you once it's done."

His brow furrowed. "No, I must see this through. I have come too far to turn away now."

They remained staring at one another for a while, neither prepared to leave their shelter because as soon as they did, everything would change.

But Luelle's stomach growled, reminding them the world was still turning, even if they wished it otherwise.

She crawled away from the overhanging ledge and got to her feet. She held out her hand. Malcolm followed and grasped it, letting her pull him to his own feet. His weight tugged at the cuts on her core but she suppressed her wince.

They gathered their things in silence and Luelle led them to the waterfall she'd remembered from years before, finding it after ten minutes of stumbling through overgrown bushes. Collecting nuts and fruits as they walked, they ate as they travelled to avoid acknowledging the tense atmosphere that had fallen over them.

Malcolm took the first lookout, letting her wash first. He sat a few steps away with his back to the water, offering as much privacy as he could.

Luelle made short work of washing and redressing into the same dirty clothes. She didn't remove her bandages, once again only scrubbing at herself with handfuls of water and soap around the fabric of her bandages. When she was ready, she walked to the patch of grass where Malcolm was waiting. He started to unpack his clothing from his bag.

"I think you should wear your armour today," she said, the weight in her chest returning at the thought of his earlier question. Would the others trust her word if she defended the prince against any that might take a dislike to him? "Just in case."

He swallowed and nodded.

# 28

Once Malcolm had washed and redressed, they walked in silence. Their path was steeper than before, but the loose dirt and stones transformed into carved steps, designed to lead people to the old pilgrimage site Luelle was taking him to.

The breeze was a blessed relief as they climbed. A sheen of sweat adorned Malcolm's forehead. Their breathing grew heavier as they pushed on, accompanied by the regular beat of their footsteps and the occasional birdsong.

Anxiety grew like a sickness in his gut. If Luelle didn't return his Power, as she'd sworn to earlier in their trip, he would have no choice but to take her back to Cerulya by force, even if he was outnumbered in the cave.

He struggled to see many outcomes that involved him making it home. If he made it back alive to tell the tale, Viv might kill him herself for such recklessness.

He shouldn't have let things get this far but he couldn't back out now.

"Did you live here before you came to the capital?" He didn't enjoy topics linked to Luelle's deceit against his family but even thinking of that was better than dwelling on the ways he might die today.

She glanced over at him and nodded. "Not in the main cavern. There's a system of caves and tunnels further in. We only lived here for a few years before I came to Cerulya, though. Before that we were constantly moving around, going anywhere Zeke knew people or thought he might find new evidence to support his theories."

Malcolm's concern spiked. "How many of you are there?"

Luelle pulled a face. "There were only about ten of us when I lived there, but I don't know if things have changed since then."

"Are your friends the ones who maintain this path?" He gestured to the stones they walked on, untouched by the surrounding plants and vegetation that obscured their way lower down the mountain.

She frowned. "We never cleared it away when I was living here. I didn't notice it then, but it's never been overgrown. I don't know why."

That fact did little to settle Malcolm's nerves.

Silence returned as they concentrated on their hike. They reached the entrance to the cavern all too soon.

Luelle turned to Malcolm, stopping him before they descended into the darkness.

"You should let me do the talking when we get inside."

"I thought you said your friends meant me no harm." His heartbeat picked up its pace.

"They do," she reassured him, too quickly. "But, they'll expect me to arrive alone. Honestly, they might not recognise you. You don't look like yourself at the moment." One side of her mouth tilted up but the smile didn't reach her eyes. Her fingers tugged at the frayed edges of her backpack strap.

Malcolm glanced down at his dirty armour. He knew he looked awful, having had no opportunity to bathe and few proper meals since leaving the castle. It was embarrassing to know his inability to adapt to a traveller's life was so obvious to Luelle.

"Are you ready?"

"No." After last night's blunt honesty, there was no point in lying any more. "Are you?"

Luelle pressed her lips together and shook her head.

"But, unless you are finally ready to concede and return to Cerulya with me, we have no choice but to go down there." He shrugged.

Something about the answering smile she gave him prompted a pang of sadness in Malcolm. He took a deep breath and followed close behind as Luelle stepped into the shadows of the cave's entrance.

His legs trembled as their direction changed, descending rather than climbing. Veins of moonstone snaked along the stone walls on either side of them, directing them deeper into the cave.

Time lost its meaning in their descent but, eventually, their path levelled out. Malcolm pushed away thoughts of the giant mountain looming above him. If anything happened to bring that rock down on them, they'd suffer a painful, claustrophobic death. It was as suffocating as the crypts beneath his castle. He concentrated, instead, on the regular drips of moisture tapping on the floor and the way their footsteps echoed through the tunnel.

He was closer than ever to having to make a decision about Luelle and his Power but felt no surer of the best course. Deep down, he hoped she was telling the truth, that the Power could be shared with others. Training every Veseile in his kingdom to use it would be time-consuming, not to mention the legislation he'd have to invent, and he couldn't guarantee all would use it for savoury purposes, but even a small collection of dedicated soldiers able to wield the Power would strengthen his kingdom in a way no monarch before him had. He could station trained Veseile wardens in villages and towns to provide aid. He could leave a legacy of good and improve lives across the realm. No one would needlessly suffer cold nights or go hungry.

Or, it could all be a lie, as he'd first suspected, and he could be walking to his death.

"It's not much further," Luelle whispered.

Sure enough, a faint glow lit the corridor ahead. Malcolm's breath caught in his throat as they reached the end of the tunnel. A vast cavern opened before them.

Moonstone veins stretched over the walls of the cavern, ascending to a rounded ceiling that reached higher than any halls in the castle at home. Not far from where they stood was a short plinth, atop which sat a crystal ball, similar to but larger than the one Malcolm's father should have used to pass his Power down. Beyond it, a lake spanned the furthest half of the cavern. The water was dark and still, unmarred by a single ripple. A narrow walkway was the only thing interrupting its surface, leading to a circular island.

In the centre of the island stood a single stone arch, large enough that Malcolm would be unable to reach the top even if he jumped, and behind it was a tall statue.

"It's of Vesanya," Luelle said as Malcolm peered at the parts of the statue visible from behind the archway.

"Can we go closer?"

Luelle nodded. They left their bags tucked in the tunnel they'd travelled down and walked into the open space.

None of her companions revealed themselves, though Malcolm could see her searching for them from the corner of his eye. As they walked, he scanned the vast room for exits but, besides the entrance they'd emerged from, there was only one more tunnel, on the far right side of the cavern.

They crossed the narrow path over the water so he could examine the statue.

Carved into stone, the God was beautiful. She stood as if she'd been frozen whilst stumbling back a step, one arm held up to shield her face, which was already half obscured by an unfamiliar intricate mask. He frowned at it. Other than that mask, every other detail was the same as the drawn and painted depictions he'd studied growing up. Malcolm was no small man, but the statue loomed a foot taller than him, towering over Luelle.

"This is so detailed," he murmured, eyes travelling over the design of the statue's armour and the pieces of stone chiselled into strands of hair as fine as a real person's. "How long do you think this has been here?"

"Since before we discovered it." Luelle stood closer to the edge of the island, rather than investigating the statue up close, as Malcolm was.

"It's incredible."

"It always creeped me out, to be honest." She stepped forward and peered at the God's expression. "Why wouldn't they carve her to look happier, or at least more powerful?"

"She looks plenty powerful to me." He admired the statue's strong build. "Why is she wearing a mask? And why is there only one of her? What about the other Gods?"

"I'm not sure. None of the sources we've found have explained the history of the statue or who carved it. Some of them mention the arch but nothing about a statue. Zeke thinks it's a sign the site is dedicated to Vesanya and explains why her Power originated here."

The urge to touch the statue washed over Malcolm but he held back.

Luelle swallowed. "Can we go back across?" She glanced at the walkway, wrapping her arms around herself.

Malcolm nodded, realising it was foolish to be on the island at all when they could be ambushed by her companions at any moment. He trusted Luelle more than he had at the start of their journey but that trust didn't extend to the strangers she was expecting to find here.

They walked in single file along the walkway. Malcolm resisted the urge to look back at the statue, feeling a pull towards it as strong as he could to the Power inside Luelle.

Instead, he turned his attention to the rest of the cavern.

Lines and circles were engraved into the floor, forming shallow grooves in the otherwise smooth stone. Something about the positioning of the circles and the surrounding dots nagged at the back of his mind.

"What is this?" he asked Luelle.

She turned to see what he was referring to. They stood side by side after stepping off the walkway, gazing at the patterns on the floor.

"I don't know. It's always been here, like the statue."

Malcolm followed one of the many curving lines. Each curved line was intersected by a single circle but each circle varied in size. There were five circles in total, lined in a neat row in front of the plinth. The dots surrounding them stretched the entire floor of the cavern, seemingly at random.

"It's a map," he realised.

Luelle strolled forward to stand at his side again.

"What do you mean?"

"It is a map of our solar system." His voice sped up, spurred on by his excitement. "Look, these are the planets." He pointed to the circles in a line. "The curving lines are their orbits. Every twenty years they align like this. The smaller dots are stars—the ones without lines interrupting them. Look, you can see the constellations." He moved his pointing finger further along the floor.

"Huh." She spun in a slow circle, looking around the room. "I never realised. We never paid much attention to it."

"There must be more information about this place somewhere." He frowned. "This map is extensive. Who would have created it?"

Luelle didn't respond. He glanced over at her. She was gazing towards the tunnels further in the cavern, picking at the skin around her nails.

"How are you meant to return the Power?" He walked over to her, hoping to distract her so he didn't have to think about his own stresses.

"The orb." She kept her voice as low as his, nodding towards the plinth set behind the diagrams of the planets.

They stood mere inches from one another, despite having plenty of space to step away. Her presence was a comfort to him, when something else about this cavern felt wrong, almost sinister. How had she and her friends lived here for so long? Was the feeling to do with whoever had carved the star map into the ground?

"How does it work?"

"I'm not sure." Luelle frowned. "I would assume the opposite of how I absorbed it in the first place, just by willing it into a new vessel. It feels stronger here." One of her hands drifted to her chest. "I feel like it's pulling me towards the orb."

"What will happen to it if you are unable to transfer it?" Malcolm stared at the transparent sphere resting on the plinth. "If you fail to transfer it into that orb, you might not be able to pass it back to me."

Luelle opened her mouth to answer, but another voice, deep and menacing, sounded from behind, startling them both.

"I hope you aren't planning to return Vesanya's Power without us, Luelle."

# 29

Luelle and the prince spun towards the voice in unison.

Numerous times over the past five years, she'd thought she might never hear Zeke's voice again but here he was, sounding as charismatic as always. It felt like she'd never been away. Her heart raced.

He stood in the entrance to the tunnel systems, his pale hair tied back to show off angular cheekbones and sharp, calculating eyes. He wore the same simple clothing he always had, with a single short, sheathless blade strapped to his waist. To his right, Imbryl towered, a hulking mass of muscle and power, and to his left was Freya, somehow more intimidating than either of them, despite her slight physique. Fresh pink battle scars decorated her exposed skin.

Tears burned Luelle's eyes and welled in her throat at the sight of them—her family. She swallowed, searching for the right words but finding none that were adequate to describe how much she'd missed them. Seeing them here, she was whole again.

"It's so good to see you." Her voice caught as she spoke. She smiled at them, blinking hard to keep her tears from spilling over, onto her cheeks.

"Is it?" Zeke cocked his head to one side. Imbryl and Freya shifted where they stood, neither meeting Luelle's eyes. The three of them stepped forward to let the rest of their companions enter the cavern.

Their numbers had grown in the time Luelle had been away. She hadn't been close with the few she recognised other than Freya and Imbryl. Most of the approaching people were Veseile, though some, like Freya and Imbryl, belonged to different Eile races. None of them were human. The cavern, airy and open a minute earlier, became uncomfortable and confined by the time all of Zeke's numbers were inside, a small crowd spilling out at his sides.

Luelle's smile faltered at Zeke's words. "Of course. Why wouldn't it be?"

Zeke shrugged, his eyes drifting to Malcolm. "I didn't expect to hear those words from a traitor." His voice was acidic.

Luelle glanced at Malcolm, baffled by Zeke's reception. The prince's hand had fallen to the hilt of his sword but she couldn't blame him for that, not given Zeke's unwarranted hostility.

"I'm not a traitor. I'm here with Vesanya's Power, I brought it back just as we planned before I left. I did everything you wanted."

"Including bringing our enemy to us?" Zeke spat. None of the crowd spared Luelle a glance, their eyes fixed on Malcolm. "Did you think we wouldn't recognise the false prince?"

A disbelieving laugh slipped through her lips. "Malcolm isn't our enemy."

Zeke scoffed, the action replicated by some of the others in his cohort. "They're on a first-name basis."

"*Prince* Malcolm isn't our enemy," Luelle pressed, ignoring the remark. "He saved my life on the way here. I wouldn't have made it back without him. He's willing to see the Power restored."

"Then explain to me why a squadron of his soldiers was seen entering the valley yesterday." Zeke glared at the prince.

Luelle's heart stopped. She felt Malcolm tense beside her. Turning to look at him, his wide eyes suggested he knew as little as she had about the soldiers. They hadn't left one another's sights during their travels, there was no way he could've known about the people Zeke was talking about.

"I knew nothing about that," Malcolm said to Zeke. He turned to Luelle and said, in a lower tone, "I sent a letter to my sister in the Meteile camp, but I had no idea she sent anyone to help me. I did not believe the capital's soldiers could reach our destination in time."

Unease settled in Luelle's stomach, but both she and the prince had known his companions from the Great Forest would follow, if they'd survived. Soldiers shouldn't be a surprise. She'd always anticipated that he would never pursue her alone, but she hadn't expected any of his soldiers to track him so accurately. Being so open with him about their destination was a stupid mistake.

"Liar!" Zeke shouted across the space that separated them.

Luelle startled at the sudden volume of his voice. "You think your soldiers scare us? They aren't here to defend you yet."

Luelle stepped in front of the prince.

"Zeke, calm down. I've brought the Power back, that's what you wanted. Malcolm can help our cause. He's willing to learn the truth." Her heart hammered in her chest. Even together, the two of them wouldn't be able to fight their way out of this crowd. If Malcolm's soldiers found them, they might stand a chance, but how could they know which cavern their prince was in? And would they recognise Luelle as a friend or a foe? If they wanted to get out of this unharmed, she needed to convince Zeke and the others that she wasn't their enemy.

"I shouldn't be surprised you're taking his side." Zeke sneered at her.

"I'm not taking sides!" Luelle raised her voice, exasperated. "Freya, Imbryl, you trust me, don't you? You know I would never betray any of you. I'd never put you in danger!"

Neither of them met her imploring stare for more than a few seconds.

Zeke took a step closer.

"I looked further into your past whilst you were away, Luelle." His voice was soft.

She met his gaze, heartbeat still wild and stuttering.

"Do you want to know what I discovered?" He raised a single eyebrow. "Perhaps you already knew."

She frowned at him. "Know what?"

"You're half-human."

She froze with shock.

"No, I'm not," she murmured. "I'm Veseile."

"Yes, you had me fooled for a while, but I realised something was wrong when you were so eager to leave and work in the castle. Imagine my surprise when I discovered you're a half-breed, just like the prince." His mouth twisted back into a sneer.

Luelle's mind raced. She couldn't tear her eyes from Zeke. His words echoed through the cavern but they weren't true. They couldn't be true. If they were true, everything in her life would change. If she had human heritage, she might not even live beyond a few more decades.

"I wanted to go to the castle for you," she managed to choke out. "I never knew who my parents were, you know that."

"I don't know what to believe about you any more." He gave her a withering glare that made her hope the floor would swallow her.

"It can't be true," she whispered. "How did you find out? Are my parents alive?"

"No, they're both dead and for the best. I was in a mind to end their lives myself when I discovered your deceit."

"I didn't deceive you. I didn't know!"

He continued as if she hadn't spoken. "All it took was another visit to Vidamere. Ask the right questions and you can find out almost anything. Including whether there's a traitor among you."

"I'm not a traitor." Luelle's voice finally regained its strength. "Whoever my parents were changes nothing. I'm Veseile." She tried to push thoughts of her unknown parents out of her mind. How had they died? Why had they left her alone?

Zeke ignored her last claim. "If you're not a traitor, you'll let us have the prince."

Luelle's heart picked up speed again.

What was happening? She'd known things would change, had expected changes in the five years she'd been away, but she hadn't anticipated that her friends, her *family*, would ever greet her with such hostility. Why weren't they listening to her? She couldn't be half-human. She'd spent her entire life working to right the sins of the human monarchs.

"I'm not going to let you hurt him, he's done nothing wrong." Luelle didn't look at the prince as she spoke, scared she would hurt herself all the more seeing the fear and betrayal that was doubtless in his expression. She'd led him into a viper's den.

"I expected as much." Zeke's lip curled. "So be it. We do not need your consent."

Behind him, the group of Eile fanned out and drew their various weapons, edging towards Luelle and Malcolm from all angles. Imbryl and Freya hesitated, shooting Luelle imploring glances before reluctantly joining the advance.

Something nudged her hand. Luelle looked down to see Malcolm pressing the handle of his dagger into her palm, as he had before their fight with the troll. She took the weapon, looking up at his face, but his attention was elsewhere, face devoid of emotion as he appraised his opponents.

The metal of his sword rang through the cavern as he unsheathed it. Most of their opponents approached him, leaving only Imbryl and Ivor, a Veseile Luelle vaguely knew, to deal with her. Zeke's numbers had grown enough that several remained content to hang back and watch the fight from the stony walls, observing with confident anticipation, murmuring bets to one another while jeering at Luelle and Malcolm.

Luelle fell into the fighting stance Zeke had taught her almost two decades ago, balancing her weight and trying to keep all of her enemies in sight. She ignored the part of her mind pointing out their dwindling odds of escaping alive. If she fled now, Zeke's crowd might be distracted enough by the prince that she could escape, but she couldn't leave Malcolm to battle nearly all of them alone. She was no fighter, and she doubted the new additions to Zeke's crew were any less ruthless than the ones she knew. Speed and size were still her allies, and she had something none of them did, burning in her chest and roaring for an outlet. She'd levelled buildings with the Power in Tolhurst, she could use it to save them now.

Taking a deep, shaking breath to ground herself, she prepared to use the Power when it was needed, when it might deal the most damage. All she had to do was ration enough that she stayed conscious and able to fight if she didn't manage to immobilise all of their enemies with a single blow.

"Why are you doing this?" she asked Imbryl as her large friend stalked closer. He looked the same as she remembered, his brown hair close-cropped, and his dark eyes glittering. Some of his scars were new, pink and stark against his thick, green-tinted skin. He hadn't even drawn his sword, so confident he could restrain her without a weapon. Over the years, during their sparring practice, she could count the times she'd beaten him on a single hand.

"You know nothing's changed. I'm Veseile, not human. Zeke has it wrong. There were no records about my parents," she insisted.

Imbryl didn't answer her but a muscle flexed in his jaw. She continued, eyes flicking from her friend to the hoard of people approaching the prince.

"Imbryl, you know me. Please don't do this. Please trust me."

"We just wanted the prince," he said, voice pitched low.

"Why? What purpose does hurting him serve? I brought back the Power, I did everything Zeke wanted!"

"You've been away a long time, Lu. A lot has changed."

"Then stop this! Explain what's changed, don't just brand me your enemy! Not when you were the ones who sent me away."

"You know I was against that." Imbryl's jaw clenched. He glanced to where the prince was standing, to the half-circle of enemies closing in around him.

A clash of steel made Luelle's heart lurch. Her head spun to the prince, who was now engaged with two unfamiliar Veseile. They darted at him one at a time, attempting to turn him so they could drive him to where more of Luelle's old companions were waiting to hurt him. Her breath caught in her throat.

Imbryl took advantage of the distraction. He strode forward to grab her.

Luelle spun towards him, realising her mistake and retreating several steps. If she gave up too much ground, she'd be trapped against the wall. She and Imbryl circled one another, only a few paces separating them. Ivor stayed back, torn between helping Imbryl and joining the fight against the prince. Luelle gripped

Malcolm's dagger tight in her right hand.

Imbryl glanced at the dagger, his lips set in a firm line.

"Would you really use that against me?" he asked, staring into her eyes.

"Only if you make me." Her voice trembled.

Metallic clangs, strained grunts, and unfamiliar voices shrieking in pain threatened to draw Luelle's attention but she kept her eyes on Imbryl and Ivor, both now edging closer. She breathed slowly, turning her concentration inward, preparing to strike out with her Power from a distance until she heard Malcolm cry out.

Her panicked look towards him cost her.

Imbryl leapt forward, gripping her wrist and spinning her before she could process what was happening. Trapping both arms at her sides, he lifted Luelle with ease so her kicking legs were useless and her dagger-wielding hand could do nothing more than wiggle back and forth a centimetre, restricted by his iron-grip. Luelle roared with frustration at her own ineptitude. She was unable to look away as her old friend held her still, facing the battle Malcolm was engaged in.

The prince was a much better fighter than her. As she'd suspected after witnessing the humans he'd slain at the temple in the Godswood, he was vicious.

Several of his opponents lay on the ground, clutching at injuries that gushed blood, but there were too many of them for him to take out alone. The jeering crowds against the walls twitched as they spectated, tense and ready to leap into the battle if it was necessary.

Malcolm had managed to avoid becoming trapped in a circle of enemies, but he was losing ground, fast approaching the wall of the cavern behind him, chest heaving at the exertion of fighting. He defended himself against Freya from the front, keeping her at a distance to avoid her two short blades, but two other opponents closed in from each side. They lurched towards the prince, slashing and stabbing with mismatched shortswords. Malcolm kept moving, never giving his enemies an easy target. As soon as he saw an opening, he jabbed the pommel of his sword into the eye of the unfamiliar Veseile to his left. Bone cracked and the Veseile reeled backward, clutching at his face. Pink-stained sludge oozed between his fingers. The fighter to Malcolm's right darted in, but the prince twisted and deflected his blow, gutting the stranger with a deep cut across the torso.

Despite besting the two men, the distraction gave Freya an opening.

Fear choked Luelle at the thought of either of them being hurt.

Freya rushed forward, swinging one of her swords. With a grunt, Malcolm blocked it before it sliced across his face, but didn't react fast enough to stop her second blade, swinging upwards towards his sword arm.

Luelle cried out to warn him, but the tip of the blade sunk into his forearm, prevented from sinking too deep by his armour. Malcolm's hand spasmed and he lost his grip on his sword. It landed with a clatter, kicked away by Freya.

Luelle squirmed in Imbryl's arms as more of Zeke's Eile closed in to assist Freya. They wrestled Malcolm into submission, holding him still. Blood dripped from the small hole in the armour on his arm.

Zeke had been watching the fight from the crowd, unwilling to risk his own safety. Doing his own dirty work had never been his style. He didn't glance at his injured followers, nor their dark sticky blood, spilled over the cave floor. Now the prince was detained, the remaining Eile rushed to one another, pressing on wounds, lifting their fallen friends to their feet and propping them against the cave walls if they were unable to stand. Two of them were beyond help. They remained where they'd dropped.

Malcolm struggled against the hands holding him in place but they tightened their grips. Blood stained his face and armour. Luelle could only pray that not too much of it was his own.

Zeke approached his captive with a dark smile.

"Your soldiers are no use to you now," he sneered.

Malcolm met Zeke's gaze, lifting his chin a notch higher.

Zeke threw his fist into the prince's stomach, to the noisy delight of their onlookers. Malcolm doubled over with a grunt but the Eile holding him hauled him back upright.

Luelle's heart lurched. She struggled twisted in Imbryl's arms but he didn't loosen his clutches.

"What to do with you," Zeke murmured, ambling back and forth in front of the prince. Freya had retrieved Malcolm's sword. Zeke took it from her and examined it, the blade still dripping with gore. He wiped it on the prince's outer thigh.

"This is a nice weapon." He nodded at Malcolm like they were friends contemplating a new purchase. "Probably worth more than I could afford in my life." He turned and smiled at

Luelle, taunting her from afar.

"Zeke, stop this," she begged him from Imbryl's grip.

He ignored her, continuing to speak to the prince whilst he toyed with the weapon.

"The question of whether or not to kill the monarch was academic until now. I never truly believed we'd get close enough to achieve it but, now you are here, we cannot ignore the chance to send a message to the king."

Luelle's face crumpled in confusion. Had Zeke not heard of Alaric's demise? How did he think she'd managed to bring the Power back?

"So many Veseile are unaware of their true potential. Our race was designed to rule. We are evidence of the Gods' existence. Millennia of being ruled against our will by humans has erased our true history. And that suppression was only possible because humans kept us in line with our own Power!" Zeke spat at Malcolm's feet.

Malcolm glared at Zeke as he ranted, but made no move to interrupt. Luelle willed him to look at her but he was busy scanning the cavern for anything to turn to his advantage so he could escape.

"Removing the Power from the false monarchs is the first step, but my people cannot thrive until the humans are eliminated altogether. None of you can be trusted," Zeke seethed, pacing back and forth in front of Malcolm. "And I can't pass up this opportunity. Restoring Vesanya's Power is symbolic of our right to rule, but removing the crown prince is a practical step to ignite our revolution. On hearing of your demise, my people will rise up behind me and accept me as their ruler rather than continuing to bow to humans and half-breeds."

Luelle thrashed in Imbyrl's arms, gritting her teeth. He tightened his grip.

"It would be satisfying to end you with your own weapon." Zeke smiled, glancing between Malcolm and his sword. The scenario elicited a few stray chuckles and words of encouragement. "But, no." He handed the weapon back to Freya. "I think I'd rather feel this with my own hands."

He slammed his fist into Malcolm's cheekbone. The prince's head snapped to the side.

Luelle cried out, struggling against Imbryl. Zeke landed another hit. Malcolm didn't fight back. In her chest, the Power warmed.

"Stop, please!" she choked out. "Imbryl let me go!" She writhed in his arms.

"Lower him to the ground," Zeke instructed.

Malcolm's head lolled but he lifted it to look towards Luelle, who was still imprisoned in the arms of someone she'd once considered family. Blood oozed from his split lip, leaking down his chin. He struggled against the two Eile that lowered him to the ground but couldn't free his hands to form any real defence.

Her skin tingled, as it had before the Power had burst from her in Tolhurst, what felt like years ago. She was too far away for it to make any real difference. Imbryl had separated her from Zeke's show. She might injure a few of them and disrupt things for a moment, but Zeke would be able to continue when she was unconscious.

Luelle tried to slow her panicked breathing, to gain enough control over her body to use the Power dwelling within her, but it wouldn't help. She had so little practice with it and had only succeeded in using it at its extremes, to destroy buildings or to lift a pebble. Malcolm should have it.

She had to reach the orb.

She still had his dagger. Imbryl hadn't bothered taking it from her, though he was holding her wrist in one large hand.

Malcolm's captors held him on his back against the floor.

Zeke stepped forward and placed his foot on Malcolm's throat.

It was the calm acceptance of his fate in Malcolm's expression that spurred Luelle into action.

Skin burning, she leaned forwards as much as Imbryl's grip would allow and flung her head backwards. Sharp pain burst through the back of her skull, but that crunch of bone hadn't come from her.

Imbryl grunted at the impact.

His arm around her waist didn't loosen but the one gripping her wrist let go to clutch at his face. She fisted the dagger tighter in her clammy hand, drew it up and plunged it deep into Imbryl's thigh. He cried out and released her.

They collapsed into a heap on the floor.

Luelle scrambled away.

"Stop her!" Zeke snarled from somewhere behind her. She didn't look back to see who would try to recapture her.

She sprinted to the plinth and slapped her hands onto the surface of the crystal orb, releasing her hold on the Power straining to be freed from within her.

# 30

Motion in the cave stopped as Luelle's palms came into contact with the orb on the plinth.

Pain throbbed through Malcolm's face and his throat ached, but Zeke and the other Eile no longer paid him any attention. Even the two strangers pinning him down were loosening their grip in anticipation of what might happen next. Zeke had stepped away the moment Luelle had freed herself, distracting the crowd from his show.

Vibrant colour spread from Luelle's hands, filling the orb and brightening the moonstone veins in the ceiling. The Power shone inside the crystal sphere on the pedestal, creating a miniature sun that lit every inch of the cavern.

Malcolm couldn't tear his eyes from the swirling patterns.

For a second, he could no longer feel the pull of it. Loss, like he had never known, flooded him, snatching his breath, bringing tears to his eyes.

Then, warmth filled his chest. His skin tingled, the sense of something new inside him distracting from the physical pains in his face, throat and torso.

He understood what she'd done when Luelle looked over her shoulder and locked eyes with him, seconds before the large Adeile she'd stabbed grabbed her shoulders and hauled her away. Malcolm's dagger was still embedded in the Adeile's thigh as he lurched away with Luelle in his grip.

Malcolm didn't stop to think about everything that had happened before this moment—about the truth of Luelle's heritage, how she'd defended him against her only friends, or how she'd almost led him to his death.

He didn't stop to think about the Power running through his veins.

About the fact that Luelle had been right, all this time.

He shoved away thoughts of his father and the emotions they brought up but sent a silent thanks to the king for training him to be ready for this moment since he was a child. Before attacking Zeke and his lackeys, Malcolm needed to buy himself some time and space.

Instinct guided him as he syphoned the Power in his chest. He willed a burst of force in every direction. All the Eile in his line of sight were shoved away from him, including Zeke and the two who had been holding Malcolm down. In their absence, he scrambled to his feet, focusing his Power on his wounded hand and throat, willing the damaged tissue to heal faster, for the inflammation to retreat. An itching, stinging sensation spread over his injured forearm as his skin knitted itself back together faster than it naturally could and the burning in his throat lessened. As he straightened, taking his first easy breath in minutes, he locked eyes with Zeke. Breaking free from his frozen state of shock, Zeke strode towards him, flanked by others who had regained their feet and composure after Malcolm had flung them away.

Malcolm willed a thread-thin tendril of Power toward the petite woman to Zeke's left, the one who had stabbed him earlier and now held his sword. She dropped it in shock as Malcolm willed his Power to lift her off her feet. Flicking the Power like a whip, he sent her skidding backwards over the rocky floor. On its return, he willed the tendril of Power to bring his sword.

His chest heaved, a sheen of sweat across his forehead at the unfamiliar exertion. He had to pace himself.

With his weapon back in his fist, Malcolm's opponents hesitated to approach him. On the far side of the cavern, even those nearer Luelle wore more cautious expressions. The large Adeile she'd stabbed had abandoned her and backed away, limping to help the woman Malcolm had thrown. Plenty of his surrounding enemies were Veseile, their heritage clear in the stripe of unpigmented hair, but none would know how to use their Power as he did—even Luelle was a novice.

Several Veseile thrust their hands out towards Malcolm but nothing happened.

Taking advantage of their hesitation, he looked around to get his bearings. Zeke had vanished but plenty of others stood between Malcolm and his way out. He willed a miniscule thread of his Power to ascend his sword, lighting it with a searing hot flame. Spreading his weight, he analysed the strangers between him and Luelle. A grin spread from ear to ear on her face at the sight of him.

He resisted the urge to roll his eyes at her reaction.

Malcolm stepped back into battle. Adrenaline pulsed through his veins, as hot as the Power setting his core alight. He parried the desperate swings of his nearest foe. Flames danced over his sword as it swung. He considered using his Power to shove his opponents off balance, but he was such an imposing sight, they scattered from him without any need to waste his energy.

Whilst he'd been distracted, Luelle had found a sword and joined the fight. Even from afar, he could see the blood that already splattered her front.

The cavern became a mess of gore, fire, and clashing weapons.

Malcolm didn't pause to see if any of the injuries he dealt were fatal.

He and Luelle were steps from one another when a deafening crack echoed through the space, silencing all else. Fighting paused as everyone turned towards the source of the sound, toward the island at the far end of the cavern.

Liquid stone bled from the statue of Vesanya, leaving colour in its absence.

Malcolm stilled.

He felt Luelle stumble closer to him. Her fingers wrapped around his bicep, gently pulling him. Following the pressure of her fingertips, he edged backward, retreating whilst their enemies were entranced by the sight of the statue changing. Like them, he couldn't tear his eyes from the dripping stone and the tall woman emerging from it.

Little by little, the likeness of Vesanya came alive. Bronze skin warmed, black hair with a single white streak settled in waves around her shoulders, and her muscular arm lowered from in front of her face. Her eyes were as gold as the intricate mask obscuring half of her face.

She was enchanting.

"She was trapped in there the whole time," Luelle whispered.

Malcolm dragged his gaze away from the captivating figure on the island. Colour had drained from Luelle's face. During the fight, her hair had been torn from its usual braid. Shadows danced on her face from the fire still engulfing his sword. He let the flames die.

"You freed her," he murmured.

Malcolm and Luelle lingered, forgotten, at the back of the cavern. Their opponents were struck with awe in the presence of the God. Several stumbled towards Vesanya, falling to their knees and crying out to her, though remaining far from the water. They clasped their hands together and praised her with loud, emotional voices. Others remained frozen in place, staring with wide eyes, mouths gaping with unspoken words.

Vesanya peeled the mask from her face and dropped it on the ground. She walked forward. Her movements were stiff and awkward as if the stone hadn't quite dissolved from within her limbs. She stepped beneath the archway and paused. Head tilting, she examined its inner curves. Reaching up, she brushed her fingers against the stone on either side of her. When nothing happened, she turned to stare at the crowd awaiting her across the water.

With a final glance at the arch, she moved forward, walking across the stone bridge. She approached the nearest Veseile, the other man who had initially been fighting Luelle, and reached her hand out to where one knelt.

The man gazed up at the Goddess. Tears streamed openly down his face, dripping from his pointed chin.

Vesanya crouched, sliding her slender fingers against his cheek. She touched the Veseile's tears and pulled away to examine the liquid on her fingertips, her golden eyes flickering from the moisture to the man at her feet. Babbling prayers streamed from his mouth.

Others stumbled closer, leaving Malcolm and Luelle to continue their quiet retreat. Malcolm might have had an advantage over them before but if a God joined their side, he stood no chance.

Vesanya's hand shot back out.

Her fingers closed around the Veseile's throat. She lifted him until their eyes were level, a foot of space between his dangling feet and the floor.

Movement in the cave froze anew as the God examined the person's face closer, unaware or perhaps uncaring about how he gasped for breath. Colour darkened in his cheeks.

Vesanya tightened her fist. Her fingers disappeared into the man's throat, squelching as they penetrated his flesh.

He struggled, clawing at the God's hand. Vesanya tilted her head to watch his blood leaking down her arm.

Glowing light emanated from Vesanya's hand, travelling from the fingers buried in the Veseile's throat, up her arm and disappearing into her own body. As the light flowed, the Veseile's skin dried and shrivelled. His body stiffened in her clutch, nothing more than a wizened corpse after a few seconds.

The God dropped him and turned to the small crowd before her.

Her spell over the cavern broke.

Some of Luelle's old companions fled through the exit furthest from Malcolm and Luelle. They attacked and shoved one another in their desperation to escape. Some stayed, desperately attempting to face the God. Vesanya moved with eternal patience, gazing with fascination at their reactions to her movements. Nausea rolled in Malcolm's gut as he watched her study how breaking a person's arm could elicit a scream, or how their faces darkened when she closed her vice-like hands around their throats. Fists, swords, and knives hammered and stabbed at her as the Eile tried in vain to defend each other, but she was oblivious to their attacks, lost in curiosity with each new plaything.

Blades seemed more dangerous to their wielders than to the God. More than once, she swatted them away, sending them soaring across the cavern and their owner crashing into the far walls like ragdolls. Few got back to their feet, blood and brains oozing from cracked skulls.

More and more of the Eile retreated, racing from the cavern the way they'd entered.

Malcolm shook himself free of his own stupor, realising he

couldn't stay and watch her kill everyone in the cave. If they stayed, she would turn on them next.

Luelle's attention was fixed on the violence, eyes wide and glossy as she watched her old companions succumb to the slaughter.

Malcolm sheathed his sword and grabbed her shoulders, turning her away from the screams and forcing her to meet his gaze.

"We must go."

Her eyes darted over his face, settling on his throat as if she could see the faint ache still throbbing there from Zeke's foot.

"I can't leave them," she whispered, eyes flickering back to the God.

"You cannot help them. We need backup." He didn't wait for her to decide. Grabbing her hand and gripping it tight, he dragged her the final few paces to the tunnel they'd entered the cavern through. They stumbled over the rocky floor and up the stairs, abandoning their bags.

Screams echoed behind them as they retreated.

# 31

Sunlight blinded Luelle at the entrance to the cave.

She tripped as they emerged, pulling the prince to the ground with her. He dragged her further from the cavern's entrance, hiding them behind some nearby rocks and shrubbery in case anything emerged behind them.

Her legs trembled. Tears dripped from her face onto the dirt, though she wasn't sure when she'd started crying. Malcolm's hand squeezed hers. He hadn't let go once when dragging her out of the cavern, but Luelle couldn't bring herself to care about whether the contact was appropriate. The warmth of his skin against hers was a reminder she hadn't just been killed by a vengeful God brought back to life because she'd returned the Power to its source.

She'd returned Vesanya's Power to its source.

Her life's mission was complete. Well, Zeke's life mission, but she owed him everything. Or so she'd once thought.

She'd put her life and freedom at risk time and time again

for him, had willingly left the only home she knew to work and live amongst strangers for half a decade, all to help him achieve his goals. She'd always known things would be different on her return, but she had done everything right—befriending the king, fitting into castle life without suspicion, retrieving Vesanya's Power and bringing it home. Yet, rather than showing any concern for her on arrival, Zeke had branded her a traitor to their cause, spouting blatant lies about her parents to discredit her.

It had to be a lie.

Bile rose in her throat as the violence replayed in her head. Her breath was coming too fast. What was she meant to do now?

"Are you alright?"

Malcolm's soft question broke through her panic. He squeezed her hand again.

Even when she'd stumbled on the ascent as they'd fled, he'd pulled her to her feet again, tugging her away from the danger behind. He'd faced his death without a trace of fear. She led him to that, after promising she would let nothing happen to him.

Luelle swallowed hard. She shook her head. "I don't know what to do."

Her life was collapsing around her. Fresh tears spilled over her cheeks, leaving wet paths to her chin.

Malcolm said nothing but didn't loosen his grip. His thumb brushed slow circles against the back of her hand. That action was more calming than anything he could say; no words would ease the horrors they'd just witnessed.

They sat, huddled together, until Luelle's hiccuping tears subsided.

"Are you hurt?" she asked the prince, her voice husky.

His face was swelling again, around his lip and cheekbone. Blood dried on his chin from the split in his lip, though most of the blood speckled further up his face must have belonged to other people.

Malcolm shrugged. "Nothing serious. Not anymore. I will be fine. Are you?"

Luelle shook her head. "I'm so sorry they did that. I don't know why, I thought—" she broke off, chewing her lip. "I swear I had no part in that. I don't know why he thought he could send a message to Alaric by hurting you." She frowned.

He swallowed. "I made some difficult decisions to keep the kingdom from knowing about my father's death while I was away from the capital. I doubt anyone other than us knows about it, beyond the castle walls."

Luelle turned her frown to him, but he changed the subject before she could ask any more.

"I appreciate you standing up for me. I know that was not easy for you."

She swallowed. It hadn't been. "You were amazing in there, with the Power."

The prince looked away. "It's strange, being able to use it after all these years. It feels like I am finally whole." He frowned, struggling to explain himself. "I cannot believe you were right."

Luelle nodded with a small smile. "I understand." She took a deep breath and removed her clammy hand from his. "I need to go back in there." By now, Vesanya might have killed every one of her friends, but she couldn't leave without trying to help them.

Even if they hated her, they were all she had.

Malcolm turned his frown on her. "No. You would be walking to your own death. Zeke made it clear your human heritage was a betrayal. I know from experience that Veseile like him will never accept you as one of them if you are tainted with human blood."

She met his gaze, wondering how easy life had really been for him in Cerulya. She'd assumed the castle walls protected him from anything bad growing up, but it must be yet another misconception.

"We need to get to safety," he continued.

"I know what they did is wrong, but I can't leave them all to die."

"What if they are already..."

"I need to try. And I might be able to help if there are any survivors."

"Not by yourself. You heard what they said about the soldiers. If my people are in the valley, they can help us. Let us find them first, then we can see if there are any survivors. We will stand a better chance with more people."

Luelle hesitated but nodded. She couldn't take on a God alone. She let Malcolm help her to her feet.

"Do you think that was really Vesanya?" she asked.

"I don't know. If it was, I doubt it is a good thing. She did not seem happy to be here."

"I doubt I'd be happy if I'd been a statue for years."

He breathed a nervous laugh.

They limped down the mountain path, pushing their tired

bodies as fast as they could, spurred by their need to find help.

They were passing the ledge they'd slept under last night when something collided with Luelle from behind. She tumbled down, landing on her front and crying out as her cheek scraped against the rocks. Pain shot through the wounds in her thigh, which already felt sticky, as if they'd reopened during the fight in the cavern.

A heavy weight on her back pushed her into the ground. She moved to lift herself, but her arms were pinned. A hand gripped what was left of her braid, yanking her head up. Cool, sharp metal pressed against her throat. She took shallow breaths to stop the blade's edge from pressing further into her skin.

"Leena, stop!"

Malcolm's panicked voice shouted from somewhere behind Luelle. His footsteps raced closer.

"You're hurt." A gruff, feminine voice spoke from above Luelle, but she couldn't turn to look at the woman who was holding her in place without slicing her own throat.

"Not by her. Let her go, we were coming to find you." The prince's feet stepped into Luelle's line of sight.

"She is a traitor to the crown, Malcolm. She forced you all the way out here. You have been injured and Gods know what else."

"I came with her willingly, and any judgement for her crime is not yours to dole out."

The blade stayed at Luelle's neck for a heartbeat longer but was flicked away, nicking her skin in the process. The stranger released her hair with a shove and climbed off her back.

Luelle pushed herself to her feet and turned to glare at the stranger, her hand drifting up to the shallow slice on her throat. The Colleile between her and the prince was tall and lithe, dressed in plain leather armour similar to Malcolm's. She must be one of the two others that had accompanied him in the forest, though her face was no longer disguised behind a scarf.

"Do you greet everyone in such a brutish way?" Luelle muttered.

"Only those who deserve it," the woman snarled.

"Leena, stop it. Luelle, this is Leena, my spymaster and one of my closest friends. Leena, this is Luelle." Malcolm introduced them, shifting where he stood as if he'd rather face down Vesanya again than stand between these two women. "Leena, I am sorry to do this, but we need to postpone our catch-up. We know about the soldiers. I need you to bring a group of them to the cave at the top of this path. Follow the tunnel inside until you reach a large cavern. I have no time to explain everything, but I need support." Confidence and command grew in his tone the more he spoke.

Leena's brow furrowed. "The soldiers?"

Malcolm nodded, hesitating. "We were told some were seen entering the valleys."

Leena gave the prince a curt nod. "We entered from the west but there may be some from the east or south. Stay here. The others I travelled with are not far. I will send a messenger to find the soldiers and return as soon as possible."

The prince shook his head. "We do not have time for that. We will meet you there. We need to return and help any survivors. If there is no one left to help, we shall retreat and wait for you."

Leena's nostrils flared. She turned, angling more of her back towards Luelle, blocking her from the conversation.

"Malcolm this is madness. I shall return with soldiers imminently. I can send a messenger and bring the guards I travelled with here in well under an hour. You cannot keep putting yourself in danger, you are the crown prince. Wait for us here."

He rolled his eyes. Luelle fought a smile.

"Just do as I tell you for once, Leena. I shall be fine." To reiterate his point, Malcolm lifted Leena with his Power, as he'd done to Freya in the cavern, though he only raised his friend a few inches from the ground, rather than flinging her away.

Leena's eyes widened. Her arms splayed in the air to try and balance herself, her dagger almost falling from her grip.

Malcolm set her back down.

A smile stretched across her face once her feet were back on solid ground. She gripped his shoulder and stared into his eyes for a moment.

"Stay safe. I will send a scout to find and retrieve the other soldiers and will be up as soon as I can with a smaller group."

She turned from the prince, but he caught her arm.

"Is Theo with you?" he asked, urgency flooding his expression.

Leena nodded. "He's unharmed."

Malcolm pulled her into a short hug and released her with a small smile. Leena barged Luelle's shoulder with her own as she passed, taking off down the mountain path in a run.

"She seems lovely," Luelle muttered, rubbing her shoulder.

"She grows on you." Malcolm grinned. "Come on." He gestured back up the mountain with a nod.

Luelle took a deep breath, readying herself for the climb, despite her exhaustion, and for whatever they would find at the end of it.

# 32

Malcolm resisted the urge to take Luelle's hand again when they reached the dark descent into the cavern. His legs burned from the climb. They'd clambered up the rock faster than this morning, pushing through their weariness. Heavy breathing filled the silence between them as they descended through the tunnel.

Seeing Leena again, even so briefly, had been everything Malcolm had needed. Learning that she and Theo were safe lifted a weight from his shoulders that had settled there from the moment he'd left them behind in the Great Forest. He ignored the fact that he was leading them into danger once again, as soon as they were reunited.

When the tunnel began to level out, Malcolm and Luelle slowed their pace.

No sounds of conflict reached them.

Sharing a concerned glance, they hesitated at the entrance to the cavern where they'd been fighting not long ago. Part of Malcolm yearned to wait for Leena and the backup she would bring, but he couldn't let Luelle go in alone and couldn't stop her from trying to protect her friends.

They waited for several minutes, listening for any noise to suggest what horrors awaited them around the corner, but nothing came. They stared at one another, silently agreeing to edge forward, hoping to spot any remaining enemies before they were, in turn, seen.

The large, open space was as beautiful as it had been when they'd first entered, perhaps more so now that the orb and moonstone veins were shining brighter, filled with the same Power that lived in Malcolm's chest. Swirling patterns in those veins reflected in the dark water, covering its surface with shimmering, twisting currents. The statue that had once stood beside the stone arch on the small island was no longer there, nor was the violent God that had emerged from the rocky prison.

None of Luelle's companions remained—at least, no living ones.

Corpses littered the floor.

Luelle raced to the nearest one, falling to her knees to check for any signs of life.

Malcolm lingered, searching the space for anyone that could be waiting to ambush them when their backs were turned, but they were the only two living souls in the cavern.

An echoing gasp from Luelle drew Malcolm's attention. He looked up to find her beside another corpse. He strode to her side.

It was impossible to believe the body she stared at had died today.

Grey, withered skin covered the corpse, like fragile leather stretched tight over the bones beneath. The person's face was unrecognisable, eyes bottomless black caverns, lips peeled back to reveal teeth frozen in a permanent grin. Its bloodied clothes were all that suggested this body belonged to someone who had been in the cave with them earlier.

Malcolm glanced around at the other bodies, several of whom were as alien as this. Two others he recognised as Veseile he'd taken down before Luelle had returned Vesanya's Power, and one more, the first body Luelle had examined, was a Colleile. The Colleile fared little better than the others, but at least their face was in-tact. A few other corpses were scattered around the edges of the cavern, but Malcolm was certain they'd look the same.

He wandered between the bodies, footsteps squelching in the sticky blood. A knot of fear twisted in his chest. He pushed away intrusive thoughts of his own body, withered and shrunken like this.

"Why did she do this?" he found himself whispering.

"Maybe she thought we were the ones who trapped her there," Luelle murmured. She stood, her eyes lingering on the bodies. "I can't believe she was here with us all this time."

"If it truly was her."

She nodded.

"I'm sorry for your loss." Malcolm swallowed. "And for the deaths I caused."

She looked up to meet his eyes. "I don't blame you for that."

He looked away.

"Were you close to many of them?" He gestured to the

bodies.

Luelle looked around again and shook her head. "I think my friends got out. Or, they've been killed further into the tunnels." Her expression was grim.

"Is there another way out through those tunnels?"

"Yes."

"Then, you must not assume the worst. They could have escaped whilst she was distracted. We managed to, so it is possible."

Luelle nodded, brow still creased with concern. She stood, wrapping her arms around herself.

"This is my fault," she whispered. "None of this would have happened if I hadn't brought her Power back here. I can't believe Zeke was right."

He couldn't bring himself to verbalise his agreement—looking at the corpses of her friends was punishment enough, she didn't need his harsh opinion on top of that.

They turned together, staring at the orb. Malcolm stepped closer to it and laid his hand on its surface. The crystal was warm. The pulsating colours within swirled around his palm, rebounding from the curve of the sphere. He tried to will it into his body but nothing changed.

"What are you doing?" Luelle asked.

"Seeing if it can be stolen again."

She moved beside him, staring expectantly.

His hands dropped back to his sides. "I cannot retrieve it. You try."

She did as instructed but the Power didn't leave the orb.

"I suppose it is safe enough here, for now." He shrugged.

She opened her mouth to reply, but rapid footsteps startled them both.

They spun in unison towards the tunnel they'd emerged from, but it was only Leena that entered. Luelle turned from her, kneeling back beside her fallen companions, closing the eyes of any that still resembled their living selves, and murmuring prayers for the others. Malcolm left her to say her goodbyes in peace.

A short stream of guards and soldiers entered after Leena. She stepped forward from them, meeting Malcolm halfway across the space to receive instruction.

"There is only one other exit from this cavern. It leads to a tunnel system. Send scouts to search for any survivors, but have them hang back if they hear fighting. I dislike our odds in this unfamiliar terrain. I want you to stay here with me while we sort out what must happen next."

Leena nodded. Before she strode off, Malcolm pulled her into another hug, still unable to believe she was truly here with him. She squeezed him tight, pulling back with a grin. When he released her, she moved to the soldiers awaiting her orders. Malcolm recognised a couple of them as Cerulyan soldiers who had been sent to Tolhurst.

Behind them, Theo entered the cavern, cheeks flushed and chest heaving. His eyes scanned the area until they fell on Malcolm.

Relief swept over Malcolm, strong enough to make his legs tremble. He hadn't wanted to believe his friends had come to any harm in the Great Forest, but seeing them both safe in person, here and now, made it a reality.

Theo grinned and jogged forward to clasp him in a tight hug. Malcolm returned it, burying his face into his friend's shoulder.

"It is so good to see you." His words were muffled.

Theo pulled back, holding him at arm's length to examine his face. "You need a shave." He sniffed. "And a bath," he teased, crinkling his nose.

"And a good meal." Malcolm returned his grin. "We both have long stories to share, it seems. How did you track us so well?"

Theo released him and turned, revealing a nervous figure at the entrance to the cave. It took Malcolm a moment to recognise the Veseile barman from the tavern in Tolhurst. Their brief meeting felt like years ago. He had left behind his stained apron, replaced by plain clothes.

"Art?" Luelle's voice sounded from behind Malcolm. He hadn't heard her approach, too distracted by Theo's presence. Leena returned to their small cluster, having sent the soldiers on their way and stationed one at each of the cavern's exits.

"Anne?" The red-haired Eile approached, his eyes darting from Luelle, to Malcolm, to the others, wide and skittish.

Luelle pressed her lips together. "Luelle. Anne is my middle name."

"I knew you were lying about that," Art muttered. Malcolm didn't miss how Theo's lips twitched with amusement.

"Art was our way of tracking you," Theo explained to

Malcolm. "We followed you as far as the Ophidian Channel after escaping the arachnids, but we had no idea if you had crossed the river or fallen in, nor how far you might have travelled if you had, so we regrouped at Tolhurst. Leena was the one who remembered Art feeling a pull to the thief, as you had."

In the corner of Malcolm's eye, Luelle winced at the term.

"We spoke with him again and he agreed to help us. We arranged a group of soldiers to accompany us, though I do not know how the other soldiers you mentioned knew to be here. I have sent someone to speak to them with instructions to meet us here," Leena added.

"I think that was Viv," Malcolm explained. "I sent a message to her several days ago. She must have arranged a force to meet us here from one of the southern cities."

Theo nodded. "Art followed the trail until today but stopped being able to feel the pull this afternoon. That is when Leena went ahead to scout and found you. Turns out we weren't that far behind."

Pride swelled in Malcolm's chest at his friends' quick thinking. He should never have doubted them. They'd more than proven they were worthy of the positions he wished them to serve when he was officially crowned king.

"What happened here?" Theo asked, looking over Malcolm's shoulder to the bodies strewn on the floor.

Malcolm ran a hand over his face. "It is a long story, probably best kept for telling at home. To summarise, we may have accidentally freed a savage god."

Theo and Leena raised their eyebrows.

"Has he been drinking?" Theo asked her, peering at Malcolm.

"Could be exhaustion. He has had a long journey, and a few knocks to the head from the looks of things," she parried.

Malcolm glared at his friends. "I said it is a long story. But, as a consequence, I believe every Veseile may now have access to the Power my father was meant to pass on to me. That's Lu's theory."

Leena narrowed her eyes at Luelle, frowning at the shortened name Malcolm gave her. He ignored it, carrying on.

"And it makes sense. It explains why Art was unable to track us all the way here."

Art gazed at the prince, then at his own palms.

"I have the Power?" he asked.

"I think you will." Luelle nodded to him.

"Have you decided how you are going to deal with the thief?" Leena asked, continuing to ignore Luelle's presence. Theo pinned Luelle with a glare.

Malcolm took a deep breath, shooting Leena an irritated glance. They really shouldn't be discussing this in front of a civilian. Though, if Art could wield the Power, Malcolm might be able to use him.

"Luelle is returning to the capital with us. She is the only other person we know with experience using the Power, and I want her to speak to Graman about what she knows. There is clearly more to our history and the Gods than any of us knew. This site has to hold some sort of significance." He gestured to the star map on the ground and the island, where Vesanya's golden mask still lay. "Vesanya was trapped on that island, but she expressed some interest in the archway before she attacked anyone. I want to find out more about it all."

Leena sneered at Luelle but didn't challenge Malcolm's decision in front of the others. He hoped she wouldn't give him too much grief about it when he and his friends were finally alone.

Luelle was chewing her lip when Malcolm looked over at her. Perhaps she didn't want to return to Cerulya with him, she might resent him for making that decision for her, but it had to be a better option than following friends who had just threatened her life and branded her a traitor for being half human. And, since she was the reason so many people had the Power that once only belonged to his lineage, the least she could do was help him make sense of their new world. Besides, he still hadn't decided how she should be punished for stealing it in the first place.

They waited in the cavern, resting until Leena's soldiers returned from the tunnel system further into the cave. They'd found no other people, but some bedding, supplies, and stacks of texts that Luelle confirmed belonged to Zeke and her old companions. Before long, after their return, other soldiers arrived from the valley, informing Malcolm they'd been sent to aid him from Vidamere after an urgent instruction from the castle.

Malcolm instructed his soldiers to wrap the corpses and carry them back to the capital, for their coroners to examine. He used some of Zeke's supplies to pen a letter to his sister and instructed the soldiers from Vidamere to send it urgently to Cerulya. For the majority, he instructed them to remain in the cavern and guard against any other threats. He took one last look around the space as the soldiers prepared everything, including the new texts they would take to Graman. He offered Luelle a smile. She returned it, arms wrapped around herself, standing away from his friends.

It was time to go home and receive his crown.

## The Gods

**Adagna** — God of Wisdom and War
**Collatus** — God of Hunt and Healing
**Dilectya** — God of Love and Invention
**Meto** — God of Harvest and Fertility
**Mortus** — God of Death
**Vesanya** — God of Chaos

## The Eile

**Adeile** — A race descended from Adagna

**Colleile** — A race descended from Collatus

**Dileile** — A race descended from Dilectya

**Meteile** — A race descended from Meto

**Moreile** — A race descended from Mortus

**Veseile** — A race descended from Vesanya

# Cast of Characters

**Alaric** — The king of Arazia, *human*

**Anwyn** — Leader of a small Meteile tribe in the Godswood, *Meteile*

**Arthyr** — A barkeep working in The Horseshoe inn in Tolhurst, *Veseile*

**Benjamin** — A guard working in the royal household, *human*

**Clarisse** — A guard working in the royal household, *human*

**Edwyn** — Prince of Arazia. Fourth in line for the throne, *half-human and half-Veseile*

**Elena** — Advisor on King Alaric's council, *human*

**Fee** — A barkeep working in The Horseshoe inn in Tolhurst, *human*

**Freya** — One of Luelle's oldest friends and a member of Zeke's crew, *Colleile*

**Graman** — Tutor to all royal children and advisor to the king, *Adeile*

**Imbryl** — One of Luelle's oldest friends and a member of Zeke's crew, *Adeile*

**Ivor** — A member of Zeke's crew, *Veseile*

**Leena** — Prince Malcolm's closest friend and spymaster, *Colleile*

**Luelle** — A thief disguised as a servant in the palace who steals the Power from King Alaric on his deathbed, *Veseile*

**Malcolm** — The crown prince of Arazia, *half-human and half-Veseile*

**Pansy** — Daughter of Anwyn, *Meteile*

**Philip** — Palace seneschal, *human*

**Shela** — A tutor to the royal children and nobles in the palace, *Adeile*

**Theodas** — Malcolm's closest friend and captain of his personal guard, *human*

**Trent** — A tutor in Anwyn's tribe, *Meteile*

**Tym** — Advisor on King Alaric's council, *Colleile*

**Vivyenne** — Princess of Arazia, second in line for the throne, *half-human and half-Veseile*

**Vonya** — Queen of Arazia, *Veseile*

**Zasha** — Princess of Arazia, third in line for the throne, *half-human and half-Veseile*

**Zeke** — An extremist that believes the Power belongs to all Veseile, father-figure to Luelle, *Veseile*

# Acknowledgements

It's strange to realise quite how long I've been working on this book when I look back over the process, and even harder to comprehend the fact that it's reached this point. There are so many people who I am grateful to for helping to shape this novel into something I feel so proud of, and no words that can really convey how grateful I am, but I will at least try.

Firstly, I would like to thank all of my family and friends for being so supportive of this pursuit and for offering constant encouragement with every update. I definitely would not have gotten this far without you all! Thank you, especially to my mum, who read through my early drafts, which were far from the quality of this final version.

Thank you to Stu and Felipe for the time and effort you spent providing feedback in my earlier drafts. I can't tell you how grateful I am and how beneficial it was. Every suggestion you made was gold and strengthened the plot and feel of this book immensely.

Perhaps my most important thanks goes to Dan. You have been the driving force getting me to this point, and have made the whole process so enjoyable. I cannot express how grateful I am for the hours you've spent listening to me talk about my writing and helping me work through plot holes and dilemmas on our long car journeys. I would not have finished this without you. Like every other part of my life that you've touched, you have made this better. You are so supportive of my work, and I can only hope that you know just how much it, and you, mean to me.

And finally, thank you to anyone who picks up this book! It's as exciting as it is terrifying to know that other people might read about the little world I've created, but I hope that you have as much fun reading about these characters and their story as I did writing them.